# Mercy, Mercy Me

# Mercy, Mercy Me

## Ronn Elmore

Walk Worthy Press

West Bloomfield, Michigan

WARNER BOOKS

An AOL Time Warner Company

Published by Warner Books, Inc., with Walk Worthy Press™

 Walk Worthy Press

*Real Believers, Real Life, Real Answers in the Living God*™

Walk Worthy Press, 33290 West Fourteen Mile Road, #482, West Bloomfield, MI 48322

Warner Books, Inc., 1271 Avenue of the Americas, New York, NY 10020

Visit our Web sites at www.walkworthypress.net and www.twbookmark.com.

 An AOL Time Warner Company

Printed in the United States of America

First Printing: October 2003

10  9  8  7  6  5  4  3  2  1

Library of Congress Cataloging-in-Publication Data
Elmore, Ronn.
    Mercy, mercy me / Ronn Elmore.
        p. cm.
    ISBN 0-446-52984-2
    1. African American psychologists—Fiction. 2. African American men—Fiction. 3. Widowers—Fiction. 4. Grief—Fiction. I. Title.

PS3605.L48M37 2003
813'.6—dc21                                                    2003043264

*For my parents,*
*Pastor A. J. and Ann Elmore,*
*who taught me what it means to deeply love God*

# Acknowledgments

I am supremely grateful to my publisher, Denise Stinson and Walk Worthy Press, for giving me the opportunity to tell this story, which has long lurked about in the shadows of my imagination.

To Victoria Christopher Murray, Lisa Collins, Frances Jalet-Miller, Bill Betts, and Bob Castillo, for their helpful editorial contributions and encouragement.

To my beloved family—Aladrian, Corinn, Christina, and Cory—for their uncommon patience and support.

Finally, to my Lord and Savior Jesus Christ, whose love and, yes, mercy continue to overwhelm me.

# Mercy, Mercy Me

# *Prologue*

To Dr. Dwayne Grandison, the last forty-eight hours had felt like he was walking through a dream. An awful dream, but a dream nonetheless; one that would, like all dreams do, end shortly. His eyes would open and real life, his own normal life, would return. Familiar. Reassuring.

Until this very moment, Dr. Grandison was not fully aware of the magnitude of what had happened. It felt as if an earthquake had erupted two days before, and those closest to the epicenter were still struggling to comprehend what happened long after others drove by to gawk at the devastation. *So this is what it's like to be at the center of a scandal.* Already it had propelled the unlikely TV therapist into the Christian media spotlight, then made him pay for it with the loss of his popular television ministry and, quite possibly, his thriving Beverly Hills counseling practice. Worst of all, it had served to cast doubt on his integrity—and even his manhood.

Dwayne entered the massive wooden double doors of the New Covenant Assembly Church, just as he had thousands of times before. Crossing the empty foyer, past the large portrait of his late father, Bishop John Paul Grandison, he cracked the doorway that opened to the brightly lit sanctuary and peered inside before entering. A score of reporters and a confused jumble of camera equipment, microphones, and electrical cords had taken over the sanctuary. They were waiting for him. Clearly, this was no dream.

How could he have gotten so caught up in this web of deceit and betrayal? Was it the price he would have to pay for the success that had bought him fame and a high six-figure income? This success had trapped him, and his heart, between two extraordinary women: the almighty Beverlyn Boudreaux, famed televangelist and gospel music artist, and former TV child star Nina Jordan. His success was also helping to bring down R&B-turned-gospel recording sensation Sean Wiley, his best friend.

Recomposing himself, he considered that he had spent the bulk of his thirty-seven years working hard and steering clear of the limelight, although in this moment he wondered if—having not followed his heart and his father into the pastorate—he hadn't unwittingly set in motion the drama that had now taken center stage in his life.

He proceeded down the long hall and toward the conference room, where everyone would be gathering. As Dwayne entered the room, he could see that Sean had not yet arrived, but everyone else seemed to be in place. He was greeted by his brother, Lafayette, who had succeeded their father as New Covenant's pastor. The two were then discreetly pulled into the corner by Mark Mansfield, a prominent attorney who attended the church and who not only handled Lafayette's affairs but also had a thriving corporate practice in Century City.

His heart pounded as Mansfield began to speak, but he couldn't seem to concentrate on any more than the commotion surrounding him. Just three days before, he had been on a fast track to national fame and untold fortune—then to have a scandal painting him to the world as a promiscuous homosexual, thanks to rumors planted by his archrival who had patiently plotted Dwayne's demise. It all seemed so unreal.

"Are you okay?"

Dwayne's hands trembled as he looked up at Lafayette, who had circled the room and now returned to stand squarely in front of him. Lafayette's eyes, too, had dark circles under them, revealing how little sleep he'd had since the scandal broke.

"You can handle this. You've done nothing wrong. You've got to hold on, little brother."

As the brothers embraced, Dwayne searched the room once again. Still no sign of Sean. The press conference had been Sean's idea. It had been set for noon. It was now eleven-forty-five.

"Has anybody spoken to Sean?"

"No." Lafayette paused. "Look, man, I know things have been pretty crazy for you since Yvette's death, and now this; but you gotta believe me . . ."

Lafayette fell silent as they both turned to see Sean Wiley and his entourage arriving. There was his publicist, a bodyguard, a stylishly dressed Sean, and a man whom Dwayne surmised to be a physician at his side. Sean acknowledged Dwayne with a calm, determined look that allayed his fears, at least momentarily. In the years he had come to be Sean's best friend, Dwayne had come to trust his judgment.

Still, in that moment, he could only think of all the time Sean had spent building and then safeguarding his image. This scandal, which had been covered by every major media outlet, had hit hard. What would the former R&B-superstar-turned-gospel-superstar have to say?

As what seemed to be a sea of broadcast reporters trained their cameras and microphones on the podium and Sean, Dwayne scanned the print journalists just as they poised their pens and pads in unison. None of them really knew his best friend's story or the truth behind what had brought the two of them to this moment.

In just two short years, Dwayne Grandison had seen both his and Sean's lives turned inside out. The seeds of this catastrophe had been planted long ago by Dwayne's wife, Yvette.

As the news conference prepared to get under way, Dwayne's thoughts flashed back in time. How ironic, he thought. The conference was being held in the very room in which he and Yvette had formally announced their intentions to wed nearly two decades before.

Yvette English had been Dwayne's childhood sweetheart. The two had grown up together at New Covenant Assembly, the church pastored and founded by Dwayne's father, Bishop John Paul Grandison, and everyone had always taken for granted that the two attractive, exceptional young people would eventually marry each other.

An only child, Yvette had thrived in a family prominent not only in the church but also in the community, her father a judge and her mother a church socialite who'd never had to work a day in her life. Yvette, the primary object of their affection, was a beautiful child who had grown into a compassionate, intelligent woman, with anxious brown eyes, slim build, and supermodel looks and style. Though she often played down her good looks, set off by curly red shoulder-length hair that perfectly framed her red-bone complexion and striking facial features, it was her flair for high fashion—her penchant for couture designs and trendy high-heeled footwear—that set her eye-turning style.

Dwayne, the unexpected child of his parents' middle age, was the pride and joy of the Grandison family, including his older brother, Lafayette. Spiritually mature at an early age, compassionate, and extremely bright, Dwayne seemed to excel at everything. He loved people and idolized his father, wanting nothing more than to follow in his footsteps. Upon discovering his gifts in counseling, he graduated from college with a B.A. in theology, before going on to attain a Ph.D. in psychology, with the hopes of joining his father in the ministry, counseling people.

Yvette, however, had something different in mind. She pushed Dwayne toward success—more particularly the outward signs of it. Though Yvette was kindhearted and considerate, prestige, material gain, and notoriety were priorities to her. Yvette's determination was surpassed only by her father's. Judge English wanted his only child to go to Yale, and that was where she went, convincing Dwayne to enroll there as well.

It was during his college years that Dwayne's dreams began to fuse with Yvette's objectives. It was her idea for him to go into clinical psychology. He'd protested at first, but Yvette had been persuasive.

"Think of how many people you could help to know the Lord and make a big difference in their lives in the process by being a psychologist, and you would be a great psychologist. Besides, your father and brother are helping everyone at New Covenant, but who's there to help the ones who may be lost forever without guidance? Take, for example, people in the entertainment industry. They have spiritual needs. You could build a practice in Hollywood helping people face the challenges that they have to overcome daily. And you can help them find the Lord at the same time. Changing them might also affect the negative images that shape our society, since they're so instrumental in the transmission of the morals that determine what is and is not acceptable."

Owing to Yvette's ambitions and savvy, as well as her skillful administration of his career, Dwayne had become the most prominent psychologist of the black celebrity crowd, with a thriving practice in Beverly Hills and a client roster that read like a *Who's Hot in Hollywood*. Many of the entertainment industry's elite were quick to boast that Dr. Dwayne was the reason they'd gotten through some pretty dark days and out of some pretty tight spots.

If the outward trappings of success were any indication, Dwayne had stepped into his calling well. But though he and his pretty and stylish wife were part of the A-list in Southern California's African American community, with every material possession he'd ever wanted, he'd remained unfulfilled. Though deeply committed to his clients, he was indifferent to the fame and fortune that were so compelling to Yvette, often becoming bored with his practice and the ambitious plans Yvette had designed.

What had started out as a starry-eyed, heartfelt, optimistic kind of youthful love was, it seemed, disintegrating as more and more they found themselves at odds with each other in such critical areas as goals and priorities, not to mention money and status. As time went on, they seemed to become each other's worst enemy.

The growing tension between them was exacerbated by the mention of children. "Why are you so focused on children?" Yvette would exclaim in exasperation. "There will be plenty of time for children." Then in her classic manner, she'd walk toward him and put her arms around his neck—an attempt to defuse the tension that over time seemed to have become permanent. "Trust me," she said.

But, at least in his sight, she had done little to warrant his trust, and while she bitterly denied it, he was sure she'd had an affair with one of his clients. It had been the basis of many of their numerous fights. Fights that had grown more frequent and caustic. Not that he hadn't had his own flirtations, though he had never acted on them.

Early on, Dwayne fought back with stubbornness, then his own verbal counterattacks, until he settled into conscious indifference and detachment, resigning himself to the notion that his wife was spoiled, selfish, controlling, and an all-round status seeker. Confrontational and calculating, she accused him of lacking ambition and often wrote him off as too passive.

"You're not going to turn me into some hat-wearing church lady like your mother," she had once told him.

Truth was, she liked his mom and his family and she couldn't see why he thought of her as selfish. So she wanted nice things. Shouldn't Christians have nice things? Shouldn't they aspire to set a new standard? Where did it read in the Bible that you have to sit back and wait for things to come your way? After all, doesn't God bless the child who's got his own?

Sometimes privately, Dwayne wondered if maybe she was right and he was guilty of missing opportunities in her pursuit of a wealthier life. Those nagging thoughts were about as constant as Yvette's never-ceasing flights of fancy.

"You stay out of my way and I'll stay out of yours" was the resolve the two came to adopt, and so, eighteen months before, disgusted with himself and the way he had gotten caught up in trying to please Yvette without being true to himself and the calling on his life, Dwayne announced his intentions to go into pastoral ministry.

Yvette wouldn't hear of it, vowing to take everything in divorce. Once she'd made that vow, he realized his life had begun to unravel. While Yvette eventually calmed, her outburst left painful scars that even he had been helpless to heal. He had long feared his marriage might be in trouble. And he'd been right. He'd never gotten over the most surprising reversal in their marriage, on an issue he thought they'd agreed upon: having children.

He'd never been able to determine the source of dissension in his marriage, especially when it came to children. When they were teenagers, he and Yvette often talked of the children they would have. Even when they first married, their plans were to wait no more than a year or two. But as his practice thrived, Yvette's desire for children waned, and with each passing year Dwayne's frustration grew. The resulting tension exploded into a final conflict that precipitated Yvette's departure.

It all started after Yvette had dragged him to an exclusive A-list party thrown by an actress girlfriend of hers who'd been dating Brian Granville, weekend anchor for CNN West Coast. After two drinks, Yvette was speaking pretty freely about her views on just about everyone at the party and what she knew of their business. Then, after drink number three, things got worse: Dwayne returned from the bathroom to find Yvette flirting with the tall, picture-perfect anchorman.

"You know, Dwayne," Brian said, "you really should branch out with your practice. Network a little more."

"I tell him that all the time," Yvette said.

"Life is more than business," Dwayne said.

Yvette jerked her head back. "Oh, not more baby talk. I am not thinking about kids right now."

With that, Dwayne had left the party. Still seething at her putting him down, he'd gotten into his car and driven home without her. The next morning he realized he should have handled it differently, but the night before, he knew he was about to blow and had to get out and clear his head. He'd also realized that the distance between them had become too substantial to bridge.

Two weeks later, she packed two suitcases and was checking to see if there was anything she'd overlooked when she stopped suddenly— as if she only then realized the gravity of the moment.

"Dwayne, I wish there was another way," Yvette said, strapping on her Jimmy Choo sandals. The sadness in her eyes matched the silent ache in his heart. He searched for words to say. After all, he was a doctor counseling people through all kinds of trials and tragedies, saving lives and marriages. But he couldn't save his own and it was tearing him apart, though he knew all too well that they had both contributed to the demise of their marriage and he had hardly been the innocent partner.

He stood and approached his wife. As he gently pulled her close, holding her face in the palms of his hands, she closed her eyes, a tear making its way down her cheek. It was closer than he had held her in months. In fact, sex had been infrequent since her indiscretion— his way of communicating the disdain he sometimes felt for her.

"There is no reason for you to go," he said. "I can leave for a couple of days."

She opened her eyes and shook her head. "It's better this way, Dwayne. I've wanted to spend some time with my parents and it will only be for a few days. I pray you'll see that I am right."

Abruptly, he'd stuffed his hands into his pockets. Uncomfortable seconds of silence hung between them, and Dwayne knew that his wife's thoughts were not far from his. How could a marriage that seemed to have been ordained from the time they were children— and a love still deeply felt—come to this? Yet they held on to their respective stances, even as they were being torn apart.

It was Yvette who broke the silence. "Dwayne, we have so much we need to work out." It was her final attempt to convince her husband. "A child isn't going to cure our problems."

He pulled away and the stubborn veil that often masked his feelings was back.

"You're right about that," he said tersely.

Yvette's eyes once again teared as she kissed Dwayne's cheek. She let her lips linger on his sullen face before finally pulling away. She reached for her suitcases, but Dwayne stopped her. "I'll get them." His voice sounded heavy.

She shook her head. "It's fine. I can handle it. The car is probably here." She turned and walked toward the elevator. Dwayne wasn't sure how long he had stood in that place, wanting to change the outcome of that moment, to bring back the woman he'd fallen in love with. But she never returned. Two weeks later, she was dead from a crushed chest and lacerated liver, the victim of a collision that had occurred, ironically enough, after she'd left the office of a doctor who had just confirmed her worst fears: She'd been eight weeks pregnant.

# Chapter One

Through the vertical blinds that hung from the ceiling to the floor, the city lights shone, sparkling brightly as the night's darkness descended upon Los Angeles. Over the past year, this had become Dwayne's favorite time. In the darkness, he could hide—from his family, his friends, and his clients. With practice, he had even learned to hide from himself the overwhelming grief that mingled with his guilt and still—after almost three hundred days—flooded his mind.

The shrill of the telephone interrupted his thoughts. With Monique gone home for the day, he reached for the phone, punching the speaker button.

"Hey, guy, I'm surprised I caught you."

"Lafayette, what's up, man?" Dwayne asked flatly.

"I was calling to see how you're doing. We haven't heard from you."

"I'm fine." Dwayne slumped into his chair. "You don't have to keep checking on me . . ."

"I'm not checking on you," Lafayette objected softly. "I need to talk to you about something. Do you have some time tomorrow?"

Though he already knew his calendar, Dwayne glanced at the leather book in the center of his desk. "I've got a full day," he said as his eyes washed over the Thursday appointments that were set for every hour beginning at 8:00 A.M. He hadn't even scheduled time for lunch.

"Hmm. This is really important." Lafayette paused. "What are you doing now? The kids have really missed their Uncle Dwayne, and you know how Robbie and I always love to see you. Why don't you come on by?"

Dwayne hesitated, gathering his thoughts.

"I wouldn't be calling if this wasn't important," Lafayette pressed, looking for the answer he wanted. "It won't take long and I think you'll like what I have to say. Or if it's more convenient, I can come to you."

Knowing there was no escape, Dwayne gave in. "That's okay, I'll come there. I'll see you in about thirty minutes."

He put the phone down. Seeing Lafayette, Roberta, and their four children was not something he relished. The house was always so full of love and he felt so empty. It was hard for him to be there, thinking always what could have been had things been different.

In a gesture of resignation, he closed his calendar and dropped it into his briefcase. He walked slowly through the massive office and then stepped into the anteroom, decorated like a living room with the velvet scarlet plush couch and matching chairs. Though they didn't have much money when they'd opened this office, Yvette worked with an interior designer, insisting it was a professional necessity.

Yvette had carefully planned every aspect of their lives. Unfortunately, there was no backup—no strategy for spending the rest of his life alone. He ran his hand over his face, trying to wipe away the fatigue that seemed to envelop him constantly. He stepped into the hallway and, like a robot, took the elevator down to the parking garage.

Dwayne turned his car into the long driveway and pulled behind a metallic blue Escalade. He peered for a moment at the darkened front of the two-story, three-year-old custom-built home and then set the car into reverse. A second later the porch light was on. Sighing, he parked his car and turned off the ignition. The front door opened before he could slam the door of his Jaguar.

"I was about to come to you," Lafayette said as he extended a hearty hug to his younger brother.

"Uncle Dwayne!" Nicole, the youngest of Lafayette's children, rushed through the hall toward the front door.

Dwayne grinned and lifted the six-year-old into his arms. "How's my favorite girl?"

Nicole giggled as Dwayne kissed her cheek and Roberta sauntered into the foyer to greet her brother-in-law. Dressed in a gray jogging suit and white Keds, and with her long reddish-brown hair pulled into a ponytail, Robbie, as everyone fondly called her, didn't look much older than her fifteen-year-old son.

"Hey there. How are you making out?"

Dwayne nodded okay as he lowered Nicole to the floor and then gingerly pulled her pigtail. "Where is everybody else?"

"In their rooms watching TV, no doubt," she said as she took Nicole's hand and headed toward the kitchen, calling behind her, "Dwayne, come for dinner on Sunday. We've been missing you."

Dwayne settled into the full-cushioned chair and let his eyes wander around the living room as Lafayette sat facing him on the adjacent sofa.

"So how's it going?" Lafayette peered into his brother's eyes. His elbows rested on his knees and his hands were folded just below his chin, as if he were about to pray.

"Hard at work, trying to keep moving forward." Dwayne looked up into his brother's eyes, knowing full well that Lafayette was scanning his face for signs of distress.

"So what's this about?" Dwayne asked, shifting the attention to whatever was so important it couldn't wait.

"I need your help." Lafayette glanced over a yellow pad Dwayne hadn't noticed until just then. "We're expanding the counseling ministry at New Covenant."

Dwayne sat up straight in his seat. "And . . ."

"Well, I need a little of your time and a lot of your expertise. We brought a new director on staff about a year ago," he continued, hoping to give Dwayne the full scope of what he was planning before Dwayne would object. "You know her—Nina Jordan."

Dwayne frowned "The name sounds familiar."

"She grew up in church with us, though she was a few grades behind you, but you remember her from TV. You know, that series—*Everyday People*."

Dwayne thought back, trying to remember. "Oh, yeah. She's not acting anymore?"

"Don't you remember . . . she was caught with drugs, lost her money? It was in the tabloids."

"She's in charge of your counseling ministry?"

"Well, who better than someone who's been there—married early, divorce, drugs, fame, partying. She's determined to use her experience to help people avoid what she's been through. Last year she got her master's in psychology from Marymount and graduated with honors. She's worked hard to turn her life around. Remember our women's program?"

Dwayne nodded slightly.

"Well, Nina came in, expanded the project, changed the name to Sister 2 Sister, and it's going well."

"What can I do?"

Lafayette handed Dwayne a thin folder before he continued. "The other day Nina brought me this proposal to beef up the men's program you once led. It will be called Man-to-Man, and like Sister 2 Sister, it will be a support system and provide mentoring as well."

Dwayne opened the folder and glanced at the first page of the proposal.

"We want to do the same for the men as we've done with the women—group counseling, one-on-one sessions, and mentoring. Like Promise Keepers or Jakes's Manpower, a strong men's fellowship."

"So it's really working with the women?"

"Man, you wouldn't believe the inroads Nina has made. Our women's fellowship has tripled in size, and these women have gotten serious. So many of them have turned their lives around. Nina doesn't play, and the women seem to respect her for that. I've sat in on a few of the sessions.

"Problem is, the program's out of balance without us doing the same for the men. Since you left, our men's ministry has stalled and I can't seem to find the person with the dynamics it takes to get and keep the men motivated."

"But aren't you overseeing that?"

"In name, yes, but in practice . . . Man, my hands are full. I need someone to really develop this thing hands-on. Borrowing from Jakes and Promise Keepers, Nina's outlined a strategy."

"Makes sense."

"Well, Nina's going to need some help and I thought, who better than you?"

"Man, it sounds great and I'd love to do it, but you know how busy I am and what I just came through. I don't know that I'm ready for this."

In truth, Dwayne had been looking for anything to fill his time and didn't know why he was so hesitant. As if Lafayette was reading his mind, the elder brother replied, "What are you talking about? For the last year, all you've done is work and go home.

"Not only do we need your help," Lafayette continued, "but I thought this would be a great way for you to get into some form of ministry, like you've always wanted. You could have your practice and just give New Covenant a bit of your time. It's the best of both worlds.

"You could make such a difference in the lives of these men and the church. Besides, Mom was the one who suggested you. She thinks it's what you need and was going to make the call herself."

With the mention of their mother, Dwayne's eyes wandered to the silver-framed picture on the desk. Their mother, Bernice Grandison, was standing stoically and stylishly (as was her custom) behind their father, one hand placed squarely on the shoulder of the man who had been her husband for nearly half a century. It was the last picture ever taken of Bishop John Paul Grandison, or Bishop, as everyone called him.

"At least give it some thought," Lafayette persisted.

This was the opportunity he'd been seeking a year ago. It had caused dissension between him and Yvette. Suddenly, Dwayne stood, still holding the folder in his hand. "I'll get back to you."

"You're not leaving already? We haven't talked about what's going on with you."

Dwayne opened his mouth but stopped when Lafayette held up his hands. "I know. You've been busy."

"Tell you what. I'll be by for Sunday dinner. I'll let you know for sure then."

"Now you're talking." Lafayette smiled widely before tugging gently at the folder that Dwayne tucked under his arm. "I really need you, man."

As they walked silently toward the front door, Dwayne contemplated the idea of working with his brother at New Covenant. Maybe this was what he needed. At the door, the brothers hugged.

"See you Sunday. Take care of yourself."

"I will," Dwayne said. He walked toward the car knowing that Lafayette had the best intentions, but he also had Robbie and the kids. His heart sank with the aching reality that he had no one.

It was the final night of the Dallas crusade. The overflow crowd nearly came to a complete hush as a giant screen was lowered to the middle of the huge arena, a drumroll marking its descent.

The blank screen suddenly filled with a close-up of Beverlyn Boudreaux in profile; she was leaning against a brick building.

"I grew up on these streets . . . New Orleans . . ."

Beverlyn turned toward the camera and began walking. She pulled her leather jacket tighter, and as the camera followed her, Jackson Square came into view.

"On these streets and in that park, I did things I am not proud of—I stole, I drank, I did drugs. I was only a few weeks away from selling my body for money." She paused, taking a deep breath. "There are lots of reasons why my life went that way, but there's only one reason why it turned around." She turned back to the park, but this time, when she returned to the camera, her eyes were watering, then gave way to a glow that lit up her face while seeming to radiate through the screen.

"Who I am today is only through the power of God. He revealed Himself and His plan, and my life was transformed."

The camera zoomed in on Beverlyn's face. "God wants you too. We'll share with you stories of victory, of tribulations overcome, of souls redeemed. We're the Jubilee Network. If you're in a place where you have more questions than answers, give us a call. We have a direct line to the man who knows. Tune in this spring."

An 800 number appeared on the screen and then the picture slowly faded. Once again, the Jubilee Network came into view. Thunderous applause arose from the crowd.

Then a roving spotlight scanned the crowd before settling on Beverlyn, who stepped from a haze of smoke in a copper Donna Karan gown, her hair pulled off her face into soft curls, accented by a pearl and diamond headband. A booming baritone voice offstage announced, "Ladies and gentlemen, please welcome a visionary woman of God, Evangelist Beverlyn Boudreaux." As Beverlyn strode confidently toward center stage, the overhead lights slowly brightened.

"Extend your arms toward this stage and believe for a miracle," she proclaimed. The audience roared their approval. On cue, another Beverlyn Boudreax Empowerment Crusade was under way. Every service was a carefully orchestrated progression of music and ministry in finely tuned synchronization, building toward a dramatic climax and calculated to spur huge product sales out in the lobby.

"I feel the power of angels . . ." Beverlyn shushed the crowd, raising her hand as a glow rose over the crowd now caught up in a wave of euphoria.

In that instant, the anointing—God's living spirit—moved through her to touch the throngs who had come to hear her minister to their sorrows, hopes, dreams, and pain. Something was happening in the heat of the moment. While no two people responded the same, all were feeling as if a hugely significant event was taking place, that they were experiencing a divine presence—as real to them as their own dreams. Onstage and off, people were breaking through pain barriers.

"God is here all around us. Ah . . . this is holy ground."

Shouts of "Hallelujah" reverberated throughout the hall.

Beverlyn stretched forth her hands. "Your people are hurting, Father. Heal them right now in Jesus' name."

Suddenly, a ceaseless flow of men, women, and children with heightened expectations moved to the front of the stage, which had become a makeshift altar.

One woman's entire body went numb, and as though someone had plugged her into electricity, she fell back into the arms of another, setting off a chain reaction, confirming and reconfirming the expectations culminating from widely felt sensations of ecstasy.

"The power of God is working its way through this crowd tonight," Beverlyn shouted. "Embrace it."

It was at moments like this that Beverlyn Boudreaux was most at home. Awe-inspiring, her five-octave vocal range thrilled audiences. Her powerful oratories and sermons were even more moving, and the presentation was both electrifying and seemingly flawless, transforming the thousands who flocked to see her into active participants. All of which were a big part of the reason why she was the most sought-after black female evangelist in the country.

Like her idols Benny Hinn, a Palestinian who'd fled with his family to Canada after the Six-Day War, and T. D. Jakes, who while being raised in a one-room shack in West Virginia watched his father slowly die of a debilitating disease, Beverlyn had experienced a childhood filled with pain. Because of the overwhelming circumstances she had overcome, she was convinced that God had chosen her, like Esther in the Old Testament, *for such a time as this.*

She had created the kind of excitement in religious circles that had been reserved for secular superstars, partly because of her uncharacteristic beauty, but mostly because she had asserted a vision that was nontraditional in approach and yet universal in its appeal. There was also her explosive gospel music career and an uncanny ability to navigate black and white fellowships, with a widespread cross-denominational appeal.

It was a style she'd developed over the last decade while building her multimillion-dollar, multimedia Beverlyn Boudreaux Ministries.

It was a flair displayed in earlier speaking engagements that caught the eye of a cadre of leading televangelists who invited her to appear on their TV broadcasts and at their conventions. Her astounding popularity had been fueled by a string of hit records, more than a dozen inspirational conferences and religious crusades, numerous TV appearances, and by one Linson William Lejohn, known to all as L.W., Beverlyn's uncle and manager: publicly recognized as the man who single-handedly choreographed her rise to fame; and privately derided as the puppeteer who pulled her strings.

Backstage, L.W. paced in the backdrop of the giant arena as production people scurried about tending to every detail of the massive crusade that had drawn upwards of thirty thousand. While the complete numbers weren't in yet, the $250,000 they'd pulled in so far was more than enough to make him smile.

Lejohn, an overweight, balding, middle-aged former storefront preacher, was often characterized by those who'd worked with Beverlyn as a paranoid, vindictive adversary who was accountable only to himself, tolerated zero dissent, and exerted a frightening level of control over Beverlyn. Together with her, this relentless self-promoter had built a multifaceted empire, which had in turn boosted her own profile in black religious circles.

Many saw him as the Svengali who, from scratch, had created a new phenomenon: a powerful woman of God with movie-star allure. It was rumored that he lived vicariously through Beverlyn's fame. Indeed, he shared in her every triumph. But L.W. didn't care what people said.

She was, after all, his creation.

It was he who had recognized her gift early and nourished it and the empire that came of it. Getting her to the top was all he'd ever done that worked, and he'd done it well.

Now Lejohn—with Beverlyn Boudreaux Ministries in tow—was rolling the dice on their biggest gamble to date, the Jubilee Network. A lot was riding on the high-risk cable TV venture whose flagship program, he hoped, would feature a Los Angeles–based therapist and author who'd created quite a stir when he appeared as a guest on *Oprah* just nine months before. His name was Dwayne Grandison.

"Mr. Lejohn," a stage assistant called out, "didn't you want Mr. Wiley to go on a little early?"

"Yeah," L.W. called out. "Signal for Beverlyn to intro him now."

The tech disappeared from view as a makeup girl rushing to put last touches on a tall, blond-haired, and gruffly handsome man scurried to keep up with him as he brushed past L.W. and headed to the stage.

Beverlyn hushed the audience before proceeding. "Now I have a real surprise for you. This man's testimony we've all had the pleasure of watching unfold. There is no greater singer. Please join me in welcoming Grammy Award–winning Sean Wiley to the stage to sing his current hit—number one on *Billboard*'s gospel chart—'For Love Alone.'"

Deafening cheers, screams, and applause filled the auditorium as Sean took his place onstage and, as the spotlight came up, began to sing.

For most of Sean Wiley's thirty-five years, his business had been music. He first rose to fame in the 1980s with a sultry blend of blue-eyed soul rivaling the success of those like Michael Bolton and the sound of Luther Vandross. If you closed your eyes and just listened, you wouldn't have guessed that Sean, like Bolton, was white. Nor could anyone have predicted the kind of success that followed his 1984 debut, including a string of hit albums, numerous awards and accolades, and several TV appearances.

But it was nothing compared to the success and fulfillment that came with his conversion to gospel in the mid-nineties. Adding to the gold albums were three platinum awards, a string of Dove and Stellar Awards, a performance schedule that had him booked up to 150 dates a year, and profiles in leading Christian and mainstream publications, including *People* and *USA Today*. And as the former R&B sex symbol continued to mesmerize the gospel and Christian community, there had come the kind of adulation that was reserved for secular artists.

"You were great," a man said as Wiley walked offstage past a throng of waiting admirers to the backstage area. The evening nearly over, the greenroom was packed with prominent pastors and their wives, socialites, and local celebrities looking to say hello to both him and Beverlyn. At least half an hour would pass before the diva made her entrance, so he went to his dressing room to change.

When he reemerged forty-five minutes later, some of the crowd had waned and Beverlyn was doing what she did best: working the room and turning on the charm. These pastors were her lifeblood: a network of people she depended on to get the word out about her ministry and her soon-to-be-launched Jubilee Network. She knew how to nail every angle, yet it was also very important to her that everything be first-class. With the help of her trusted personal publicist, Kim Steele, everything always was.

Steele, invariably at Beverlyn's side in public venues, was somewhat a chameleon. While at times you hardly knew she was there, there were those times when she took center stage, making sure everything ran with precision, timing, and the right results. She, too, appeared to be first-class—an attractive, professional type with a seemingly unshakable demeanor, who dressed conservatively, in perfectly coordinated designer suits.

"Well, I've got some good news for you," Beverlyn said to Sean as he approached her and Kim. "Ticket sales were going well for the Women's Crusade, but when we announced you were added to the show, we sold out the Georgia Dome within twenty-four hours. I thought we were going to have to book the World Congress Center for the overflow."

Sean grinned. "You're giving me way too much credit."

"Oh, please . . . You know you're way bigger now than you ever were when you were singing that 'groove with me' stuff and gyrating your hips."

He chuckled. "Well, just call me the Elvis of gospel."

"Yeah, right." It was Beverlyn's turn at sarcasm.

"How's the Jubilee Network coming?"

"Well, we're just weeks away from the first telecast. Can you believe it?" Then, not giving him a chance to answer, Beverlyn continued, "I just keep thinking of all the things I'll be able to do—so many people I can help and lives that can be saved and changed if things go well."

"You do quite a bit of that now."

"But I'm talking huge," she said, spreading her arms wide and almost bumping into the mayor, who'd been standing to the side awaiting her acknowledgment. "Excuse me," she said, turning back to wind down her conversation with Sean as Kim turned to greet the mayor.

Sean took her hand. "God's blessed everything you've touched. Why should this be any different?"

"Because it's L.A., Sean, and L.A., I've heard, is a tough nut to crack. A lot of megachurches. A lot of homegrown celebrities. It's just not the same."

"Nothing's the same in L.A. That's why you'll fit right in."

As he bade good night to Beverlyn, Sean remembered there was a call he needed to make. Stepping into the hall, he pulled out his cell phone and dialed the L.A. number. He was mildly disappointed when he called Dwayne's office and the voice mail greeting came on.

"Hey, man. Sorry I missed you. Just wanted to give you the heads-up on the concert next week. I've reserved two VIP tickets and all-access passes, so bring a date. There'll be a party afterwards and of course, I'll expect to see you there. By the way, Beverlyn Boudreaux's been after me to introduce you two. She has some big project she wants to talk to you about. Well, got to run. I'll talk to you when I get back to L.A."

As he tucked away his cell, Sean was hopeful Dwayne would be up to going out. He had been worried about his best friend, hoping in some small measure to help pull him through the gloom that had cast a dark cloud over his life since the death of his wife.

"Good evening, Dr. Grandison," the valet said as he opened the car door.

Dwayne nodded. "Thank you, Edmund." He handed his keys to the valet and entered the Wilshire-Pacific Towers. The heels of Dwayne's polished shoes clicked against the marble floor, breaking the silence in the opulent lobby. It was almost eleven, so Dwayne wasn't surprised to find the lobby empty, though even during the day, this high-priced high-rise condominium complex was often conspicuously bare.

Once inside the elevator, he put the key into the panel granting him access to the seventeenth floor—the penthouse. As the chamber rose, his eyes held his own reflection in the mirrored doors. On the outside, he appeared fine; he hid well all that was brewing inside. The dark circles that had once taken up residence under his eyes had all but faded. And his return to his four-times-a-week workouts helped his chestnut skin regain its luster, making him appear younger than his thirty-seven years.

As the elevator doors parted, he stepped into the circular foyer of the penthouse condominium and dropped his briefcase at the base of the round granite table. Loosening his tie he walked slowly into the living room and clicked the dimmer switch, allowing streams of amber light to radiate through the room. At the same time, Kirk Whalum's mellow jazz filled the air, the result of an electronic gadget Yvette had installed when they first moved into the three-bedroom unit.

Dwayne flipped through the mail that had piled up on the dining room table. Moments later, he tossed the envelopes aside and slumped onto the glove-soft leather couch.

He closed his eyes and leaned back, stretching his legs onto the glass coffee table in front of him. With his eyes still closed, he breathed deeply, taking in the music. Opening his eyes, he allowed them to move through the room, soaking up every bit of the surroundings. Though Yvette had been dead now going on eleven months, she was still very much alive in his heart—and surroundings. From the furniture to the original paintings that covered the walls to the Chinese vases they had collected during their travels— even the plants that still flourished under the windows due to the weekly visits from his cleaning woman—it was all Yvette. Dwayne was sure that even his wife's favorite perfume, Tiffany, still hung in the air.

Slowly, he lifted himself and shrugged his jacket from his shoulders. He went into the extra bedroom, which had once been his home office. Today it was a storage area, filled with empty U-Haul boxes, waiting for him to take the first steps.

Dwayne roamed through the room with boxes in hand. In the living room, he began to pack away the pictures that filled the mantel and covered the piano, leaving just their wedding picture alongside a photo taken a few weeks before Yvette passed. Next he moved through the long hallway into the guest bedroom, where books Yvette had been reading were still stacked on the dresser. In one of the two bathrooms, he removed bottles of scented shampoos and fragrant lotions that had sat unused for a year.

It was well past midnight by the time he went into the master bedroom they'd shared. Bernice and Robbie had mercifully spent the week after Yvette's funeral packing the clothes that lined her two walk-in closets, and carted them off. Still, he'd kept some of her personal trinkets and much of her jewelry spread across the dresser, next to her picture.

He gathered the jewelry into a pouch before returning to the guest room, emptying its contents onto the bed and then spreading the pieces until he found the one he was looking for. He stared at the diamond-studded Rolex he'd given Yvette nearly one year before on her thirty-fifth birthday. It had been among the personal effects he'd claimed at the hospital where she'd been pronounced dead upon arrival.

He rolled the gold band through his fingers and then laid it on the pillow. Lifting the rest of the boxes, he took them into the guest room. It took him another hour to seal all the boxes, and when he finally lay down, still fully clothed, the grandfather clock in the foyer chimed four times.

# Chapter Two

*W*hen God came into our lives, we were dead in trespasses and sins. Now"—Lafayette paused—"a dead man can't be sorry that he's dead. A dead man cannot wish to live and a dead man certainly cannot contribute anything to coming back to life. In fact, we—as sinners—were so dead that we couldn't have come to God without God drawing us. And some of you all are sitting up in here dead right now."

Dead is surely what Dwayne felt inside as Pastor Lafayette Grandison continued his sermon while holding the gaze of the nearly seven hundred worshipers who'd gathered in the sanctuary of New Covenant Assembly for Sunday morning service. Dwayne sat in the front row, his shoulder rubbing against his mother's. Bernice Grandison sat with her back pushed against the high pews, her chin jutted forward, her eyes following her older son as he strutted across the altar.

With a flick of her wrist, Bernice threw up her hand and offered an amen, the sleeve of her salmon-hued, crepe-chiffon suit flowing so fluidly and setting off her impeccably styled silver-gray hair. Ms. G, as some of the kids in the congregation had nicknamed her, was known for her expensive and stylish collection of hats. Though she had aged gracefully, she insisted on remaining a style-setter; she wore the somber wisdom of her years only in the advice she gave her children.

She hoped Dwayne was hearing all Lafayette had to say. She had known about—but not commented on—his failing marriage to Yvette. She'd liked Yvette, though she knew instinctively that she wasn't the right woman for Dwayne, even if the girl was a beauty.

"That's right, son." She flicked her wrist again, turning her attention to Lafayette's words.

"God wants you to stand on your own two feet because of His love alone," Lafayette continued. "God looks at us and says, 'I love you just the way you are. You are incapable of doing anything for Me.' And in order to love and get nothing back, you've got to have something behind you, in you, around you, over you, under you, above you, and all through you. Nobody in here loves like that. Now, we might *lie* like that, but we don't love like that.

"It's human to want to be replenished, but when you have a relationship with God, you have strength you didn't know you had. We seek intercession because sixty percent of our trouble is relationships. Like the words in the refrain of a Teddy Pendergrass song, 'Love TKO,' aren't you tired of getting beat up by love?

"I want to tell you that you don't have to throw yourself at anybody, at any time, because no matter what you think you need, God is saying, 'Start looking to Me like you've been looking to others and I'll give you the sense of peace you have never had.' "

As Lafayette pulled a white handkerchief from his pocket, pressed the cloth against his face and announced that the doors of the church were open, the congregation bowed in prayer. Throughout the altar call and then the benediction, Dwayne held his head in his hands, bowed in prayer. It wasn't until the rest of the congregation stood and his mother softly placed her hand on his shoulder that Dwayne lifted his head.

"Are you all right, son?" Bernice's thin eyebrows were creased together with concern.

He nodded, then smiled and stood. Dwayne put his arm around his mother's shoulders as the choir filed from the stand, followed by

Lafayette and Minister Leslie, the assistant pastor. Then Dwayne took his mother's hand and led her toward the back.

At the end of every Sunday service, Bernice Grandison made her way to the doors of the church to stand with her son and daughter-in-law and greet the parishioners who patiently stood in line, waiting to address the Grandisons. While Roberta stood on one side of Lafayette, Mother Bernice, as she was lovingly called, stood on the other, with the stature of a First Lady, shaking hands with everyone, just as she'd done with her husband, Bishop John Grandison, for more than three decades.

Dwayne kissed Bernice's cheek—his sign that he had delivered his mother to her place. As members and friends strolled by, Dwayne attempted to step aside, but was met at each turn with greetings from people who had known him all his life.

"How are you doing, Dwayne?" Mrs. King, one of the church's founding members, asked.

"Very well, ma'am. And how are you?"

He nodded as he edged from the silver-haired woman and the others, seeking refuge in Lafayette's office. For the past year, right after the close of service, Dwayne would make himself scarce, fleeing the curious gazes from people who openly wondered how well he was getting on since the passing of his wife, some of the unmarried women seeking the prime opportunity to make their moves.

He walked into the office, settled into Lafayette's chair, and turned toward the window. An overnight storm had pelted the city and had still been raging earlier that morning as Dwayne maneuvered his way through the rain-soaked streets to church. But now the sun glowed brightly, all signs of the severe weather gone. Dwayne turned the chair away from the window and the memories of Yvette that had flooded his mind during the service. He looked at the oversize picture of his father across the room. Bishop Grandison never looked more regal, sitting stately at his massive desk and draped in his classic black robe with red collar.

A peaceful calm came over him as it had whenever he spent time alone in this office. It pleased him that Lafayette had not changed much since taking over, though the church had thrived, growing from four hundred active members to upwards of a thousand.

Los Angeles respected grandeur, and nowhere was it more evident than in its astounding array of African American megachurches. "Whatever your thing is, you can find it in this town," John Grandison would say, while not totally buying into the characterization that the city's church community had been affected by, and perhaps even infected with, a Hollywood mentality, energized by worshipers who looked to where "the action" was—celebrities, progressive programming, exciting worship services, and ministers who themselves had acquired notoriety.

While Lafayette's status in L.A. bordered on celebrity, he was well liked among his peers. And while the preaching social chain could be quite treacherous, it was said of those envious of Lafayette that they might circle the wagons, but they didn't dare attack. Dynamic, magnetic, and contemporary, he knew how to politic his way from South-Central to City Hall, and while the strength of his name alone at a press conference guaranteed the attendance of every major TV station, he steered clear of controversy.

Perhaps the most powerful side of his appeal was his pulpit charisma. His style was a rousing, "wake up, I'm talking to you" delivery, punctuated by an apparently boundless generosity that seemed to permeate every action and word, a powerful one-two punch to the worshipers who packed his Sunday morning service and a Wednesday night Bible study as well.

Then there was the youthful exuberance of his forty-five years, his striking good looks, keen intellect, and community activism, all of which had helped to thrust Lafayette into a circle of high-profile black preachers often cast as community leaders. They were part of a new breed of savvy pastors who had—to a point—discarded a traditional and more denominational regimentation to embrace a fuller expression of worship while utilizing new technology and expanding church services to better serve the needs of parishioners.

Though wise beyond his years, the six-foot-two light-complexioned man, whose muscular build bespoke a demanding daily exercise routine, was completely oblivious to the fascination driving the attendance of some of his female worshipers. He was, after all, a family man, particularly on Sundays, when he took pleasure in a Grandison tradition: Sunday dinner.

"Hey, Dwayne, Mom was just asking where you were," Lafayette said, jarring Dwayne from the window and his thoughts.

Dwayne turned around to face his brother and Deacon Miller. "I thought I'd wait in here."

Lafayette smiled as he took off his robe and handed it to the deacon.

"Is Mom outside?"

"No. She went ahead to the house with Robbie. Wanted to spend extra time with the kids. In fact, let's get going," Lafayette said as Deacon Miller left the room.

Dwayne stretched as he stood, and they walked from the church shoulder-to-shoulder.

"Have you given any more thought to what we discussed the other night?"

"A little."

"Well, I'm not trying to rush you, but Nina will be joining us for dinner."

"Bringing in the troops, huh?" Dwayne said, searching his pocket for the car key.

"Not really. Robbie had invited her to dinner before we knew you were coming. But I think meeting her will help you decide one way or the other."

"So I'll meet you at the house in a few."

As Lafayette opened the front door, laughter mixed with the sounds of pots and pans clattering in the kitchen, and the aroma of fried chicken and greens filled the room.

"Uncle Dwayne!" His nieces, nephews, and cousins rushed him.

"How's it going?" He lifted Nicole as Robbie and Lafayette's other three children flanked him. He kissed Deborah and shook hands with Brandon and Joshua, then high-fived Mario and Eric, Monique's foster sons.

Monique, Dwayne's and Lafayette's first cousin, had come from

Texas to live with the Grandisons when she was four years old. Her mother, who had married too young, suddenly left her teenage husband and their daughter and took up residence with the local drug dealer. Monique's father got drunk and, in a jealous rage, went with gun in hand to force his wife's return. When she refused, he shot both her and her new boyfriend, then turned the gun on himself. All three died instantly. The family's neighbors pooled their money to send Monique to Los Angeles to live with her uncle and aunt and their two sons. She had been raised as if she were the boys' natural sister.

"What's up with the sad face?" Dwayne asked Joshua, the eldest of the Grandison grandchildren, who had marched into the living room like the Pied Piper.

"My friends are going roller-skating and Mom won't let me go," Joshua said, pouting. "She said we're having a family dinner and since I'm family, I have to be here."

Joshua pleaded his case with the hope that his uncle would speak to his mother on his behalf. Dwayne chuckled, remembering the many occasions he'd done the very same thing with his aunts and uncles.

"Let me see what I can do," Dwayne said, slipping Nicole from his lap.

"Don't even try." Robbie smiled as she entered the room. "Tell your uncle the whole story." She placed her hands on her hips.

Joshua sulked from the room, and his brother and Monique's two young sons followed.

"I'm really glad you made it."

"C'mon now. You see me every Sunday."

"I know," Robbie said, slapping him playfully on his arm. "But today seems like old times . . . almost." She paused. "Take off your jacket and get comfortable. Where's your brother?"

"Upstairs, I think. Where's Mom?"

"In the kitchen. Where else? But don't worry. I'll get her out of there. The moment she hears you're here, she'll come running." She turned. "Deborah, I need some help in the kitchen."

Deborah obediently followed her mother, with Nicole in tow.

Dwayne leaned back on the couch. He always felt at home here, though View Park was miles away from the South-Central corridor where he had grown up. Still, Lafayette and Roberta had created a space just like his childhood home. So unlike the high-tech, elegantly designed home that Yvette had created. He remembered when Yvette first surprised him with their new home. It was his birthday and Yvette told him that she had a surprise.

"So it's a party," Dwayne had surmised as they entered the Wilshire-Pacific Towers, which had been well known for housing many of Hollywood's elite, especially New York–based actors who maintained bicoastal homes. Dwayne searched his mind trying to remember which of his clients lived here. "I can't remember, who lives here?"

Yvette smiled as they entered the elevator. "What are you talking about?" She ran her hand over her hair, which was curled into a flip.

When the doors opened to the penthouse, Dwayne blinked in confusion. The massive space was empty.

Yvette took his hand and smiled again. "This is our new home. Happy birthday."

He walked along the deep-piled carpet toward the long windows that faced the Hollywood Hills. Several minutes passed before he turned back to his wife. "Our new home?"

She bobbed her head like an excited schoolgirl. "Yes, sweetheart. I wanted to surprise you. Isn't this magnificent?" She spread her arms wide.

He didn't answer at first.

"You said it was time to start looking for a place so that we could get out of that cramped apartment."

"But we agreed to buy a home—a house, with a backyard, where our children could run and play."

The ends of Yvette's smile turned down a bit. "Yeah . . . but there's so much we have to do before we have children. This is a great place to start." She took his hand and led him from the living room into the formal dining area. "And there's more than enough space here. There are three bedrooms and it's almost three thousand square feet."

Dwayne followed as Yvette rushed through the apartment, taking him through the kitchen, the extra bedrooms, and the two bathrooms.

"You gotta love this," she gushed. "I know you do."

Dwayne pulled her hand, stopping her dead in her tracks. "Honey, this is nice, but it's not what we talked about."

"I know, but for now, isn't this place just perfect? Just the right address for a successful young psychologist and his thoughtful, gorgeous"—she posed playfully—"and ever-so-brilliant wife."

Dwayne shook his head, giving in.

"Hey, wait a minute," she said. "I have something to show you. Come right this way, sir." She kissed him softly as she led him into the master bedroom. Dwayne gasped as they entered a circular sifting room, then stepped into the massive bedroom. On the wall opposite the floor-to-ceiling windows was a black granite fireplace crackling with flames. In the middle of the empty room was a large blanket spread across the carpet and a silver bucket, holding a bottle of champagne, and two Baccarat flutes they had received as wedding gifts.

Yvette took her husband's hand and gently pulled him toward the center of the room. He knelt beside her, taking her chin into his hands and kissing her deeply. He loved her so much, even if she was pushy and ambitious. But then again, everything she did was for them, to nurture their success and help the business to thrive. To help them build a secure future.

"Wake up," the voice said, and Dwayne sat up, stirred from his daydream. It took a moment for him to focus on Lafayette standing in front of him and a young woman smiling at his side.

Trying to hide his embarrassment, Dwayne stood and extended his hand toward the woman, who looked familiar. "Hello, I'm Dwayne Grandison. Obviously, I have better manners than my brother," he said, taking a jab at Lafayette for not making the introduction.

The woman's earnest expression broke into a wide smile, revealing her perfectly aligned teeth. "Dwayne, you don't remember me. I'm Nina Jordan," she said softly, taking his extended hand.

Dwayne once again surveyed the slender, demurely beautiful

woman, dressed stylishly in a tailored gray pantsuit and accenting scarf draped over one shoulder, her dark brown shoulder-length hair pulled back off her face. He had been instantly struck by her stunning looks, and, yes, there was a familiarity, though he at first thought her to be one of Robbie's girlfriends. It took a moment for him to realize that he was still holding her hand.

"Nina, it's good to see you again," Dwayne said, now recalling the many times he'd seen her on various television programs some years ago.

"Let's sit down," Lafayette said, "and talk about this counseling program a bit before we eat."

"No, you don't," Robbie said, entering the living room with a silver tray containing garlic dip and crudités. Bernice followed with small plates. "There will be no talk of business now." Robbie put the tray down, then wrapped her arms around Lafayette's neck and kissed him. "This is a family affair and we're all going to have a good time."

Dwayne followed Lafayette into the kitchen and filled the water glasses with cider, juice, soda, and sparkling water. When they returned to the living room, Dwayne looked around. Monique had just gotten up to chastise her two young sons, who had been fighting. Bernice sat in the high wing-back chair next to Robbie, who was on the love seat. Before Dwayne could sit next to his sister-in-law, Lafayette sat, put his arm around his wife, and smiled at his brother. The only place left for Dwayne to sit was on the couch next to Nina.

For a moment, he'd considered that they might be setting him up, and then just as quickly he realized he might be overreacting. After all, everyone knew that he wasn't ready for any kind of relationship. This was only a gathering of family and friends who'd come together for conversation and dinner. It made sense that Nina was invited, since Lafayette was trying to sell him on joining the ministry. Dwayne knew that Lafayette was confident he would close the deal before sundown.

Casually, Dwayne sat on the couch and crossed his legs. When Nina glanced at him and smiled, he took a sip of his soda.

As they settled in, taking pieces of vegetables from the tray, the children played outside with the other neighborhood kids, the sound of their laughter and screams filling the air.

"Dwayne, I called Sean to see if he could join us, but his assistant said he's on the road," Robbie said.

Dwayne nodded. "He's in Atlanta. I think he's singing with Beverlyn Boudreaux this week."

"Now, that woman can sing!" Bernice raised one hand in the air and shook her head. "You know the Holy Spirit is moving when she opens her mouth."

"She's really doing some things down there in New Orleans," Robbie joined in, "with all of her crusades and speaking on top of her singing. But Lafayette said he heard she was moving to L.A."

"Really?" Nina raised her eyebrows.

"The word is, Beverlyn and her uncle are putting together some kind of gospel television network," Lafayette said.

"That's going to take a ton of money," Robbie said.

"Well, you know she's got it," Bernice noted.

"They all look kind of phony to me," Monique chimed in.

"Now, Nikki," Bernice said.

Lafayette turned to Dwayne. "What has Sean told you?"

Dwayne had been surprised. He didn't really follow Beverlyn Boudreaux and knew nothing of her plans. Taking a sip of his soda, he replied, "Sean did mention something about her to me."

"Well, you know both she and Sean have a concert in Los Angeles coming up," Lafayette pointed out.

"Mommy, Mommy!" Nina's seven-year-old son, Omari, came running into the room, interrupting the discourse.

"Omari!" Nina shrieked. "You know better than to interrupt us like that. Where are your manners?"

"I'm sorry, Mommy. I'm sorry, Pastor Lafayette."

Dwayne smiled. "And who is this young man?"

"Omari, this is Dr. Dwayne Grandison." Nina introduced the two of them as Robbie and Bernice turned their attention back to the kitchen.

"How are you, Mr. Dwayne?" Omari said before blurting out, "When are we going to eat?"

"Soon. Go back and play with the children for now."

"Okay, Mommy." The little boy, full of energy, scurried from the room.

Just Dwayne and Nina remained in the room as Bernice and Robbie prepared to serve and Lafayette went to check on the kids.

"So what do you think?" Nina inquired, moving forward in her seat. "Did you get a chance to go over the proposal?"

"Yeah, I did. I'm impressed. You've put together quite a program," he complimented her.

"Thanks, but I know you could bring so much more to it," Nina stressed. "And we'd be more than happy to work around your schedule."

"Well, I've always wanted to get involved. I'm just not so sure that now is the time."

"I promise it won't take much of your time. Besides, I'll be doing the bulk of the work," Nina added.

Dwayne looked at Nina and then Lafayette, who'd returned, wondering if they knew what they were offering him. A chance to return to the place he'd always thought of as home.

"I'd be honored to work with you," Nina said.

When Dwayne looked at Nina, he could see the sincerity of her compliment in her eyes.

"I hope you guys are finished," Robbie yelled from the dining room. "We're just about ready in here."

"Maybe we should get together and discuss this a little more," Nina said.

"Let's do that." Dwayne responded almost instinctively.

Nina pulled a small black book from her purse. "When would you like to meet?"

Dwayne laughed. "Boy, you don't waste any time."

She shook her head. "I try not to. Why don't we do lunch tomorrow?"

Her timing was perfect. Monday was the only day he allowed himself free time, not taking his first appointment until late in the afternoon. It gave him time to catch up on paperwork and return phone calls. "That'll be fine."

As Nina jotted the appointment down in her date book, Dwayne glanced over at Lafayette, who was giving him a thumbs-up.

"It's great to have you on board, man."

Dwayne smiled as he shook his head. Just like when they were children, his big brother knew how to get his way.

# Chapter Three

Dwayne looked at his watch and sighed. This was a side effect of his business—punctuality to the minute. He pulled his cell phone from his suit jacket, checked again to see if it was on, then laid it on the checkered tablecloth. He looked up and smiled as he caught sight of Nina rushing through the doors of Cafe del Rey.

"Dwayne, I am sorry," Nina said as she approached the table. "Just as I was about to leave, my sitter called with an emergency, so I had to get someone else to watch Omari."

"Oh, you could have brought him. I enjoyed meeting him yesterday. He's a good kid."

"Yes, he is." She sat back in the booth as a waitress handed her a menu. "Thanks again for meeting with me. I'm so excited that you'll be working with us."

"Hungry?"

"Not really. I'll just have a salad."

Dwayne wasn't all that hungry either, opting for a bowl of the eatery's famed black bean soup. He turned his eyes back to Nina as the waitress maneuvered through the maze of tables in the crowded restaurant, finally disappearing from view.

Dwayne smiled at the way Nina's eyes gleamed and the way her hands punctuated each of her words. And the way she pumped him up and made him feel good about himself. He had also liked that she, like him, wanted little of the limelight, opting instead for the things that, to him and now her, were most important: God, family, and making a difference.

"I know you're a busy man so I think I've devised a way to both minimize and maximize your time."

Dwayne sat silently as Nina presented her case. She was really quite pretty, he thought, understanding, as he sat before her, how as a child star, she'd been such a hit with adolescent boys.

"We would set up the general sessions for the entire group to meet just once a month. The private sessions, which are generally made up of three or four men, could be customized to your schedule. In fact, everything can be scheduled around you."

Time, however, was hardly Dwayne's concern. He'd had way too much of it on his hands lately. Nina finished her proposal just as the waitress put the crab salad with mixed greens in front of her and the bowl of soup in front of Dwayne.

"So what do you think so far?"

"Sounds like you've put together quite a program. I'd sure want you on my team."

She smiled shyly, but he was serious. Nina had the same passion he once held for his father's church.

They continued to chat through lunch, until Dwayne finally asked, "Is there any way you can put together a calendar so I can get an idea of exactly what kind of time we're talking about?"

"No problem. I can work on that this afternoon and get it to you in the morning."

"Take your time. I'm in no hurry."

"Well, thanks for lunch. I'll talk to you tomorrow." Nina took the napkin from her lap, put it on the table, gathered up her things, and rose.

"Wait, I'll walk you." Dwayne rose to his feet, hustling to take care of the bill.

"That's okay, I'm late," she called back. Nina had something a great deal more important on her mind as she turned her attention to her next appointment and the news her doctors were about to share with her.

She thought little about Dwayne and more about Omari as she got into her car and put an inspirational tape in, reminding herself that God was in control. Then she made a left onto Hughes Street, pulled into a parking lot, took one of the automatic tickets, and parked. She looked in the rearview mirror, and with her fingertips, blended the makeup under her eyes. She took a deep breath and tried to turn her lips into a smile, but the blue-lettered sign on the building behind her came into view—Brotman Medical Center. Her weak smile disappeared. All that now filled her mind was the news the doctors were about to share with her. She picked up her purse and walked unflinchingly into the hospital and headed, as always, to the radiology department for the latest test results.

As he headed back to the office, he knew he'd been struck by Nina's professionalism. But there was more. She stirred something deep within him. Something he hadn't experienced in a very long time.

Why had she left so soon? Was she not attracted to him in the least bit? Then almost instantaneously, he realized that not until today had it ever mattered whether or not a woman was attracted to him, for since Yvette, there were none he had been attracted to.

He arrived at his Beverly Hills office suite moments before his next clients. He'd received an emergency call from them that morning and had agreed to see the high-profile couple—she an anchorwoman and he a successful entrepreneur.

Renee and Jamal believed a quick, friendly divorce was the answer to what they saw as their irreconcilable differences. They were angry and fed up and came to see him for some eleventh-hour marriage counseling on the way to a high-powered Century City divorce attorney's office.

Actually, it was clear to Dwayne that there was plenty they could do to save the marriage. With the right help, he had seen relationships far worse go on to flourish.

Renee and Jamal's problems with each other weren't so terrible they couldn't be remedied. The real problem was that neither knew what to do about them. Though they loved God—and even each other still—they had few reliable tools to work with. To paraphrase the lament of the apostle Paul: They had the will to deal with each other lovingly, but when it came down to how to perform it, they were clueless.

Neither Renee nor Jamal had come from a household where the skills of a godly marriage (good communication, conflict management, mutual submission and respect, and demonstrated affection) had been modeled before them. So when they grew up and went out on their own and jumped the broom, they ended up trying to do something they hadn't seen done very well themselves.

When you ain't seen it done before, it ain't so easy to do. The sad part was that their children were watching them twenty-four/seven and learning, for better or for worse, the way a husband and a wife were supposed to treat each other.

Dwayne dropped his head in his hands and rubbed his face as they left the room after their session had come to a close.

"What's up, boss? Boy, do you look tired," Monique teased as she sauntered into the office, her blond hair twisted back into a French roll and her trademark short skirt rising along her long mocha-brown legs, and handed him a stack of clients' folders for the next day's appointments.

"I'm not tired. I just have something on my mind."

"Well, I'm out of here. Got a date. Don't work too late."

"I won't."

Monique rolled her eyes as if she didn't believe him and then walked out of the door. She had grown to know his moods quite well, and though it seemed that different worlds had always separated them, Monique was closer to Dwayne than she was to most anyone and could tell him most anything.

Dwayne had always been surprised at Monique's resolve and cheeky outlook in spite of all she'd been through, but then again, he attributed that to the time she'd spent in the Grandison home. Still, having had two young children and divorcing only recently, he couldn't help but feel she didn't take life as seriously as she should.

Yet, surprisingly enough, she had worked out perfectly for him, the perfect mix of sister girl panache and down-home Texas wit with sound uptown judgment. When he heard the front door close and lock behind her, he leaned back in the reclining chair.

He'd been this way since lunch—not able to concentrate as Nina's smiling face lingered in his mind. There was something about Nina that Dwayne could not erase from his psyche. Maybe it was the way she looked at him, with those intense brown eyes. He'd felt an immediate connection.

Nina sat at the round dining room table and took off her glasses. She massaged her temples, then put her reading glasses back on and returned to the yellow sheets of paper stretched in front of her.

The floor creaked behind her and Nina turned. "Omari, what are you doing up?"

He rubbed his eyes with his fists. "I was thirsty. May I have a glass of water? I'm really thirsty." He put his hand to his throat and coughed weakly.

Nina twisted her lips in doubt, but stood and walked to the adjoining kitchen, taking a small glass from the dish drainer on the counter and half filling it. A minute later, Omari handed the glass to his mother, but stood in place.

"Go back to bed, young man," she said, pointing in the direction of his room.

Without argument, he hugged Nina tightly. "I love you, Mommy."

She kissed his cheek, then turned him around, slapping him playfully on his butt. "It's almost midnight. Back to bed, buster."

She watched him scurry down the long hall to his bedroom and she sighed. "Thank you, Lord," she whispered.

Omari was the treasure that had risen from the rubble of her life. From the outside looking in, anyone would have thought she was blessed, but most people didn't know the rough road she'd taken. Shaking her head, even she was amazed that she'd made it.

When she spoke at high schools now and told how she wished her life had been different, her words were always met with shocked stares. Thanks to cable networks like TV Land and reruns, Nina's face was still known, even to this new generation of youngsters.

She knew all too well what they were thinking. How could someone who had been lucky enough to be acting in a top television series at the age of six say she wasn't lucky?

But by the time she explained her two suicide attempts, her battles with drugs and bulimia, and her failed marriages, the students' stares always switched from shock to sympathy. But it wasn't their sympathy she was after. She only wanted them to hear her message—that luck had nothing to do with her life. It was only the grace of God that had granted success so early and His mercy that had pulled her through when it seemed life had let her down. Nina wanted her testimony to help others, providing hope for deliverance from drugs, drinking, and promiscuity.

She shuddered at the thought of her "not distant enough" past—days that were further behind her spiritually than in years. A chapter of her life that had, since its closure, given way to a robust resilience that had brought maturity, earthiness, and the confidence of one who had been to hell, survived, and then lived to tell about it. She pushed her five-foot-four, 115-pound frame from the table and tiptoed down the hall to check on Omari. Though he had only gone to bed five minutes before, he was sleeping soundly, his arms wrapped tightly around his pillow. She kissed his forehead, pulled the comforter over him, then tiptoed from the room.

As she returned to the dining table, she looked at the clock. Nine-thirty. She'd work just a half hour more, then go to bed. But when she finally rose from the table, it was almost one.

# Chapter Four

*A*s the men continued their argument, Beverlyn twirled the glass of water she held, then sighed and stood, walking to the enormous windows of her Canal Street Plaza office. Her ankle-length purple chiffon sheath flowed gracefully behind her. The debate continued, but Beverlyn tuned the voices out, focusing in on the soft lights of the park below. Darkness was descending, but from her twenty-seventh-floor window, she could still see Jackson Square illuminated by lights from the surrounding Hilton and Marriott hotels.

She reveled in the thought of being on top of the city that once held her beneath its feet. She now sat in a top-floor office, overlooking the same park where she used to beg and steal.

"Do these people realize who Beverlyn Boudreaux is?"

With the mention of her name, Beverlyn turned around.

"L.W., we need the equipment, but this has to be a good deal for everyone." She returned to her desk and ran her fingers through her short-cropped layered hair.

The stern look in L.W 's eyes told her to let him handle this, and as she took a sip of water, he turned back to Michael Grossman, the man in charge of procuring the production equipment. He handed Michael a folder.

"I'm sure you understand my concerns, Mr. Grossman. These

numbers are not good enough and we're running out of time. We move to Los Angeles in less than a month. The production facilities are ready and the scheduling is set to go; the only thing missing is what you told us you could handle."

Michael, flushed red with L.W.'s reproach, turned to Beverlyn for support. But she dropped her gaze, confirming what he already knew—indeed, what everyone knew: that Linson William Lejohn really ran Beverlyn Boudreaux and the ever-expanding enterprise that bore her name and was said to be pulling in millions of dollars annually.

Michael turned back to L.W. "Mr. Lejohn, I'll keep working on this—"

"You have forty-eight hours." L.W. abruptly cut him off and then stood.

Michael stuffed the folders into his briefcase and nodding in acknowledgment, swiftly exited the office. Beverlyn swiveled her chair around, facing the window again, her back to L.W. She could hear him as he returned to his seat.

"Beverlyn, I know you think I'm being hard."

"Not at all, Uncle Linson." She turned toward him, calling him by the name she used only when they were alone. "I just believe he presented a good deal and we should be fair."

"We need to be smart. I don't want people taking advantage of us because we're Christians and they know we have a lot of money." The sardonic wit riddled with insecurity was part of L.W.'s persona. His smile faded so easily into a grimace that it was hard to tell them apart.

"Now, Uncle Linson, I'm hardly going to let anyone walk over me."

"Listen, what's this I hear of your agreeing to appear at the Glory Time Conference in Jackson, Mississippi?"

"Well, I have the time and I made a promise."

"Beverlyn, you're way beyond that conference. They can't pay your rate. You'd have to fly coach to meet their budget, and it would be sending a signal that people can offer you just about anything. That conference won't draw more than five hundred people. We've worked too hard to get you top dollar on the circuit and here you are!"

"Oh, Uncle Linson," she cut him off. "I really hadn't wanted to do it anyway. The woman just caught me off guard. I'll have Kim make my apologies. However, I will be doing the Spirit Alive Conference."

"But they're not even paying."

"Yeah, but Kim thinks she can get a cover story if I agree to do the conference."

"Well, let's see if we can't get them to nail that commitment down, and if they have dollars for performers in the budget, I don't see why they can't pay you, even if they're doing a cover story."

"But," she started to argue, and then stopped. She knew that despite anything she had to say, her uncle was going to do this his way, just like he'd been doing for the last twenty-five years. Besides, there was little for her to complain about. L.W. had moved her into areas she hadn't considered, including a highly successful spoken-word ministry that grossed upwards of two million annually, and book publishing. Her latest book, *Sex and the Single Christian Woman,* was selling out at all the nation's Christian bookstores.

Now L.W. was taking her beyond anything she could have imagined. The Jubilee Network was an idea presented just twenty-one months ago. He'd worked endlessly to make it a reality, but now as this latest achievement was at hand, she had her doubts, and worried that they might be in over their heads.

"Beverlyn, let me handle all of this," L.W. said. "This is a great move. You've seen the projections. We're talking a lot of money, and I'm not going to kid you, there are some risks involved, but God hasn't failed us yet."

The numbers—that was her hot button and L.W. knew it. She needed money so she could do all the things she dreamed of: starting a Christian camp for children whose families were too poor to send them away, or scholarships for poor young men and women who aspired to major in music. She wanted to fill in all of the gaps she had faced when growing up. And she also wanted to call her own shots. For too long, she'd not been taken seriously on the Christian front. She was either too pretty or too young or a woman. She was finally close to letting people know just how wrong they'd been about her and what she could do. Yeah, she was about to give the African American church world something to talk about.

"Beverlyn." Kim entered the room. "Your two P.M. with *Gospel Alive* magazine is here."

# Chapter Five

*A*nd the final question," Nina said. "Should we and, if so, how will we attract men beyond our church members?"

Dwayne leaned back in the seat and intertwined his fingers behind his head. He had rolled up the sleeves of his starched shirt two hours before when his meeting with Nina had first begun. He smiled as Nina answered her final question the way she had addressed all of his concerns—professionally and succinctly.

"Well?" Her forehead crinkled with anxiety as her eyes searched his for the answer she wanted to hear. When he remained silent, she tried to smile through the grimace that betrayed her concern. "So, Dwayne, what do you think?"

Dwayne leaned forward, resting his hands on the conference room's cherry wood table. From the sanctuary, they heard the faint sound of a keyboard and soft voices as the youth choir practiced. The words of the song settled into their silence:

*Order my steps in Your Word, Dear Lord.*
*Lead me, guide me every day.*

Finally, he said, "Well, I don't know . . . um," prolonging her suspense. "I, um . . . well, actually"—he stood up, turned away from her, then slowly turned back around—"nothing would please me more." With that, he could hardly contain his laughter.

At once, she playfully nudged him, then lunged her arms around his neck. "All right!"

It was an automatic reflex when Dwayne returned her hug.

"I hope I'm not interrupting anything."

Both Nina and Dwayne jumped at the voice behind them. They turned almost simultaneously to find Lafayette leaning against the doorpost, a wide grin occupying his face.

"Dwayne has agreed to join us, Pastor."

"That is good news." Lafayette swaggered toward them in a casual black Georgio Armani slacks set. "It's good to have you back home, man."

"And Dwayne has shared some good baselines for the dialogue," Nina explained to Lafayette.

"Who knows? I might have to move over."

"Don't get any ideas," Dwayne said, reacting to the smirk on Lafayette's face. "I'm taking this one step at a time."

"I know." Lafayette got serious. "Then again, who knows what could come of this?" He stopped, his eyes darting between Nina and Dwayne as he turned toward the door. "You guys just keep doing what you were doing before I interrupted you."

Dwayne squinted as he stared at the door, wondering about his brother's comment.

"There is just one thing to discuss," Nina said, her voice still filled with excitement.

Dwayne turned his attention back to her.

"We should meet regularly for the next few weeks until the program is up and running," she said. "And it would be good if you could come to one of the sessions I lead."

Dwayne pushed away from the table and began rolling down his shirtsleeves. "Great," he said, surprised by his own excitement.

"So when should we meet again?"

"I have to check my calendar." He stood and lifted his jacket from the chair next to him. "Call my office tomorrow and Monique can schedule something in."

"Okay." Nina tilted her head. "Is something wrong?"

"No, I just . . . have somewhere to go."

"I have something for you two." Lafayette came into the room with two gold-inscribed cards and gave them to Nina.

"These are VIP passes to the Beverlyn Boudreaux concert and after-party," she said. "These are for me?"

"For you and Dwayne." Lafayette smiled. "I thought this would be an excellent way for the two of you to celebrate. Sean Wiley donated a block of tickets to the church and I can't think of a better way to thank you both."

Nina's gaze dropped. "Well, I don't know . . ."

"Lafayette . . ." Dwayne's voice was tight.

"You don't have to thank me," Lafayette said, oblivious to the tension that now choked the room. "I'm glad to do this." He walked out, leaving Dwayne and Nina alone again.

"I don't know why Pastor did that," Nina said nervously. "Listen, we don't have to go. Besides, I'm not so sure I could get a sitter . . ."

"It's not that . . ."

"Dwayne, you don't owe me an explanation." She paused and looked up at the clock. "Speaking of sitters, I think I'd better get home and relieve mine."

Dwayne watched in silence as she filled her briefcase with the folders scattered across the table, his hands stuffed deep in his pockets. He stood by helplessly, lost in the awkwardness of the moment.

Her smile was weak as she put on her jacket. She'd known that Lafayette had meant well, but in the heat of the moment, it seemed he'd ruined everything. She put the strap of her briefcase over her shoulder and extended her hand. "Thank you, Dwayne, for joining the team. I'll give your secretary a call tomorrow."

"Uh, well . . . ," he countered as he watched Nina step from the room. Once alone, he fell against the wall. How could Lafayette have done something so stupid? After snatching up the invitation, Dwayne straightened his jacket and went to find Lafayette.

Dwayne's breathing was somewhat labored when he entered Lafayette's office, and the peace that he usually encountered upon entering the room escaped him now as he paced back and forth in front of the desk. He still thought of this as his father's office, even though Lafayette had been senior pastor for over eight years. Not that he didn't respect his brother, though at this very moment, respect was the furthest thing from his mind.

"I didn't know you were still here," Lafayette said, entering the room and letting the door close behind him. "I saw Nina leave and assumed you'd left as well."

With Dwayne's silence, Lafayette knew something was wrong.

"Something on your mind?"

Dwayne shook his head and then looked at his brother. "How could you do that?"

Lafayette drew back, his eyebrows raised in surprise. "What are you—"

Before Lafayette could finish, Dwayne cut him off. "How could you embarrass Nina and me like that?"

Lafayette raised his hands and reached toward his brother, but Dwayne stepped away. "Dwayne, calm down and lower your voice. I only came up with the idea after you and Nina told me the news. It was a knee-jerk reaction and, I thought, a pretty good idea. I'm sorry, but why are you so angry?"

Dwayne paused, not quite sure. "You embarrassed both of us. Besides, Sean had already sent me passes. I gave them away." Exasperated, he charged, "Are you trying to set me up with Nina?"

"Is that what you think I'm doing?" He shook his head. "Look, I just thought it was a good idea. I'm sorry if I put you in a bad position. You two are friendly, aren't you?"

"There you go again." Dwayne glared at his brother.

Lafayette held up his hands. "Hey, you and Nina are going to be working closely together. I thought it might be a good way to break the ice, but just for the record, you couldn't do any better."

Lafayette had a point, but Dwayne said nothing.

"Okay Dwayne," Lafayette gave in. "Look, it's getting late. Just take the invite, think about it, and if you decide to go, go. And if you don't . . ." He shrugged, then picked up the phone. "I have a call to make before I leave."

Without a word, Dwayne stood and walked out the door.

Lafayette shook his head before smiling. His baby brother was interested. He hoped whatever was going on between him and Nina would flourish. Nina might be just what the doctor ordered.

It took Dwayne twenty-five minutes to drive home, reflecting on the question Lafayette posed—and he still couldn't answer. What was the problem? What his brother had said made sense. He just wished Lafayette had checked with him first. But even if he had, Dwayne would have said no. He wasn't sure that he was ready to date.

But it wasn't really a date, the other side of his brain argued. In fact, if he did decide to go to the concert—after all, Sean was performing and was expecting him to come—Nina was a safe choice. She'd never be able to look at this as a date, at least not seriously, and maybe taking her to the concert would be a great way to break the ice—with Nina and his new life. By the time Dwayne handed his keys to the valet and took the elevator to the penthouse, he'd decided.

He clicked on the lights and headed for the bedroom. Turning on the lamp on his nightstand, Dwayne pulled the card that Nina had given him from his wallet and dialed the number before he could change his mind.

"Hello."

"Nina, this is Dwayne. I hope it's not too late to call." He looked at the clock. He hadn't thought of the time.

"No, it's okay. I was just getting Omari settled in. Hold on?"

As muffled sounds came through the phone, Dwayne closed his eyes. It wasn't until that moment that he realized his leg was shaking. He held it still. A few minutes later, Nina returned, sounding rushed. "I'm sorry, Dwayne. I'm back."

"That's okay." He cleared his throat. "You left before we could talk about the concert." Dwayne wondered if he sounded as awkward as he felt. Why did it feel so unnatural? Maybe because he hadn't talked to a woman in this fashion in over fifteen years, and the silence he felt from the other end of the phone did little to ease his awkwardness. He realized in that instant that he really was asking her out on a date, but it was too late to back out now.

"I think Lafayette had a good idea. So if you're not doing anything next Saturday, I would be most honored to have you attend the concert with me."

There was a long pause. "I don't know what to say. I really would like to go to the concert, but earlier this evening, you—"

"Please, no more about that. It was just a little awkward for me."

"Believe me, I understand and I'd love to go to the concert with you," she said softly. "I've been wanting to see Beverlyn Boudreaux for some time."

Dwayne took a deep breath and relaxed, leaning up against the headboard. "You know, Sean has spoken so highly of her, I'm anxious to see if she's all people say she is."

"Then we'll go. I'm looking forward to it, Dwayne."

"Well, I don't want to keep you."

"Good night." Nina clicked off the phone before he could say another word, and for several minutes, Dwayne sat clutching the receiver. Slowly, he dropped it into the cradle, then walked to the dresser. He lifted Yvette's picture and stared at the photo as his fingers traced the lines of her face. She had truly been beautiful, and for all of his noble and spiritual priorities, he was undeniably drawn to her. With her at his side, he had been the envy of every man he'd known. The thought of that had bothered him, causing him to examine his own superficial yearnings.

What, he thought now, had been so very wrong with wanting, as she had, the best of life? There they were again, the second thoughts that had clouded his grief with self-doubts. Perhaps, if he had been more aggressive, she would be alive. He placed the picture back, sighing as he always did.

Nina stared at the phone. She certainly hadn't expected that call. In fact, after she had left Dwayne, her only prayer was that he wouldn't back away from Man-to-Man. But as she drove home, picked up Omari, and checked his homework, nagging questions distracted her.

As she filled the teapot and then put it on the stove, she wondered aloud, "So what is this all about, Dwayne?"

She knew about his wife's death, though she hadn't said anything about it. It just hadn't seemed appropriate. She hadn't really known Yvette, but couldn't help but wonder if Dwayne's reaction tonight had something to do with his wife. Could it be that he hadn't been out socially since her death?

No, Nina thought. That wasn't possible. It had been over a year, as she remembered, and as good-looking and successful as Dwayne was, surely there were legions of women swarming, ready and willing to do his bidding. The shrill of the teapot's whistle made Nina jump and she grabbed the handle.

"Ouch!" she shrieked, and dropped the kettle back on the stove. She shook her head, scolding herself as she looked at her reddened palm. If only she had been paying attention, instead of daydreaming about Dwayne Grandison.

After blowing on the tips of her fingers, she put a Mint Medley tea bag into a cup and, this time using a pot holder, poured the hot water over it. She placed the cup on a saucer and gingerly carried it to the couch. After taking a small sip, she sat down and curled her legs under her.

She continued to contemplate the phone call, replaying every word. Then suddenly, it hit her. She couldn't get involved with Dwayne, or anyone else for that matter. No, she would concentrate on the ministries and Omari. She was after all on track, and the tests had, for now, indicated that the treatment was working and the tumor had not returned, but she was not yet out of the woods and she knew it. No, she had enough on her hands without the added drama of a relationship. Besides, she wasn't moving, in any area, without God. And He hadn't yet said anything to her about Dwayne Grandison. She stared at her reddened palm. Why—she shook her head—had she said yes?

# Chapter Six

*D*wayne felt as if he were a young man again, preparing for his prom. He straightened his bow tie, then stepped from the limousine after the driver had opened the door, and looked up at the Spanish-motif building before moving toward the entrance. He buzzed the button next to 2F, Nina's apartment number, then stuffed his hands into his pockets. As he waited, his eyes glanced across the block that was lined with middle-income apartments. When Nina had given him her address, he'd been surprised, expecting a luxury building, similar to where he lived.

Instead, he was standing in the small entryway of one of the look-alike buildings that sprinkled the Westside of L.A. Nothing about it suggested a former child star who'd once had her own series and become a household name.

"Hello."

Dwayne smiled at Omari's voice and leaned closer to the speaker.

"Hello, Omari. It's Dwayne Grandison."

"Hi, Mr. Dwayne," Omari responded as if he were settling in for a long conversation.

"Dwayne," Nina spoke over Omari, "I'll be right down."

"Okay." Dwayne was surprised at his disappointment. Once he heard Omari's voice, he'd hoped to get a chance to see the boy.

The door behind him opened and he turned around, relieved that Nina had come down so quickly.

"Dwayne, I'm sorry I kept you waiting."

A smile instantly filled his face. He'd only seen Nina dressed in the most professional business suits, but standing before him now, she was both elegant and sexy in an off-the-shoulder beaded cocktail dress. A matching shawl was draped over her arm, and her hair was pulled out of her bun, and the way it fell softly onto her shoulders made her look like she had not lost the unmistakable star quality he remembered.

"You look great, Dr. Grandison."

"I was just thinking the same about you. I'm glad we decided to go tonight."

"Me too. I'm surprised I'm so excited." She folded her hands under her chin. "It's going to be fun." Yet, as the stretch limousine turned onto the 10 Freeway, Nina and Dwayne found themselves unable to resist the urge to turn their talk to business.

"Did you imagine growing up that you would ever be in ministry?" Dwayne asked.

"Not until after I'd made every mistake known to man, it seems. Then I realized how alone people feel when they're going through things. That is when I knew I had to do something where I could have an impact. If they only knew they are not alone, they might feel more comfortable facing their shortcomings head-on. When I think about what I went through, the things that I did . . ." Her voice faded, and she shivered thinking back.

Dwayne recognized the look of life's pain. It was one he saw often in his clients who claimed Hollywood as home. Gently, he covered Nina's hand, and even though her eyes remained on the window, he said, "When you think back to all of those times, all you have to remember is that what you've gone through is helping others now." He kept his voice soft, soothing, professional. "That is your purpose."

A moment of silence passed, and when she turned toward him, the brightness in her eyes had returned. "Always the doctor."

"Well, I don't want to be tonight. I just want us to have a good time together." He reached for her hand and entwined her fingers in his.

"Thank you."

The limousine exited onto Prairie Street, and they slowed to a crawl. The streets surrounding the Inglewood Forum, recently purchased by a pastor friend of Lafayette's, were lined with hundreds of other stretch limos. And though the silence had returned, their hands remained entwined on the leather seat between them.

As the limousine moved slowly away from the curb, Nina and Dwayne walked forward at the same slow pace, crushed between the bodies of the music world's royalty.

"This is a madhouse," Dwayne yelled, though he was barely audible above the hovering hum of the helicopters. He squeezed her hand tighter. Nina tried to keep her head high, though the lights continued to blind her. The crowd on the sides screamed names that melted into a continuous drone.

"Who's this coming toward us?" Nina heard one of the cameramen from E! Entertainment Television ask the young woman with the microphone in her hand.

Nina watched as the young woman with short blond hair moved her microphone into position. She squinted in their direction. The young woman's shoulders dropped. "Isn't that Nina Jordan?" She paused, then turned to the cameraman.

"Who?" he replied.

"Never mind. Maybe we should move further to the front."

Nina smiled. There was a time when she would have demanded the attention of the cameras, but she was pleased the cameras no longer sought her, though at times she wished they did—to make up for all the compromising photographs they had captured in her past. However, there was little real desire to seek redemption from the tabloid press. The work that she now did had helped her to find a personal peace, which years ago she'd been sure would never be part of her life.

Nina was so deep in her thoughts that she didn't realize Dwayne had maneuvered them to the front, where they were blocked by two men, dressed in matching black suits and wearing earphones. The larger one stood sullenly as the tall, thin, Kareem Abdul-Jabbar look-alike checked VIP passes. When his partner nodded, the burly one stepped aside and directed her and Dwayne through the security barriers.

Though they were now inside, the outside commotion had followed them. The entry, adjacent to the backstage area, was thick with celebrities mingling with other VIP ticket holders.

"Should we find our seats? Or would you like something to drink?" Dwayne still gently held her hand.

"Let's find our seats." But before they took two steps forward, they were stopped by a voice.

"Hey, Dr. Grandison."

Dwayne turned toward the voice. Arden Parks, an actor and one of Dwayne's clients, stepped toward them.

"Arden, how are you?"

"Great, thanks to you." His words were directed toward Dwayne, but his eyes were focused on Nina. He squinted, then his eyes opened wide in recognition. "You're Nina . . ." He snapped his fingers as if his memory would return with the action.

"Jordan." Nina completed Arden's sentence and stretched her hand forward. "Nice to see you again, Arden." Years ago, they'd worked together when Arden made his acting debut in an episode of *Everyday People*. The ten-year-old Arden had swooned over the thirteen-year-old Nina, who was already a star.

"It's been a long time." Arden's eyes moved from Nina to Dwayne.

"Yes, it has," Nina said softly.

"Well, Arden, we're going to find our seats. Good seeing you."

"Yeah, Doc. It was good seeing . . . both of you." He tapped Dwayne's arm as if he were sending him a coded message.

They hadn't gotten two feet before they heard Dwayne's name called again. As they turned, Sean Wiley, gospel music's reigning sensation, approached. Eyes turned as the six-foot-two, handsome, thirtyish, blond-haired, blue-eyed man approached, wearing a trendy Armani slacks set. Dwayne dropped Nina's hand and extended a warm embrace to his friend.

"I hadn't heard from you. I wasn't sure you'd come."

"I got your message late and thought I'd just see you here. This is Nina Jordan." Dwayne introduced the two.

Sean hesitated for a moment, then a wide smile crossed his face as he shook Nina's hand. "It is a pleasure."

"Excuse us a minute." Sean pulled Dwayne to the aisle.

"Man, you've been holding out. You're dating Nina Jordan?"

"Sean . . ."

Before Dwayne could continue, he was interrupted by a voice behind him. "Sean, where have you been?" The voice echoed through the stadium. Beverlyn Boudreaux floated down the aisle toward them. Her gold chiffon gown sailed behind her, as did Kim Steele, elegant in a black satin Tuxedo slacks suit, an earphone accentuating her coiffed pageboy. Beverlyn held out her hands and Sean took them. "I looked for you at sound check," she said.

"Sorry, I just got here."

Her eyes had already left Sean's and were fixed on Dwayne. "You must be Dr. Dwayne Grandison," Beverlyn said, smiling broadly as her face lit up.

"I've been trying to get the two of you together," Sean said excitedly. "Beverlyn, this is a man I have the pleasure of calling my best friend, Dwayne Grandison."

Beverlyn's eyes dropped to Dwayne's feet and slowly moved up. Photos didn't do him credit, she thought to herself. She extended her hand. "It is incredible to finally meet you. Sean tells me such wonderful things about you."

"He speaks well of you too."

"We'll have to get together and compare notes."

"Hello, Ms. Boudreaux. It is an honor to meet you."

All eyes turned toward Nina, who suddenly appeared at Dwayne's side. The wide smile on Beverlyn's face faded, but only for a moment. She took Nina's hand. "You are . . ."

"Nina Jordan, and I am a big fan of yours."

"Thank you." Beverlyn's eyes lingered on Nina, but then she returned to Dwayne. "Dr. Grandison, I've been looking forward to meeting you for some time now. There are some things I'm working on that I'd like to discuss with you. You will be at the after-party, won't you?"

"Beverlyn, you need to get to your dressing room." L.W. stood behind his niece, for the first time entering into the small circle they'd formed in the backstage lounge.

"You're right, L.W.," she said before turning back to Dwayne. "I hope you can join us later."

"We're not sure." He looked at Nina and then looked back at Beverlyn. "But thank you for the invitation."

"Well, I hope to see you later."

"Beverlyn, we really have to go," L.W. said strongly.

She hugged Sean, then smiled and walked away with her uncle and entourage in tow. All eyes followed her as she stopped every few feet to greet her friends and fans.

"I've got to go too," Sean said as Beverlyn finally disappeared through the stage door. "I'll see you at the party. Try to make it so that we can . . . chat." He grinned.

"Okay." Dwayne patted Sean on the back.

Sean gently took Nina's hand. "I'll see you later."

Dwayne put his hand in the small of Nina's back and led her to their seats.

"I didn't know it was going to be this kind of evening," Nina said, exhilarated as they took their near-front-row seats. "How long have you known Sean?"

"Years. It started as strictly professional, but we really hit it off and became friends."

"Well, he sure can sing," Nina exclaimed. "From what I've read, though, he's had a pretty tough time." When Dwayne's eyebrows furrowed together in question, Nina continued, "You know—from the streets of Hollywood to the pews of the church."

"Yeah, Sean has made quite a turnaround."

"So are you going to accept Beverlyn's invitation?"

"Do you want to?"

"It's not a problem if you want to go." She paused, then added, "Besides, aren't you the least bit curious about that . . . proposition she has for you?"

Seconds later, the lights dimmed three times and there was darkness. The music began and the crowd sat back waiting for a rousing and spirited two-hour performance that, during its course, brought the crowd to their feet at least a half dozen times, culminating with three standing ovations.

It took several minutes for the audience to leave after the final standing ovation. Nina glanced at Dwayne as they moved into the aisle and was pleased at the wide smile on his face. This was just what he needed, she thought. But as they piled back into the limousine for the ride to the party, she had a feeling this night was going to be important for her too.

The hotel suite was nothing short of palatial. The select gathering that Beverlyn had told them about seemed to have turned this into the place to be. Nina held on to Dwayne's hand as they stepped through the throng of bodies that filled the space, finally settling at the edge of the room near the balcony.

In the sophisticated roar of the industry's elite, elegantly dressed men and women hovered in small clusters with glasses in their hands. In between, tuxedoed men and women passed through the crowd with trays covered with smoked salmon, soufflé-filled potato skins, and shrimp pastries.

"Champagne, wine, or sparkling cider for anyone?" A waiter balanced a silver tray of several bottles.

"I'll get us some glasses," Dwayne said. "Wait here."

Nina nodded as Dwayne pressed his body through the crowded room. She smiled, amused, as she watched other women zoom in on Dwayne, some stopping in midconversation as he passed.

*Who is he?* Nina couldn't exactly hear their whispers, but she didn't need to. Their eyes told the story. She turned away, her smile still intact as she now watched Dwayne's movements through the reflection in the sliding glass door to the balcony. She wasn't surprised at the women's reaction. It wasn't just his stunning good looks and build. It was the way he held his shoulders square, strutting with a confidence that oozed sexiness.

This wasn't the first time Nina noticed the stares. Throughout the night, she'd observed the envious glances, but they hardly fazed her.

"A dollar for your thoughts."

Nina jumped at the sound of Dwayne's voice. "Only a dollar?" she asked, recovering quickly. "I'm worth far more than that, Dr. Grandison."

He laughed, handing her a crystal flute. "I bet you are. So how much would it cost to find out what you were so deep in thought about?"

Nina took a sip of her cider and lowered her eyes, letting her lips linger on the glass for a long moment. Just as she raised her eyes to speak, she saw Beverlyn over Dwayne's shoulder, and almost simultaneously Dwayne turned.

His mind went back to their earlier conversation. What had Beverlyn wanted of him? He'd only met her hours earlier. What was this proposition about? Beverlyn was drawing closer, en route stopping to greet the growing number of clamoring guests jammed into the posh hotel suite awash in marble, eighteen-foot-high ceilings, warm, muted earth tones, and sweeping views of Los Angeles.

In one sense, Beverlyn Boudreaux was exactly what he had expected. Yet there was a magnetic quality he couldn't now put his finger on, and it had taken him quite by surprise. A flawless light olive complexion surrounded her dark, piercing eyes and was framed by her shoulder-length hair, not a strand of it out of place, layered in a voluminous upsweep that seemed to perfectly frame her oval face. She was prettier than he had expected. Though he'd seen her many times on the TBN Network, her good looks had been lost in her conservative appearance, the power of her words and song, and her forceful beckoning of a better way through salvation to the thousands watching. The characteristic shrilling vocal runs had translated into a string of hit albums, the latest of which, *Unconditional Love,* was skyrocketing her to the kind of mainstream success that was afforded secular superstars.

To a small degree, he'd been there (done that), having been catapulted to notoriety by two appearances on *Oprah,* which he'd believed to some extent had occurred on a lark. (But as his brother,

Lafayette, and his mother had reminded him, "All things work to-gether for good to those who love the Lord," and so, they had sur-mised, it was no lark.) He had traveled to Paradise Island with Sean, who was slated to appear on the show shortly after Yvette's sudden and untimely death. Dwayne had been recommended to the produc-ers by a publicist who was a former client of his.

The audience had loved his advice—a combination of his family's homespun wit, biblical teachings, and a strong dose of unfiltered common sense—and while he was one of five guests on the show, he found himself fielding most of the audience's questions with what appeared to be Oprah's unconditional approval.

"You were great. They loved you," Sean had said as the taping ended, and taking a deep breath, Dwayne had removed the mike and walked off the set.

A producer had approached him with Oprah in tow and said, "Great show, Doc."

"Write a book and we'll make it a best-seller," Oprah had said as she interlocked her arm with Sean's and pulled him forward, turning back to say, "It was nice meeting you."

While it was a whole lot less interaction than they had shared dur-ing the show, he knew he'd scored points with her. A book, he pon-dered.

One of the show's producers had alerted a friend at Excelsior Books who was excited to take on the project, and he received a call within the week. Without thinking, Dwayne, who'd operated on au-topilot since the death of his wife, said yes, later reasoning that the challenge might take his mind off the enormous grief he'd been suf-fering.

For the next few months, he'd poured his energy into his practice and the book. And just as Oprah had hinted, a producer called as it was completed and he was booked on the show.

Sean had been told that the show had been deluged with letters in-quiring about Dr. Dwayne Grandison, everything from marriage pro-posals for the handsome, young, and recently widowed doctor to desperate letters seeking his guidance on a variety of issues. He had been oblivious to the attention, awash in the sorrow and guilt of

Yvette's passing, for despite their differences, he couldn't see life
without her, and still somewhat naively believed that what he and
Yvette had enjoyed together as teens could have ultimately been re-
captured.

Tagged "Dr. Dwayne" by Oprah, he took the stage at Harpo's
Chicago-based set, and for a full hour, he engaged the audience with
his sage life counsel, at one point rolling up his sleeves and loosening his collar to dispel any notions that he was there to do anything
but help, a move that made him all the more attractive to viewers.

Sales of his newly penned book briefly went through the roof, and
his high-profile private practice became all the more elite, with his
celebrity clients now thinking he could relate all the more to them.
But he was quite frankly relieved when he didn't receive another call
from Oprah's producers.

It was like he'd told Yvette, he wasn't cut out for all that, yet while
he'd yearned to follow his father's footsteps into the ministry—just
like his brother—he wasn't so sure pastoring was what God had in
store for him either, and the whole notion of what he should be
doing perplexed him.

Beverlyn, on the other hand, was comfortable with growing mainstream appeal. She seemed born for it.

"I'm glad you could make it," she said, approaching with Sean.

"Congratulations on your performance. We wouldn't have missed
it," Dwayne said politely, with Nina echoing the sentiments. "You
were great."

Disregarding Nina's acknowledgment, Beverlyn moved in closer to
Dwayne and only then turned to Nina. "Mind if I steal him away for
a moment? There is something important I'd like to run by him."

Taken aback, Nina could barely respond before Sean came to her
rescue.

"We'll be just fine," he said as Beverlyn drew Dwayne across the
room and the two disappeared from view.

Sean Wiley shook his head in response to Nina's bewilderment.
"Don't let Beverlyn get to you. That's just her way. She's a great person, just a bit over the top."

"Oh, so that's what it's called?" Nina took a sip of her cider. "I have to admit, she's not what I expected."

"People say that, but Beverlyn is just one of those women who have to be at the center all the time. That's really why she's so successful. But I don't want to talk about her. It's hot in here. Let's go out on the balcony, where you can tell me what's happening between you and Dwayne."

Nina smiled coyly, somewhat embarrassed to say that there was little to tell.

"Yeah, right." Sean coiled back, examining Nina a bit closer.

She was beautiful and one couldn't help but notice that together she and Dwayne made a stunning couple. Something had to be happening between them, though after having heard unofficial accounts of Nina's checkered past from those who'd read supermarket tabloids, he was somewhat surprised that Dwayne and she had much in common.

Yet there was something about her. Nothing like the girl who'd grown up right before his eyes on TV, whom he'd felt sorry for ten years earlier when they'd canceled her once top-rated TV series after reports that her on-again, off-again battle with drugs was on again. No, this beautiful woman wasn't the same girl at all. He found her easy to like and suddenly knew why Dwayne was with her.

They went through large French doors onto a wide platform where white cast-iron chairs with thick black cushions circled matching tables. Though a light wind swirled gently onto the terrace, Nina felt relief from the stuffiness of the suite.

"Well, you really had the crowd rocking tonight!"

"Thanks." He directed Nina to a chair at the far end of the terrace. "I get so much more out of singing now than when I was doing secular music. There's nothing better than knowing you've had an impact and that you may have played some role in people's lives being changed for the better."

"I know. That's the charge I get every day."

"Oh, yeah? Do you sing?"

Nina laughed and shook her head. "Not hardly, but I do work at New Covenant with Dwayne's brother. About a year ago, we set up a women's mentoring and empowerment ministry and recently we added a program for men. Dwayne will be working with me in developing it."

"Oh." Sean sang the word out. "Well, Dwayne has been keeping secrets," he said before taking a sip of champagne. With a smirk, he added, "In more ways than one."

"He's not. This just happened last week. It's been like a whirlwind romance." She blushed at the slip. "I mean . . . you know what I mean."

"No, I can't say that I do. Why don't you explain it to me?" he teased.

"It's all business." Her words were deliberate, even if not convincing. "The idea for Dwayne to work with us came about so quickly, that's why I made the analogy . . . to a romance."

Sean took a long sip of his champagne. "And romance was the first thing that came to your mind?"

"You're teasing me." Nina frowned, then laughed at the smile on Sean's face.

Sean joined in her laughter. "I am. But my man Dwayne is going to be quite busy."

Nina tried to hold back the question, but once again, words escaped her lips before she could stop them. "What does Beverlyn want?" she asked, feigning a casual tone.

Sean leaned against the balcony rail. "She's starting a television network . . ."

"I heard about it," Nina interjected.

"She's been after me to introduce the two of them, so I'm sure she wants Dwanye involved in some capacity . . . maybe for one of the programs. That would be something," he mused. "My friend, a star."

While Sean chuckled at the thought, Nina felt the whip of the wind, stronger now than it had been moments before. She shivered.

"Do you want to go back inside?"

"Yes. Dwayne might be finished and I want him to know where I am."

"I understand," Sean said as he took her hand, helping her up from the chair. Still holding her hand, he guided her back into the penthouse suite, where Beverlyn had earlier been swept up into the crowd.

Nina couldn't get over how down-to-earth Sean had been. She had actually seen him once or twice at the church but had never gotten close enough to say hello.

Dwayne felt for a moment as if he were being swallowed up. Beverlyn's aura had completely filled the room. He sat quietly as she went on about the twenty-four-hour gospel television network that Beverlyn Boudreaux Ministries was about to launch in Los Angeles. He had to admit it was ambitious but had little doubt that Beverlyn, who was set to relocate to the City of Angels within the next month, could pull it off. What role would he play in her Jubilee Network? Finally, she stopped talking, handed him what appeared to be a proposal, and said, "Here's where you fit in."

He scanned the document, which was attached to a packet of written materials detailing every aspect of the Jubilee Network, and shook his head in disbelief. "You want me to host a television show?"

"I saw the show you did with Oprah. You're a natural."

He looked back down at the paper.

She continued, "You're successful. You established quite a following with your book. You're well known in the Christian community. You'd be great, and the best part is that I know that you have a heart for ministry and this is an opportunity for you to help so many." She paused for a moment. "And, Dr. Grandison"—she drove the point home before he could object—"the Jubilee Network will be the first Christian network owned by African Americans. Speaking of which, you'll see there," she said, pointing to the package, "we're prepared to pay you a quarter of a million dollars for the first ten shows. That's twenty-five thousand dollars per episode, not including monthly bonuses based on ratings."

He said nothing, though inside he couldn't believe his ears.

"Ms. Boudreaux—"

"Beverlyn," she interrupted.

"I'm just a therapist, and I'm pretty good at what I do. I like to help people with their problems. It's what I do. The Oprah thing was a lark. I'm sure there are any number of more qualified—"

She cut him off. "I won't take no for an answer. I know you'd be perfect. Say yes," she said, moving in closer to him.

Was she flirting? He dismissed the thought almost as quickly as it had popped up. Was she even his type? Surveying the long and fitted designer red dress that displayed a tasteful bit of cleavage, she had—at least this night—shed her more conservative image. In that instant, all that was healthy and natural in him, the homebody who held close to family and God, cherished his wife, and yearned for family, was now buying into the fast-track, high-profile Beverly Hills psychologist image he'd long resisted. He wondered if he hadn't subconsciously fostered it with his natural good looks, well-toned physique, *GQ* flair, always-in-control demeanor, and cool intellect, which had translated as "tight" to those who had not really known him. While he shrugged off the label readily cast upon him by his younger, hipper clientele, it was quietly appreciated.

Why not do it? he thought, fearful attraction overtaking him, shaking the inner intellectual protests and tempting him forward toward a door Yvette would have been thrilled to walk through. It was in deference to her that the consideration became all the more real. But while he liked to say that this kind of success had been Yvette's dream only, he was flattered. Perhaps this was God's plan for him. After all, what Beverlyn was suggesting was ministry. It seemed the best of both worlds.

"So what do you think?"

"I don't know," he mused. "Nina started a program at my brother's church that I'm going to be helping her with."

"That's sweet, but think about what I'm offering, Dr. Grandison. I'm sure that if you had to choose between this proposal and Nina . . ." She left her sentence unfinished.

"Oh, there will be no choice." He paused briefly. "If I were to do this with you, I'd have to find time to make everything work. I'm already committed to Nina."

The ends of her smile turned down and a knock on the door interrupted his thought. As L.W. entered, both he and Beverlyn stood.

"Let me get back to you," he said, a smile hinting she might just get what she wanted.

"L.W., I think we've got our man," she said as Dwayne turned to leave.

"We'll see." He extended his hand to L.W. "Nice meeting you. I promise I'll give this serious consideration."

Taking a deep breath, Dwayne made his way back to Nina. Though flattered, he didn't like the feeling of being worked. It was part of what had driven a wedge of tension between him and Yvette. When he spotted Nina and Sean across the room, a wave of calm swept over him. He wanted to get out of there. He had some thinking to do. "Let's get out of here," he said, taking Nina's hand.

As they made their way to the car, Nina couldn't help but notice the folder tucked under his arm and wondered what was in it.

"So how did it go with Beverlyn?"

"Interesting." He offered no more, and as it wasn't her business, she let the matter rest, at least for the moment.

"Did you have a good time?" he inquired, hoping she'd enjoyed being with him as much as he had with her.

"Yeah, everything was wonderful, the show, the party, and Sean is great."

But Nina was not in the mood to be engaging. Why hadn't he told her what he and Beverlyn had discussed? Then again, it was none of her business. What was she thinking?

As cameras flickered in the throng of partygoers awaiting their cars, Nina thought about her old friend Todd Bridges. The tabloids still haunted him. But since she had given her life over to God, they could surely find no interest in her. At least so she hoped. Still, she knew that they could make life difficult, and because reruns of her old series still aired, she was hardly immune. Humph, she smirked to herself. All for filler material. While she no longer held the title stories or big news, any secrets revealed in her life could still be, if nothing else, filler and the tabloids wouldn't think twice about printing news of her medical crisis. And while she could have survived the intrusion, she was most concerned for Omari. For that alone, she hated this scene.

By the time the car slowed to a stop in front of Nina's home, Dwayne's mind was racing. Both women had given him a great deal to think about.

He held her arm as she lifted her gown and moved up the stairs to the second level. Nina put her key in the door, opened it slightly, then turned back to Dwayne.

"I really had a nice time. Thank you, Dwayne."

"Believe me, it was my pleasure." He hesitated before leaning over and kissing Nina's cheek. "Thank you."

# Chapter Seven

As he looked up, Dwayne was relieved that Vanessa was the last client he'd booked for the day. At thirty, and financially well off, having recently divorced a major R&B performer, Vanessa was attractive, intelligent, saved, sanctified, filled with the precious Holy Ghost, and angry enough to bite somebody!

It seemed "for the fifty-eleventh time" (her words), she had fallen head over heels in love with yet another positively wonderful, spiritually mature, truly caring man at her church. After about two minutes together—oh all right, two weeks—they'd both begun to use words like "commitment," "our future together," "marriage," and, oh yeah, "God sent us to each other" in their late-night four-hour telephone conversations and their fervent Day of Pentecost–style prayer sessions.

Problem was that by mutual decision, the relationship had ended with great drama (God had "unsent" them to each other?), and Vanessa's ex-beloved had struck up a starry-eyed courtship with some other sweet young thing in the choir or the singles' group, or on the usher board or the prayer team.

Vanessa considered herself a poor innocent victim who was made to fall in love with a wolf in sheep's clothing. To hear her tell it, she had been abused by this Christian Casanova who was now, according to her, "running through every woman in the church." All she wanted to know was what the Lord Himself, the pastor, the LAPD, or the resurrected prophet Isaiah were going to do to make sure it didn't happen again.

Vanessa's beef was one he'd heard a thousand times over the years from his clients as well as men and women at his seminars. That she had been made to fall in love with someone. Dwayne was always frustrated that he couldn't seem to get her to understand that nobody makes anybody else fall in love, challenging her to determine what she was going to do to make sure this didn't happen to her again . . . and again and again.

Just one hour after he'd ended the session, Dwayne was back home, the frustration of his failed attempt to get Vanessa to see what she was doing now behind him. The lights above were as soft as the music that drifted through the room. Dwayne sat in one of the eight Queen Anne chairs at the dining room table, staring at the papers and folders in front of him. But he didn't need to read any more; he could recite most of what was in front of him from memory.

For the last six days, he had thought of little else. Even as he moved through his day, listening to and counseling his clients with the professionalism they'd come to expect, the television proposal was foremost on his mind.

It wasn't just his own musing that held him hostage. Beverlyn Boudreaux had not made it easier for the thoughts to loosen their grip. She'd called four times before he finally returned her calls, though he'd done so at a time he knew she wouldn't be available, leaving a message on her voice mail and ignoring the home number she'd given him.

Dwayne had a feeling that Beverlyn would pursue him until she got the answer she wanted, but he would make his own decision. He pushed back from the table and walked to the window overlooking Hollywood Hills. Even though the hour was late, lights twinkled, flickering in syncopation, like Morse code. Dwayne stared at the glittering mountain for several minutes, before turning away in puzzlement.

He lifted the folder labeled "Dr. Dwayne E. Grandison, Host," then tossed it on top of the rest of the clutter. As he stared at the disorder, he could almost hear Yvette's voice.

"I told you, Dwayne, you were destined for television."

Dwayne smiled slightly. Indeed she had told him that, predicted it the day he moved into his office.

"You know, Dwayne," Yvette had whispered as they'd watched the last of the orange-uniformed movers place the coffee table in the middle of the reception room, "this may be our first step forward, but I know it's just the beginning. First, you'll be helping people here, but one day, you'll be reaching people in greater numbers."

He looked up at her.

"I'm talking about television," she said. "A program that . . ."

Dwayne had laughed, but his amusement ended with her somber glare.

"A program that would minister to millions across the country. One that would provide healing for the hurting and deliverance for the lost. People need to hear you, and you have to reach the most people in order to best serve God. You have a higher calling than this practice."

Now, as he stood in the middle of their home, he felt as if Yvette were standing beside him. Her words were clear.

*People need to hear you . . . you have to reach the most people in order to best serve God.* The words were similar to those Beverlyn had used.

In fact, both had said he had a higher calling. The music in the room's background interrupted the reverie, and Dwayne smiled before walking to the stereo and turning up the volume. Sean's voice came through the Braun speakers as if he were performing in the middle of the living room. Dwayne sat down on the couch and listened as the background singers joined in, clapping their hands to the upbeat tune, declaring God's Word to be true.

Dwayne loved hearing his best friend sing, but it was the words to this song that made him smile. There was no doubt in his mind that even with all he'd been through, he was blessed. It had been hard to see his blessings when Yvette was snatched from his life. But if there was one thing that he was sure of, it was that God was faithful. And as the days had turned to months that had now suddenly flowed into a year, it was God's hands that allowed the passage of time to slowly heal him. It was the Lord's love pouring all over that was making him feel whole again.

Just a few weeks ago, he had packed away Yvette's things. Not to rid himself of her memory, but to move forward. Now doors were opening to opportunities to serve the Lord in ways he'd never dreamed. But how would he do it?

"You only have to tape once a week," Beverlyn's words rang in his ears.

"Dwayne, you're always saying you're not ready for this or that. But you know that God has your back! Look at all you've accomplished." This time it was Yvette's voice he heard when he'd told her he didn't think he could really handle a private practice without working someplace else first.

Dwayne leaned forward, holding his head in his hands. Exhilaration, shock, fascination, and amazement all mixed to form an emotional volcano ready to erupt. But after a few minutes, he sat back, letting a smile settle on his face. Suddenly, he jumped up from the couch and turned down the volume on the stereo. He reached for the phone, punching in the numbers quickly.

"Hey, Lafayette. What's up, man?"

"It's about time I heard from you. I give you tickets to the concert and you don't even call me to tell me how things went."

"Lafayette, we need to talk."

"Hmm . . . sounds serious," Lafayette said with mock alarm. Dwayne could hear papers shuffling and figured his brother was preparing for Sunday's sermon. "Robbie and the kids have turned in. Why don't you come over?"

"It's not like that." He paused and took a deep breath. "It's time for a family council. Can you call Mom and set it up for tomorrow?"

A low whistle escaped from Lafayette's lips. "Okay, Dwayne. You got it."

As Lafayette returned the receiver to its cradle, he didn't know whether to be concerned or elated. Over the last year, he had come to be more protective of his brother. He'd known for some time that Dwayne's marriage to Yvette had been on the rocks, although his brother, for the most part, remained characteristically quiet on the matter, preferring (he'd guessed) to confide in Sean.

Dwayne's marriage had been a sore point between them, as Lafayette had advised Dwayne against marrying Yvette in the first place; he felt that she was much too worldly for him, and he resented the way she pushed Dwayne toward superficiality.

Not that Lafayette didn't like nice things. His near-million-dollar home in the best section of Ladera Heights had in its driveway his Lexus, Robbie's Mercedes, and an Escalade, which either he or she used to taxi the children, all thanks to the money he earned from tapes, books, and engagements on the high-profile and charismatic African American church circuit. With an average five thousand to ten thousand dollars per appearance, there was additional income of twenty thousand to thirty thousand dollars each month.

But his brother had always been more reserved, and Lafayette had been turned off by Yvette's hold on him as well as her constant reaching for the success ring.

# Chapter Eight

*D*wayne dated the file notes from his last client, Autumn Jones (known to her fans as Jade), a chart-topping and beautiful R&B star caught up on the fast track of the hip-hop industry with all the trappings: fast cars, foul language, trendy wardrobe, premium exposure on the gangsta rap scene, high stress, and self-destructive habits including her on-again, off-again addiction to cocaine and abusive relationships.

Jade swore that she did all she did for her current fiancé, Trey, because she loved him. Trey wouldn't work (or even work hard enough to find work). So as her schedule permitted, Jade hunted down and followed up job leads, chose (and often bought) his outfits, and drove him—or let him drive—to appointments in her red convertible Porsche. And when Trey blew yet another interview with his "don't care" demeanor, Jade (hush-hush) paid Trey's rent yet another month—her version of unconditional love.

Closing her folder, Dwayne massaged his temples with the tips of his fingers.

"That bad, huh?" Monique walked in, catching him unaware. "You look worn out."

"Yeah." He let out a sigh of exhaustion.

Stacking a pile of manila files neatly in the out-tray to the right side of the large maple and glass desk, she announced, "Here's to-morrow's lineup."

Dwayne didn't even look up.

"Okay, boss, what's going on?" Monique folded her arms in front of her.

"It's just been a long day."

"For the past few days—or should I say since the Beverlyn Boudreaux concert—you've been acting strangely . . . like you're holding back on me." Monique slumped into the chair adjacent to the desk. "C'mon, fess up. Was it your date with Nina?"

Monique's stern stare was just one indication of her determination to get an answer. The other was clear in the frown lines in her fore-head. Dwayne stood and gathered the files, dropping them into his briefcase.

"Please don't tell me you're going to walk out of here without say-ing a word."

Dwayne picked up his briefcase and walked around the desk. "You're right—something is going on." He put his arm around Monique's shoulder as they walked into the anteroom, stopping at Monique's desk. "In a day or so, I'll share it with you."

"C'mon, you can tell me now. You can't just leave me hanging since I'm going to find out anyway. What's a day or two?" Dwayne laughed when she swatted her hand at him in feigned anger and told him, "Get out of here."

He turned toward the door, putting his hand up to gesture his de-parture. He was still smiling when he got to his car, but by the time he turned the ignition key and pulled out of the parking lot, a new uneasiness had washed over him. Dwayne was ninety percent sure of his decision, but he still felt obliged to discuss it with his family. Sharing news of this sort had been a long-held family tradition.

John Grandison established the family councils to discuss issues that affected the family. "I want us to sit down and talk about things together," his father had said. "It's important because there are things I do that will affect you, and the opposite is true too."

Days later, they had their first official family council meeting, initiated by Lafayette. The only topic Dwayne wanted to discuss was his comic book collection and how he could earn extra money to buy a new skateboard. But his brother convinced him they should boycott the family dinner to convince their parents to get a dishwasher.

"This will work, Dwayne," Lafayette said as he made a sign reading, "Down with dirty dishes," with a red marker.

"But I like helping Mom with the dishes," seven-year-old Dwayne whined.

Lafayette, then fifteen, grimaced. "That's now. In a year or two, you'll be thanking me."

When their parents sat down for dinner, the brothers entered the dining room with their picket signs. Dwayne and Lafayette marched around the table twice, with their surprised parents' eyebrows raised. Then Lafayette presented their demands.

"Dad, you said whenever we had any issues, we could bring them to the family council. Well, Dwayne and I have an issue. We want a dishwasher. All our friends have dishwashers. We're the only ones still doing dishes by hand."

John Grandison glanced briefly at his wife (who could hardly contain her laughter), then his sons. Trying to keep a straight face, he delivered his reply in earnest. "Boys, thank you for bringing your issues to me. Now, let's sit down and have dinner."

Lafayette grinned at his father's response. Surely, that meant that he'd agreed. After Lafayette and Dwayne had taken their seats, John said grace, then was silent as Bernice filled their plates with baked chicken, mashed potatoes with gravy, and green beans. Just as they began to eat—the aroma of the dinner tickling at their noses—their father announced, "Boys, I want you to know that your mother and I are very happy with the dishwashers we have. There will be no change in the near future. Now, let's eat."

It hadn't bothered Dwayne. He'd been able to eat everything on his plate, but Lafayette barely touched his food—an openmouthed, stunned look on his face.

There had been many family councils after that first one—all more serious. They'd discuss marriages and even when and how Lafayette would join his father in the pulpit. As a family, they'd shared every major decision, up to the last family council, which was held almost five years ago upon the death of Bishop John Paul Grandison, head of the family, the victim of a massive coronary.

Dwayne turned onto Mount Vernon Drive and parked his car behind Lafayette's Lexus. Robbie's Mercedes was in the long driveway. Dwayne closed the car door, trotting up the concrete stairs to the front door, and used the key he'd had from childhood to let himself in. He stood silently in the foyer for a moment, listening to the muffled voices emanating from the dining room. The voices fell silent as Dwayne moved past the stairway toward the back of the house, his heels clicking against the hardwood planks.

Even with the darkness of night and the heavy oak dining and buffet decor, the room seemed filled with light. His mother sat at the head of the long table and Lafayette and Robbie sat on either side. Their faces were filled with concern and questions. Dwayne smiled, hoping to ease the tension.

"Hey, everyone." He relaxed his shoulders and walked to his mother, leaning over to kiss her cheek, then greeted Robbie before casually unbuttoning his jacket and sitting next to his brother. But even with his easy manner, their faces revealed worry.

"So how are you, son?"

"Great." Dwayne answered cheerfully, hoping to ease the concern that had shadowed him for the past year. Maybe the news would erase their uncertainties with regard to his future happiness.

"Well, Dwayne," Bernice began, her voice trained to be steady in even the most stressful situations, "we're waiting. What's this important news?"

Dwayne took a deep breath. "No long faces. I'm about to make a major decision and I just wanted some input from my family. I've been offered a big opportunity. Beverlyn Boudreaux has purchased a television network—the Jubilee Network—and she's asked me to host one of the programs."

Bernice released an audible breath and then began to mull over what she'd just heard.

"That's wonderful," Robbie said. "What kind of show?"

"Kind of an extended and yet different version of what I did on

*Oprah* last summer. The details haven't fully been worked out because I haven't given my answer."

"Well, this meeting means you're interested." Bernice's was a leading statement.

"I think it's great," Robbie interjected. "You've done well, Dwayne, and television will mean a great deal more exposure for your book and your practice. I can't wait to tell the kids. They'll be so excited. Their uncle—a TV star."

Dwayne turned to his mother, then back as Lafayette began to speak. "Sounds like a great opportunity, but will your schedule allow for this plus your practice and the commitment you've made to Man-to-Man?"

"My commitment to you is solid," Dwayne reassured his brother. "That's why I'm here. I wanted to see what all of you thought before I gave my answer."

"Sounds like you've already made up your mind, son," Bernice surmised.

"I think I'd like to try this. I don't know just yet how it's going to work with everything else on my plate, but I'd be lying if I said I wasn't intrigued. And they're offering me a lot of money."

"And, of course, you've prayed about it," Bernice asked.

"Not as much as I should, but I won't do anything before I do."

"Well, that's where you'll get your answer. And we'll all be in prayer with you." While she'd always directed her children to pray, a twinge inside told her that there was something disturbingly seductive about this deal. She would pray too, but for now she knew the only role she could play to the son who for the last year had been drowning in his sorrow was to be supportive.

Dwayne exhaled, but his relief was short-lived when Lafayette stood and stepped to the other side of the table, staring directly at his brother. "You're moving awfully fast on this. We don't know anything about the program, who will be on it—"

"He said they haven't worked out the logistics," Bernice broke in. "I think he brought this to us so that we would know what he was doing and he wanted us to know first."

"But what he does will affect us . . . as a family."

"I know that," Dwayne said. "What's really bothering you?"

Lafayette shook his head. "I don't know." He paused and leaned over the back of the chair. "I'm not so sure about Beverlyn Boudreaux."

"Now, Lafayette," Bernice said, looking up, "I may not know Beverlyn personally, but everything she's done seems to be top-notch. I'm sure she hasn't gotten this far without having people around her who know what they're doing."

Bernice turned to Dwayne to get his agreement, not quite sure herself.

"I don't know her either," Dwayne said, looking at Lafayette, "but she's hardly walking into this blind. It's an opportunity for me to make a difference. At least, that's how I'm looking at it. If you've heard something about Beverlyn Boudreaux or the Jubilee Network, let's hear it. Otherwise, I don't understand where this is coming from."

Bernice turned to Lafayette, her eyes piercing her elder child's. "Son, why don't you tell us what's bothering you?"

Lafayette walked around the table and took the seat next to Dwayne, thinking that this probably wasn't the best forum to discuss what he'd heard and known of Beverlyn Boudreaux Ministries, especially since he had not cared enough when he heard it to check it out. "It's nothing I can put my hands on. Something about this just doesn't sit well with me."

Robbie reached across the table and covered her husband's hands. "I think you're concerned because of all Dwayne's been through," Robbie said softly.

Lafayette looked at his wife and smiled. Then he turned to Dwayne and shook his brother's hand. "Maybe that's it. That whole world seems so different and I don't want to see you get caught up."

"Appreciate it, man. But I don't think you have that much to worry about. This feels good to me."

"Be careful of what feels good. Just do what Mom said. Pray and we'll be in agreement with you, not for what you want, but what the Lord wants."

As Lafayette spoke, Dwayne felt a chill run through his body, and he shifted in his chair, trying to shake the feeling. He leaned over and hugged his brother. Lafayette sighed, but was disturbed by his brother's attraction to women like Yvette and now Beverlyn.

"Well, if this family council is about to come to a close, I have something for everyone," Bernice announced. She disappeared into the kitchen, returning a minute later with a pan of peach cobbler.

Robbie laughed. "This is the way I like to celebrate."

"But before we dig in . . ." Bernice stretched her hands forward, taking Lafayette's and Robbie's hands into hers. Lafayette took Dwayne's hand. "Let us pray."

As they bowed their heads, Dwayne was thankful to be part of a family who cared about every facet of his life and who knew how to take everything to God in prayer. That's what he would do. He would pray as soon as he got home. And he would continue until God directed his steps and he got a definite answer.

# Chapter Nine

*B*everlyn inspected once again the boxes that cluttered her office. This time she carefully checked the labeling against her own list to see that nothing had been overlooked. More than twenty brown corrugated containers, filled with personal papers, private trinkets, and other memorabilia representing her life in New Orleans, surrounded her.

She let her eyes roam the room, determined to hold back her emotions, having gone through the same process at home. Even with the assistance of two helpers and a maid, it had taken over a week to pack what should have taken just days. But the process had been filled with emotion as she packed up her life for the journey to Los Angeles.

Beverlyn walked to her favorite place in the office, her eyes taking in the activities below. The sun shone brightly on the streets that led from the Riverwalk to Jackson Square. As always, the French Quarter was filled with pedestrians, tourists and residents alike, roaming each block, soaking up the sights and sounds of this Cajun metropolis.

How many days had she spent the same way? Only her strolls hadn't been leisurely. Her time on the streets was for personal survival. She spent hours eyeing the crowds, then following the most inattentive person she could find. Someone so wrapped up in the flavor of the city that he wouldn't discover his missing wallet until she was long gone. It had been a tough job for her, but at seven, eight, and nine years old, it was her only means of survival.

Ah, the streets below held her secrets. No matter how hard she tried to rid herself of the bad memories, they stuck to her. Thankfully, she knew that God had forgiven her long ago. But getting rid of the shame and guilt wasn't so easy. That's why she worked so hard now.

Even if she couldn't shed the memories, she knew that in a few hours, New Orleans would be history, with little left to connect her to this city. Even the New Orleans Children's Mission, her first major purchase more than ten years ago, was in the hands of new owners with the condition that she stay on as one of the directors. She had to make sure the Mission never reverted to the kind of place it was when she called it home.

"Beverlyn, are you busy?"

She turned toward the voice. Whenever she seemed to think of her early days, her Uncle Linson would appear, as if to take her away, as he'd done all those years ago.

"No, I just finished closing these last boxes. Do you need something?"

L.W. looked around the large office that seemed to have shrunk with the clutter of the boxes. His thin lips eased into a tight line that was meant to be a smile. "Looks like you're all packed up. We're on our way."

Beverlyn sat at her desk, devoid of the papers and folders usually scattered across the top. "I can't believe we're really leaving New Orleans."

L.W. perched himself on the side of her desk. "You're not getting butterflies?"

"No . . . It's just how do you leave a place you've called home for thirty-seven years?"

"On a jet plane with a multimillion-dollar enterprise in your hands and a new venture that will bring millions more. And," he added softly, "with an uncle who will always take care of you." L.W. lifted Beverlyn's chin. "You know that, don't you?"

Beverlyn tried to swallow the lump in her throat. "I know, Uncle Linson."

"There's nothing to worry about." He stared into her eyes, trying to reassure the grown woman whose eyes were filled with the same fear he'd seen when she was nine years old. Finally, he lifted himself from the desk. "I told the limousine to pick us up at four." He looked at the Rolex on his wrist. "That gives us about three hours." He turned toward the door. "By the way, any word from Grandison?"

"Not really." Shrugging her shoulders, she winced. "Maybe he's not interested."

"Don't give up yet. I'll give him a call when we get to L.A. After I talk to him, he won't be able to turn us down."

At once, Beverlyn felt relieved. Few men turned L.W. away. With the influence he wielded as president of Beverlyn Boudreaux Ministries, few men wanted to. Then again, if there was anyone who might not succumb to Linson Lejohn, it was Dr. Dwayne Grandison. And as much as that intrigued her, it also shook her confidence.

Just as L.W. put his hand on the doorknob, the voice of Beverlyn's assistant sounded over the intercom.

"Ms. Boudreaux. Dr. Grandison is on line one."

She slumped back in her chair as if preparing for bad news.

L.W. stood in place as she picked up the phone. "No need to worry, honey. He's smart enough to know what this deal could mean for him."

"Dr. Grandison, I'm glad to hear from you. I hope you're calling with good news," she said, her voice full of confidence she didn't really feel.

"Actually, I hope it's good news for both of us. I've decided to take you up on your offer to join the Jubilee Network."

"This is good news. When I didn't hear from you, I wasn't sure you were interested."

"Are you kidding? Ms. Boudreaux, it's a very attractive offer, but there was a lot to consider. I needed time to sort everything out."

"Listen, we'll work this out together. On our end, we'll do all we can to ensure this works within your scheduling considerations. We really believe in you and this show."

"Well, I still have a lot of questions . . ."

Beverlyn smiled, looked at her uncle, and then swiveled her chair slightly away from him, missing the frown that instantly filled L.W.'s face. "That's no problem, Dr. Grandison. All of your questions will be answered. I'm flying into Los Angeles today. Can we meet the day after tomorrow?"

"It's good, but please call me Dwayne."

"Only if you call me Beverlyn."

As Dwayne and Beverlyn continued to talk, L.W. left the office, making the way to his own down the hall. Boxes cluttered even the doorway, but he stepped over them, moving to his desk. He sat down and tapped his fingers along the walnut top. Beverlyn had sounded a bit too elated to hear from Grandison. Granted, it had been his idea to have Dwayne host the program. His research told him that Dr. Dwayne Grandison would be an asset to their team. The man was highly respected, well known, and good-looking—the latter being important because of the high premium the TV industry put on looks—and he had recently been widowed, which would render him inaccessible on any other level.

He had assumed that building a relationship with anybody—including Beverlyn—was out of the question. But he sensed Beverlyn had something more on her mind. Something, he feared, that could leave him, L.W., out of the loop, and he would never stand for that. Yes, Grandison would be an asset, just as long as he didn't cross to the other side of the balance sheet.

L.W. mulled the options over in his mind. From the beginning, he'd establish that he was in charge—the president—or as he and his boys used to say back in Mississippi, the head-Negro-in-charge. Dwayne Grandison would get the message quickly. But there was no need to take chances. L.W. pulled the Palm Pilot from his jacket and scrolled the list of telephone numbers, but then quickly closed it. Why was he letting a little conversation between Dwayne and Beverlyn get to him? Then again, why had she told Grandison she'd answer all of his questions personally, when she always left the business to him?

Not two seconds passed before he reopened his PDA and began dialing. If L.W. could put his finger on what had helped him to get to where he was, it was his caution. The phone call, he reasoned, was a simple insurance policy, and if Dwayne Grandison ever overstepped his boundaries, L.W. would just as surely cash that policy in.

Dwayne was still smiling minutes after he'd said good-bye to Beverlyn. She had been as enthusiastic as he. She had so much faith and her words warmed him. And reminded him of Yvette—especially during the early years of their marriage. Dwayne buzzed the intercom, and a moment later, Monique appeared at the door.

"You called me, boss?"

He nodded. "Come in. I need to rearrange my schedule a bit."

Monique walked in, a pencil and pad in hand. "Shoot," she said, poised to take notes.

"I need to free up some time." Dwayne leaned back, clasping his hands behind his head. "I'm thinking Tuesdays and Fridays." He paused, returning Monique's curious stare. "What's wrong?"

"You already have Mondays free. Now Tuesdays and Fridays? The way you're going, I might not have a job in a month."

Dwayne laughed at her straightforwardness. "As long as I'm in practice, you'll have a job. In fact, we may need to expand your responsibilities in the near future."

Relieved, Monique lightened up, tapping her pen against her leg and teasing, "Here we go with that undercover stuff."

"I've gotten an offer to do a television show with Beverlyn Boudreaux's new network, and I'm going to take it."

The telephone rang and Monique sighed. "Don't think you're getting off. I want some answers, mister," she said before she picked up the phone, then cupped her hand over the receiver. "It's Nina Jordan. Do you want to take the call or call her back after you tell me what's going on?"

He motioned for the phone and waited until Monique stepped from the office.

"Nina, good to hear from you. I've been meaning to call . . ."

"I hope I'm not interrupting. I wanted to schedule time so that we could review the materials for the first Man-to-Man meeting."

"That's a good idea. And—"

"My day is full tomorrow, but I was hoping you'd have some time Thursday."

Dwayne took a breath. Why was she being so professional? He glanced at his calendar even though he already knew he'd scheduled Beverlyn in the 7:00 P.M. time slot.

"Dr. Grandison?" Nina called his name.

"Thursday would be fine as long as we're able to do it late afternoon."

"I have a meeting with Pastor at three. How's four o'clock?"

"That works," Dwayne said, still smarting over the unwanted formality. "Nina, I'm looking forward to getting this project started. So . . . I'll see you Thursday."

"Thank you."

Dwayne still held the phone, with only the sound of a dial tone in his ear. What might he have done wrong? Why was she being so businesslike? He buzzed the intercom for Monique again.

"So how's it going with Nina?" She smiled coyly.

"I honestly don't know. I've gone from being her date to Dr. Grandison again and I thought we had a good time."

"I don't know"—Monique shook her head—"'cause she sure seems to like you."

"Has she said anything?"

"It's not that. Women just know these things. Believe me, she likes you."

Well, he was not going to try to figure this out. It was beyond his comprehension. If he was going to reduce his office hours, he'd better get to work.

# Chapter Ten

*E*ven though I still want to watch one of your sessions, I think some of what I outlined will work well in the men's sessions."

Nina's eyes rested on Dwayne's lips.

"I really want to focus on how men can more effectively deal with the pressures and responsibilities that so often seem to be closing in on them. How we can remain godly in the face of so much worldly temptation and how we can better interact and mentor young men, as well as the kinds of things we can do to strengthen our resolves and each other, while handling the emotions we tend to keep inside."

When she noticed his lips had stopped, Nina coughed and moved her eyes away. "Great. It sounds like what I'm doing with the women. When do you think we can make an announcement about the first meeting?"

Dwayne tapped the pen against the table. "I'm not sure. By the end of today, I'll have a better idea."

"Still working out your schedule."

"Something like that."

"I'm glad you're excited." Nina matched his smile. "I believe this is going to make a real difference."

"I hope so." He looked at his watch and began pushing his papers into a single pile.

"So all that's left to decide is when you can observe one of my sessions. Actually . . ." Nina looked up. "I have a session in about an hour." She moved from the conference table to her desk and picked up the folders. "You'll have a chance to meet—"

Dwayne stood and put on his jacket. "I won't be able to do that tonight. I have another appointment."

She dropped the folders back onto her desk. "Oh, of course."

He looked at his watch again. "Do you have a moment?" he asked somberly. "There is something I'd like to discuss with you."

Nina slowly lowered herself into the chair, staring at him with piercing eyes. "This sounds serious. Is everything okay?"

"Sure. I just wanted to tell you about a new project I'm working on. Why would you think that there was something wrong with me?"

"Forget I even said that." She smiled, embarrassed at the slip. "Tell me your news."

The smile returned to Dwayne's face and he leaned back in his chair. "It looks like I'm going to take a few small steps in tracks you set a long time ago. I'm being given an opportunity to host a television show."

"That's great. Tell me everything. Where? How?"

Dwayne laughed at her enthusiasm. "Well, you make me feel good. Maybe I *am* doing the right thing."

"I'm sure of that, but tell me about the show."

"I'm joining Beverlyn Boudreaux's new television network."

"Oh." Nina leaned away from him and folded her arms in front of her. "That's nice."

"I believe it's going to be an important venture. Not just for me but for the Christian community. I'll be doing a talk show mixing celebrities with ordinary citizens giving their testimonies, telling about their struggles and triumphs. We'll do some counseling, some preaching, and a whole lot of praying and praising."

Nina dropped her arms. "Dwayne, this sounds incredible."

Nodding excitedly, he continued, "The best part is that though it's a Christian show to inform and entertain believers, our prayer is to reach nonbelievers. And, though they may never enter a church, they might find deliverance through this show."

Nina smiled.

"I apologize. I've just gone on and on."

"And you should. This is an exciting project."

"I'm on my way to a meeting with Beverlyn." He pushed back his chair. "Their timetable is aggressive. She wants the show to air in a month or so." He glanced at his watch. "I'm running a bit late."

"Then you better get moving. I am so happy for you." She hugged him.

"And you don't have to worry about our men's ministry. I am as committed as I was when I agreed to do this."

Nina playfully punched his arm. "You better be. But I'm not worried. I know you, Dr. Grandison."

"Oh, you do, huh?"

A rush of blood warmed her face. "We still need to agree on a time for you to watch a session," she said quickly. "Maybe next week?"

"Sounds like a plan. I'll call you tonight and we can set up something when I have my calendar in front of me."

"Great."

She smiled widely as he walked through the door. It wasn't until she no longer heard his footsteps that the smile completely disappeared. She slipped into the chair behind her desk. It appeared Ms. Beverlyn Boudreaux had found a way to ease into Dwayne's life, after all. So what? It was a great opportunity and a perfect time for him.

She tried to pull joy from deep inside, but she couldn't shake the ambivalence that had underscored the news. She began shaking her head and hands vigorously—an acting exercise she learned years ago, to clear her mind for complete character immersion.

I must have been out of my mind, she thought, remembering the smile that had lit Dwayne's face as he talked about Beverlyn. That memory persuaded her fully. Emotionally she needed to return to where she was before she ever met Dwayne Grandison. Where she felt blessed with everything in her life: Omari, her growing role at New Covenant, and most importantly, the Lord.

Besides, she had a much bigger battle to fight. It had begun five years ago with a recurring pain under her armpit. Omari was two and she'd filed for divorce just months before. She thought the stress of a failed marriage, wrestling with a two-year-old, working full-time, and taking courses for college credit had all taken their toll. But when she complained to the doctor of her symptoms during one of Omari's routine visits, he arranged for her to see an internist, who immediately had her admitted to Cedars-Sinai, where they discovered a growth.

Surgery to remove the tumor was scheduled, but the attempts of the surgical team were thwarted and the procedure aborted when doctors discovered that the tumor had connected itself to vital blood vessels and could not be removed. Hours later, Nina was given the grim news: The tumor was malignant.

Devastated, she sought refuge with God at New Covenant, where Lafayette and Robbie took her under their wing, arranging care for Omari and emotional support during her hospitalization, as Nina had no family to speak of and few close friends, having been burned by people who'd said they were her friends—but instead took advantage of her—when she was a TV star. She'd at first reasoned that she deserved the cancer that was ravaging her then twenty-seven-year-old body for all the things she'd done wrong: the promiscuity, the drugs, the arrogance, and most of all the indifference to the God-fearing upbringing her parents, now deceased, had instilled at New Covenant Assembly in what seemed to be a lifetime before her discovery by Hollywood.

And while Nina had become accustomed to living out her private pains in the public eye, thanks to the now-waning interest of the tabloids, she trusted that Lafayette and Robbie would keep her secret.

Nina began chemotherapy: once a week for twelve weeks. Within one week, the tumor began shrinking. The chemotherapy was followed by five weeks of radiation therapy. Although the curative measures were deemed successful, the tumor and subsequent treatments had taken a toll on her body over a two-year period, causing her to make some major changes. She recalled crying at one point when she was so weak it took her an hour to eat a piece of toast.

A distant aunt was enlisted to help care for Omari, then an over-active three-year-old. Then came another hit: Nina was informed she would have to have surgery to repair nerves that had been damaged by the tumor.

With the success of the surgery, the hardest part had been put behind her. But tonight she was not so sure. Until she could celebrate five years in remission, it was as if a death sentence hung over her, never know-ing from one moment to the next what was brewing inside her body.

Still, she was grateful that a disaster had been avoided. She could only imagine what Dwayne had gone through with the loss of his wife. With all he'd suffered, didn't he deserve more?

The first thing Dwayne noticed when the elevator doors parted on the eighteenth floor of the International Commerce Building were the two workmen putting up three-foot-high gold letters on the wall. "Beverlyn Boudreaux Ministries" was already plastered on the wall. Underneath, three letters, "JUB," were set in place. Within a few hours, the opulent reception area would be aglow with the gold let-ters spelling out "Jubilee Network."

"Dwayne, I was hoping to meet you as soon as you arrived." Bev-erlyn hugged him. Uncanny, he thought, that the perfume she wore was Yvette's favorite, Tiffany.

"I just got here."

"Let's go to my office." She squeezed his hand.

They moved through the long carpeted halls, past workmen ar-ranging furniture into cubicles and employees unpacking dozens of U-Haul boxes. Finally, Dwayne followed Beverlyn into a corner office with windowed walls overlooking Sunset Boulevard.

"This is quite a spread."

"Yeah, I love this place. It's much bigger than our offices in New Orleans."

"So you've moved your entire operation here?"

She nodded. "We'll be able to do so much more in Los Angeles. Why don't we sit over here?" she said, sitting on the couch and pat-ting a space next to her. "It's less formal."

He hesitated momentarily before sitting down next to her and pulling a folder from his briefcase.

"You're all about business, aren't you?" she said.

"Well, I don't want to take up too much of your time."

"Your program is our flagship, the most important one we're putting on the air. So you don't have to worry about that."

He opened the folder, but before he could say a word, she touched his arm.

"Dwayne, I want you to know how happy I am to have you join us. The Lord saved my life," she said soberly, "and I've always wanted to reach millions with the same message that delivered me. Your show is one of the ways I'll be able do that."

"Not only my show, Beverlyn, but your entire network. You have a great vision and I'm pleased you asked me to be part of it. So how exactly is this going to work?" Dwayne pressed. "Am I correct in assuming that major decisions will be made by you and me?"

"That's true. As executive and senior producers, all roads lead to us. Believe me, this is your show, but it's still going to take a team to put this program on. You know what they say about two heads. Well, what about ten? That's how many we've hired to do production on the show. You'll get to meet them at the first production meeting."

"There'll be ten people in the meeting?"

"At least. We're putting everything we have behind this show, Dwayne. So tomorrow we can brainstorm with the team."

"I see."

"And it's best if we do this with L.W. He's going to be an executive producer on your show."

Dwayne raised his eyebrows. "I didn't know that."

"It's a formality. Speaking of which, I'll buzz L.W. and he can bring the contracts in. I'm sure you'll want to go over them with your attorney."

As Beverlyn phoned her uncle, Dwayne moved slowly through the spacious room. He thought his office was large, but two of his could fit into this space. Impressive, he thought, yet something was making him feel uneasy. He couldn't pinpoint where the doubts were coming from. Maybe he hadn't asked enough questions. Things that

Beverlyn had never mentioned were now being revealed. But maybe that was the way the entertainment industry worked—constantly changing, moving fast. And the Jubilee Network was brand-new. Things were bound to change as they moved along.

He paused at the window, looking at the tower above the Capitol Records Building, and pushed his doubts aside. He wasn't going to give room to the devil. His prayers had been answered. So he would make this work no matter what it would take on his part.

"L.W. will be right down," Beverlyn said, interrupting his thoughts.

"Okay." He returned to the couch and began putting papers back into his briefcase.

"I hope you're not planning on leaving already?"

"Since we're meeting tomorrow . . ."

"I have an idea. I haven't eaten yet, and I don't know many places in Los Angeles. I certainly don't know many people. Why don't we have dinner?"

When he didn't respond, she continued nervously, "This would give us a chance to get to know one another—as executive producer to senior producer."

"Okay, let's do it."

"Do what?"

Dwayne and Beverlyn spun around at the sound of L.W.'s voice. L.W., it seemed, had been standing by the door for a moment.

"Dwayne and I just decided to go to dinner."

L.W. moved toward Dwayne and stretched his hand forward. "Good to see you again, Mr. Grandison."

"Same here. Glad to be joining the team."

"Here's your contract." He handed Dwayne a manila envelope. "There are three copies. We'll need your signature on all three and then we'll give one back to you."

"I'll need at least a day or so."

"Of course."

"I appreciate that," Dwayne said as he tucked the envelope into his briefcase. Then he looked at Beverlyn. "If you have work to do, I can take a rain check."

"Absolutely not. I can't wait to get out. L.W. has been working me too hard, isn't that right?" She smiled at her uncle.

Dwayne and L.W. exchanged silent glances as Beverlyn moved to her desk. "Just give me a minute, Dwayne. I need to make a quick call."

After a few more silent seconds, L.W. said, "I need to get back to my office." He turned toward Dwayne. "Good seeing you . . . young man," he added condescendingly.

Dwayne's eyes followed L.W. until he closed the door behind him. He didn't know why but he just didn't feel good about the man. He returned his attention to Beverlyn, who was winding up a phone call.

"Thanks for understanding," she was saying. "We can do dinner next week."

When she hung up, Dwayne said, "You already had plans?"

"Not really. And even if I did, there is nothing more important than the two of us getting together, wouldn't you agree?"

Dwayne neither agreed nor disagreed. He simply smiled.

L.W. sighed as he walked back to his office. He wondered why Dwayne Grandison made him uncomfortable. Maybe it was because he didn't yet have the information he needed. He paused in front of his office and watched the young woman unloading boxes.

"Are you sure all of the boxes that should be in my office are in there?"

The young woman looked up. "Yes, Mr. Lejohn."

He opened his office door and stepped inside, and just as he was reaching to close it behind him, Kim Steele brushed in.

"What are you doing here?" L.W. asked through clenched teeth.

"You said you needed to talk to me," she answered.

L.W. marched to his desk. "Oh, yeah." He shook his head.

"So what do you need, boss?"

"I told you about calling me boss. I can't afford for people to put together that you're really working for me and not Beverlyn."

"Sorry, L.W."

"I need some background information on a Dr. Dwayne Grandison."

"What kind of information?"

"The kind one tends to keep in their closet. You know what I mean."

"Sure, I'll get right on it. Give me a day or two."

"Make sure that nothing can be traced to me."

"You know me better than that. I'll say we need it as part of due diligence with regard to high-profile personnel." Kim slipped from the office before L.W. could say another word.

L.W. finally relaxed, knowing he could count on Kim for results. Normally, he didn't go to such lengths, but concerned that Grandison might prove to be a problem, it wouldn't hurt to put together a backup plan.

There was something about him with Beverlyn . . . something that made L.W. believe that Dwayne would be a threat to all he'd built. He, L.W., was the mastermind behind Beverlyn Boudreaux and it would remain that way. There was room for only one man in Beverlyn's life, and if Dwayne Grandison ever had other thoughts, L.W. would be there to blast those thoughts away. He had worked too hard to have Grandison ruin things.

No, he thought. He didn't like the way Beverlyn played up to Dwayne.

# Chapter Eleven

*O*n Saturday, Kim had called Dwayne informing him of a special last-minute appearance she was able to arrange with KJLH to promote the new network. He and Beverlyn would be appearing on Aundrae Russell's *Spread the Word* radio show. He agreed to the meeting, willing to do whatever he could to help get the word out about the Jubilee Network.

Dwayne pulled up at KJLH just as Beverlyn's limousine arrived. Outside, awaiting his arrival, stood Kim, who'd advised him that it might be better to meet at Beverlyn's new offices so that they could arrive together at the radio station. But he decided against being part of Beverlyn's entourage, opting to meet them there, telling Kim he had an engagement directly after the interview.

In fact, he had a long-standing Sunday tennis engagement with Sean, whenever Sean was in town. And this week Sean was in town.

As he got out of the Jaguar, Beverlyn approached in a tapered Donna Karan cream dress suit. They were running late and immediately entered the station, where they were met by Aundrae Russell and ushered to their seats in the studio.

For the next hour, Beverlyn and he talked about the show, exchanged views on the Christian community with Russell, took calls from listeners, and engaged in Dwayne's renowned Bible Jeopardy! quiz.

Dwayne saw another side of Beverlyn, a more relaxed, down-to-earth evangelist who—for a moment—had let her hair down with him and Russell, trading jokes, coming out from behind her carefully constructed facade. As she talked more and more about her world, what she was saying was right on, and he felt a strange attraction; briefly, a childlike—and more feminine—vulnerability seemed to emerge from her.

"It was uncanny," he was explaining to Sean later that afternoon. "But I'm beginning to enjoy the prospect of doing the show."

"How's Nina?" Sean snatched up a bottle of Evian as they put their rackets down and headed into the sprawling Beverly Hills mansion the singer had purchased a decade before.

"Man, I can't figure her out. I know she likes me—or at least, I think she does—but she's holding back. Monique says she likes me. I can't figure it."

"That's surprising. I clearly picked up some interest when I was talking with her. Maybe something else is going on that has nothing to do with you."

"Yeah, maybe that's it. How's everything with you?"

"Well for now. I'm doing really well. Just got to keep exercising, eating right, and living right."

# Chapter Twelve

"Man, that's good news." Lafayette grinned widely as he placed the call on speakerphone. "What do you think the chances are that the deal with the station will go through?"

"Looks good," the voice continued. "We have yours. We're talking to Evans and Bishop Taylor about getting their financing in the next two days, and in about a month, Los Angeles will have its first church-owned gospel radio station."

"I love it. Listen, I'm with you on booking more Christian and family entertainment events. The Forum will become the premier venue for them."

"That's exactly what we have in mind." The voice belonged to Bishop Kenneth Ulmer, whose church had made history with their acquisition of the Great Western Forum, former home to the L.A. Lakers. "Look, man, I've got to take a call. Let's talk tomorrow."

"You got it. Thanks again for the info on Beverlyn Boudreaux." Lafayette hung up.

The crease in Lafayette's forehead became all the more pronounced as he sat in his office and prayed about Dwayne's decision to join the Jubilee Network, imploring God to impart the discernment he was sure his younger brother would need. As he opened his eyes, Lafayette thought about the rumors he'd heard surrounding

Beverlyn Boudreaux Ministries. Most of them had centered on what went on behind the scenes involving her business dealings—not those of Boudreaux directly, but those of L.W. Lejohn, the man whom they credited with pulling the strings. Several of Lafayette's friends had not-so-pleasant run-ins with L.W.

Additionally, while raking in uncounted millions, L.W. had been accused of financial indiscretions and yet had refused to open his books to the scrutiny of independent auditors in compliance with the standards mandated by the industry with regards to evangelists and nonprofit organizations. Beverlyn Boudreaux Ministries had operated with little interference—at first because of L.W.'s renowned vindictiveness and later because BBM had grown so successful that few in the Christian world would challenge it.

Lafayette had always been wary of operations like hers. Glitzy, savvy, and highly commercial, they gave new meaning to the business of ministry, and in an era when high-octane scandals, plus scores of routine ones, had shaken public faith in televangelists, he was hardly excited about the prospect of his brother being linked to them. But with no hard evidence, and reports that Boudreaux herself was on the level, there was little he could say, so instead he stomached the foreboding that raged in his gut.

He got up from the desk and proceeded toward Nina's office for an update on how Man-to-Man was coming along.

Nina pursed her lips as she turned the handle on her Rolodex. When she found the number, she dialed.

"Dr. Grandison's office."

"May I speak with Dr. Grandison, please?"

"I'm sorry, Dr. Grandison just left. May I take a message?"

"This is Nina Jordan."

"Oh, Ms. Jordan," Monique said. "Dr. Grandison apologized for not getting back to you last evening, but he wanted me to ask if you had an evening session next Wednesday he could observe?"

At least he remembered he was supposed to call, Nina thought. "Yes, next Wednesday will be fine. I'll plan on him coming." Nina bit her lip, hoping she didn't sound anxious.

"He's looking forward to it. He told me to make sure nothing gets scheduled on that day if it was available for you. So I'm going to put this on Dr. Grandison's calendar now."

"That'll be fine." Nina resisted the urge to ask to have Dwayne call her.

"I'm sure Dr. Grandison will give you a call later today or tomorrow," Monique said, as if reading Nina's mind.

"Thank you." Nina let the phone drop into the cradle and then leaned back into her chair. "Argh!" she yelled just as the door of her office opened.

"Boy, I don't know if I should come in and save you or turn around and run," Lafayette kidded, peering into the room, then seating himself in the armchair in front of Nina's desk.

"Come in, Pastor. I'm sorry. It's nothing."

"How are things going with you and Dwayne?"

The question caught her off guard, and she knew that he had purposely framed it to be taken two ways in the hopes that she would open up.

"Great, Pastor." Nina turned to the credenza behind her, removing a folder from the top of the pile. "Dwayne is coming next week to observe one of my sessions. We should be able to get going by the beginning of April."

Lafayette was more than pleased. "Well, I'm glad you and Dwayne are working well together."

Nina was sure he was still fishing, but she kept a straight face. "Yes, it's working out fine . . . between us."

Lafayette eased forward in his chair as if he wanted to ask another question, but changed his mind. He slapped his hands together against his legs and stood. "Well, I just wanted to check in. Keep me posted."

"Sure will. By the way, it's pretty exciting that Dwayne will be doing a TV show."

"Yeah, it's interesting." Lafayette's smile faded. "I have a board meeting to get ready for. I'll see you on Sunday."

"Thanks, Pastor."

The night before when she found herself watching the clock as the minutes passed, until finally realizing she wasn't going to get Dwayne's call, Nina had once again vowed to keep a professional distance between herself and Dwayne Grandison. Pulling her digital recorder and pad from the desk drawer, she began recording the notes from last evening's session. It was time to get back to work.

Dwayne shifted uncomfortably at the head of the conference table. Beverlyn sat to his right as nine others, seated around the large mahogany oval, gave him the once-over. At the other end of the table sat L.W., who was staring intently in his direction. Dwayne closed his eyes and again wondered if he had made the right decision. The doubts he'd had the day before didn't compare to those he felt now. After all, he wasn't familiar with the world of television.

Beverlyn touched his arm and stood.

"We've already made the introductions, but I wanted to say how pleased I am to have Dr. Dwayne Grandison join our team. As all of you know, this program is important to us because we bring the name of Dr. Grandison, which is well known in the Christian community. Our prayer is that this show reaches the top of the ratings."

Just pile on the pressure, Dwayne thought.

Before he could respond, another voice intervened, and all heads turned, facing L.W.

"I want to join my niece in welcoming Mr. Grandison," L.W. drawled, looking directly at Dwayne. It was the first time Dwayne noticed his accent. He glanced briefly at Beverlyn, whose own inflections sounded as if she'd been raised in the Northeast.

"We have a lot of confidence in you, son," L.W. continued. "We know you're going to do a fine job for the Lord."

"Thank you, Beverlyn," Dwayne said, turning toward her. Then his eyes moved to L.W. "And thank you, L.W., for your confidence in me. I am most appreciative for this opportunity. Like you, my prayer is to bring glory to God.

"When Beverlyn brought this idea to me, I was more intrigued than anything. After hours of thought and many more hours of prayer, I came to see the purpose of not only this show but also this entire network. As I don't know much about television, I will be depending upon most of you. I trust that I'm in good hands, so let's get to work."

The discussion around the table was brisk—with the exchange of concepts and concerns. The show would have a serious talk show format.

"Remember, what's key," Maria, the producer, pointed out, "is that along with the people who are on the show to discuss their issues, we'll have a celebrity—a major entertainer or someone in the news—talking about how God saved them. We will show that God is the solution."

"I think the thing for us to do now," L.W. interjected, "is to have Maria work on a mock-up script, complete with guests."

"We can do that," Maria said. "Then we'll all feel more comfortable that this is feasible." As a new thought came to her mind, Maria eagerly jotted something on the pad in front of her. "Has there been a final decision on the name for the show?"

"We won't be able to come up with a name today," L.W. observed.

"How about . . . 'Word Up'?" Dwayne leaned back in his chair and looked straight at L.W. "I like 'Word Up' because of the play on words. Obviously, 'Word' means Lord. And 'Word Up' means lifting the name of the Lord."

"I like it," Beverlyn said.

"It's the play on words I like," Maria added. "It's young and hip and—"

"That's the part I like," one of the interns interjected. "If we're trying to attract a young crowd, this name could help us do it."

"That name is ridiculous!" L.W. exclaimed. "It doesn't have anything to do with what we're doing. There is nothing about that name that works. First of all," he noted raising a finger in the air, "our market is Christians. If we get others, that's fine. But we should provide the highest-quality programming for the Christian market."

"I agree," Dwayne countered. "However, who said that Christians aren't young and hip and—"

"That's nonsense. We want to glorify the Lord. That's our primary objective."

"That's what we're trying to do, L.W." Beverlyn had watched the exchange and was confused by her uncle's forcefulness. They'd had other meetings on other shows, most of which L.W. had attended, but he'd had little to say, leaving decisions to her and the producers. Why was today so different? She didn't know what was up, but she was going to end the confusion here.

"I think we have to consider every option, L.W., so that we have the best possible name. I don't think we should categorically dismiss anything."

L.W. stared at Beverlyn with what she'd come to know as "the look." But unlike when she was a child, it fazed her little now.

"I agree," L.W. retorted. "We should look at all options. I've compiled my own list of possible names."

Both Beverlyn and Dwayne were silent as L.W.'s list was passed around the table.

"I believe these names will glorify the Lord," L.W. boomed through the room as if he were about to give a sermon. "The one I like the best is first. 'Higher Ground.' That encompasses all we want to do." He raised his hands in the air and made a circular motion. " 'Higher Ground' says this is a show that is not going to take the low road. That the solutions we offer—Christ-centered answers—are the highest road you can take."

Suddenly, the sun's rays filled the room with their heat. A few very long moments passed. Only the sound of people moving outside of the conference room was heard. Most heads were dropped, roving over the sheets in front of them and at the same time avoiding the eyes of L.W. Only Dwayne's and L.W.'s heads were raised, their eyes—and egos—locked.

"So what do you think of 'Higher Ground'?" L.W.'s tone was serious, but it was the smirk on his face that annoyed Dwayne.

"Like you said before, L.W., we don't have to make a decision today," Dwayne responded without breaking eye contact.

"You're absolutely right, Dwayne, but if we find a name we all agree on, we might as well move forward." He paused for a moment. The doctor was tougher than he had imagined. "Well, let's have some feedback."

"No," Beverlyn said strongly. "We have the names on the table and we'll let it rest for now. This has been a really good start. I want to thank everyone for their time."

Chairs scraped against the floor as people pushed from the table. It took less than a minute for the room to clear—except for L.W., Beverlyn, and Dwayne, who remained in their seats. L.W. finally pushed his chair back and stood. He moved toward Dwayne and stretched his hand forward. "That was a good meeting, Mr. Grandison," he said, shaking Dwayne's hand. "I hope you didn't take offense with anything."

"No offense taken. This is business."

"That it is." L.W. held Dwayne's stare for a moment and then turned away. "Beverlyn, when you're finished here, may I see you in my office?"

When the conference room door closed behind him, Beverlyn rolled her eyes. "I'm sorry about that name thing, Dwayne. L.W. didn't mention it to me." She rested her hand on his shoulder. "I'll see you later," she said simply, and walked out of the room.

Dwayne slumped in his chair. This had been a tough meeting. He'd been nervous and he was a novice, but it was L.W. who made him uneasy. He'd felt set up. Was he overreacting? He leaned forward, holding his head in his hands. Yvette would have been perfect for this. Boardrooms, corporate meetings, executive sparring—that was his wife's forte, not his. All he wanted to do was to help people with his brand of ministry.

He lifted his head. This show was part of what he was called to do. He'd just have to muddle through all of the tricks and traps that were obviously being set in his path. He gathered the loose papers, staring for a moment at the list L.W. had prepared.

"Welcome to show business," he said aloud.

With a leather portfolio stuffed under his arm, L.W. rushed back to his office.

"Mr. Lejohn," Kim called, but he closed his office door before she could finish her sentence.

He locked the door behind him, moved across the lush mauve carpet, and tossed the portfolio onto his desk. He left the room darkened, even though the only light was from the sun that was partially blocked by the surrounding concrete buildings. His keys jingled as he lifted them from his pocket and unlocked the door on the left side of the credenza. Gently, he removed the bottle of Hennessy cognac and filled one of the plastic cups he kept with his liquor stash.

Then he leaned back in his chair and lifted his feet onto the desk. His polished wing-tip shoes shined in the room's dull light. He swallowed two small sips of cognac and grimaced slightly as the smooth, hot liquid slid down his throat. It wasn't until his cup was empty that he allowed himself to gloat. He had done it—set the rules and laid down the law. And he could see in Dwayne's eyes that the good doctor had gotten the message.

L.W. got up from the desk and turned to look out of the window. His office was just half the size of Beverlyn's, but he didn't care. Superficial signs of success never impressed him. He and Beverlyn had built an empire, and the outer trappings of it were never at issue. He was more concerned about anyone who would dare upset the apple cart. He had worked way too hard to get them where they were. And with what lay ahead with Beverlyn Boudreaux Ministries, there was no doubt that in a few years he'd be one of the most powerful men in the Christian community.

L.W. shook his head as he watched the traffic below crawl along Sunset Boulevard. That was exactly the way his life had been: a slow crawl, a long journey, but one that always had purpose. Life had been a battle, but finally, he was winning.

Fact is, any way you looked at it, L.W. had come a long way from his humble beginnings in Bayou St. Jacques, Louisiana, to New Orleans and now Los Angeles. This was his dream as much as Beverlyn's—if not more. After all, it was he who had turned a waif into a star. He who had saved Beverlyn from a life that might have ended before she was a teenager had he not rescued her. And he who had come from nothing now held the keys to a multimillion-dollar enterprise.

Oh, if they could only see him now, the uppity Negroes that used to call him a short, high-yellow, bootleg country preacher: his new apartment in Westwood, his seven-figure bank account, the finest duds, a driver, and a burgeoning business empire. Ironically, he really owed this success to his mother. It was she, Beverlyn's grandmother, who had urged her son to find his niece. "Go to Nawlins and get that child. Bring her home," his elderly mother had croaked. L.W. remembered how his mother paced the wooden floor of the three-room shack they called home. She had paused and pointed her cane in his face. "You're a man of God, Bubba. Go find your niece."

L.W. had winced at his despised nickname but hadn't said anything this time, because her words interested him more than what she'd called him. He was thrilled to leave home, though he was still angry that his older sister, Niecy, had left more than ten years before, never keeping her promise of returning for "little L.W."

"You have my word, Bubba," his sister had said. "As soon as I find a job, I'll come back for you. And we'll both get out of this hick town."

"Promise, Niecy?" twelve-year-old Linton asked with tears in his eyes. What would life be like without his beloved sister? She was the only one he looked up to.

"I promise," Niecy said, hugging him before she walked out the door.

But within six months, Niecy had written home announcing that she was pregnant and that she wouldn't be coming back.

L.W. hated his sister from the moment he read the last word of her letter. But ten years later in death, she was providing the escape she'd long ago promised.

"Are you going to do this for me?" his mother had asked with tears in her eyes.

"Yes, Mama."

He didn't tell her that it would be impossible to find a child when he only had a name and no address. But he kept his doubts to himself.

"And don't you worry nothing about that church," his mother continued. "Ol' man Stan or Uncle Julius can take over while you're gone."

L.W. almost laughed out loud. Surely, his mother couldn't really believe that he truly cared about Country Baptist. He only started the church because she encouraged him to—and because he couldn't find another job to his liking. L.W. had no formal training, only finishing high school. His sole credential was that he studied the Bible. Probably more than anyone in Bayou St. Jacques, except for his mother. And even his Bible study was simply because his mother made him and Niecy sit in front of the fireplace every night, even before they could read, and listen as she read chapter after chapter.

In reality, few of the twenty-five or so members of Country Baptist took Pastor Linson Lejohn seriously. Most still called him Bubba, a gesture he found disrespectful. As he sat in the creaky rocking chair that day, he watched his mother limp to their "safe"—a loose plank under the kitchen table—and pull out a stack of bills. When his mother handed him the large roll, it took L.W. only minutes to pack his small suitcase and call a friend to drive him to the bus station.

He kissed his mother good-bye, bestowing on her the same promise that Niecy had given him. "Don't worry, Mama. I'll find her and bring her home." He said the words, but he intended never to return. And L.W. had fulfilled his intention, returning for the first time six years later to bury his mother in the small weed-filled cemetery behind Country Baptist.

When L.W. arrived in New Orleans, he made only cursory inquiries to find his niece. But to his dismay, within a week he stumbled upon Beverlyn at the New Orleans Children's Mission. And from the staff, he learned that he'd located her five days before her tenth birthday and two weeks before she was to be shipped to a home for delinquent girls in Lone, Louisiana.

Even though he had no desire to have children, he couldn't allow a child with his blood to be sent away. So grudgingly, L.W. found a small apartment over the Royal Pharmacy on North Rampart Street, checked his niece out of the Mission, brought her home, and set down the Lejohn law.

"I don't know what you're used to, young lady," he said, pointing his finger in her face. "But now you're going to follow some rules. You will go to school and come straight home," L.W. continued as he paced in front of her. "When you come home, you will do your homework, then complete your chores I will set out for you every day. After that, you'll read this." He picked up his Bible.

"What's that?" Beverlyn crinkled her nose and tugged at one of her thick braids.

"This . . . is a Bible. It is the Word of God."

Beverlyn rolled her eyes. "Oh, brother."

"And we will read this together every day."

Beverlyn put her hands on her hips. "You can't tell me what to do. You're not my father."

His lips spread into a smile, but it was the menacing message in his eyes that made the young girl drop back silently onto the chair. "You don't even know who your father is," he said through clenched teeth. "From now on, I am the only father you'll know. Do you understand?"

That first conversation would set the tone for their relationship. L.W.'s next order of business was to look for a job. So he did the only thing he knew how to do: He opened a church. While he had not been successful with his church at home, L.W. believed he could turn that around. He was no longer working with country folks. This was New Orleans, a big city—the Big Easy. Sin flowed freely through these streets. Surely, on Sunday these people would need a place to acknowledge their transgressions and get saved.

Like everything else that happened since he'd come to New Orleans, he found a home for his church right away. It was a small pink building with two rooms—shotgun style—on Dauphine. The building was fine—except for the fumes that seeped through the thin walls from the gas station next door, but L.W. could not be picky. Despite his lack of credit and references, the owner had still agreed to rent the building to L.W.

"It's good to meet a Christian man," the old man said to L.W. "Ain't nothing but sin roun' here. We need more preachers like you in this city."

L.W. signed the lease. He knew the offerings would pay the rent. The next week, he opened the doors of the Alpha and Omega Greater Baptist Church. Only five attended that first week. They had heard of the new church from handwritten flyers that L.W. had tucked inside the portals of neighborhood houses. L.W. preached as if he had an audience of thousands. The next week, eleven came to Sunday service, one of them, Ms. Anna, offering the use of an old piano for the church.

"Pastor Lejohn, it's not the Lord's house until we can lift our voices in song. I haven't touched my piano in years. I'm willing to donate it to you for the good work you're doing for the Lord."

L.W. graciously accepted Ms. Anna's offer, gathering a few men to help him move the piano into the church, and when Ms. Anna sat down at the bench, Beverlyn joined in singing the tunes that Ms. Anna played. At first, L.W. was startled at the sheer power of Beverlyn's voice. Hers was a little girl's body, but with a woman's sound. He quickly recovered himself and put Beverlyn to work.

For the next week, Ms. Anna worked with Beverlyn every day, teaching her how to project from her diaphragm, how to read sheet music, and how to invite the Holy Ghost to every performance. "You have to lift your hands and stomp your feet," Ms. Anna told her. "Do that and people will fall out in the aisles. And if you can add a tear or two, that's even better."

When Beverlyn finally stood next to Ms. Anna two Sundays later, the thirteen people in the congregation stood and raised their hands in praise to the Lord. The next Sunday, there were twenty-five in the sanctuary, and by the end of the next month, almost fifty filled the mismatched folding chairs that members had brought from their homes.

L.W.'s income doubled, and he began to give great thought to how he could make better use of Beverlyn, who was a big part of the reason why the church had begun to grow. He decided to change the program, having her sing just before the offering.

"Now, before we bring our tithes and offerings to the Lawd, I want to bring forth a young lady whom I'm very proud of—my niece, Beverlyn Lejohn."

Beverlyn's singing dazzled the new members while still amazing the old ones. The change in program had worked. The offering doubled that Sunday. The next month, L.W. put in two offerings, one right before Beverly sang and one shortly thereafter.

"Blessed Assurance. Jesus is mine . . ."

The money flowed. Not only were there now more than one hundred people sitting in that small building, but he collected almost a thousand dollars every week.

One night, as L.W. watched Beverlyn wash their dinner dishes, a revelation came to him. She was a gift from God. That had to be the reason why he had found her so quickly. As he sat, he was sure he even heard God's voice.

"This is my gift to you, Linson, for your faithful service to me."

That was all L.W. needed to hear. He sat up all night, and before the sun's first rays burst into the apartment, L.W. had his plan. That morning, he found a friend of a friend who knew someone with a recording studio in the back of their house. It took much of the money he'd collected and some he had to borrow, but making Beverlyn's recording demo was an investment he was sure would pay him back a millionfold.

And he had been right on target. Her first record had gone straight to the top of the charts—as did her next two. It made it easier when a few years later L.W. was able to introduce Beverlyn to the speaking circuit. However, it still took him nearly a decade to break her onto the megachurch circuit, where speaking and/or preaching engagements brought anywhere from ten thousand to twenty-five thousand dollars, and the exposure was phenomenal.

The top speaking slots were few and far between, and it wasn't so easy for L.W. to break Beverlyn in. He'd done a lot of sucking up to get her the plum dates: the T. D. Jakes conventions, Pastor Eddie Long's conferences, the Full Gospel Baptist Church Fellowship's annual convention, Bishop Kenneth Ulmer's Rev. Sister Conference, Ernestine Reems's women's conference, Dennis Leonard's "Fire in the Rockies," Rod Parsley's annual meet, Marvin Winans's convocation, the National Baptist Convention, and Dr. Beverly "BAM" Crawford's annual LAMPS convention.

Small wonder that the slots on the megachurch circuit were coveted: Why, she'd sold nearly eight thousand copies of her third album at the Extraordinary Woman conference the year before she set out to launch her own crusade.

Competition was stiff, with names like Bishop Noel Jones, Myles Monroe, Mark Chironna, Juanita Bynum, Jacqueline McCullough, and Creflo Dollar, dominating key dates on the conference circuit, but after a decade of trying, L.W. broke Beverlyn Boudreaux into the inner circle—one of his biggest accomplishments and something Beverlyn had wanted more than anything.

"Uncle Linson, why can't we get T. D. Jakes?"

"We will, Beverlyn," he'd tell her. "But we've got to pay our dues first."

He and Beverlyn had been through so much together. They were a team, and nothing but nothing would get between them. He had worked too hard raising her and getting her to the top. It's all he'd ever done that worked.

A hard knock on the door pulled him from his sea of memories. He saw the knob of his door turn, but the door was still locked.

"L.W., it's Beverlyn."

Slowly, he lowered his feet from the desk, threw his empty cup in the trash, locked the secret place that hid his liquor, then opened the door for his niece.

"Why was it locked?"

"I don't know. I guess I did it out of habit."

"You said you wanted to speak with me."

L.W. returned to his desk. "Did I?"

"Yes, when you left the meeting, you asked me to stop by," Beverlyn said as she slumped into the overstuffed leather chair.

L.W. rubbed his eyes. "I can't remember what I wanted."

"Well, there is something I want to discuss with you."

He looked up.

"What was that all about in the meeting today?" She leaned forward. "Why did you challenge Dwayne? I thought you weren't going to be involved."

Finally, he met her eyes. "Beverlyn, honey, I'm the president of this business. My job is to make sure that every aspect of this company reflects well on Beverlyn Boudreaux Ministries."

Beverlyn leaned back in the chair adjacent to his desk. "I know that, Uncle Linson. But everyone could feel the tension at the table.

You seemed to be challenging Dwayne. Do you have a problem with him?"

L.W. chuckled inside. No one gave him problems, because he never allowed anyone to give him problems. "Of course not," he said with practiced sincerity. "I know that his is our most important program. That's why it's so critical that everything go well, right down to the last detail—particularly the name."

Beverlyn shook her head in doubt.

"If it seemed like I had a problem or I caused one, I'm sorry. Do you want me to apologize to Dwayne?"

"No, maybe I'm just overreacting." Then she peered into his eyes. "Uncle Linson, one of the things that attracted Dwayne to this project was that it was completely his."

"Now, honey, we can't turn over everything to him, or anyone else for that matter. This is our vision. Besides, Dwayne knows nothing about television—"

"I know," she said, cutting him off. "Dwayne is not interested in the technical aspect. But the actual show—the format and its name . . ." She paused, letting her words hang between them. "Those kinds of things he should play a key role in."

L.W. held his niece's gaze. Finally, he said, "That's fine, as long as I know you'll be involved." He paused for a moment. "And you'll come to me if you need my help."

"Uncle Linson, can't I always count on you? By the way, did you talk to Pastor Milton about our take on the Spirit Alive Conference? I'm not so sure he was all that clear on the way the deal was set up."

"Yeah," L.W. noted. "He tried to get me down to twenty percent of the take, but I told him that your standard on dates like this where you were a huge part of the draw was thirty percent."

"That includes the hotel bookings as well, right?"

"Beverlyn, I got it all straight. I told him before he passes any offering plates, he'd better have our cut. So don't you worry your pretty little head about it. Let me do my job."

"I know. It's just sometimes it makes me mad. They think because I'm a woman that I'll take less." She turned to leave, then stopped suddenly and turned back. "What do you think about including Dr.

Grandison on some of the crusade dates? It would be a great way to promote the new show." Beverlyn smiled for the first time since she'd come into the office.

"You're taken with that young man, aren't you?"

"What if I am? Look at him. Successful. Brilliant. Good-looking. Single. He's a good man who loves the Lord. I'd like to have a family. Maybe it's time for me to make time for a relationship. I don't know that he's the right man for me, but I do know that since I met him, I've been thinking maybe it's time."

"Maybe it's not," he said sternly. "There's a lot going on in your life right now. With the Jubilee Network and your speaking and singing, I don't want you overwhelmed."

"You don't have to worry about me, Uncle Linson."

"I don't know any other way to be," L.W. said honestly. Long ago, he'd had another revelation—he really did love his sister's child.

Beverlyn stood, walked around the desk, and kissed her uncle on the cheek. "That's why I love you. I'll see you later at the house."

L.W. watched Beverlyn walk across the office. He smiled as she waved and slowly closed the door behind her. Ever since incorporating Beverlyn Boudreaux Ministries, L.W. had become one of the few enterprising evangelists able to turn lucrative speaking engagements and concert dates into a multimedia empire. He'd learned long ago that enterprise is about generating streams of revenue far beyond any one single entity, and he left little space for others to err. He waited only a minute before he picked up the phone and buzzed Kim.

"Do you have any information for me yet?" he said when she entered the room.

# Chapter Thirteen

*N*obody is loving you for no reason." Lafayette pointed at the congregation as he paced the pulpit. "People get to know one another for reasons. And I don't think there's anybody here today who simply loves somebody for what they can do for them and not get anything in return. I love you because you stimulate me. I love you because you're attractive to me. One writer says, 'There is desire in all who admire.' There is no way to compliment and admire without a modicum of desire—because it is coming out of the desire of the flesh and the desire of the mind. You do not hang too long with anybody who does not give you something in return.

"The bigger the bank account, the more I love you. I love you because you have something I want, something I want to identify with, or something I want to get close to.

"Now, here comes the frustration. Often, we make deals in relationships. We say okay, I'll invest a little up front, but I have to receive some dividends. And if we aren't paid back, we'll find somebody else. But God doesn't play games. The love I gave Him back is the love He gave me. It's the love of the Lord—that's the only reason I'm here. He loves you so much that He's getting ready to open the windows of heaven and bless you. That is your salvation today."

The congregation shouted as Lafayette stepped from the pulpit and walked toward the back of the sanctuary. Everyone stayed in place until the final note was played on the keyboard. Dwayne hugged his mother, then took her hand and escorted her to the back.

"I'm sorry you won't be joining us for dinner, son," Bernice said. "But give Sean my best."

"I will. I'll call you tomorrow."

Dwayne kissed his mother and Robbie on the cheek, exchanged greetings with Monique and her two sons, and slapped his brother on the back. "Great word, man."

After Dwayne had finished with the familial good-byes, his eyes searched the sanctuary. He weaved through the maze of exiting worshipers, stopping occasionally to speak to familiar members, as his eyes focused on the west side of the sanctuary until he was standing in front of them.

"Mr. Dwayne!"

Dwayne hunched down. "How are you, Omari?" he asked, running his hand along the boy's navy-blue suit. "You look great, young man. I was wondering if you like basketball."

"Boy, do I! I love the Lakers."

"Then you might like these." Dwayne pulled two tickets from his pocket and handed them to Omari.

"Mom, look!"

Nina smiled at her son, then looked at Dwayne.

"I tried to get three, but I could only get two. Those are floor seats."

"We're going to be sitting on the floor?"

"Yup. You and your mom should have a good time."

Nina frowned. "Oh, I thought you . . . ," Nina started.

"I thought you'd never ask. If you want me to take Omari, I will."

Nina playfully slapped Dwayne on the arm. "I had a feeling that was the plan. It's very nice of you, Dwayne."

"My pleasure!" He patted Omari's head. "Listen, I have a meeting."

Nina's smile faded slightly. "No problem. By the way, I got your message about Wednesday with the women's group."

"We'll be getting together on Tuesday too. That's the day of the game. I'll call you to make arrangements."

"Well, we'll see you then," Nina said, taking Omari's hand.

"Thank you for the tickets, Mr. Dwayne."

"No problem, kiddo."

Dwayne's eyes followed Nina as she led Omari toward the front doors. He watched the gentle sway of her hips and the way she threw back her head, tossing her hair over her shoulder when she stopped to speak to others. Wow, she was a beautiful woman.

But, he thought, should he chance ruining their professional relationship? Turning quietly, Dwayne slipped out of the side door to his car. He looked at his watch. He would still get to brunch at Le Grille on time.

He turned on the radio and smiled as Aundrae Russell announced the beginning of *Spread the Word,* tapping his fingers along the steering wheel as the intro melody played. It was a beautiful day—a great choice for Sunday brunch with Sean.

Brunch had been Sean's idea. He hadn't been up to their weekend tennis match. Besides, this time they could really catch up—something they so often didn't do while playing their usual fierce and competitive tennis matches. Besides, there was a lot he wanted to run by Sean, who had ironically enough once been a client, and though Dwayne referred to many of his former and current clients as acquaintances, only Sean did he consider a friend.

After all, they had become best friends as they'd grown to know each other over the past five years. Sean's need for therapy waned and their conversations were now reciprocal. Dwayne was not always the doctor, especially during the past year, when Sean had allowed Dwayne to be the patient many times.

Sean Wiley had first come to him—broken and on the verge of suicide—referred by Harrison David, the star of NBC's new hit drama, *Garry and Me.* David's frantic call implored him to schedule an emergency meeting with Dwayne.

The next evening when Sean Wiley walked into his office, Dwayne barely recognized the soulful singer who had wowed audiences for more than a decade and whose claim to fame was a body that could gyrate in six different directions at once. From his unkempt, unshaven appearance to the way he held his head uncharacteristically down, Sean looked like a man on the brink of permanent collapse. It didn't help that Sean's eyes only occasionally met Dwayne's—instead seeming to focus mostly on the large windows. For a moment, Dwayne had wondered if the singer was considering how he could get outside to the ledge.

"I don't even know why I'm here." Sean's voice shook when he spoke.

"I hope you're here so that I can help."

It was one of the only moments when Sean looked directly into Dwayne's eyes. "I've been told that I'm going to die. Unless you're God, you can't help me."

Dwayne hesitated, then said, "First, you've been told something we all know—death is a journey we're all going to take. Second, I'm not God, but I do know Him."

Sean's astonishment confirmed to Dwayne that he had caught the Grammy-winning singer off guard. With that, Dwayne leaned forward and began the first in a series of sessions that eventually led Sean to the Lord.

In the beginning, Dwayne had been worried about his friend, particularly after Sean had revealed that the womanizing reputation he'd earned had brought a deadly force into his life—AIDS. Keeping it out of the press had been difficult. Lately whenever they'd spoken, Sean reassured his friend that he was in a place where many Christian entertainers find themselves: between knowing of God and knowing God. Then he'd say, "I know the Lord now and I know what I have to do to stay close to Him. Just keep me in your prayers."

To Dwayne's relief, Sean met Beverlyn only months later, and with her encouragement, he converted not only his life but his music too. Given his newfound passion, Sean found himself at the right place at the right time. Contemporary gospel was exploding thanks to Yolanda Adams, Kirk Franklin, Donnie McClurkin, and others. Seven months later, he released his first self-titled contemporary gospel album, soaring to heights above any he had achieved before. Sean and Dwayne had since come to share a kinship closely resembling that of blood brothers.

Dwayne rolled his Jaguar into the valet area of Reign, and before he could pull to a complete stop, a young valet opened his door and handed him a ticket. He walked through the large glass doors and was greeted by one of the hostesses, who led him through the maze of tables. His eyes finally rested on Sean at one of the small round tables in the back.

"My man . . . ," Dwayne said.

Sean stood and warmly embraced his friend. "Looking good."

"So tell me, what's going on?"

"Same-o, same-o. But I hear you're the man."

"So you heard the news . . ."

"Somewhat, and I'm happy for you. It's time things started moving for you. And this is what Yvette would have wanted. I know she would have wanted you to find love again."

"Whoa, what are you talking about?" Dwayne leaned back.

"You and Nina . . . She seems to be a really nice lady."

"You got the 'nice' part right, but there's nothing going on between us. At least, not now."

Sean cocked his head as if he didn't believe his friend. "Yeah, that's what she tried to tell me at Beverlyn's party, but I wasn't buying it then and I'm not really buying it now."

"Well, she was telling the truth." As he spoke the words, it was almost as if he were trying to convince himself. At the same time, he was conjuring up images of Nina and Omari in church that morning.

"That's too bad." Sean glanced down at the menu.

"I've got quite enough on my plate right now."

A waiter brought two mimosas and Sean raised his glass. "I want to make a toast. To all the blessings God has given us and to conquering the challenges ahead."

Moments later, servers placed a platter of lobster crepes in front of Sean and smoked salmon Benedict in front of Dwayne. They bowed their heads in silent grace and then eagerly tackled their food.

"So the television show is a go, huh?" Sean asked between bites.

"Yeah, I'm excited about it. You realize that Beverlyn wants to revolutionize Christian broadcasting?"

"Ambitious plan. But that's Beverlyn—bigger than life."

"She seems that way. So what's the real skinny on her?"

"Interested?"

"More like curious. She reminds me a lot of Yvette."

Sean frowned. "I don't think the two of them were alike at all."

"Really, I look at their ambition and their drive. And like Yvette's, Beverlyn's heart is with God. I like that about her. I think I'm going to enjoy working with her."

Sean chewed for an extra moment before he said, "I'm sure you will."

Dwayne couldn't decipher the look in his friend's eyes, so he decided to change the subject. "When are we going to see you at New Covenant again? I get such grief about us being friends and not being able to get you to church."

Sean laughed. "Well, maybe I can get there next Sunday." Then his tone sobered. "I have to stay in town this week. I'm taking some tests . . ."

"Are you okay?"

"So far and we're trying to keep it that way."

When Sean didn't continue, Dwayne knew to let it go. His friend would tell him when he was ready. They ate in silence for a few moments before Sean said, "Have you had the pleasure of meeting the great Linson Lejohn?"

Dwayne nodded and then shook his head. "What is that man's story?"

"All I can tell you is that he's a control freak. And," Sean cautioned, "he's not about to let anyone get close to Beverlyn—especially not someone who could have any influence with her."

"I can see that. He showed me that he was in charge the other day. But what I don't understand is, according to Beverlyn, he was the one who really sought me out."

"If I had to make a wild guess," he said, reclining back into the chair, "I'd say he felt you were pretty harmless having recently lost your wife. But having met you and realizing you might be a threat . . ."

"How?"

"Doc, you can't be that naive. You must be too close."

"Beverlyn . . ."

"You got it. And make no mistake. The man's no fool. He wants the best people around, but he remains in control. Believe that. I've known him for years and he's not too crazy about the friendship Beverlyn and I share. Now here comes some good-looking, successful guy that for once is on Beverlyn's level."

"But there is nothing going on . . ."

"Not yet. But I've seen the way she looks at you, and believe me, he's noticed it too. Don't buy into the cocky, confident demeanor. He's a scared little man whose whole reason for living is Beverlyn and the little empire, he reminds you over and over again, that he built. He's desperate enough to do just about anything—I believe—to ensure that nothing shakes the control he has over her."

"Well, he's the only thing that makes me hesitate a bit about this project."

Sean laid his hand on top of his friend's. "Look, you're a man of God, and L.W. can't stop anything that God has ordained."

"Excuse me . . ."

When Dwayne and Sean looked up, they couldn't believe their eyes. Standing before them was L.W. In rushing to push his chair back from the table, Dwayne's knee hit the edge, knocking over his half-filled mimosa. As the liquid splattered onto the tablecloth, Dwayne and Sean reached for their napkins to halt its spread.

"I'm sorry," Dwayne said to Sean, noticing the puzzled look on L.W.'s face.

"No need to get up. I saw you gentlemen sitting here and wanted to say hello. But it looks like I interrupted something."

"Sean and I were having brunch," Dwayne said, finally standing, but still patting the napkin across the table as the waiter rushed to take over.

"Yeah, just two good friends having lunch," L.W. said cynically, and paused. "Well, like I said, I don't want to interrupt . . ."

"No more than you already have," Sean muttered under his breath.

L.W. stared at Sean for a moment, then rolled his eyes before turning back to Dwayne. "I'll see you later this week in the production meeting."

Dwayne stretched toward L.W. and shook his hand. "I'm looking forward to it."

"I'm sure you are. You gentlemen . . . enjoy the rest of your day," he said, smirking as he walked away.

Sean shook his head. "All I can tell you, Dwayne, is to be careful."

Dwayne laughed, but it was a nervous laugh. He knew there was nothing funny about Linson "L.W." Lejohn.

L.W. walked quickly through the restaurant to the valet stand. There was a line as he waited to hand over the ticket for his car; and while waiting might have annoyed him on another day, it didn't bother him today. He tried to peek back through the restaurant's windows, but he couldn't see their table.

How interesting, he pondered. Something must have been going on or the two of them wouldn't have jumped as they did when they saw him. He wondered what. As he reached the front of the line, he handed his ticket to the man in the red vest, paid his fee, then pulled his cell phone from his jacket.

Normally, L.W. had rather deal with a message machine than a tiresome real person, but today he grimaced when the answering machine picked up. "Kim, this is L.W. I need you to give me a call on my cell—" He kept his voice as low as he could over the sound of the busy traffic on Robertson Boulevard. Before he could finish, he heard Kim's voice. "L.W., I'm here."

L.W. was relieved to hear Kim's voice. "Kim, I need you to check something out for me quickly."

"Why are you whispering?"

"Just listen," L.W. hissed. "In addition to what you're researching for me, I need you to expand your search to include Sean Wiley."

"Sean?"

"Yeah. It seems he and the good doctor are better friends than we know. And my instincts tell me that there is something going on."

"Something like what?"she asked incredulously.

"That's your job, Kim. Just get back to me. I'm going to need this information quickly." L.W. pressed the "end" button before Kim could say another word, and just as his money-green Mark VIII rolled in front of him, he trotted to the driver's side and handed the man holding the door a dollar bill.

"Gee, thanks," the young man muttered sarcastically.

L.W. stared at the young man. Any other day, he would have asked for his supervisor and demanded that he be reprimanded. But today he let it roll off his back, jumping into the car. He screeched onto Wilshire Boulevard, turning a few blocks later onto Rodeo Drive. He slowed, passing Cartier, Christian Dior, and Gucci. Soon he'd be shopping here—not only on special occasions but regularly. This was certainly going to be his town. As he continued down the street, he thought, L.A. truly does have streets paved with gold. And he was on the brink of getting his fair share.

# Chapter Fourteen

Though he treated her badly, Kim almost felt sorry for L.W. The way she figured it, without Beverlyn he was nothing. All indications were he had few, if any, friends. She'd never seen him involved in a serious relationship—forget marriage. He had no kids. Nope, it was all about Beverlyn. He seemed to live vicariously through her. Perhaps she was all he had set out to be but never achieved.

However, there was little doubt in Kim's mind that he genuinely cared for her. In fact, he had his moments where he wasn't all that bad. At times, he had been rather generous with her and more than generous with Beverlyn, but L.W. was indeed a very strange bird. She'd known from the first that it was going to mean big trouble if Beverlyn ever found a man, and lately, she'd noticed the way he reacted whenever Dwayne Grandison was around.

Alas, when threatened, there was none more conniving than L.W. She'd hated doing his dirty work. She'd grown to love Beverlyn, considering her to be one of her closest friends, and while she didn't know what L.W. had up his sleeve, she knew it couldn't be good.

For Kim, the situation was as close to being caught between a rock and a hard place as ever it could have been. Unbeknownst to Beverlyn, part of Kim's job description was to "keep watch over her." When L.W. hired her five years ago, she'd been indifferent to the task, but having come to know Beverlyn, she resented having to spy on her, reporting back to L.W. what she'd heard.

Quite frankly, there had—until now—been little to report and so, no conflict. But she knew all too well that Beverlyn was falling for the doctor. Who wouldn't? The man had it going on and she was happy for Beverlyn, but at the same time, she knew the painful ramifications, part of which would begin with the information L.W. wanted on Dwayne. And now Sean? She liked them both, especially Sean, who'd been singing on Beverlyn's crusades on and off for the past five years. Sean had been so impressed after hearing Beverlyn at one of T. D. Jakes's conventions that he'd said yes when first approached by Lejohn to appear on Beverlyn's first crusade.

Kim's thoughts were interrupted at the sound of someone entering the room, and she turned to find Beverlyn in her doorway.

"What are you doing here so late?" Beverlyn inquired.

"I could ask the same of you," she countered.

"Oh, for sure," Beverlyn said, easing onto a leather sofa adjacent to Kim's desk. "What's my travel schedule like this month?"

"You've got Jakes on Thursday, then on Friday, you go to Houston for Saundra Montgomery's women's conference, and on Sunday, you're with Eddie Long. Later this month, you're in Nashville to do some studio work with Shirley Caesar for her next album, and on the twentieth, you're back in New Orleans with Deborah Morton. Montgomery—that's Yolanda Adams's church, right?" Kim asked.

"Yeah. Okay, I'm glad you booked them. I like the pastor, Ed Montgomery. He's really coming up in that city."

"Of course, you know you're also scheduled back at Carlton Pearson's in Tulsa and then you're back in Los Angeles for Fred and Betty Price's Inner City Church Confab on the twenty-fifth," Kim added.

"Pretty light this month."

"Well, considering we're still getting settled, I thought it best to keep your engagements down. Something on your mind?"

"What do you think of Dr. Dwayne Grandison?" Beverlyn asked.

Kim had known that question was coming. "Impressive. Dynamic. Handsome. Single."

Beverlyn laughed throatily. "Yeah . . ."

"Interested?"

"Well, he's certainly not like anyone I've ever known. Not even close."

"Really?"

"Unfortunately, yeah." She paused for a moment. "Sometimes I think it's good to marry young." She gazed directly at Kim, who was a divorced single mother of an eight-year-old daughter. "Because when you're young, one doesn't have to consider what the other brings to the union—the ramifications of mixing lifestyles and those lifestyles being compatible—because no one has anything. Of course, there's always the chance that one outgrows the other, but at least motives aren't a particular concern."

"Well," Kim considered, "I guess you have a point there. Were you ever close to getting married?"

"Not really. Well, I had a first love . . . but I don't think it would have worked out over the long haul."

"What happened?" Kim asked.

"Uncle Linson saw before I could that it wasn't going anywhere and talked me into breaking it off. Oh, I hated him for it then, but—as always—he was right. Since then, there have been flirtations, but nothing really meaningful. Then, too, there's my work . . ." Her voice trailed off. "And quite frankly, I hadn't met anyone I was all that interested in. Sure there are a lot of single pastors, but some of their motives—as you well know—have been questionable, and I don't want a business merger, I want a marriage."

"So you do want to get married?"

"Why do people assume that if a woman hasn't married by a certain age, she doesn't want to be married, instead of assuming she just hasn't found the right man?"

"And is Dwayne Grandison the right man?"

"Could be," Beverlyn said, her eyes twinkling.

"Does L.W. know that?" Kim inquired, as if in surprise.

"I suppose so," Beverlyn said, wondering why she'd even have to ask.

\*   \*   \*

*Daaaaah!* The horn signaling the end of the Laker game mixed with applause and cheers. Omari stood with the crowd as Shaquille O'Neal, Kobe Bryant, and the rest of the team members—and their opponents—filed off the stadium floor to the locker room.

"Mr. Dwayne, that was so good," declared Omari, whose purple and gold Laker jersey was covered with melted cheese from his nachos and caramel-covered popcorn that had spewed over onto the playing floor of the Staples Center.

"You had a good time?"

"Boy, did I. Thank you."

Within five minutes after their ten-minute press through the crowd to Dwayne's car, Omari was fast asleep in the backseat, allowing Dwayne's thoughts to drift. Dwayne continued to look at Nina's son in the rearview mirror. With four nieces and nephews, he was used to being around children, but there was something about Omari. Every time he saw the boy, he was reminded of the child he and Yvette never had. Was the breakdown of their marriage really tied to children? And which one of them had been right? Had Yvette been correct—was he too passive about success and achievement? Was that why he had lost all that was important to him?

He pulled in front of Nina's building. When he turned off the ignition, he glanced at Omari, his head dropped toward his chest and a soft snore coming from his lips. Dwayne pulled Omari from the backseat. The boy stirred, but only for a moment, and nested his head on Dwayne's shoulder. As Dwayne rang Nina's buzzer, then carried Omari up the stairs, he buried himself in the feeling of the boy against his chest. He took in his breathing—and the way Omari's heart beat against his.

When he reached the top of the stairs, Nina was already in the hallway. His demeanor changed when he saw her—dressed in jeans with holes at the knees and her hair pulled back in a loose ponytail, a stark departure from the professional pantsuits and conservative look he had grown accustomed to seeing her in.

"Let me take him."

"No." Dwayne shook his head. "Just show me where to lay him."

Nina smiled and led Dwayne down the long hall to Omari's bed-room.

"Just put him down. I'll come back and change his clothes," she whispered.

Dwayne gently laid Omari onto his bed, covering him with the blanket, then followed Nina from the room.

"He's a good kid. Thanks for letting me take him."

"Are you kidding? I really appreciate it."

Dwayne glanced across the living room to the dining table covered with papers and folders. "Do you ever get out and have any fun?"

"Well, I had fun when I went to the party with you." Her words had come quickly. It wasn't until they were hanging in the air that she realized what she'd said. "I mean I don't have much time to get out. Between Omari, my job . . . and the women's ministry."

Dwayne held his hand up, silencing her. "Don't explain. I know what you mean. Well, it's getting late." He paused for a moment and then turned. "I'd better go."

"Thanks again."

She followed him to the door and he paused somewhat awkwardly again before finally leaning over and hugging her. While she felt strangely familiar in his arms, he was at a loss for the proper good-bye.

"Dwayne," she said, calling him back.

He turned, his eyes meeting hers.

"Be careful. It's easy to get caught up in that world."

He acknowledged the admonishment with a nod, then stepped through the door and waited to hear the locks click. Still, he did not move from the door, wondering if Nina was standing there on the other side, and wondering if the moment had been as awkward for her as it had been for him.

He walked back to his car. Inside, he clicked on the radio, turning the volume up as loud as he could stand, hoping to drown out the confusion in his head. Yvette. Nina. Beverlyn's TV offer. So much was going on.

# Chapter Fifteen

*D*wayne smiled as he watched Nina through the observation glass.

"You're the first to use this," Lafayette said, pride filling his voice. "After sitting in on the first few sessions, we knew we needed an observation room."

"New Covenant is big-time," Dwayne teased.

"I'm trying. Dad had such a vision for this church."

Dwayne turned his gaze back through the mirror at Nina. She was bent over her desk wearing a black two-piece knit suit, with her hair pulled tightly in a braided bun, looking every bit like a schoolteacher. Less than twenty-four hours ago, he'd seen her without makeup looking like a twenty-five-year-old. At the concert, Nina was at her most glamorous, as sophisticated as a cover girl. No wonder she'd been a star. Whatever look she chose appeared to have been achieved effortlessly and at the same time was stunning.

As if she could feel his stare, Nina lifted her head, looked toward the glass, and smiled slightly. Then she returned to the notes on her desk.

"She's good," Dwayne commented.

"That, she is." Lafayette followed Dwayne's glance, then looked back at his brother. Moments later, Lafayette left his brother alone in the room to observe the session that was about to get under way.

As women slowly began to file into the room, Nina's posture became more formal. She pulled her chair around from her desk to close the circle the dozen or so had formed, and after joining hands for an opening prayer, the session was under way. They dropped their hands and Nina leaned back in her chair.

Six months had passed since the beginning of their sessions and the women had all gotten to know each other. But over the last month, Nina had attempted something new. Realizing the women's issues were very different one from the other, she had decided to split the women into two groups: those married and those single.

Tonight Nina was working with the single women. Several were looking for relationships. Many had been divorced. Some had children. Some were in relationships and others were not. Most, however, were seeking serious, meaningful change in their lives. All had professed a deep desire to be viable and vital independent women, while confessing they had some things to work through.

In the last few minutes, just when they expected some opening words of inspiration, Nina posed a bombshell question to each of them: "If you were to marry today, what is your number one piece of emotional, spiritual, or relational 'excess baggage' that your mate would be subjected to?"

At first, they all tried to avoid the question, but Nina insisted and finally each offered an answer: "My temper," "My insecurity," "My jealousy," "My lack of confidence," "My out-of-control mouth," "My laziness." Each quickly acknowledged that her trait was regrettable. And, in her own way, each of them pronounced her excess baggage to be "just the way I am and probably always will be."

Nina followed the first question with another: What kind of man are you looking for? This time, even as Nina insisted, no one could provide a sufficient answer. One woman said, "Well, no one knows exactly." Then Nina paused, looked each of them (it seemed) in the eyes, and said, "Well, if you don't know exactly what you're looking for, how will you exactly know when you find it?"

Suddenly, they were on the defensive.

"Oh, I'll know," said Denise.

"Well, then, Denise, just what is it?"

For Denise, it was a precarious question. Most of the men she'd been attracted to had been as successful as she was brilliant, but few of them lasted past six months. Oh, it would be hot and heavy in the beginning and then nothing—no dates, no calls—and then finally if they did by chance cross paths, no words were exchanged.

"I'm looking for someone successful, loving—someone who would make a good father and someone who is godly. I can't think of anything better, can you?" Denise answered.

"Not really. Except perhaps you might have put the last quality first."

"With all due respect," Gloria declared, "there are a lot of godly men who aren't so 'godly.'"

"Then they are not godly men," Nina countered. "There is an old saying: 'Just because a mouse gets into the cookie jar doesn't make him a cookie.' The thing is, people aren't always who they say they are. That's why it's so important that we know enough about who we are and what we want to not just fall for anything. And believe me, I know."

Nina continued, "When I was younger, I wanted it all. And you know what? Because I didn't know God the way I know Him now, I suffered. I got sexually transmitted diseases, I had an abortion, became involved with men who cared little for me other than for my looks or body . . . I had unprotected sex. It's only by God's grace I'm not HIV-positive. That's what you can look forward to when you try to live without God. The world has made its own rules. And those rules have led to trouble: unwanted babies, destroyed marriages, sexual diseases. None of these were in God's plan.

"We get so blindsided by the things of this world. The 'ooh, he's fine'—the big house, the big cars. Not that all these things aren't nice, but we can't look to others for the fulfillment of our needs.

"I recall when my young niece—not saved—called me up to have dinner. It turned out she wanted to confide in me that she'd had sex for the first time. I asked if she needed advice about birth control or HIV and she said no. I took a deep breath and asked if she was scared she might be pregnant and she again said no. Perplexed, I asked, 'So tell me, Gina, did you have some questions you wanted to ask me?' 'No,' she replied. 'I just wanted to share this with you.'

"Now, mind you, I'd never met nor had I seen this boy, and I don't believe that they were dating. Furious, I put my finger in her face and said, 'What you're telling me is you got screwed, because since I haven't seen this boy, he can't have much respect for you, and neither, quite frankly, have I. You're my niece and I love you, so I want more for you than someone who uses you to get off. So the next time you get screwed, I don't want to know about it. Tell a friend.'

"I believe that's how God feels when He sees us giving away the very essence of ourselves to men who haven't proved they deserve the time of day from us. Many of us think that if we lose ten more pounds, or if we had this outfit or could impress him with our accomplishments, could make him jealous . . . if we could only get him in the bedroom . . ."

The room was suddenly abuzz with outspoken agreement. Gloria shouted out, "You better say that, girl."

"Well, I've got a news flash for you," Nina continued. "Like a male friend of mine once said, 'You can't nice your way into a man's heart.' Either he likes you or he doesn't. If he likes you, all you need to be is yourself. If he doesn't like you, it won't matter what you wear, how much you make, or how many men are after you.

"God wants us to be the unique women that He made us— Oops, where did the time go?"

"Ain't it the truth," said Johnetta. "Seems like I just turned around and I'm forty."

Nina laughed and then went on. "I want to close with this: Pray about all of your decisions and rejoice in the knowledge that what God gave you uniquely is all you need."

Silently, Nina hugged each woman as they hugged one another and then departed. It wasn't until she heard the knock on the door, and Dwayne peeked into her office, that she remembered he had been watching.

"You were great."

Her heart sank recalling some of the personal disclosures she'd made.

"I just hope I'm making a difference."

"Trust me, you are. I could see it in their faces." He took her hand. "Let me take you to dinner."

Nina smiled for the first time since the session ended. She held so much of what she felt inside. It was good to talk to someone who understood. She reached for her purse, but the sound of Dwayne's cell phone made her pause.

"Excuse me," he said. "Hello . . . Hello, Beverlyn."

Nina almost chuckled as she turned from her desk, gathering papers from folders on her credenza. With her back to Dwayne, she wouldn't have to look into his eyes.

"I won't be able to do that, Beverlyn," Dwayne said, making no moves to keep his conversation private. "I have plans tonight."

When Nina turned around, Dwayne was looking at her. She tried to smile.

"We can meet tomorrow," he said into the phone.

A few days before, Nina would have been upset with Beverlyn's timing. Now all she wanted to do was remove herself. She had seen all the signs. Beverlyn was after Dwayne and would try to mow over anything that got in her way. Not that Nina wasn't up for a good fight, but she was saving it for the cancer. Besides, Dwayne would have to find out for himself whether Beverlyn was what he wanted. Nina was way too removed from that kind of drama to sign up for it now.

"I'm sorry, Beverlyn," Dwayne said, then hung up abruptly.

"So where would you like to go?" He tucked his cell phone into his pocket.

"I don't really feel like going out tonight. I still have the session notes, and unless you had questions or something else you wanted to discuss?"

"No," he said, surprised. "I didn't plan for this to be a working dinner. I thought we'd go out and have fun."

"I'll take a rain check."

Dwayne's eyes darted around the office as if he didn't know what to do next. Finally, he stood and straightened his tie. "Well, then, I'll get out of here so that you can get home at a decent hour. Good night."

"Good night, Dwayne."

When he closed the door, Nina smiled. This had been a good day. She'd made headway with the women and she was pleased that this time she hadn't allowed Dwayne or Beverlyn to get to her. She was proud of herself.

Beverlyn let the telephone fall gently into its cradle.

*I'm sorry, I have plans, Beverlyn.*

Those were not words she was used to hearing. She eased back onto her bed and looked at the papers spread across the covers. She'd simply wanted to ask Dwayne about the name of his program before Friday's production meeting. It wasn't until she heard his voice that she suggested they get together. Still, she couldn't believe he'd turned her down.

Beverlyn pushed the papers on her lap aside. Obviously, Dwayne had been preoccupied, but with what . . . or with *whom*? She'd called his office first and gotten his service. So where was he? Perhaps visiting a friend or having dinner with a business associate. Or was he with Nina Jordan?

Beverlyn stood and walked to the window of her eighth-floor suite at the Beverly Wilshire. The corner of Wilshire and Rodeo was still full with traffic as shoppers scurried and executives exited the busy intersections, heading home. For a girl from New Orleans, the bright lights of Los Angeles were mesmerizing. If only she could get out of the hotel and be out there—a part of the city that now held her attention.

Beverlyn walked into the living room and stretched across the green brocade couch. She turned on the television and flipped through the channels, revealing a potpourri of seemingly mindless entertainment. She clicked the television back off. It was time for her to find her own place. Her uncle had already moved into a spacious apartment in Westwood, never having been one who enjoyed hotels—not even one as opulent as the Beverly Wilshire.

On the other hand, Beverlyn enjoyed spending time in A-rated hotels throughout the world. Such posh accommodations vividly distinguished her past from her present—reminding her of who she was and at the same time never allowing her to forget who she'd been. Besides, on the church circuit, top hotels were significant. If you were really valued as a speaker, you were offered the best: first-class travel accommodations all the way around. So she'd come to expect the best. She looked around the room, at the antique furniture, gold-plated lamps, and Oriental rugs—and the privilege and wealth they represented. All of it was part of her testimony.

But now Beverlyn felt transient. Maybe if she'd had her own place, Dwayne would have agreed to meet her tonight—if he wasn't with Nina. She winced at the thought of the two of them together, though they never seemed like a couple to her. At the party, they'd almost acted like business associates.

Not that it was any of her business—except that she would never pursue the man if he was involved with Nina Jordan. Beverlyn laughed aloud and looked in the mirror. Who am I kidding? she thought. If she really wanted the man, it didn't matter who else was interested. He's not married, that's all that counts.

Beverlyn thrived on competition. But if she was going to toss her silk scarf into this ring, she needed to know all the vital statistics. She smiled as a thought came to mind. Quickly, she moved to the phone and was relieved she got him instead of an answering machine.

"Sean, it's Beverlyn. How are you, honey?"

# Chapter Sixteen

'Higher Ground' works for me," Dwayne said simply as he remembered the way L.W. had bulldozed the beginning of the meeting.

Beverlyn began to protest. "L.W. . . ."

Dwayne reached over and touched Beverlyn's hand, stopping her. He knew what was going on and he also knew that he had to be the one to end this battle. "L.W. is right," Dwayne said, keeping his eyes on him. Ten pairs of stunned eyes turned toward Dwayne, and he knew he'd just gained major points with his team. Beverlyn raised her eyebrows, then shook her head in defeat.

L.W. slapped his hands against the conference table. "Well, then, 'Higher Ground' it is," he said, and stood. "I have another meeting." He'd made his point and the room was silent until he exited.

As the others filed out, Beverlyn turned to Dwayne. "Before you go, there is something I want to show you. Do you have a moment?"

"Sure." Dwayne closed his portfolio and stood.

They walked shoulder-to-shoulder down the long hall, past carpeted cubicles and Beverlyn's office into the room just next door. She stepped into that office and Dwayne followed, scanning the spacious room decorated in rich mahogany complete with oversize desk, matching credenza, and bookcases lined with burgundy binders that seemed to blend in. The adjacent wall of the room was a complete window, offering a breathtaking view of Los Angeles.

"Nice office," he said.

"Think you could get comfortable here?"

He looked at her in disbelief.

"This is your office," Beverlyn said.

"Beverlyn, I have an office. I don't need another."

"Yes, you do." Beverlyn walked toward the windows. "Dwayne, once this show gets going, there's no telling what demands are going to be made on you. We have to be ready."

"Ready for what, Beverlyn? I'm simply going to be meeting with the production team once a week . . ."

"Well, you may need to interview potential guests or handle business that we haven't even thought of."

"There are plenty of conference rooms . . ."

"Dwayne, it's only natural that you should have an office here, even if you choose not to use it. However, you are important to us, and should you choose to use it, I just want to make you comfortable."

Dwayne looked at Beverlyn and then moved his eyes away. Was she making a good point? he asked himself. The office was very nice. Still, he didn't want to be swallowed up by Beverlyn Boudreaux Ministries. He didn't like that she seemed to be giving too much, almost as if she were bartering for his affection or entrapping him. Besides, he didn't want to be anywhere near L.W. Yet what she was saying made sense. He looked back at Beverlyn and forced a smile. "You have a very good point. I was just concerned about wasting the space . . ."

"Dwayne, there is nothing that's a waste when it comes to you. We're committed to making the show successful and you a star in the process." She paused and stepped closer to him. Dwayne wondered why he hadn't noticed in all the weeks they'd been together just how tall Beverlyn was. She only had to tilt her head slightly to look him directly in the eye.

He coughed lightly and stepped back, putting space between them.

"You're an asset," she argued persuasively. "Even if *you* don't realize it. I know who you are and what you're going to be."

The words came out before she could stop them, and instantaneously, she wanted to take them back. She had said too much.

Her words made him take another step backward. They were Beverlyn's eyes but Yvette's words. Silent seconds passed before he picked up his briefcase. "Beverlyn, thanks. Listen, I've got to run. I will talk to you later."

Dwayne walked past her, moving swiftly through the halls—his eyes trained on what was directly in front of him—and only when he entered the elevator did he breathe. It was uncanny the way Beverlyn's words reminded him of Yvette: *I know who you are and what you're going to be.*

Beverlyn fell back into the plush chair behind her massive desk and put her head in her hands. She felt cheap, like she had been trying to buy him when all she really wanted him to see was how good a team they made together . . . and to draw him closer in a way that was comfortable to her.

But Dwayne Grandison was not like those before him who'd been impressed by the generosity that masked her desire for true affection. She wondered, had she come on too strong? Oh, well, she thought, if he wasn't God's desire for her, then she didn't want him. Then again—she stood and walked to the window—he was perfect for her. But how, she wondered, would she get him to see it?

The weeks moved forward at a furious pace. Sessions with Nina, production meetings with Beverlyn, and maintaining his practice packed the hours of Dwayne's days. Some of his clients had even gotten caught up in the excitement.

"I read in the *Hollywood Forecast* about your new talk show," Jasmine Charles gushed at one of her sessions.

"Yeah, it's pretty exciting. Quite a change for me."

"Well, if you ever need a guest . . ."

Dwayne laughed halfheartedly. "*Higher Ground* is a Christian take."

"How do you know I'm not a Christian?"

"Because you told me that there wasn't a thing a Christian could do for you."

Jasmine was a "stuffer." Whenever there was a hard-to-talk-about issue she knew she needed to raise with her husband, Kirk, who like herself was an actor, she had a tendency to keep it stuffed inside, seldom taking the risk of bringing it up to him. She figured that speaking up would do more harm than good.

Kirk, on the other hand, was a "skirter." Whenever there was a potential conflict in their relationship, he was prone to using an endless stream of vague, indirect words instead of saying what was really on his mind, skirting around the issue, fearful that he might set off an argument.

Both wrongly suspected that their marriage would go under if they ever rocked the boat. Dwayne's job had been to persuade him and now her that their relationship was more likely to sink if they *didn't* rock the boat, to remind them that they were two separate individuals—individuals who had been brought up in two different homes, who had differing experiences, motives, and personal preferences, and who were subject to seeing the same issue in two vastly different ways. But today, with Jasmine's mind seeming to be more on Dwayne's show than her problems, Dwayne was struggling to stay focused.

"So how'd you get this gig?" she asked.

"Jasmine, we're not here to talk about me. We're here to talk about you. After all, you pay me for that."

With that, Dwayne settled back into his chair, much more comfortable as a listener than the center of attention—particularly in a world he still didn't feel part of. Fact was, outside his practice, Dwayne felt most comfortable with New Covenant's Man-to-Man ministry, his first official session scheduled to begin the day after the first taping of *Higher Ground*. Ironic that they were both debuting at the same time.

With everything on track, all that was left to do was to wait, hold his breath, and pray that this would all turn out the way God wanted.

"You've been working on this four weeks and you have nothing?" L.W. looked directly into Kim's eyes. "You didn't look deep enough. Everybody has some skeleton in their closet."

"L.W., it was an extensive background check that included everything from his bank records to his childhood friends to some distant family members—even talked to some of his patients, who all seem to want to nominate the man for sainthood or something." Kim could read the disappointment in L.W.'s face. "So what now?"

With nothing to hold over Dwayne's head, L.W. found himself at a distinct disadvantage. There had to be a way, he thought, looking across the table at Kim in disgust. No one, not even Dwayne Grandison, could be perfect. "You have to give me something, do you hear me? Now, how about Sean Wiley?"

"Nothing yet. I'd been devoting my time to Dr. Grandison."

"Well, get working on it."

Without waiting for a response, L.W. stood and stomped past Kim out the door.

In another part of the building, production assistants scurried about as studio technicians trained their cameras and lights on the stage. A crowd of eagerly waiting onlookers had been seated in the studio audience, and Dwayne paced nervously backstage.

"You're going to be great," Beverlyn reassured him.

"Are you sure?" he countered with the first hint of vulnerability she'd observed in him. Nice, she thought as both of them rushed to take their places. He was coming to depend on her.

The room filled with music as the stage spotlight zoomed in on a duet with Beverlyn and Sean. As the duet came to a close, another camera and bright light shone on a now-visible Dwayne.

"Good afternoon. My name is Dr. Dwayne Grandison. Welcome to *Higher Ground*."

The show focused in on the ravaging results of drugs on the families, and the confessions of those whose actions had devastated the lives of their loved ones. He quickly forgot the cameras, focusing in only on the people in front of him and Sean. Sean began to disclose for the first time—before a national audience—the harrowing five-year battle with drug abuse that nearly killed him and how he was finally delivered through Jesus Christ.

"I lost my job," one of the women said, "because my son came to my office ranting for money. He threatened my colleagues and attacked my boss."

As the woman spoke, her son, Robert, dropped his head.

"What's so painful," the mother continued, "is he's still using. He says he's not, but I know the signs. It's like he doesn't care about his family."

"I care, Mom," the seventeen-year-old said softly. "I just can't help it. But I would never hurt you."

Another young woman turned to Robert. "You say that you don't want to hurt your family, but you will. Crack made me so paranoid that I put my two-year-old out of the house. I left him standing on the steps, bawling, in the middle of winter. I didn't care. I was sure he was conspiring with the neighbors to kill me. I was out of my mind."

The talk continued, each declaration sounding worse than the last. Sean's riveting testimony provided the knockout punch, bringing everyone to tears.

"Drugs became more important than my music. They were my lovers, and I would do anything for them. I knew I was killing myself, and I didn't want to die. But I couldn't stop. I gave up, but the blessing was that God never gave up on me."

On the screen, Sean lowered himself to his knee and turned to Robert.

"Christ saved my life, and He came to save yours."

As Sean led the young man to God, Dwayne gave a number for viewers to call if they desired to speak with prayer counselors.

"This is not the end for Robert, or any of my guests," Dwayne said to the camera. "God is the beginning. And He gives us tools to handle challenges. So we are going to help our guests get what they need. We will do our best to take them to a Higher Ground. I'm Dr. Dwayne Grandison, and I'll see you next time."

As the audience applauded in a standing ovation, Dwayne smiled broadly, thinking to himself that this wasn't all that bad. In fact, he was pretty good at this. He had grown to like the attention. Wow, he thought to himself. Suddenly, he scanned the room for Beverlyn and with the cameras still trained on him, walked over, clasped her hand, and brought her front and center for the continuing ovation.

Beverlyn took it all in, breathing deeply and silently celebrating the fact that Dwayne had just officially crossed over into her world. Even if he didn't know it, they were now a team, just as she had wanted.

# Chapter Seventeen

Nina looked up from her desk and glanced at Dwayne, sitting at her conference table.

"You've been working for hours." She smiled. "You've got to be tired."

Dwayne made a final marking on the paper and then looked up. "I am tired," he said, rubbing his eyes. "This has been one of the longest days of my life."

Nina walked across the room to the conference table. "Tiring but exhilarating, I'm sure. You're officially a TV star," she teased. "How did it feel to be in front of all those cameras?"

Dwayne motioned for Nina to sit next to him. "It was surreal. You see this stuff on TV, but then you're the one with dozens of cameras pointed at you. Thousands of lights beaming and people yelling instructions . . . makeup . . ." He paused, rubbed his hand against his cheek, then checked his fingers. "I have a new opinion of show business."

"It's a different world."

"Let's just say I have new respect for my clients," he quipped. "Seriously, though, I can't wait to see how it turns out. They said they'd have the final edits by morning. I can't stop wondering how it will look."

"It'll be fine. I know you don't know anything about television, but you're doing the part you know well—you're talking to people."

"I hope that's enough for the cameras."

"You have charisma, Dwayne. The cameras will love you."

He paused, thinking of how she was speaking from her own experience.

"Just look at everything you do," she continued. "You don't take a project unless you can give it your best. Everything you touch does well. Look at Man-to-Man."

"Now, this I'm sure of. I can't wait for tomorrow. Do we have a final count for the meeting?"

Nina returned to her desk and picked up the file. "Fifteen confirmed."

"Well, however many, I'll be ready."

"I know you will. And on that note let's get out of here. No matter how hard we try, we're not going to be able to script every minute of the meeting."

Dwayne laughed as he packed the papers into his briefcase. They chatted as they walked to the church's parking lot, pausing at Nina's Toyota Camry.

"Nina, thank you for being such a good friend these last few months."

"I haven't really done anything."

"You may not realize it, but getting me involved with Man-to-Man and encouraging me with *Higher Ground*, you've helped me to see a future I'm now looking forward to."

"You really do seem happy, and I couldn't be happier for you. But remember what I said, Dwayne. It's so easy to get caught up in that world—without ever knowing it. And it's not so much the money or the outward success as how, before you know it, you find yourself off course."

Dwayne silently reflected on Nina's words, reasoning that this would not be the case with him. Besides, he was finally happy. The dark cloud that had hung over his life for the past year had lifted, and Nina was part of it all. There was so much he wanted to say to her, but moments between them were still awkward. So as had grown to be his custom with her, he held back, analyzing every word and motion, often opting to play it safe.

"Thanks."

"Whatever I've done, it was easy," Nina said, peering into Dwayne's light brown eyes. "I believe in you." She paused and stepped closer.

Suddenly, it became quite clear that they were in kissing range. As the realization sank in, the moment seemed to hold them in a stark eternity. Slowly, Dwayne leaned forward. His lips were within mere inches of hers when Nina abruptly turned away.

"We'd better get going," she said, fumbling with her keys. "If you thought this was a long day, wait until tomorrow." She hoped her tone lightened the moment.

Dwayne cleared his throat. "I wanted to ask you . . . Beverlyn is hosting a screening for the first show of *Higher Ground*. I'd like you to go with me."

Again, the seconds stretched, with Nina's gaze still lowered to the ground. "I don't think so. I'll be working."

"I haven't even told you when."

She finally looked at him. "It doesn't matter. I can't go."

"It's the day after tomorrow," he said anyway. A moment later, he nodded. "I understand." He opened her car door and then closed it after she had slipped inside. Without a final good-bye, Nina drove away, leaving Dwayne standing in the dust of the gravel that her car wheels left behind.

Dwayne raised his head a bit and peeked through half-opened eyelids. Only one of the chairs was empty. Dwayne lowered his eyes once again with a smile. The only thing that would have made this night better was if Nina had come. But when he arrived at the church an hour or so earlier, she was not there. He waited in her office, until Lafayette arrived a half hour later, and together, the brothers christened the first official gathering of Man-to-Man.

Instead of the fifteen or so they'd expected, nearly three dozen turned out for what would be the first of a series of intense sessions designed to support and encourage men through all the challenges they faced as breadwinners, fathers, husbands, and Christians. Just as with the women, their open and honest communication was encouraged.

"I want to applaud you for coming out tonight. After ten years in private counseling practice, I am accustomed to the hesitation many men have in admitting that they need help, when in reality, we all do.

"Unfortunately, some men let that self-sabotaging kind of pride stop them from seeking assistance when the stakes are far higher than just trying to get to a destination in their cars. Some of us flat-out refuse to say 'Help!' even when our lives, our mates, our families, finances, or spiritual growth are at risk.

"The pride that keeps men from seeking needed help is based on a lie that says a man ought to handle every facet of his life all by himself. If he can't, his excessive pride convinces him he's a failure and less than a real man. And, of course, we avoid doing anything that might make us feel like a failure. A good friend of mine, Frank Wilson, says men are like turtles. Inside—soft, sensitive, and vulnerable, yet choosing to construct a tough outer covering for protection. We call them shells, he calls them masks.

"Let's start by taking off our masks tonight. I want to have everyone stand up and say a little about themselves."

"Good evening," Deacon Sloan said. "My name is Isaac Sloan and I came here tonight to stand in support with the men of this church."

"My name is Don Adams," said the next, "and I'm here out of curiosity, mostly."

Dwayne chuckled, as did the rest of the men, and one by one everyone shared—some just their names, others more. Then came the last introduction. "I'm Milton Wright, and I'm here because I need somebody to walk with me. I'm going through some difficult times and I may be the cause of them. I just don't know how to turn around some of the destructive things that I do."

"Ah, man, we all know what you're going through. Nearly everyone has at least one emotional slave master. It's the psychological black hole that you trip into over and over in the normal course of living and loving. It's that troublesome and persistent emotion you feel far more intensely—and more frequently—than you wish you did. You hate that you feel it, but you don't quite know exactly why you feel it. You do suspect that it—and any other excess baggage you may be carrying—might be robbing you of too much of your peace and joy.

"Maybe it's jealousy, or insecurity, or anger, or resentment, or worry, or fear, or . . . Whatever it is, you return to it often, even when you try your hardest not to. In relationships with the opposite sex, you're likely to try to get your mate to keep you from ever having to feel that negative feeling.

"When you are a slave to a particular emotion, you spend huge amounts of time defending yourself, denying the feeling, or demanding the one you love order his or her steps to make room for your excess baggage. All of this, of course, leaves little time—or energy—for love.

"If you're a slave to insecurity, you'll unknowingly require others to allay your fears.

"If you're a slave to jealousy, you'll insist that your mate or girlfriend prove that you are more desirable to them than anyone else on the planet.

"If you're a slave to anger, you'll demand that those around you make the world, and everything in it, work just the way you dictate.

"If you're a slave to self-doubt, you'll look to others to do for you what you're afraid to do for yourself.

"The emotion that enslaves you won't politely go away on its own. Freedom comes with a fight. I offer you this Emancipation Proclamation: Over the course of these sessions, ask for help. We will arm you with the skills necessary to free you from 'emotional bondage.'

"All around you in the Body of Christ are those whom God has placed to help you become, inside and out, more like Jesus. Pastors, and prayer partners, counselors, and intimate friends who know you well enough and love you deeply enough to encourage, rebuke, and support you in changing your style. You really don't have to live your life enslaved to an ugly emotional or behavioral trait. If you stretch, freedom is within reach, by the grace and power of God. It can be yours if you will.

"One, admit the need. Conviction followed by confession is the starting place. Resist denying, justifying, or excusing your excess baggage. These things only work to keep you stuck where you are.

"Two, explore the origins of your problem. Often, knowing where you began to feel and act so angrily, fearfully, vengefully, selfishly, et cetera, helps you to determine why you are so attached to your excess baggage. You do what you do for a reason. Probably a distorted, self-deceptive reason that is inconsistent with what God says about you and about Himself. Here some sensitive, supportive help from others and consistent Scripture intake will be very beneficial.

"Three, repent. Call your negative emotional, behavioral, and relational patterns 'sin,' not 'just the way I am.' Make a sincere, faith-filled commitment to participate in God's purifying work in your life. Commit to no longer speaking and acting in accordance with your excess baggage. Keep the commitment when it feels good and when it doesn't.

"And finally, pray for God to reveal and heal you in that area. Then act, speak, and relate to others in ways that are the opposite of what your old habits dictate.

"Remember"—Dwayne held up his hands—"what we are focusing in on here is strengthening ourselves to become men of God, not men of the world. That leaves one question for you privately to answer: Which do you really want to be? The goal of these sessions is to clearly delineate the difference.

"Now, I really have talked too much. Are there any questions?" he asked, scanning the room, his eyes falling with surprise on a familiar face—that of his friend Sean Wiley, seated in the back. He'd only briefly discussed the first meeting of the group with Sean over the weekend.

From the corner of his eye, Dwayne saw Lafayette stand. He had forgotten that he was there. When he faced his brother, Dwayne was pleased with the smile on his face. Lafayette raised his thumb in the air. Dwayne watched as he moved up toward the podium, indicating that the first session of Man-to-Man was about to come to a close.

After taking three or four questions from the attendants, Dwayne handed the microphone back to Lafayette, who closed out with a congratulatory word to the men for turning out and making a commitment pledge to grow with the ministry and a word of prayer.

"Great job." Lafayette turned and embraced Dwayne before greeting some of the men who'd turned out.

Dwayne was deluged by a group sitting in the front but kept an eye out for Sean, now making his way toward him—also stopped by men every few steps.

"Hey, man, this is great," Sean said, finally approaching Dwayne.

"I didn't know you were coming."

"Well, I didn't say anything because I didn't know if I could make it, but I sure am glad I did."

From behind the observation window, Nina had gathered up her things and was preparing to leave. She had seen what she had come to see. Dwayne had done just fine, and Man-to-Man was on its way. She'd come well after the session had started and left without Dwayne ever knowing she had been there.

# Chapter Eighteen

The Jaguar purred as Dwayne slowed to a crawl, eased next to the curb, then turned off the ignition. He turned and smiled at his mother.

"Are you ready, son?"

"Yeah. Thanks for being my date, Mom."

"I wouldn't miss this for anything." She patted him on the shoulder. "My son the TV star."

"I'm the one who's proud, Mom."

"What have I done?"

"It's because of you that I am who I am. You provided the foundation . . . you taught me how to know God. How to pray."

"Thank you, son."

"I just wish Lafayette could be happy for me too."

"He's not happy about the show?"

"He hasn't said he was unhappy, but you know Lafayette. When he's behind something, you know it."

"Lafayette is just concerned that you're overextending," Bernice theorized. "He worries about you. We all do."

Dwayne looked up ahead through the windshield. The street where Beverlyn had moved, in exclusive Hancock Park, seemed deserted. Few cars were visible; most were probably parked behind the gates of the vintage mansions lining the streets.

"I'm fine, and I'm not just saying that. And that is why so many great things are happening. Like this TV show." He looked down at his watch. "We'd better get inside. I'm sure Beverlyn is waiting."

The April evening's breeze blew cool, and Bernice adjusted her black azalea floral silk wrap before they moved forward. At the six-foot-high wrought-iron gate, Dwayne pressed the lit but unmarked button over the intercom to the home, which sat back a dramatic distance from the curb. There was no voice response, only a nearly imperceptible buzz signalling that the gate's lock was released and they could now enter. He took his mother's hand and they slowly strolled along the winding, sloped driveway, finally stopping in front of the massive gated Tudor complex, an 8,500-square-foot main house on beautifully landscaped grounds, a three-bedroom guesthouse, and maid's quarters. They stepped between the concrete pillars, to huge double doors. Dwayne's hand barely touched the doorbell before a lanky, bald-headed gentleman dressed in a black tuxedo opened the doors, then stepped aside, allowing Dwayne and Bernice to enter into the large foyer.

The tuxedoed man bowed slightly. His chestnut-colored scalp glistened in the glow of the crystal chandelier that hung above. "Come in, Dr. Grandison."

Dwayne raised his eyebrows.

"My name is Harris. May I take your wrap, Ms. Grandison?"

It was Bernice's turn to raise her eyebrows as she slipped the matching cashmere silk wrap from her shoulders. Dwayne's eyes followed his mother's as she scanned the massive entryway. Her eyes glanced up the long staircase, centered in front of them, then moved to the portraits that lined the walls. From the soft "umph" that seemed to involuntarily escape from his mother's throat, Dwayne could tell that she was as impressed as he was. Not that either of them wasn't accustomed to the lifestyle, but Beverlyn's home was truly impressive—a page right out of *Architectural Digest*.

"Ms. Boudreaux asked me to let her know when you arrived. If you will wait right here, I will get her."

Before he could answer, a voice came from above. "Dwayne, you're here."

Beverlyn stood at the top of the landing in a periwinkle jeweled and beaded Empire gown—then proceeded toward them. With the grace of a Hollywood movie star, her steps perfectly choreographed, she held the handrail with the tips of her fingers.

Dwayne couldn't take his eyes off her as she moved toward him. At the very moment their eyes met, she knew she'd scored some bonus points in the fifteen-hundred-dollar b. Michael original.

"I'm so glad you're here." Beverlyn took Dwayne's hand. Immediately, she turned to Bernice with a wide smile. "You must be Mrs. Grandison. I cannot tell you what a pleasure it is to meet you."

Bernice held her hand out. "The pleasure is all mine, Ms. Boudreaux."

"Please call me Beverlyn. I have a feeling we are going to be great friends." She locked her arm through Bernice's. "Let's go into the parlor. Our guests are waiting." She led them across the foyer into the living room.

Dwayne's professional training taught him the importance of keeping his face and body neutral, no emotion discernible. But he found it difficult to conceal his surprise when he entered the expansive space and elegant "great room." In the sitting areas throughout the room, people chatted while sipping chardonnay and cider and snacking on skewered grilled shrimp. At the far end of the room, Sean sat at the ivory grand piano, playfully fiddling with the keys. All eyes turned as they entered the room.

"Everyone, our guest of honor is here," Beverlyn announced, dramatically spreading her arms wide as if she were about to sing.

The group applauded enthusiastically. Dwayne had been to many celebrity events, but Beverlyn's small gathering was exceptional. Andrew Campbell, a top aide to the mayor, and Rosalyn Saunders, a Los Angeles councilwoman, were the first to approach him and Bernice. "Dr. Grandison"—Councilwoman Saunders offered her hand—"it is a pleasure to meet you."

Within a moment, Dwayne and Bernice were surrounded, each guest wanting to offer his or her own congratulations. After a few moments and the signal from Kim, Beverlyn clapped her hands. "Now that Dr. Grandison is here, it's time for the viewing." There were mutters of agreement. "Don't worry about your drinks. There are refreshments in the media room." The group parted like the Red Sea, allowing Beverlyn, followed by Dwayne and Bernice, to lead the way. As they passed the piano, Sean stood and grabbed his friend's hand.

"Breathe deeply. You deserve this," Sean said.

"Thanks, man, for all your support."

"You were there for me when I needed it. Isn't that what friendship is about?"

"Thanks again, man."

Dwayne couldn't thank Sean enough for agreeing to be the show's first celebrity guest. Even though Sean had turned toward what he referred to as God's music, he'd never lost his mainstream appeal, so his appearance on their pilot episode had been a major coup for *Higher Ground.*

"I feel like a fish out of water."

Sean chuckled. "Relax, man. You're doing just fine. How are you and Nina, or should I say Beverlyn?"

"Why?"

"Because she's got it bad for you."

Dwayne shook his head. "A great lady, but I don't know."

"You'd be surprised. There's a lot more to Beverlyn than meets the eye. Deep down," Sean reflected, "she's just a little girl looking for acceptance . . . to belong. And apart from all this and her ministry, I'm not so sure she is all too sure of just who she is. So don't buy into all this."

Beverlyn's media room was like a small movie theater, with twenty-five cushioned chairs facing a large screen. She motioned for Dwayne and Bernice to take seats in the front row as the rest of the gathering sat throughout the room. A few minutes later, Beverlyn stood on a slightly raised platform, raising her hands to silence the gathering.

"I want to thank each and every one of you for coming out this evening. You already know about the Jubilee Network, but what you may not know is that the show we are viewing tonight is the flagship program for the network."

Bernice squeezed Dwayne's hand, and it wasn't until that moment that he realized how nervous he was.

"I'm not going to say much because this show speaks for itself. So now I am proud to present the first show of *Higher Ground*." And with a slight twist of her hand, Beverlyn motioned to the projection room, and the lights slowly dimmed. She took her seat, and the screen was instantly covered with the opening title.

Dwayne shifted in his seat as the crowd took in the opening duet with Beverlyn and Sean. This was one of his favorite parts—and it was even better because he had defeated L.W., who wanted more traditional gospel music. The picture faded, and slowly his image filled the screen.

"Good afternoon. My name is Dr. Dwayne Grandison. Welcome to *Higher Ground*."

Dwayne couldn't tell if the cheers came from the audience in the studio or from those who were with him now, but his eyes stayed glued to the 120-inch screen. As the show proceeded, he analyzed every motion, every gesture. He was pleased that he didn't look as if he were wearing makeup. That had been a major concern, especially under the heat of the studio lights. He squirmed a bit as he watched his hands move with his words, a bit too much, he thought.

The self-critiques continued, and the group became engrossed in the show. When—forty-three minutes later—the screen faded to black, there was silence. From the corner of his eye, Dwayne watched his mother wipe a tear from her cheek. Then Sean stood, turned to Dwayne, and began to clap. In the darkness of the room, the others followed and, similar to what had happened in the studio, Dwayne received a standing ovation.

The lights came on and Dwayne stood.

"I am so proud of you," Bernice said as she put her arms around his neck, her eyes still tearing. He was surprised at the emotion, his own as well, but as he watched, he saw what the others saw: a moving drama played out before their eyes.

Beverlyn stood again in the spot where she'd started. "The show made its point. We want to take people to a better place—a Higher Ground. For your information, we've taped another show, but this one will air tomorrow. Please keep us in your prayers." Beverlyn paused and dabbed her eyes with her fingertips. "Many of you have invested time and money in the Jubilee Network because you believe in what we're doing, and from the bottom of my heart, I'd like to thank you. Without you, we couldn't have done it. Now," she continued, directing the crowd to where Kim was standing, "let's go into the living room."

Dwayne stood, and as the others filed out, he stared at Beverlyn. When they were alone, he pulled her into his arms, hugging her and seeing her with brand-new eyes.

# Chapter Nineteen

Dwayne looked up when he heard someone knocking at his door. He glanced at his watch, surprised. Monique usually announced his clients, and today Jade was early. He frowned, wondering why Monique didn't keep Jade in the waiting room for the next ten minutes. Before he could say, "Come in," Beverlyn entered. She held the door open wide and looked stunning in a perfectly fitted ivory shirt jacket and flared pants set that perfectly complemented her size 6, five-eight frame.

Dwayne's frown deepened. Beverlyn had never been to his office, and since he was supposed to see her in three hours at their production meeting, he assumed something was wrong. But the broad smile on her face as she walked toward him and laid a computer printout on the desk told another story.

Dwayne stared at the paper filled with numbers, then shrugged his shoulders. "What's this?"

Beverlyn sat on the edge of the desk and twisted around to face him. "Dwayne, these are the overnight ratings. It's unbelievable. These are the kind of numbers that a fourth or fifth network like Fox or UPN would love to see. We got over a three share."

Beverlyn leaned back and laughed. "You weren't kidding when

you said you knew nothing about television. Dr. Grandison, you are a hit!"

"But it's just the first show . . ."

"And that's what makes it so great. It will get better from here. Yesterday we only had a little advertising. But with word of mouth . . . You might not grasp it yet, Dwayne, but this is huge. I'm so happy." She wrapped her arms around his neck. "You're a success, Dwayne."

"Excuse me!"

Dwayne pulled away from Beverlyn and saw Monique and Jade standing in the open doorway, both with the same question in their eyes: *What is going on?*

"Beverlyn was just giving me some news."

"Oh, that's what it's called." Jade snickered.

"Dwayne, call me as soon as you're free here." Beverlyn laughed throatily, swooping past Monique and Jade, whose eyes followed her until she was out of sight. Then, as if they were performing in a synchronized dance, they turned back to Dwayne, with their arms folded.

"Doc, you've been holding out on me." Jade strolled into the office, taking a seat. "How can I get some of what you've been giving that client?"

Dwayne almost laughed. The eighteen-year-old rap star didn't even recognize Beverlyn Boudreaux.

"Jade, let's get started."

The young girl smoothed her skintight leopard leggings. "No problem, but for my sessions, I want the door closed."

Dwayne chuckled, but as he settled into the session with Jade, he couldn't dismiss Beverlyn's words.

"You're a success, Dwayne."

# *Chapter Twenty*

*B*y the end of the first month, not only was the Jubilee Network increasing in popularity, but its flagship program, *Higher Ground*, after just four shows, had ratings that rivaled those network programs in the same 8:00 P.M. time slot. Armed with the latest viewer survey and demographic data, Beverlyn announced that it was time to capitalize.

"Our viewers can't get enough of Dr. Grandison." Beverlyn leaned over Dwayne's desk. After the first show, Dwayne had agreed to use the office at the Beverlyn Boudreaux headquarters. It hadn't taken him long to realize that the office was a necessity with the number of meetings and all the research that had to be done.

"So many people are calling in that we've had to put in additional lines, and I can think of at least two ways to make even more money from this. One way is books. The sound way is perhaps more important: We can make your message more widespread through audio- and videotapes. We should start with tapes because we can rush to market with those. We just need to come up with subjects.

"Themes you've found to be common issues," she continued. "We need tapes people will rush to buy. For that, I'll put you together with Kim. She's great at that. Besides, she'd be great at beefing up your publicity. This could mean big dollars, and by the time we're finished, Dwayne, your face will be plastered from billboards in L.A. to subway stations in New York."

"Yeah, right." He chuckled.

"Laugh now, but you'll see."

He remembered when Yvette had brought grandiose plans to him. He would laugh, but she would just look at him saying the exact words that Beverlyn had just uttered. It continued to be uncanny how similar the two were, not only in words but also in the abundant energy they directed toward what each saw as his ultimate success. And she was almost irresistible standing before him in a honey-colored sleeveless georgette silk blouse with contrast flounce collar and a floor-length slim skirt.

One look said to any red-blooded man that there was more to this Bible-totin' woman than the business and ministry that had become her lifeblood. Since her days at the orphanage, her life had been about survival and getting ahead. So much so that she didn't know how to shut down. It was a trait he didn't find particularly attractive in women, though with Beverlyn, he'd understood its core and found himself drawn by the vulnerability that so often had arisen from it.

Still, he found refuge from the grind of producing a daily TV show in other projects: his practice, his weekly tennis matches with Sean, and working with Nina. Even though the sexual tension of the "near kiss" hung between them, Dwayne looked forward to their meetings. When he and Nina met, it wasn't about bigger, better, and faster, but about family, God, and helping others. When he had agreed to meet Nina today, he hadn't known that he would have to endure four client meetings and a three-hour audiotape session before he could do so. Now, as he eased his car around the corner onto King Boulevard, his shoulders slumped with the weight of the day. But he forgot his fatigue when he pulled in front of the church to find Nina standing on the steps. As he turned off the ignition, she ran toward his car.

"Dwayne, we have to change our plans."

He hoped Nina missed the relieved sigh that escaped his lips.

"The offices were painted last night," she continued. "But the fumes are still bad. Would you mind if we worked at my house?"

There was no need for an interpretation of Dwayne's hesitation. The reason had been more than obvious.

"We can go somewhere else if you prefer."

"No, your apartment is fine. But what about Omari?"

"He's hanging out with his favorite aunt tonight. I thought we might be working late." Then, giving Dwayne another look, Nina said, "You're tired. Maybe we should postpone this."

It was what he'd been thinking. The past weeks had been exhaustive, but the exhilaration of accomplishment kept him going.

"I'm fine. I'll just follow you to your place." He waited until Nina jogged to her car, then followed the burgundy Camry across La Brea to La Cienega, heading toward West L.A.

Dwayne glanced at the dashboard clock and calculated the time in his head. If he stayed no more than two hours, he'd be home before ten. He'd still have time to relax, watch a little television, and get seven hours of sleep—just one hour less than what he recommended to his clients, but more sleep than he'd had in over a month. The traffic was post-rush-hour light, and within twenty minutes, Dwayne was following Nina up the red brick stairs to her second-level apartment. Once they were inside, Nina's face was flush with embarrassment.

"I ran out so fast, I didn't clean up." She lifted a red and white afghan from the floor.

Dwayne glanced around the living room. Except for the afghan, there was nothing out of place. "What are you talking about? It's fine."

She smiled. "At least, I should have turned off the radio." She moved toward the curio.

"No, it sounds nice. Leave it on."

She reduced the volume and motioned him toward the couch. "Some tea?"

"That's fine."

As Nina opened and closed kitchen cabinets, Dwayne settled onto the couch and looked around the room. Though the space was laid out like a typical two-bedroom apartment, there was nothing ordinary about what Nina had done with the nine hundred square feet.

The centerpiece of the large living room was a cream-colored 1940s high-style sofa flanked by cocoa-colored chairs with walnut arms. The walnut curio had probably been specially designed to fit the wall it perfectly stood against. A three-tiered walnut coffee table sat in the middle of the room. Cream silk curtains on the French doors that led to a small balcony matched the deep-piled carpet that Dwayne figured had to date from Nina's television-star days.

"Milk or lemon?" she asked as she returned from the kitchen with two brown teacups and a sugar bowl on a wicker-trimmed tray.

"Just sugar is fine, Nina."

She sat next to him on the couch. "Isn't that a great shot of Omari?"

"It's amazing how much he looks like you." Dwayne put down the framed picture of the precocious seven-year-old.

"Thanks." She leaned back, gingerly holding her cup.

"I have a question," he said, looking again at the picture. "You can tell me if I'm getting too personal, but where's his father?"

The question caught Nina off guard. Not that she hadn't expected him to ask. Frankly, she'd thought he would ask way before now. It didn't matter; she wouldn't have known what to say before, and still didn't know now.

"I don't know." She looked down. "He walked out on me when Omari was a year old. I haven't seen or heard from him since."

"Does Omari ask about him?"

"Oh, he used to . . . but not anymore. Did you ever want to have children?" she inquired.

The dark veil that suddenly covered his eyes made Nina regret her question. Before Dwayne could respond, she said, "You know, we should get started." She stood and, still holding her cup, walked to the small round table that separated the living room from the kitchen. "We can work over here."

Dwayne followed and they sat at the table, silently sipping tea and avoiding each other's eyes. It was a comfortable rhythm they'd developed over the past months. And for the next hour or so, it continued as they tossed ideas back and forth, whizzing through the unfolding program outlines, developing a schedule and topical ideas for the church workshop on relationships that would merge their two groups into one big conference session. Lastly, they established a budget to present to the board.

Dwayne looked at his watch. Ten-thirty. Not bad. Only thirty minutes past his self-imposed deadline.

"Well, I have an early morning and—" he began, rising to leave, but he stopped midsentence and began bobbing his head to the Marvin Gaye cut that had just begun on the "Old School" station Nina kept her radio dial set to. Dwayne was surprised by the playful mood that seemed to have come over him spontaneously. "Do you remember this jam?"

For the briefest instant Nina was taken aback. Then, smiling her recognition, she scooted over to her sound system and turned up the volume as the signature Motown bassline reverberated throughout the room.

"'Mercy, Mercy Me' was my song," she said, recalling the lyrics and snapping her fingers, "especially when I was going through all my drama. For the longest time I thought it was a church song Marvin was singing."

"You probably weren't even born when the song came out."

Nina rolled her eyes but continued swaying to the music. "I didn't have to be, because Marvin sang it again and again and again . . ."

Dwayne pushed his chair away from the table and joined Nina. As the tune continued, Nina and Dwayne swayed and dipped, each trying to outdo the other.

"Look at the old man." Nina giggled, raising her arms above her head.

"Who you calling old?" Dwayne replied, matching her moves.

They laughed and danced to the last note, then fell onto the couch, taking the next few minutes to catch their breath.

"That was one of my favorite songs. Yvette's too."

Nina didn't know if she was supposed to speak or smile. She chose the latter.

"The thing is, she just died so suddenly . . ."

"An accident?" Nina treaded softly, remembering what she'd heard at church.

"Killed instantly," he went on. "She had just called me at the office to say there was something she had to tell me. I didn't know it, but she was pregnant. That was her news."

Nina gasped and gently touched his arm. "Dwayne, I'm sorry."

He acknowledged her words and dropped his eyes.

"Dwayne, at least you know that the last moments of Yvette's life were happy ones. She was carrying your child."

He opened his mouth, then shut it suddenly without a word escaping. He couldn't tell Nina he had no idea what Yvette might have been thinking.

"Dwayne?"

He opened his eyes and was surprised to see Nina leaning close to him. She did care more than she'd let on, after all. His hand rose to her cheek and his heart melted as she closed her eyes and pressed her face into his palm. Slowly, yet determinedly, he moved in toward her until his lips met hers. It was a tender, delicate kiss, but it felt familiar and altogether right. It was Nina who pulled back first, only slightly, allowing just inches of air to hang between them. His hand still held her face and she could feel his breath on her lips.

"I'd better go," he whispered without moving.

He stared at her mouth and resisted returning his lips to the spot where he'd felt whole again. Long moments passed, and still they had not moved. Finally, Dwayne inched forward, but paused when Nina pulled back slightly and lowered her head. He could tell something was wrong. But what? He removed his hand, letting the tips of his fingers linger briefly on her skin. Dwayne stood, but her head was still bowed, her eyes turned away.

"I'll leave the notes with you." His voice was husky as he reached for his jacket and slipped into it. Still Nina did not raise her head. Slowly, he lifted her chin with his fingertips, forcing her to look into his eyes.

"Thank you, Nina."

The lump in her throat stopped her words.

"I'll speak to you tomorrow." He turned away and walked to the door.

Though she wasn't looking, Nina could feel Dwayne pause before he stepped into the hallway and closed the door behind him.

She stood and walked to the window, watching as he trotted to his car. She knew he felt her gaze; she was just thankful that he couldn't see the tears forming in her eyes. So far, she was surviving the cancer that had completely turned her life inside out, but she wasn't altogether sure what the future held. She'd survived by keeping her life as uncomplicated as possible, by keeping her emotions—and romantic entanglements—at a safe distance. She couldn't afford to slacken her resolve now. Besides, she had to be strong for Omari. Her plans did not include the complications that were part and parcel of developing a relationship—especially one that involved a man who'd already experienced a devastating loss.

Her doctor had encouraged her to move forward with her life— that all necessary precautions had been taken. That there was no imminent threat of her losing her life or a breast. "At least, not now," the doctor had said as he clasped her breast. The dark cloud of a possible mastectomy down the road brought a wave of anxiety. She breathed deeply, reciting, "By his stripes, I am healed."

And while she felt better, she was more resolved than ever that there could be nothing between her and Dwayne. At least, not now.

The concierge smiled as he opened the door for Dwayne. "I recognize that tune."

"What?" Dwayne stopped.

"Marvin Gaye, right?"

Dwayne hadn't even realized he was whistling. Once inside his apartment, he turned on the lights but left off the stereo. He didn't need any music tonight. His mind was completely occupied by Nina. That kiss had been long overdue, pushing its way from the background where they had both hoped it would stay. He stood in front of the bathroom mirror, and for the first time since Yvette's death, he could say his smile was genuine.

The memory of Nina's lips lingered when he climbed into bed. Their kiss had been gentle and sweet, but the intensity made him feel alive again. Nina had begun awakening passion in him a long time ago. First professionally and now personally. Dwayne lay silently, reflecting on the past, wondering how to step forward to the future. Should they talk about it? He shook his head. No, it should just progress naturally.

He glanced at the clock—approaching midnight. He would only get six hours of sleep now, but what he felt inside would ease any morning exhaustion. Dwayne rolled over onto his stomach and closed his eyes. He couldn't wait to see Nina tomorrow.

# Chapter Twenty-One

Cassandra, a high-powered entertainment law attorney, had sought Dwayne's counseling services because she was convinced that her husband, Carl, one of Hollywood's top black executives (and "all other guys I dated before marrying him") were insensitive, lazy, and thoroughly resistant to giving a loving and supportive Christian woman like herself the high-performance love she needed. She frequently used words like "trifling," "inconsistent," "selfish," and "undermotivated" to describe her man in particular—and all men in general.

According to Cassandra, Carl wasn't taking adequate care of one thing or wasn't following through on another. He didn't take her feelings into consideration and was completely oblivious to her efforts to beautify herself and their home. And, of course, Cassandra voiced the number one most common complaint of all Dwayne's female clients: "He just refuses to share his feelings with me."

Dwayne had heard it all before. Whether it was about money or parenting or the division of responsibilities or communication or sex or dating habits or even getting to church on time, Cassandra was only expressing the frustrations of countless girlfriends and wives (and countless more ex-girlfriends and ex-wives) everywhere: "Why won't my man do what he's supposed to do? I've tried everything."

After Cassandra had gotten adequate time to vent and complain, Dwayne, as always, informed her there was, in fact, something she could do that could ignite a fire under even a "semicomatose" (her word) man like hers.

"Whatever the behavior is that you deserve from him, lavish your applause and commendation on him when he does it, even the least little bit."

"You mean, that's it? That's the secret?"

"It won't happen overnight, but start making it a practice, and before long, you'll begin to see a difference."

Dwayne looked at his watch. It was eleven-thirty. He would have to leave now in order to be on time for his lunch with Nina.

Cassandra picked up the cue and they closed out the session, gathered up their things, and he walked her to the elevator, bidding Monique good-bye. Exactly twenty minutes later, he was shifting in his seat, feeling like a fourteen-year-old on his first date. He didn't know why he felt that way. This wasn't a date. He'd simply invited Nina for lunch when he'd called her that morning. She'd sounded strangely stiff, but he chalked it up to the same nervousness he'd been feeling. Perhaps this talk would be the perfect icebreaker.

He scanned the Beverly Hills Cheesecake Factory, but Nina was nowhere in sight. Maybe she'd gotten stuck in traffic. Or maybe she had changed her mind. As he thought about it now, what he'd interpreted as nervousness this morning could have been doubt.

"Hello, Dwayne."

He looked up, not having seen her come in. He stood and pulled out the chair next to him.

Nina looked at him with a slight smile as he leaned over to kiss her cheek. They sat, and Nina immediately picked up the menu.

"Busy morning?"

"A bit," she answered, her face hidden behind the enormous two-fold card.

Dwayne opened his mouth, then closed it when Nina didn't look up. He picked up his menu and pretended to scan the lunch items. It was odd, this disconcerting air that suspended between them. They'd become very comfortable together, but it was clear the relationship had changed. He was sure it was momentary. After this lunch, they'd get back to where they'd been—only on a different level.

"Do you know what you want?" Dwayne asked.

For the first time since she'd come in, Nina looked directly at him. "I'm not very hungry."

Aha. The flutters in his stomach had almost taken away his appetite as well. He looked down at her hands, which lay gently in front of her. But before he could reach across the table, she pulled back, hiding her hands on her lap.

"We don't have to stay here," he said, suddenly fidgeting in his chair. "We can go for a walk or anything else you'd like to do."

The ends of her lips slipped upward. His considerate nature was one of the first things she'd noticed—from the night of the party. She remembered how he'd treated her with care and consideration. Then it struck her like lightning—the memory of what she was here to do. "No, I have to eat something," she said, smoothing her hand over the sleeve of her suit as if she were distracted. "Maybe I'll have soup or a salad."

Neither noticed the waitress approach the table.

"I'll just have the asparagus-walnut soup," she said.

Dwayne said, "I'll have the same and the seafood Caesar salad. And tea for both of us." He looked at Nina for her approval.

She dropped her gaze as the waitress left with the orders.

"I wanted to talk to you," they said simultaneously.

Dwayne laughed; Nina only smiled.

"You first," Dwayne said.

Nina took a deep breath. "I never expected what happened last night," she said softly, her fingernail tracing the red lines in the table-cloth.

"Are you talking about our kiss?"

When Nina looked up, his eyes were sparkling, teasing her.

"You can't tell me you were totally surprised," Dwayne said.

His words made her think back to all the times they'd come close, probably more times than he even realized. She shook her head no.

"Exactly." He moved his chair closer to her. "You have to admit, there's been . . . tension between us. Is something wrong? Are you concerned about how it's going to affect our working together? I don't want what happened to get in the way . . ."

She should have been relieved, but it felt like he had tugged at her heart. His words told her that he didn't want a relationship either. It was only then that she realized she'd held hope that maybe they'd had a chance. She shook her head to rid her mind of those thoughts. "Well, this shouldn't affect our working together. We're two adults."

"Who got caught in the moment . . ."

"Exactly. We understand what happened."

"Like you said, it's been coming for a long time."

"And we should just look at it for what it's worth and move on."

Dwayne was prepared to respond, but then closed his mouth and frowned. He paused. "Well, for what it's worth, it meant a lot to me."

Nina's frown matched Dwayne's. Her heart felt like it was beating a hole through her chest.

Dwayne covered her hands with his. "I don't know where this is going," he whispered. "But you awakened something in me, Nina."

As he spoke, her face softened with desire. But as his words seeped in, Nina's resolve became all the more clear—she could not spring the cancer on Dwayne, nor was she one hundred percent sure of what Dwayne really wanted. He didn't seem too sure himself. She stiffened up and said sharply, "Dwayne, there is no way we can have a relationship."

"Nina, I could tell when we kissed that you felt . . ."

She held her hands over her mouth to hide the trembling of her lips. "I can't do this," she said, fleeing from the table before Dwayne could stand.

"Nina, wait," he called, finally rising. His chair fell backward as he stood abruptly, but it was too late. She was already gone.

Nina searched her purse for the parking ticket and took a deep breath, willing her hands to stop trembling. Then she remembered the ticket in her pants pocket. By the time she finally screeched from the lot, her heart was beating so fast she could hardly breathe.

As she moved slowly through the streets, she played the restaurant scene over in her mind. Dwayne was probably going out of his mind. How could she get things back to where they had been? She could have kicked herself. What could she do now? As she continued driving, she searched her mind for answers. Then it hit her.

She ran a few errands, and by the time she turned onto the church parking lot a little more than an hour later, she had a plan.

The way she figured it, if their lunch date could have gone normally, then by now they would have agreed that any personal relationship would not be good for business. She knew Dwayne would have agreed. The ministry was too important—mixing church matters with personal affairs never worked. People would be in their business; it would be complicated . . . She'd had a complete list to convince him. But her intentions had gone astray. Unexpected emotions had arisen inside. Her new plan was this: She would call him and say what she had to say. The phone would keep distance between them and would prevent unexpected emotions from arising.

Across town, Dwayne sat on the bed, his legs stretched forward. The latest issue of a trade magazine lay on his lap, but nothing could hold his attention. It had been that way since he'd left the restaurant and returned to the recording studio. After several unfocused attempts, the technician agreed to reschedule. Dwayne decided to go home, and for the first time in months, he entered the apartment while the sun was still shining.

For the rest of the afternoon, he'd fidgeted about—scanning a magazine, straightening his clothes, turning on the TV—but nothing could take his mind off Nina. Several times he picked up the phone, then returned the receiver to its place. But as the hours passed, he was still confounded.

The ringing phone startled him.

"Dwayne, this is Nina."

Relief filled his sigh.

"I wanted to apologize for this afternoon," she said quickly. "There's a lot going on with me right now."

She stopped and he waited for her to continue, to give him more. But when she said nothing, he prompted, "Are you all right, Nina?"

"I'm fine now, Dwayne." She paused. "I'm just worried about you and what this does to us . . . I mean . . . our working relationship."

"We're fine, Nina. As long as I know you're okay, we can move forward as if this never happened."

"Thank you for understanding," she said, offering no more, though she wished with all her heart that she could explain and wanted Dwayne to press for more. But when neither said anything, she broke the silence with "I'll see you on Wednesday."

"Yes. Have a good evening, Nina." He hung up. For several minutes, he stayed still, wondering what had not been said.

Nina let the phone drop into the cradle and slumped back onto the bed. At least, Dwayne hadn't made it difficult, asking her to explain. What would she have said anyway? She looked at the papers on her lap. Maybe if he had asked just one question, she would have told him about the cancer. But that would be selfish, sentencing him to the same day-to-day uncertainty that tortured her.

Half the time, she didn't know how to feel, though the test results had been encouraging—the cancer had not come back. She had a lot to be thankful for, even though the only real good news would be the doctor telling her that the breast cancer was gone from her body forever.

# Chapter Twenty-Two

As L.W. sat in his office awaiting news from Kim, he grew more and more impatient. L.W. needed the information to plan his next move. For the last month, he had listened to his niece constantly sing the praises of Dwayne Grandison.

"Uncle Linson, can you believe the success of *Higher Ground*? And the income we're pulling in with his tape ministry? Getting Dwayne to join the team was the best decision we ever made," Beverlyn boasted. "Thank you for thinking of him, Uncle Linson."

L.W. had said nothing and grunted even now as he recounted the conversation and the developing relationship that drew Beverlyn and Dwayne closer. There were very few times his niece was alone when Dwayne was in the building and even fewer times when she was free to join him in the evenings.

"Mr. Lejohn."

L.W. looked up, then followed Kim with his eyes as she entered his office and took a seat.

"You're late."

"I'm sorry, but I'm sure this information is just what you were looking for."

Without another word, he snatched the envelope from Kim's outstretched hand. He opened the package and slowly read the first page of the report. His eyes moved from the paper to Kim, then back to the paper. He read the words again. Then he sifted through the pictures. Finally, he stuffed the materials back into the envelope.

"Kim, this is great," L.W. said, rubbing his hand over the envelope as if it were fine silk, then reopening it and once again reviewing the one-page report. The words were already committed to his memory, but he read them again, unable to believe the contents. *This is sweet,* he thought, smiling as he put the papers back into place. *This is oh so sweet.*

In the back of her mind, Kim knew that the information she'd given L.W. was dynamite. She also knew that dynamite could sometimes backfire. But there was no use in warning L.W. She would lose her job if he viewed her as a threat. She already knew too much.

"Look at these numbers," Beverlyn exclaimed as she marched into Dwayne's office.

"More Nielsen's?"

"No, these are from the sales department." She looked up. "Your video sales are phenomenal. They're moving almost as fast as the tapes."

Dwayne hit the power button on his laptop and closed the computer. No matter how often Beverlyn talked to him about numbers, he couldn't get into it. And Beverlyn's driving ambition hadn't prepared him for the way his life was changing.

Beverlyn, on the other hand, thrived on success, obsessed with the finer things in life. For some of her fans, it was difficult to reconcile her music and ministry with her lifestyle. Though her ministry stressed empowerment, its strength lay in her ability to get to the heart of people's fears, insecurities, and hurts. Her uniqueness was that she was honest enough to let them see hers. It was that current of hope that was interwoven into her songs and ministry—that faith in the human spirit's ability to transcend such stuff. But while that conviction was the key to her image, a close look at Beverlyn revealed a woman driven to finding the one missing piece that would bring fulfillment after many lonely years on the ministry fast track.

"You know what I think, Dr. Grandison?" Beverlyn said, interrupting his thoughts. "It's time for another book."

"Like I really have time for that."

"Come on, Dwayne. We have to strike while the iron is hot. I've already spoken to my agent and he agrees that we could get quite an advance."

"Beverlyn, the television show is enough for me."

"But not for the Jubilee Network. Dwayne, all of this is tied together. A book would help. We can introduce you to people who've never seen the show. And that would mean even higher ratings."

This wasn't what he had signed up for. He'd agreed to the tapes and the sale of the show's videotapes, but a book was out of the question. He crossed his arms over his chest and stared at Beverlyn. "No. There just isn't time."

"I know a way that we can make more time."

"What are you thinking? Asking God to add more hours to my day?"

She laughed. "Nothing that drastic. I was thinking about a driver."

He frowned.

"Like I have. You would not believe the amount of work I get done as I'm going from home to work or meeting to meeting."

"I don't want a driver."

"I'm not talking about what you *want,* Dwayne, I'm talking about what you *need.* Think about it. How many hours do you spend in your car?"

He shrugged. "I don't know. A couple, but still . . ."

"Do you know how much work you could get done? Just the book alone—you could dictate chapters and then have them transcribed. The book could be finished in less than a month."

His silence told her that he wasn't convinced.

"Dwayne, think about the show."

He nodded slightly. From the beginning, he'd made a commitment to do all that he could to make *Higher Ground* a success. And though he didn't know whether tapes or books added to the success, Beverlyn said they did. And she knew this business. The numbers proved it. So did the bonuses he'd received each month.

Beverlyn continued, "And another thing, Dwayne. You have to start seeing this the way God sees it. He's not pouring these blessings onto you for no reason. You're doing His work. He wants you to be a success. Having a driver is all part of it. It's who you are now. It's who God wants you to be."

"Beverlyn, God doesn't care about my having a driver." Dwayne blinked in confusion, realizing it was all the same to her.

"Not about a driver per se, but God does care about your success." She paused. "Trust me, Dwayne."

Finally, he said, "I'll think about it."

Her smile widened. "Good." She walked toward him. "That's all I can ask." Her steps brought her so close there was barely air between them.

"Trust me, Dwayne. Everything I do, I do for you," she said huskily.

He wondered if he closed his eyes and then opened them, would Yvette be standing in Beverlyn's place?

It didn't seem possible, but Beverlyn moved even closer. "You believe me, don't you?" she asked softly. Only the ticking of the clock could be heard as they waited to see where the next moments took them.

Dwayne coughed and turned away. "Have you eaten yet? Maybe we should go out . . ."

Beverlyn backed up. "That would be nice." She stared at him for a moment before she walked to the door. "Give me five minutes."

He nodded and watched her leave. It wasn't until she closed the door behind her that Dwayne finally breathed.

Dwayne glanced at Beverlyn without turning his head. She was silent but smiling, intently watching the shops they passed on Wilshire Boulevard.

He returned his eyes to the road and smiled. Beverlyn had been this way through most of their dinner. Though she chatted some, she'd shown a side he'd never seen. She had remained uncharacteristically pensive throughout dinner, never mentioning her crusades, gospel music, Beverlyn Boudreaux Ministries; and even talk of

*Higher Ground* never crossed her lips. Now, as he stopped in front of her house and turned off the ignition, she remained silent.

"I had a nice time tonight, Dwayne."

"I'm glad, because for a while there I wondered if you were okay. You seemed . . . different."

She dropped her eyes coquettishly. "What do you mean?"

"You didn't mention a word about the show or the videotapes or the book. You didn't even badger me about a driver."

"Is that what I do?" Her smile vanished with the thought. "I just want what's best for you."

He stared at her for a long moment. "I know."

Then without saying a word, he walked around to the passenger side, opened her door, and helped her from the car. She opened the gate and they strolled up the winding driveway, with only the sound of their heels clicking against the concrete, echoing in the nighttime silence.

"Missing New Orleans?"

Beverlyn stopped as they neared her front door. "I haven't had time to think about it, but there are things I miss, like the food. But mostly, it's strange not being in the place you've called home."

She lowered herself onto the front steps of her two-million-dollar estate as Dwayne leaned against one of the giant pillars.

"You're not too cold out here, are you?" Dwayne asked. "I didn't mean to keep you out in this night air." (Nor did Dwayne want to go in and encounter L.W., who for all he knew may have been just on the other side of the door.)

"No, I'm fine. I'd like to sit here and talk for a while, if that's all right with you."

Almost mechanically, Dwayne sat next to her, their shoulders nearly touching.

"If we were in New Orleans, there'd be a swing on the porch and we'd be swinging."

"Did you have a swing on your porch when you were growing up?"

"You haven't been paying attention to the vignette that's been running on Jubilee."

"I've wanted to ask you about it, but—"

"You're too much of a gentleman?"

"That, and I didn't want to play doctor."

She looked at the ground, all traces of her smile now gone. "Well, that three-minute commercial says just about everything. My mother died before I was one. The really sad thing is I don't even remember her. I was raised—"

"In a foster home?"

"I wish," she said softly. "An orphanage with people who didn't care, so I ran wild. I always knew what I was doing was wrong. And even before I knew God, I made promises to Him that I would make up for those times. I was only seven when I made my first promise."

"Looks like you kept it," he said simply.

"I did and L.W. was a big part of that."

Dwayne lost his professional stance at the mention of L.W.

"L.W.?"

"My uncle has been the most important person in my life. He saved me physically and spiritually. He brought me to the Lord. When I was nine years old, he took me off the streets and cleaned me up. Then he opened up a church."

"L.W. was a pastor?" Dwayne asked, all decorum gone.

"Yeah, we struggled for a time. Then my uncle heard me sing and sacrificed everything so I could pursue a life in gospel music. I started singing locally. He got me a contract, and the rest . . . Well, let's just say, I would be nothing without my uncle."

Bells went off in Dwayne's head, but he said nothing.

"You have much to be proud of," he said gently and sincerely. "You're an example of what can be overcome. You give so much hope to others."

"That's what I want. For people to know that what God did for me He can do for them."

They said nothing for several moments. She looked at him, and in the soft light that illuminated the entrance, he could see her eyes glazed with tears. "Are you ever afraid of being alone, Dwayne?"

Odd question coming from Beverlyn—so driven and headstrong and yet, at times like these, so vulnerable.

He answered by taking her hand. She inched closer to him, leaving only a small degree of air between them. A second later, they both leaned forward, allowing their lips to touch. Then Dwayne put his arm around Beverlyn, pulling her closer.

"It's time for me to go inside. Do you want to come in?" she asked softly.

He stared into her eyes, then brought his lips to hers again, this time kissing her gently. He stood and pulled her to her feet.

"Good night, Ms. Boudreaux." Without another word, he turned away and began to walk to the front gate. After a few steps, he looked over his shoulder. Beverlyn was gone.

As he started his car, his thoughts were a blur of images of Nina and Beverlyn. He'd been sure about Nina, but maybe he'd been wrong. This moment felt very natural, and so had Beverlyn.

# Chapter Twenty-Three

Dwayne pulled into the parking lot and searched for Nina's car. There was no sign of the Camry. He parked and walked quickly into the church. He checked Nina's office. The top of her desk was cleared, void of the papers and folders that usually covered it when she worked. It looked as if she hadn't been in the office all day.

Well, he couldn't worry about Nina right now. The session began in an hour, and he had to direct all of his attention to the young men. He laid his briefcase on the conference table. Still, he was concerned. Was Nina still upset with what had happened? The door opened and he turned. Nina was standing there, her hand on the knob as if she hadn't decided whether to come in.

"Hi," she said simply.

"Hi, I was just—"

"Hi, Mr. Dwayne." Omari sprang from behind his mother.

Dwayne's smile was instant. "Hey, my man, what are you doing here?"

"I've been hanging out with Mom all day long."

Dwayne looked up at Nina. "You were out of school?"

"Uh-huh. A teacher conference."

"Omari, could you do me a big favor?" Nina leaned over her son.

"I have a package for Pastor Lafayette. Can you take this into his office? Besides, he told me to bring you by, so I know that he wants to see you."

"Okay, Mom."

Nina waited until Omari was across the sanctuary before she closed the door and turned to Dwayne. "I thought I would bring in the heavy artillery." She took a deep breath. "I figured you couldn't be too mad at me when you remembered I was his mother."

Dwayne laughed and Nina followed.

"I'm not mad, Nina. I just wanted to make sure you were okay."

"I'm fine."

"And I wanted to make sure that I didn't offend you in any way."

"Oh, no," she said, shaking her head. "That wasn't it at all." She sat down.

He sat in front of her desk and waited.

A moment or two passed before she spoke.

"For many reasons, this is not a good time for me to . . . get involved with anyone. But if it were a good time, you would have been the one."

"At least I know it wasn't my breath or anything like that."

She laughed. "Hardly."

"So we're friends?"

"You better believe it. As long as you don't go getting the big head or something."


As Dwayne pulled into the valet section of the Sunset Room, he wondered, once again, what he was doing here. And as he had done on the drive over, he remembered the call he'd received this morning. "Dr. Grandison, Ms. Boudreaux has changed the location of the production meeting. We're meeting at the Sunset Room in Hollywood. Do you need directions?"

"Are you sure?" he asked, doubting that his assistant, Tori, had the right information. She was new, another idea from Beverlyn to make his life easier. And though he had at first protested, Tori had become an asset, freeing him from all the administrative work associated with *Higher Ground*. However, Dwayne was sure Tori had made a mistake. He didn't know that the trendy celebrity hangout even opened before noon.

But even at 10:30 A.M., the restaurant was half-filled, although that was nothing compared to the madhouse this popular celebrity eatery would become in an hour or so, he thought. A hostess stood behind a gold and glass stand. She looked up as Dwayne approached.

"Hello," Dwayne said tentatively. "I'm Dr. Grandison. I'm supposed to be here for a meeting?" Doubt had turned his statement into a question.

She flipped her long blond hair over her shoulder. "Yes, Dr. Grandison. Follow me."

She led him through the maze of tables to a darkened patio area. At the end of the long hallway, the hostess opened a door, but when they stepped inside, she still had not turned on the lights.

"What is going on?" he asked, impatient in his tone. "Where are the lights?"

Suddenly, light beamed throughout the room.

"Surprise!!"

It took a moment for Dwayne's eyes to adjust. "What?"

Beverlyn rushed to his side. "The other night I realized that today would be the seventh airing of *Higher Ground*. And seven is a special number—God's number of completion. And, Dr. Grandison, you have completed a good work. In seven weeks, the ratings are where we'd hoped to be this time next year."

"Well, I couldn't have done that without all of you," Dwayne said, holding out his hands to the group.

"But you are the leader. Last night I realized that we needed to celebrate. So congratulations, Dr. Grandison."

As the *Higher Ground* production team applauded, Beverlyn smiled and squeezed his hand. At that moment, Dwayne realized it was no coincidence—what had happened between them two nights ago and this celebration.

"This is my way of saying thank you . . . for many things." Beverlyn leaned toward Dwayne and whispered, confirming his thoughts.

"Congratulations, son."

Dwayne turned at the sound of his mother's voice. "What are you doing here?" He hugged her.

"Beverlyn called last night and invited me."

"She called me too." Dwayne's smile widened at the sight of Monique.

"Well, I'm glad you're here," he said to both his mother and Monique.

"I hate to drag him away," Beverlyn interrupted, "but he needs to chat with the rest of the team."

"Of course," Bernice said.

"Go on," Monique added. "We see him all the time. Oops," she said, covering her mouth as if she'd made a mistake. "That was how it used to be," she added in jest.

"Now, be kind, Monique," Beverlyn chided playfully. "Dr. Grandison is busy changing the world."

Beverlyn hooked her arm through Dwayne's and led him away. As Dwayne shook hands, chatted, and thanked each person on the team, Beverlyn never left his side. Dwayne kept looking over his shoulder at his mother, but her eyes assured him that she was enjoying the impromptu gathering.

When the waiter asked all to take their seats, Beverlyn directed Dwayne to the center of the table, where she sat on one side and Bernice on the other. Dwayne glanced around the room, stopping when he saw L.W. holding a chair for Monique. But then, he thought, Monique could more than handle Linson Lejohn, who was flanked by Kim Steele.

"Dwayne, this is so nice." Bernice smoothed the oversize napkin on her lap, thinking that Lafayette had been right. She'd seen why he declined the invitation, leaving just her and Monique to be there in support of Dwayne. She didn't get a good vibe from L.W., and while Beverlyn was nice, there was something amiss . . . something she couldn't quite put her finger on.

Dwayne wasn't sure if his Mom was just being nice. Though loving and supportive, she wasn't easy to win over, and though she was Baldwin Hills bourgeois, she could spot a fake a mile away. Before he could respond, he felt Beverlyn reach for his hand under the table.

"Mrs. Grandison, what do you think of the show?" Maria, the show's producer, asked.

Dwayne turned toward Beverlyn.

"I hope you're not doing anything after this," she whispered, leaning close to him.

Dwayne shook his head. "Not really."

"Then I hope you can reserve the entire night for me."

"What do you have in mind?"

"I have something incredible planned for you." Her voice was sensuous. "I want to take you back to my office," she said slowly. "Close the door and then . . ." She paused and leaned away. "Interview the five men I've arranged for you to see as potential drivers."

Dwayne threw his head back and laughed. When others looked at him, he lifted his cupped hand to his mouth and pretended to cough.

As the waiters served the brunch of scrambled eggs with sautéed spinach, artichoke omelets, French toast, and fresh fruit topped with whipped cream, Dwayne turned back to Beverlyn. "Why, Dr. Grandison," Beverlyn teased, "you couldn't have thought I meant . . ."

"Don't you try it, Ms. Boudreaux. You aren't as innocent as you look," he interrupted. "I guess I'm just starting to see your point. And if you think a driver is a good idea, then I do too."

L.W. peered at his niece and the doctor over the rim of his water glass. Something had changed. He knew everyone in the room could feel the electricity between the two, and he wondered how far Dwayne and Beverlyn's personal relationship had progressed. Beverlyn hadn't mentioned anything to him, though L.W. was sure she wouldn't, knowing he would disapprove.

"Beverlyn, it's not that I don't think you should have a life, but you are Beverlyn Boudreaux. You have to be careful about relationships."

"Uncle Linson, I know who I am. A relationship is not a corporate merger. God has blessed me with so much. Now I pray that He will bless me with a family."

Her words made him cringe. He was all the family she needed. If anyone else came into the picture, he wasn't sure where he'd stand. Visions of Country Baptist in Mississippi haunted him like the monster nightmares he'd had as a child. There was no way he'd go back.

He would step aside for no one, at least no one as spoiled and privileged as Dwayne Grandison.

L.W. shook his head. A few weeks ago, this obvious display of affection between Dwayne and his niece would have made his blood curdle. But now he just leaned back in his chair and watched. Beverlyn whispered something into Dwayne's ear, and Dwayne laughed, just as he'd been doing all morning. Laugh now, Grandison, L.W. thought. These are your final days.

L.W. almost wanted to stand up and make the announcement now. He would bring Dwayne Grandison to his grubby knees in front of his mother. L.W. twisted in his seat as the thought tempted him. That would work—he'd destroy the entire family and maybe even bring down his brother's church. He couldn't stand how much Dwayne always talked about it.

On the other hand, Beverlyn would be hurt. And L.W. loved his niece too much to bring her that embarrassment, at least right now. No, the right time would reveal itself. He was sure he wouldn't have to wait long.

"Mr. Lejohn, would you pass the water pitcher, please?"

L.W. reached across the table and poured water into Monique's glass. As he settled the pitcher back, he said, "I want you to call me L.W." He leaned closer to her. "After all, you work for Mr. Grandison. That makes us almost family."

"Thank you, L.W. What a nice man you are," Monique said with a hint of sarcasm, trying to figure out just what his angle was. She just didn't get a good vibe from the old geezer. In fact, she didn't like him and wasn't all that sure of Beverlyn either.

"That's what they say. I'm just a charmer."

Catching Dwayne's eye, Monique signaled her distaste for L.W. Dwayne's gaze then locked in on L.W., and they held their stares. L.W. knew that Dwayne realized they were at war. Seconds passed as the sound of clanking silverware filled the room. And it was Dwayne who was first to drop his gaze.

# Chapter Twenty-Four

Beverlyn laid her head in Dwayne's lap. He looked down at her and smiled. She held the book she was reading above her head, while Dwayne read the proposal. Nina had given him two days to review the expansion of both the men's and women's ministries.

The light summer wind whistled through the magnolias and Chinese elms that provided privacy to Beverlyn's grounds. Only the sounds of an occasional passing car or the distant traffic from Wilshire Boulevard disturbed their backyard retreat.

They swung gently in the wide-seated swing Beverlyn had installed over the Memorial Day weekend, enjoying their first Saturday together without a scheduled event, and with L.W. out of town on a business trip. Beverlyn turned over, knelt on the seat, then kissed him softly. He looked up from his papers and smiled. "What was that for?"

"For making me happy."

Dwayne laid the papers on the patio table in front of the swing.

"When you say that, I know it means either you're very happy or you want me to do something."

Beverlyn sat back on the swing and laughed. "I could be insulted."

"Or you could tell me what's on your mind."

"You're going to have a break this summer?"

Dwayne folded his arms behind his head. "Yeah, and I'm looking forward to relaxing a bit and spending more time with my clients and at New Covenant. This has been some ride, but I'll go back to the life I had before—at least for a moment." He reached out for her.

She rested her head on his chest and they swung silently for a few minutes.

Finally, Beverlyn said, "You know, you can't go back. Nothing is the same."

While he didn't want to face it, Dwayne realized Beverlyn was right. Though *Higher Ground* was on hiatus, biweekly repeats of the ten original shows kept Dwayne's image in millions of households. And with the more than 100,000 videos sold, it was hard for Dwayne to walk the streets without being recognized.

"I know," he said, finally responding to her statement. "Still, I want to spend the summer with as much normalcy as I can before we rev up again in the fall. So what's on your mind?"

"I think you should do some speaking this summer. And before you say no, remember the show."

There it was. Use the show to get him to add still more to his already full plate.

"Anytime you speak it's free advertising for you and *Higher Ground*. Though we've done advertising, we don't have the budget for more. We have to do whatever we can to build and maintain viewership."

"I take it you have something specific in mind."

She paused, taking a deep breath. "I want you to be a featured speaker at my New York Crusade."

"Oh, no, Beverlyn."

"Speaking at the New York Crusade will put you on the front lines."

"That's what I don't want."

"There will be over eighty thousand people there, mostly women . . ."

"Not a selling point, Beverlyn."

"This will be added exposure to our target market. You'll be a live commercial."

He was still shaking his head, but not as strongly. He stood and walked to the edge of the redwood deck, scanning the vast grounds. A minute later, Beverlyn came up behind him and wrapped her arms around his waist.

"Sean is going to be singing, and we might be able to spend an extra day or two and hang out—just the three of us."

He remained silent.

"Just think about it?"

He still didn't turn around, keeping his eyes on the petunias and sunflowers planted around the yard's perimeter. Their colors were brilliant, almost blinding. "There's not much time to decide. The crusade is in a month."

"I don't want to pressure you . . ."

"Yeah, right."

His sarcasm caught her off guard. She stepped in front of him with her arms folded. "Dwayne, I was talking about *Higher Ground*, but what about you? You haven't come close to reaching your potential, and speaking will put you on the right road. There is so much I see that you can't."

Dwayne turned away and returned to the swing. He dropped his face in his hands.

Beverlyn frowned. "What's wrong?"

"Nothing," he said, looking up and half expecting to see Yvette. "Beverlyn, I need you to do something for me."

"Okay."

"Stop trying to direct my career. I know what I want and was doing fine before you came into my life."

"Dwayne, I'm not trying to—"

"Yes, you are," he interrupted her, straining to keep his voice even.

Beverlyn held up her hands. "Is there something wrong with making suggestions?"

"No, the problem comes when you try to manipulate me by using *Higher Ground*." He was yelling now. "I know the importance of the show. I'm committed to its success. End of discussion."

"There are just some things that you may not know."

"Then bring them up in a production meeting," he shouted.

Beverlyn drew back from his anger. "I'm sorry."

He nodded, then began packing papers into his weekend back-pack.

"I thought we'd spend the day together," she said. "This is the first Saturday I've been home."

He turned away, gripping the handles of his backpack tightly, and walked to the back door without looking back.

"That's game, man. What's on your mind today?"

"Beverlyn."

"What about her?"

"Sometimes I just feel that she's trying to control my life."

"So what's new?"

Dwayne put down the racket and motioned for a glass of the lemonade Sean Wiley's maid was approaching the two of them with.

"So what are you going to do?"

"Got any ideas?" He paused for a moment and then got serious. "Enough about me, man. How are you?"

"Up and down. Had a minor complication, but I think it's the stress of all the traveling, so I may be cutting back. I go to the doctor this week, so we'll see. And before you pick up the latest copy of one of the tabloids, I just want to say that I've been spending some time with a lady that I'm coming to like a lot."

"And does this lady have a name?"

"Ashley Allen."

"Do I know her?"

"No, she's a non-pro, but when and if the time is right, I want you to meet her."

"I'd love to," he said, pausing. "Have you told her . . ."

"Not yet."

"I'm sure it will all work out, man."

"Now, let me ask *you* something." Sean looked directly at Dwayne. "Do you think it's time for you to give up Man-to-Man?"

"Are you kidding? I love working with the men."

"I'm not talking about walking away totally. But you're sure juggling a lot. You've trained Deacon Miller and the others. They're doing great. It might be time for you to step down and concentrate on what's happening with the network."

"I don't want to do that."

"Perhaps I used the wrong word. Not step *down*, but step *back*."

Though he didn't want to admit it, he agreed. His schedule had become too full, and Man-to-Man was the most logical place to cut time.

"It's an option, Dwayne," Sean offered. "Still see Nina?"

The words elicited a sarcastic chuckle from Dwayne.

"Oh, is that why you don't want to give up Man-to-Man?"

"Man, I don't know. But you were right. Something's going on with her. I just wish I knew what it was. At any rate, she's not ready, she says, for a relationship with anyone."

"And Beverlyn . . ."

"Oh, she's more than ready. And there's something about her . . . We're getting close, but sometimes I just feel like I'm getting swallowed up when I'm with her."

"Well, you take it easy. Just remember to think everything through. There's a lot on the line."

"Yeah," Dwayne said, now standing. "And you keep me informed about everything, including Ashley."

Returning to his high-rise penthouse, Dwayne picked up the cordless in the foyer and then put it back down. He had been thinking about Beverlyn all day. Dwayne walked to his bedroom, took off his clothes, and settled into bed with his Bible. As he read, he felt his eyes being drawn from the pages. He looked up and Yvette's eyes stared back at him from her photo. He gazed at the picture, letting himself feel the moments of her last breath, and wondered what death snatched from them.

Ten minutes passed before he picked up the phone and dialed Beverlyn's number.

"Beverlyn, I've decided to do the New York Crusade."

"Yeah!" she screamed so loud he had to pull the receiver from his ear.

"What's the topic?"

"Oh, no. This is your career. You decide."

"Very funny," he said.

"Tell you what. Tomorrow I'll give you all the information on the workshop topics, and if you need some help . . ." She paused and added softly, "You can let me know."

"Good night, Beverlyn. I'll call you in the morning."

# Chapter Twenty-Five

*A*s the flight attendants secured the jetliner's door, Dwayne took his cell phone from his suit jacket and dialed Sean's cell number once again. Still just voice mail. His concern for Sean had now grown serious. Dwayne looked out the window as the L-1011 backed away from the gate. What could have happened? He'd called his friend countless times over the last few days, and though he'd left messages, he hadn't received a return call. That was not Sean's way, but until this moment, Dwayne had been too busy to be concerned.

Dwayne pushed the first-class leather seat into the fully reclined position, declining the flight attendant's offer for dinner or a snack. Even the opportunity to watch a movie didn't interest him now. His mind was filled with images of Sean. By the time the plane landed five hours later, Dwayne's concern bordered on panic.

He was met at baggage claim by a uniformed driver holding a placard that read, "Dr. Grandison." Within fifteen minutes, Dwayne and his bags were secure in the limousine and headed into the city. As they crept through the afternoon traffic on the Long Island Expressway, Dwayne checked his messages. Sean had not called.

The car stopped in front of the Trump International Hotel and Tower. As Dwayne checked in at the front desk and signed the registration paperwork, he wondered how many five-hundred-dollar-a-night suites Beverly Boudreaux Ministries was paying for.

"Will you be needing one key or two, Dr. Grandison?"

Dwayne thought about Beverlyn. "One key will be fine."

Within minutes, Dwayne opened the door to his one-bedroom suite and was instantly struck by the smell of fresh-cut flowers. As he stepped inside, the grand vintage buildings that lined Central Park West came into view. The bellman disappeared into the other room when Dwayne glanced out of the nine-foot-high windows. Central Park stretched out before him.

"Will that be all, sir?"

Dwayne nodded, handing the man a twenty-dollar bill.

"Thank you, sir." The bellman disappeared into the hallway. Dwayne threw his jacket on the plush white sofa, then reached for the phone. But Beverlyn was not in her room.

He loosened his tie, then made his way into the bedroom. The Jacuzzi tub was more than inviting, but he resisted, knowing his schedule was too tight for that. He opted instead for a quick nap, pulling back the heavy bedspread and laying his head against the softness of the feather-down pillows. His eyes weren't closed for a minute before the phone rang.

"Darling!"

"Beverlyn."

"Just get in?"

"Yeah."

"Boy, I'm glad you're here. You wouldn't believe my day."

"Things not going well?"

"Well, everything is fine now, because of course, L.W. took care of it—but I don't want to talk about that. Are you up for an early dinner? We can go downstairs to Jean Georges. It's fabulous."

"That's fine. Listen, Beverlyn." Dwayne's tone grew serious. "Sean missed the plane. Have you heard from him?"

"I thought you knew." She paused, continuing when he didn't speak up. "He canceled his appearance at the crusade."

Dwayne sat up straight in the bed, now worried. "Is he all right?"

"I didn't speak to him directly, but his assistant, J.T., said something important had come up."

"What could be that important?"

"Any number of things, Dwayne. Why are you so worried? J.T. said that all was well and that Sean would make it up to me."

Again, there was nothing from Dwayne.

"Dwayne, things happen. I'm sure it was nothing. He's canceled before."

"I don't know . . ."

"Well, there's nothing we can do about it here and now."

"You're right about that."

"Let's forget about the crusade and Sean and everything else tonight. Let's just have a good time."

"Okay. He hesitated before adding, "I'll meet you in the lobby in one hour."

Dwayne had barely hung up when he dialed J.T.'s number.

"J.T., this is Dwayne Grandison. I need to get in touch with Sean."

"Oh, Dr. Grandison, Sean asked me to call you. His doctor ordered him on a much-needed hiatus to get some rest."

Though he could read no reason for alarm in J.T.'s voice, Dwayne didn't believe a word. He paced the floor. "J.T., give it to me straight. Is Sean all right?"

"He's just fine and doesn't want you to worry."

Dwayne paused. Sean hadn't talked to many people about his life. He didn't know what J.T. knew. "The fewer the number of people who know," Sean had once told him, "the better chance I have of keeping my personal life personal."

"Sean will be back on Wednesday," J.T. continued. "He'll call you then."

Dwayne hung up the telephone. The best thing for him was to believe J.T. If he did that, he wouldn't have to believe that his friend's illness had taken over and begun to ravish his body as he imagined over and over in the past hours. Sean probably just needed some rest as J.T. said.

Anyway, if Sean was sick, Dwayne was sure he, Dwayne, would be the first person Sean would call. Sean had long ago lost touch with his own family except for an occasional relative who popped up from some obscure southern town requesting financial aid, in the name of the Wiley family.

Dwayne sat down on the bed. Now that he thought more about it, his worries were probably without cause. He looked at his watch and dashed into the bathroom for a quick shower. He'd relax and unwind later tonight.

Seconds after the waiter who'd served them removed the last of the fillet of salmon and braised lamb they shared, another waiter followed, and with three swift swoops of his table scoop, removed all signs of crumbs from the white linen tablecloth.

"Are you as stuffed as I am?" Beverlyn asked.

Dwayne nodded and reached for her hand. "Let's take a walk."

After signing the check, Dwayne took Beverlyn's hand and led her through the restaurant still filled with people, many of whom had come in from the Wynton Marsalis concert at Lincoln Center.

"Excuse me, Ms. Boudreaux." The young Puerto Rican man who had served them came up behind them. "Would you mind if I had your autograph?"

Beverlyn smiled, took the paper, and signed her name.

"Thank you," he said. He stared for a long moment at Dwayne, then shook his hand before he turned and walked away.

Dwayne followed her as they walked outside, taking her hand as they ran across Central Park West. Silently, they strolled at a leisurely pace along the park's western perimeter. The sweltering heat of the hot July day had cooled and was now replaced by a comfortable seventy-nine degrees that was enhanced by a light breeze.

Central Park West was packed with the usual evening rush of cabs as they dashed across driving lanes and through red lights in their quest to take passengers to downtown destinations. The air filled with sounds of horns blaring, people yelling, and whistles from doormen of surrounding hotels and apartment buildings vying for the next vacant cab.

"I love New York," Beverlyn said, putting her arm around Dwayne's waist. "When I was little, I dreamed of living here."

Dwayne looked down at her. "Really?"

Beverlyn paused and pulled Dwayne to the waist-high brick wall. She stuffed her hands deep inside the pockets of her wide-legged denim slacks.

"Yeah, right after I snatched my first purse." She laughed at the irony of her words. "There was this girl, Sara, at the orphanage. She told me that snatching purses was the easiest way to get money. She was older than me, so I looked up to her.

"She had me practice on some other girls and then I went with her out on the streets to try." She paused, but his eyes told her to continue. "It's a wonder we never got caught, but all the kids knew those back alleys and passageways almost better than the police. And the smaller you were, the better.

"Anyway, I was supposed to snatch the purse, run to the nearest alley, take out the money, then dump the purse. But I found three brochures about New York. I stuffed them into my pockets, and that night, I waited until Sara was asleep and then I read the pamphlets. I couldn't understand all the words but I knew I wanted to come here. That was the first night I made a deal with God."

"What was the deal?"

"I told Him that if He would just send someone to rescue me and take me to New York, I would get a real job."

"And how old were you?" Dwayne inquired. "Seven, eight?"

"Yeah, the joke was I thought what I was doing was work. I wanted a better job."

Together, they shared a good laugh. This was when he liked her most, though he wasn't sure if the attraction was based on the doctor in him or the vulnerability in her.

"At least half of my dreams came true. Did you know that L.W. came to New Orleans just to look for me?"

"I didn't know that." Dwayne hoped his tone didn't reveal his doubt.

"He said he searched for months and was determined to find me."

As Dwayne pulled Beverlyn into his arms, he wondered what the real story was. The man whom Beverlyn described was hardly the same man who stared him down in meetings, barely speaking to him if they were to pass each other in the halls and refusing to refer to him as "Dr. Grandison," only condescendingly as "young man" or "Mr. Grandison."

"Oh," Beverlyn said, jarring his thoughts, "there's Tavern on the Green."

"Don't tell me you're hungry. We've barely walked—"

"Oh, come on. They have the best cheesecake. You just have to taste it." Beverlyn ran ahead of him, and when he caught up with her, they stepped inside. Even though it was after ten, nearly every table in the main dining room was occupied.

"I don't think we're going to get in here tonight," Dwayne whispered.

"Watch this." They stepped to the hostess stand. "We'd like a table for two. Just for dessert."

"Do you have reservations?" the woman asked without looking up.

"No."

When the hostess looked up, her recognition was instant.

"Dr. Grandison." She smiled. "Welcome to Tavern on the Green."

Both Beverlyn and Dwayne raised their eyebrows in surprise.

"Follow me."

They were seated at a windowed corner table facing Central Park West. It didn't take long for a waitress to take their orders for the mixed-berry cheesecake and crème brûlée. Over dessert, they chatted about the crusade and the fall's season plans for *Higher Ground*. Their initial strategy was to produce another ten shows. But with the explosive ratings, they decided to double new show production and change the time. The show would now air twice, both critical time slots: once at 9:00 A.M. and then again at 8:00 P.M.

Dwayne looked at his watch. It was almost midnight.

"I need to get you back," Beverlyn said. "You have to be up early. I'm so excited about Saturday. The women are really going to love you."

They walked silently, arms hooked, back down Central Park West. Even though the hour was late, people strolled and traffic flowed almost as if it were the middle of the day.

"Dwayne, what are your dreams, what is it that you want?" she asked, laying her head on his shoulder as they walked slowly down the boulevard.

He thought for a moment. "My dreams have changed so much. They're different now from when I first started out with . . ." He stopped himself from saying his wife's name.

"So tell me, what did you dream in the beginning?"

It didn't take him a moment to answer. "I wanted to become a pastor like my father."

"I didn't know that. Why didn't you?"

"It's a long story, but I'm not unhappy with what I've done."

"You shouldn't be. You're reaching people who may never enter the church."

Once again, Yvette's words.

"What about you?" he asked.

She was silent for a moment. "There is not much more for me to dream about. I have more than I could ever imagine. What God has done for me gives new meaning to the Scripture's 'exceedingly, abundantly' . . ." She let her voice trail off.

"Yeah, me too. Everything has changed so drastically in the last few months. It's hard to get used to, because this kind of success has never been my focus."

"You more than deserve it, you know . . ."

"I don't know. My heart has always been with helping others. That's how my father lived his life and that's how I wanted to be."

"Then it's a good thing you have me, because while you're thinking of everyone else, I can be thinking about you."

"So"—Dwayne stopped and took Beverlyn's hand—"why do you do all of this? The concerts, crusades, the Jubilee Network."

"It's the way I survive. I work to give back to the children and . . . because of where I grew up. I never want to go back there," she said, shaking her head forcefully.

He took her hand, and when she looked up, he saw the tears in her eyes. "Beverlyn, you don't have to worry."

She laid her head on his shoulder as they paused in the hotel lobby. "Sometimes I feel like this could be taken away."

"Why?"

"Maybe it's because I wonder if I deserve this." She fingered the gold and diamond Rolex on her wrist.

"Beverlyn?"

Their heads snapped up at the voice.

"L.W.," was all Beverlyn said as she stood and straightened her sweater.

"I've been calling your room for hours," he said, as if he'd forgotten Beverlyn wasn't a teenager. "Tomorrow's keynote speaker backed out. When I couldn't reach you, I got worried. Remember, we have a crusade to run . . ." He looked at Dwayne with disgust.

"If you'll excuse us, young man." L.W. moved in between them.

Dwayne held his temper, clutching his hands at his side.

"Hey, wait a minute, L.W.," Beverlyn said. "You're being rude to Dwayne."

With a lethal glare, L.W. stomped away, leaving the two agape, standing in the middle of the opulent lobby.

"Dwayne, I'm sorry," Beverlyn said when L.W. disappeared into one of the elevators.

"You don't have to apologize." Dwayne unclenched his fists. "You need to speak to your uncle. I'm too old for this."

"I will," Beverlyn said, trying to calm Dwayne. "He's probably just worried. There's so much at stake doing the crusade here in New York. Everybody's freaking out." She paused. "Walk me to my room?"

They rode to the seventh floor in silence, and when Dwayne walked Beverlyn to her door, he kissed her lightly.

"Dwayne, please don't let what happened downstairs ruin the great time we had."

He looked into the brown of her eyes. She was right. Five minutes couldn't override five hours. At that moment, as he looked deeply into her eyes, he felt a pang—a stirring he hadn't felt in some time, with the exception, that is, of Nina.

"Are you still planning to stay in New York for a few days?"

He was thinking yes, that would be very nice. She brought her lips to his and they kissed deeply.

"Let's talk about it tomorrow."

"I'm looking forward to it," she said, then stepped into her room, gently closing the door behind her.


The New York Crusade marked the first time Dwayne had accompanied Beverlyn to such an event. One couldn't help but be overwhelmed as upwards of 50,000 people crowded into the Empire Stadium. It was Beverlyn's first appearance in the Big Apple in over three years, and there was enough demand that promoters could have sold 100,000 tickets if space had permitted.

It was all handled very much like a stage production, complete with sound and visual effects. The backstage flurry of activities included the greeting of local celebrities and church leaders, many of whom requested and received VIP treatment—TV media coverage and a battalion of security.

He was surprised at how glamorous it all was, right down to the stylish fashions worn by the luminaries as well as the attendees. Beverlyn had been dressed by New York–based fashion designer b. Michael. His high-couture line of clothing and hats was carried in big-name retail outlets like Saks and Nordstrom. Beverlyn—like all of the other renowned first ladies and African American celebrities he dressed—attended his annual fall and spring showings during Fashion Week in New York City.

With the sudden withdrawal of Bishop Lawrence Biggham, one of the nation's foremost Pentecostal preachers, both L.W. and Beverlyn had been scurrying earlier to find a replacement. A lot was riding on the crusade, and without big names, crowds lost interest no matter how anointed the evening. But as fate would have it, Bishop Franklyn Grace—ranked second by most on the list of the nation's top African American evangelists—was in New York and could alter his schedule to accommodate them.

Dwayne was struck almost as much by the pecking order at such events as by the protocol. He thought it particularly strange that the speakers most often arrived at the conference just in time to do their bit and never came to the stage until just before they spoke and then directly after were taken back to their dressing rooms to change, everything handled like a production, with them as the stars. Even he had felt like one as Kim had wrangled an interview for him backstage with *Gospel Today*, whose publisher, Teresa Hairston, had been on hand to cover the event.

Still, the high point for Dwayne was witnessing firsthand the effect Beverlyn had on audiences. Watching her onstage was like watching a ball in motion, the feeling of being handed over to another force, one that may exalt you or cast you to the ground. Not surprisingly, it was hard to tell where the gospel artist stopped and the evangelist began—the synchronicity, no doubt, by design.

As he waited in the wings, he wondered how—and if—he could hold his own on that stage and then, before he knew it, came the introduction that meant he was about to find out firsthand.

The lights were almost blinding and Dwayne found himself looking into a maze, genuinely surprised at how easily the words flowed, whizzing through the twenty-minute discourse. Before he knew it, he was closing:

"As we move forward, we would do well to remember that everything begins with the individual choices we make. What most people don't realize is that faith requires something. It requires that you believe. And when you believe, you act with renewed optimism, and it is that optimism reflected in your attitude that will all too often determine your outcome. In closing, I want to remind you that the key to every man is his thought. What you can and cannot do starts and stops with you."

# Chapter Twenty-Six

*D*wayne had rushed into the office just five minutes before Walter and Latasha Winston arrived. Walter was a superstar NBA player who'd wed Latasha after she'd become pregnant with his child in their senior year of college. They were friendly, attractive, and intelligent people with two children, and very active in their church. Everybody loved them. They, on the other hand, seemed to hate each other.

Walter and Latasha had a troublesome habit of waiting until their weekly sessions—or church Bible studies—to launch a verbal attack on each other. Walter used prayer times to ask God to strengthen him so that he could deal with his "lazy and unsubmissive wife." Latasha constantly attempted to twist their session around to make it support the many bitter complaints she had about Walter. If Dwayne didn't keep them in check, he feared their sessions could become violent.

Actually, both Walter and Latasha had valid complaints about each other that deserved to be dealt with—but the couple had not learned one of the cardinal rules of loving relationships. Praise each other in public, protest to each other in private. One of the quickest ways to completely kill a relationship is to embarrass, berate, criticize, or otherwise "dis" your mate in public. To have a beef with each other was fine, he'd told them, but to serve it up in the presence of others was not.

It was only after the exhaustive hour-long session that Dwayne stood and properly greeted Monique, who was seated at her computer. "Good morning."

"So you do still work here, after all," she teased. "It's good to have you back."

"It's good to be back. How are things?" he asked as he opened his briefcase, loosened his tie, and began to review the message slips that cluttered his desk.

"Well, there's not much to do when there are no patients."

"They're not patients, Monique. They're clients."

"Whatever," she said, settling into the chair directly across from him and crossing her legs. "How were New York and the crusade? Or better yet, did you have a good time with Beverlyn?" She let the question hang in the air.

Dwayne laughed as he took his seat behind the desk. He thought of the two days he and Beverlyn spent together—running through the city like first-time tourists, eating in romantic spots like the Quiet Little Table in the Corner, flying over the city in a private helicopter. But most of their time together was spent shopping the boutiques of New York's posh Upper East Side, including Madison and Lexington Avenues.

He'd never done that before. He had the money, but spending thousands of dollars in one store seemed frivolous. "Five thousand dollars is not much money," she'd told him when he balked at the price of one suit. "Look at it this way: We represent God. We want the people who listen to our words to be able to look at us and see how God has blessed us."

It all made sense to him. People were surely attracted to success and power, and it made sense that he and Beverlyn should represent the best God had to offer. But the real truth was that Beverlyn was teaching him how to live well and he was beginning to like it.

"Not talking, huh?" Monique asked, interrupting his train of thought.

"Absolutely not." He pulled his date book from his briefcase.

Monique tapped her fingers on the desk. "No problem." She walked out of the office, but a moment later, returned holding a newspaper in her hand. "It's hardly a secret anymore." She tossed him a copy of a page from the *Hollywood Insider*, and there in the midst of Flo Anthony's "Go with the Flo" column was a photo of him and Beverlyn leaving Tavern on the Green, his arm around her waist.

"And for the record, Nina was my choice. Beverlyn's a real number, and that uncle of hers . . . what a creep."

He'd tuned Monique out, instead searching his mind—wondering how he could not have noticed someone taking a photo of him and Beverlyn. In fact, he'd been surprised that as they walked through the city, they'd only been stopped four times for autographs. He'd liked that about New York City—that New Yorkers were unimpressed and that they'd been able to fade into the background. Or so he thought.

He'd never even heard of Flo Anthony before, he thought to himself as he scanned the item that read, *Grammy-nominated gospel singer Beverly Boudreaux seemed to be looking to win over more than lost souls on a recent trip to the Big Apple on the occasion of her New York Crusade. She seems to have her hooks in the dashing Dr. Dwayne Grandison, who has become quite a sensation for her newly launched Jubilee Network.* He couldn't read any more, putting the paper down in frustration. For a brief moment, he wondered if Kim hadn't planted the item, but he dismissed the thought as quickly as it had surfaced.

"You're not mad, are you?"

Dwayne shook his head. "I just didn't know people would find my life so interesting."

This was what Monique hated about him but at the same time respected. Nothing could shake him.

"However," he went on, "if you want to keep this, it's on you. But I really don't want this kind of reading material in the office. My clients don't want to see themselves laid out in the waiting room."

Monique picked up the paper. "All right. But I just want to add one more thing: I don't trust Beverlyn or her uncle."

As Monique closed the door, he continued the perusal of the messages, searching for one from Sean. But there was none, even though this was the day Sean was supposed to return. Dwayne dialed Sean's cell phone and smiled wide with relief when it was answered on the first ring.

"Dwayne, my man," Sean exclaimed. "I've been meaning to call."

"When you didn't show up for the crusade, I got worried."

"I appreciate it, man, but no need to worry. Everything is under control. The doctor just told me I needed to get some rest."

"Why? Is something happening?"

"Nothing that wasn't expected."

"Why are you being so evasive?"

"Dwayne, it's really not all that serious. The doctor just didn't want me getting run-down. When I told him I was going to New York on top of my last tour, he asked me if I had some sort of death wish. So I thought about it and canceled."

Dwayne wanted to believe him. His words and sentiment had been persuasive enough, but there was something missing from this picture and he couldn't put his finger on just what, so he let it go, saying, "Well, you know I'm here."

"Thanks, man."

"Listen, when can we get together?"

"What about after church on Sunday?"

"Well, you know everyone is going to want you to join us for dinner."

"I wouldn't have it any other way. I'll give you a call tomorrow."

"Do that," Dwayne said.

As he put the receiver back onto the cradle, Monique peeked into the office.

"Dwayne, Tina Laws is here and Nina Jordan is on line one."

He looked at his watch. Tina was early. He had about ten minutes. "Nina."

"Dwayne, I hope you're not busy."

"Not for you. How are you?"

"Just fine. I'm calling to check on you." Her voice was light and easy. "How was the crusade?"

"Great. I was a little nervous, having never done anything like that before—in front of fifty thousand people . . ."

"You speak in front of more than that every week on your show."

"Yeah, but I don't know that they're there."

"I don't know if Pastor told you, but the fellowship went well."

"That's terrific," Dwayne said with traces of regret in his tone. The men and women's fellowship had been scheduled for the same weekend as the crusade, though Dwayne had already decided not to attend. After a lot of thought and prayer, he'd resigned his position with Man-to-Man though he stayed on the board. "You've got to be proud, Nina. This program is better than even you ever imagined."

"It is," Nina said.

"Well, let me know if I can help."

"You've done so much already. As long as you stay on the advisory board, we'll be fine."

"Done. Listen, I have a client . . ."

"Oh, I understand. I just wanted to say hello."

"Why don't we get together? I'd love to hear more."

"I'd love to, but my week is pretty packed and I know you must be busy . . ."

"What about Sunday after church? Join my family for Sunday dinner. I'd love to see you and Omari."

"That'd be great. I'll see you Sunday."

"We're on."

His smile was still in place as he hung up the phone and Tina Laws entered the office. As she did so, she looked at him as if she were seeing him for the first time.

"Is everything okay, Tina?"

"Well, I'm just so used to being the one in the news, it's a bit of a change to pick up a column and read about you. Especially since you're so tight-lipped about your private life. Shoe's on the other foot now," she said, teasing him.

"Not entirely," he countered. "We're still here to talk about you and not me."

When he looked up at the clock again, it was almost nine. When he'd told Monique to schedule a full day, he hadn't considered jet lag. He was tired. The phone rang as he was urging Monique to go home. Instead of letting it go to voice mail as Dwayne had instructed, she answered the phone at his desk. "Oh, Ms. Boudreaux . . ."

Dwayne motioned that he would take the call.

"Beverlyn," he said as he waved good-bye to Monique.

"Hey, baby. I just wanted to see how your day went."

"Great. I'm just tired. What about you? When are you coming home?"

"I'll be home tomorrow, and for once, I'll have the entire weekend free."

"Great. We'll be able to spend some time together."

"Yeah, I was hoping we could go to church. I've never been to New Covenant."

"My family reminds me of that all the time. So this Sunday, huh?"

"Yes. The day after this Saturday."

"Of course, I'd love that. In fact, after church you can join my family for one of our famous Sunday dinners at my brother's house."

"Dr. Grandison, are you inviting me home to meet the family? You know what comes after a family dinner, don't you?"

"My guess would be that after dinner comes dessert."

"That's what I'm talking about."

Dwayne shook his head. "Ms. Boudreaux. If people only knew the real you."

"Then they wouldn't fill those stadiums for my crusades," she said, laughing. "Well, it's after midnight here and I've got to get some sleep. I'll speak to you tomorrow?" she added in the form of a question.

"I'll call you."

He smiled when they hung up, but his grin faded when he realized that he had just invited three people to Robbie and Lafayette's home on Sunday. He picked up the phone. He'd better alert Robbie.

# Chapter Twenty-Seven

Dwayne held Beverlyn's hand as they walked up the steps and he opened the heavy double doors at New Covenant Assembly.

"Good morning, Dr. Grandison," the usher said, handing Dwayne a bulletin. Then instantly recognizing Beverlyn, she began to stutter, "Uh . . . good morning. Here's one for you too."

Dwayne could tell by the gleam in her eye that the hostess recognized Beverlyn, though she refused to gush over the famous singer. They followed the usher down the green-carpeted aisle to the front row, where Beverlyn joined him beside his mother. He could feel the long stares and muffled whispers.

"Hello, Ms. Grandison." Beverlyn took a surprised Bernice's hand. "It's good to see you again."

"It's wonderful to see you, dear." Bernice's eyes darted between Dwayne and Beverlyn. "I didn't know you were coming," she said, giving Dwayne a "why didn't you tell me" glance.

At exactly eleven, with the sanctuary completely full, the choir took their places to lead the congregation in praise and worship. Beverlyn's voice rose above all around them. After the final note of the first selection, the musical director, Janice Bell, signaled for the keyboard player to continue and took the microphone. "New Covenant

is especially honored this morning to have a very special visitor—
Evangelist Beverlyn Boudreaux."

Loud applause filled the sanctuary and people stretched their
necks to get a glimpse of their VIP visitor. Beverlyn turned around
graciously and waved, before the thunderous applause prompted her
to bow as well. She was absolute magic, instantly endearing herself
to her admirers with her high-voltage smile and a faintly surprised
expression as if she had no idea she would be recognized. Dwayne
was momentarily unsettled by the fact that he felt flush with pride
that by simply being with her he too was the center of the crowd's attention.

"Ms. Boudreaux," she continued, "we'd be honored if you would
join us in singing 'Ask God for the World.'"

While Beverlyn was openly pleased that the choir had chosen the
title song from her last CD, she hesitated. Was it sincere humility or
was it a seasoned pro working the crowd?

"Go on." Dwayne finally nudged her while the applause continued. "They really want you."

Having gained his approval, Beverlyn rose to her feet and stepped
onto the podium, making her way to the choir stand. After hugging
Janice, she accepted the microphone and signaled to the musicians
that she was ready. As Beverlyn sang the first stanza, it was clear she
was comfortably in her element. She closed her eyes and raised her
hand in praise. By the time she finished, the entire congregation was
on its feet. The applause, coupled with the chorus of amens and hal-
lelujahs throughout the sanctuary, was so deafening that Beverlyn remained onstage singing until Lafayette took his place, at which time
one of the male choir members escorted Beverlyn back to Dwayne.

Lafayette stood silently at the podium until the praise and prayers
waned. Finally, he raised his hand for quiet and spoke. "My brother
did not tell me that we were going to be blessed in such a way today.
Thank you, Ms. Boudreaux, for sharing with us the wonderful gift
God has so graciously extended you. We are so very pleased to have
you."

Lafayette's sermon was powerful—as usual—but it was clear that
the high point of the two-hour-long service had been Beverlyn's per-

formance. When Lafayette walked from the altar to the back of the church, he paused and asked Beverlyn to join him, Bernice, and Robbie in greeting the parishioners.

Dwayne took his mother's and Beverlyn's hands in an effort to maneuver them through the crowd toward the church's alcove, but people stopped them at every turn—some to say hello, some for autographs, and some just to get a closer look. Once in place, Dwayne squeezed Beverlyn's hand before he left her at his mother's side and returned to the sanctuary, his eyes searching the still-full room.

His face lit up when he spotted her at the other side of the church chatting with one of the women from Sister 2 Sister. He tried to weave through the maze and sidestep the women who made personal—though lighthearted—inquiries about him and Beverlyn. Mrs. King wanted to know what the real deal was. Ms. Lacy just offered a sinister smile as if she knew the real deal, while Ms. Brown wondered if Beverlyn would soon be joining the church (since she'd just moved to Los Angeles and couldn't have already found a church home).

Finally, he stood in front of Nina and Omari.

"Mr. Dwayne," the boy exclaimed.

"Hey, my man." Dwayne high-fived Omari.

"It's good to see you, Dwayne," Nina said as they hugged.

He held her for a moment, feeling a familiar stirring. Slowly, his arms relinquished the embrace.

"Well, you're a bona fide star now," Nina teased.

"Really," he said.

"Well, a driver . . . a TV show, and . . . ," she added, whispering, "Beverlyn Boudreaux."

Dwayne didn't know what to say.

The hesitation didn't stop Nina. "Are you happy, Dwayne?" she asked softly.

"I'm on my way," he said soberly.

"Well, that's all that matters."

"How 'bout you?"

"I'm on my way as well."

She said the words, but he detected sadness in her voice.

From the outside alcove, Beverlyn mindlessly shook hands and watched Nina and Dwayne through worried eyes, flustered at the sight. She couldn't put her hands on why Nina unnerved her so. Nina had always appeared calm and collected, and that riled Beverlyn even more. What was it he saw in her? Beverlyn wondered.

Even as the car pulled in front of Lafayette's home, Beverlyn couldn't manage to shake the scene she'd witnessed between Dwayne and Nina.

"Is something wrong?" Dwayne searched her eyes. "You've been so quiet since we left the church."

"I'm just thinking about the service. Your brother is a great speaker."

"Then I hope you'll come back with me sometime."

She wanted to say she had no plans of letting him out of her sight as long as Nina was around. "I hope to come back with you again and again and again."

"Well," he said, "we'd better go in or they're going to send someone out after us."

He held her hand as they stepped into the house.

"We were wondering what happened to you guys," Robbie said, coming out of the kitchen, a white floral apron partially covering her yellow sleeveless linen dress. "Welcome to our home." She took Beverlyn's hand and led them into the living room.

"Everyone is here." Robbie continued chatting, stopping in front of the love seat, where Nina sat with Monique.

"Beverlyn, you know Nina and Monique?"

Nina stretched forward her hand. "Yes, good to see you, Beverlyn. You were wonderful in church this morning."

"Thank you." Beverlyn forced the words.

"I think you know everyone else." Robbie scanned the room before wiping her hands on her apron. "Well, I'll leave you all to talk. I'd better get back in the kitchen."

Robbie—joined by Monique—scurried from the room, leaving Dwayne, Beverlyn, and Nina standing in a triangle as the kids played on the other side of the room and Lafayette greeted Sean, who had missed church that morning.

"Congratulations on the Jubilee Network and, I might add, on your recent New York Crusade," Nina said.

Beverlyn wrapped her hands around Dwayne's arm. "Yeah, it was great. Did Dwayne tell you that he was in New York with me?" she asked with a catty edge.

"Yes, he said he was one of the speakers."

Beverlyn looked at Dwayne. "He was more than that."

Dwayne coughed. "Look who's here—it's Sean."

"Oh, yes. Excuse us, Nina," Beverlyn said.

Dwayne was sure that Nina rolled her eyes as Beverlyn detoured to the rest room, leaving him to greet Sean alone. "My man, it's good to see you." He took Sean's hand.

"Boy, two women fighting over you—you are indeed the man."

"I don't think they like each other."

"What a surprise," came Sean's sarcastic response. "Anyway, you look great. Nice suit."

Dwayne stepped back and looked at his friend. His eyes shined brightly behind his glasses. To him, Sean looked healthy, except for the few pounds he seemed to have dropped.

"Looks like your vacation did you good. You lost some weight?"

"Maybe a little." Sean paused and then looked up. "How was New York?"

"Great."

"I saw pictures of you and Beverlyn together," Sean said, eyeing Dwayne over the top of his glasses.

"I'm going to get a drink. Do you want anything?" Dwayne changed the subject, hurrying from the living room to the kitchen.

"Hello, son." Bernice gave Dwayne a hearty hug. "Where's Beverlyn?"

"She's out there," he said, waving his hand. "I came to get something to drink."

"Don't hide in here. The action's out front," Monique said as she brushed past him heading toward the living room.

Dwayne took a sip of his Coke and offered to help Robbie, who was fussing about Lafayette, who was now outside throwing a football with the boys. He watched as his mother and sister-in-law worked in unison, like a well-oiled machine, preparing another traditional Sunday dinner: baked chicken, stuffing, yams, macaroni and cheese, collard greens, monkey bread, and today it smelled like his mom's famed sweet potato pie and sock-it-to-me cake. He planted himself against the refrigerator, deciding that the heat of the kitchen was much more inviting than the deep freeze building between Beverlyn and Nina.

Beverlyn stepped to the edge of the room and looked around. She smiled when she saw Sean, then noticed Nina standing alone, scanning family photos perched on the fireplace mantel.

"So, Nina, I'm so sorry Dwayne had to quit the program."

"It's just fine." Nina swung around, chuckling a bit to herself. Surely, she thought, Beverlyn couldn't be taking her on. Hardly fragile, Nina was a street-smart survivor; having been hardened by her life's experiences, she was not easily hurt.

"I'm sure you miss Dwayne."

Nina twirled the glass in her hand for a moment, wondering what would be the Christian way to respond. Oh, to hell with it, she thought.

"Not actually, Beverlyn. Dwayne is good about making himself available to me. Then, too, he's still on the board and you know how he feels about the program. So it's really great. If we need him, he's just a phone call away."

Without another word, Beverlyn walked away, almost bumping into Monique when she turned.

Nina couldn't hide her grin as Monique and she shared a little laugh.

"Girl," said Monique, "I couldn't have said that any better myself."

"If I could have just been a fly on the wall," Sean joked as he approached Nina, setting his drink on the mantel. Monique rushed outside when they heard a child crying.

"Can't say that was one of my proudest moments," Nina said.

"Oh, don't be so hard on yourself. She can be a little hard to take. She acts that way because she's had a tough time. Down deep, she's a good person . . . just has her ways."

"Well, I'll tell you. My opinion of Ms. Beverlyn has changed since

I've gotten to know her up close and personal." She paused for a moment. "I hate to say it. It's so cliché, but you expect that kind of behavior in the secular world, and it kind of catches you off guard when it comes from someone like her."

"Remember, we're all just human. But more importantly, have you considered that she's obviously threatened by you?"

Nina was silent. Sean's words had come as a revelation to her.

"Why?" she asked innocently.

"Oh, don't play dumb with me," Sean teased.

"I've been told to summon you," Lafayette announced. "Dinner is served."

Sean offered Nina his arm. "May I, Ms. Jordan?" They both laughed and joined arms together to walk into the dining room.

"I want to thank everyone for joining us this afternoon." Lafayette stood at the head of the table with ten settings. Along the wall, two card tables had been set for the children. Dwayne could not suppress a smile when Beverlyn entwined her fingers through his, and Lafayette began to say grace. This was the first time Dwayne had been with another woman around his family. What he had imagined as awkwardness had only been pleasant, except, that is, for the incident with Nina. He prayed that would change. After New York, he knew Beverlyn was going to be part of his life and he wanted everyone he loved to love her.

Dwayne lifted his head when Lafayette closed the prayer, and saw Nina smiling directly at him. He cleared his throat and turned to Beverlyn, who was complimenting Robbie on the food. Throughout the meal, Dwayne frequently found himself drifting from his conversation with Beverlyn, distracted by Nina. He turned his head whenever he heard her laugh with Sean, or he wondered what she was talking about when her head was bowed close to Deacon Miller's and Monique's. (He would talk to Monique tomorrow.) By the time Lafayette suggested that they go into the living room after dessert, Dwayne was eager to rise. As they followed the others, Dwayne said to Beverlyn, "Ready to go?"

Beverlyn frowned slightly. "Oh, honey, I'm having such a good time."

"I just thought we'd spend some time together."

She squeezed his hand. "I should have thought of that." Then Beverlyn stepped forward. "I'm sorry, everyone," she announced. "We have to leave."

Dwayne stood back, letting Beverlyn have the floor. He didn't understand why she was making such a production. As Robbie and Bernice protested and Beverlyn continued to make excuses for the both of them, Dwayne set off to find Nina, but came up empty.

Finally, Dwayne helped Beverlyn find her purse and moved her toward the door, just as Nina came out of the bathroom.

"Nina, I'm glad we got a chance to say good-bye." Beverlyn hooked her arm through Dwayne's. "We need some time together," she said, lowering her voice.

"Well, it was good to see you." Nina smiled and then turned to Dwayne. "Give me a call tomorrow," she said, running her fingertips along the sleeve of his jacket. Then she walked away.

Beverlyn scowled, opened the door, and stomped outside.

Dwayne followed. He could never have said the words that were in his mind. "You deserved that, Beverlyn."

# Chapter Twenty-Eight

*A*s Monique closed the office door, Dwayne stood and walked over to his window. Though it was August, it seemed more like June. For days, a cloud cover had taken up residence over the city, making for gray skies and cool temperatures. With Beverlyn out of town, the show on hiatus, and sans Man-to-Man, Dwayne found himself a bit down—lost without his workaholic schedule.

Maybe Monique had been right when she suggested a Palm Springs getaway. But Palm Springs . . . No, he wanted to do something different, something wild, and something that would make Beverlyn proud. Suddenly, it came to him. Paradise Island.

Within an hour, Monique had booked him on a late-afternoon flight to Miami, where he would make the connection to Paradise Island; and he had reserved one of the most expensive suites at the posh Atlantis resort.

"This is going to cost a fortune," Monique had repeated to him, confirming and then reaffirming the extravagant arrangements as she half rolled her eyes. He knew what she was thinking. That he was somehow changing—beginning to feel quite at home in the lifestyle he once detested. But strangely enough to Dwayne, it had felt exhilarating to be spontaneous. He left a message at Beverlyn's hotel in D.C. inviting her to join him—separate rooms, of course. He knew there could be no way she could up and leave on such short notice, but he got a huge kick out of playing the bad boy daring her to leave her labors and join him at play.

Twenty-four hours later, Dwayne found himself sitting on the fringe of the white sands bordering the turquoise sea. The breeze blew softly as he sipped his orange juice and took the last bite of his French toast. Pushing the plate aside, he stared out at the beach, refreshed. He'd slept until noon.

It surprised him that the beach wasn't packed with sunbathers. Instead, it seemed that most hotel occupants opted for the cool of one of the fourteen Atlantis pools scattered throughout the resort. But he wasn't going to get this close and not savor the soft-blue water of the tropical sea. He'd even considered heading to Cabbage Beach, where snorkelers the world over reveled in the forty acres of coral and sea fern just one mile offshore.

He looked at his watch. There were still many hours of daylight. He would take it easy—a stroll on the beach. Or he could hire a driver for a tour of the island. Tomorrow he would play golf. From his back pocket, he pulled the tourist brochures he'd taken from his room and spread them across the table.

"Sir, do you need anything else?"

His eyes were still on the pamphlets and he waved his hand in dismissal.

"Are you sure?" the persistent voice behind him asked.

"No thank you," he said, irritated at the intrusion.

"I think you still need something else."

"I said no." He turned abruptly toward the voice.

"Surprise." Beverlyn dropped her bag and extended her arms. She was dressed for the tropics in a multicolored cotton pantsuit.

"What are you doing here?" He stood, embracing her, and then pulled out the chair next to him.

"I was able to sneak away for a few hours." She sat down beside him. "I missed you."

"How much time do you have?"

She looked at her watch. "Ten hours. I have to be at the airport at midnight. I hired a private jet to take me back in time to get a few hours' sleep before I speak in the morning."

He shook his head. Her trip was crazier than his.

"Well, what do you want to do? I was just going to hire a driver to take me around the island."

"Why don't we rent a couple of mopeds? Then we can go where we want and take our time. I just have to change my clothes."

He took her bag, leading the way back to his suite. "I can't imagine you on a moped," he teased as they stepped inside the tower lobby.

"There are lots of things about me you can't imagine. If you give me a chance . . ."

Dwayne laughed at her words as they walked into the Great Hall of Waters Lobby with aquatic sculptured pillars and a ceiling dome of golden shells that soared seventy feet above.

She kissed him passionately while he fumbled for the key in his pocket, finally locating it, unlocking the door and then holding it open for her.

"This is fabulous," she said, breaking away from him as she took in the massive two-floor penthouse suite, with a breathtaking view of the beach below, high ceilings, and a white bow-backed sofa covered in chenille.

"I'm following your advice and learning to live well."

"I'll be ready in just a minute." She ascended the spiral staircase that led to a huge open bedroom master suite.

An hour later, dressed in shorts and tank tops, with mopeds, helmets, and an island map, they set out to explore the beautiful beaches the Bahamas were known for—from the unspoiled champagne-pink sands of North Shore Beach on Cat Island to the Grand Bahama Island's Gold Rock Beach.

They giggled as they struggled to stay on the left side of the road. They had little problem making it to their first stop—the harbor—within twenty minutes. There they ordered conch fritters from a street-side stand and shared a strawberry soda. Next they ventured downtown. Their first stop was Main Street Square. Boys of the island danced to Junkanoo music. Many in the crowd joined in, and after some prodding, Dwayne and Beverlyn were dancing too, making up steps as they went.

Their bodies ached when they returned to the hotel after traveling a radius of over thirty miles on the mopeds and shopping in the duty-free boutiques.

"I don't know if I can walk," Beverlyn whined as she flopped onto the sofa.

"Except you have to go back in five hours." Dwayne rested her feet on his lap. "Do you want to order room service?"

She opened her eyes and peeked at him. "No, I think being alone in here with you for a romantic dinner would be more temptation than I could bear."

Dwayne picked up the phone. "I'd like to make reservations at Windmills." He leaned over and kissed her. "Get up, Ms. Boudreaux. I'm going to treat you to a fabulous dinner before you jet away, leaving me here all alone."

"I hate leaving you here."

"I'm kidding, Beverlyn."

He watched as she stumbled up to the bedroom to freshen up and change her clothes. He still couldn't believe that she had come so far to spend a few hours with him, and after a moment's reflection he dashed up to the bedroom after her, reaching and pulling her into an intimate embrace. Without hesitation, Beverlyn returned the embrace, and passions were stirred, their hands leading the way to yet another level of discovery. It seemed like an eternity passed before they almost simultaneously drew back, as if considering the implications of their unfolding physical desires.

They lay back on the bed as Dwayne took her hand. "What's wrong?" he asked softly.

When she looked up, he thought there were tears in her eyes.

"I feel really special with you, Dwayne." Her voice was low.

"You are special. We're good for each other, Beverlyn." He took her hand in his.

"I pray you're right." She squeezed his hand as they lay almost motionless in each other's arms, not wanting to spoil the moment, no longer hungry.

By the time they looked at the clock, they had just one hour to get to the airport. In the back of the limousine, they held hands, but remained silent, each lost in thought, wondering how their short hours together had changed their relationship, knowing it had changed for sure. When they arrived at the airstrip, they kissed passionately, neither wanting to let go of the moment.

"I will miss you," she said.

"Hurry home," he said.

Dwayne had the driver wait until the airplane that carried Beverlyn was just a small dot in the black sky. When he returned to the car, he reveled in the realization that his relationship with Beverlyn Boudreaux was finding its own higher ground.

# Chapter Twenty-Nine

*N*ina had walked away from the fast-track lifestyle of chauf-feur-driven limousines and dining at only the most expen-sive, swanky restaurants ten years ago, but as she found herself leaning back into the leather seat while Teddy drove her and Dwayne to dinner at Crustacean, a Beverly Hills hot spot, those old memories came flooding back. She glanced at Dwayne from the corner of her eye. He looked the same, but what she saw in his face was far from the whole story. Over the last several months, Dwayne Grandison had gone from being a simple, humble man to one who was being se-duced and won over by the trappings of success.

They hadn't seen each other in a month. Observing Dwayne now, Nina realized dinner was the last thing on her mind. Closing her eyes, she said a silent prayer as the limousine wound its way up Rodeo Drive. Dwayne was much older than she had been when she fell into the trap. But she feared age was not a deterrent. Success was more intoxicating and addictive than any substance she'd taken.

They made small talk as the limo pulled up to the chic restaurant, whose list of patrons included Bruce Willis, Leonardo DiCaprio, Will Smith and Jada Pinkett, Shaquille O'Neal, John Travolta, Eddie Mur-phy, and Sean, who'd always raved about their much-celebrated gar-lic crab, which was prepared in the eatery's equally famed "secret kitchen." Both Dwayne and Nina had already decided on the ride over that they would try it tonight.

The glass floor beneath them revealed an underlying aquarium, setting the tone for the restaurant's exotic decor. The maître d' led them past tables where chatter filled the noisy open room, and held the chair as Nina sat. They were barely seated before a waiter introduced himself and pulled their napkins from wineglasses.

Nina rested her arms on the table. "So it's been a while. How are you?"

"Great. Gearing up for fall shows, but I've been able to get away for a couple of days here and there."

"Yeah, your mother told me you'd been in the Bahamas and then Maui."

"I played golf for three days straight. It was wonderful."

"I'm sure Beverlyn enjoyed it as well . . ."

"Well, I went to Maui solo. Beverlyn was able to make it down to the Bahamas for a day, but for the most part, she's been working. August is a big month for the gospel industry as well as church conferences. There seems to be a convention every other day and she has to make all of them, especially with the release of her newest CD."

Though hardly insecure, Nina couldn't help but feel a bit relieved that he and Beverlyn hadn't spent too much time alone together.

"She should be back the day after tomorrow," Dwayne continued. "Our first production meeting is tomorrow and I know Beverlyn will want to jump right back into the mix of things."

"Then I'm glad you called tonight."

"So am I. What's going on with you?"

She thought about all that had happened in a month. How she'd returned to the doctor and had him retest her, finding the results the same. "I'm fine. It's the ministry I wanted to talk to you about," she said, directing his attention away from her.

"So how's it going?"

"Good. The initial excitement died down, but I expected that. The surprise is the number of calls we're getting from people interested in our doing another combined women and men's fellowship conference."

As Nina continued to outline another strategy, he thought back to the passionate kiss they'd shared and wondered why, even now, he was still drawn to her. Even though he liked what was happening between him and Beverlyn, he cherished his friendship with Nina.

Scanning the pages of the proposal, he said, "Sounds like a good idea, but you and Lafayette must realize how difficult it is to get funding for a project like this."

"I know," Nina mused, "but with the right positioning, we might be able to pull this off. And with the Grandison name behind it . . ." She threw up her hands, leaving the sentence unfinished.

"Are you talking about the preacher or the therapist?"

"We have the pastor, but it would sure help if we had the very talented psychologist. I was even hoping we could get you to host a fund-raiser to raise at least part of what we need. Sean has already agreed, and with you, perhaps even some of your clients . . ."

"And Beverlyn?"

"Well, she was your mother's idea."

They both laughed.

"Nina, you know you have my support. Whatever I can do. Actually, I think this will be a lot of fun."

She leaned across the table and kissed his cheek. "Thanks for being such a wonderful friend."


The flight from Miami had been long and filled with turbulence— the result of a string of thunderstorms winding its way across Texas, Louisiana, and Mississippi. Beverlyn's plan had been to sleep through the flight so that she'd be rested when she surprised Dwayne with her early return. But the plan hadn't worked. She wasn't able to sleep, nor could she find Dwayne. There was no answer on his cell or at his condo.

Instead, she suggested to L.W. that they get a bite to eat before turning in for some much-needed rest. Kim had rushed home to spend time with her daughter. When L.W. suggested seafood, Beverlyn thought of the restaurant Sean had spoken so highly of. Usually, L.W. wasn't thrilled with any referral Sean made, but being from bayou country, there was nothing he liked better than good crab. So off they headed to Crustacean.

The maître d' signaled for them to follow, but as they passed the bar and entered the main dining room, Beverlyn stopped dead in her tracks when she spotted Dwayne and Nina. Perplexed by his niece's actions, L.W. followed Beverlyn's glance. An immediate smile filled his face when his eyes rested on Dr. Dwayne Grandison and Nina Jordan cozily planted at a table. He wanted to march over and confront the good doctor, particularly as Nina leaned over to kiss him on the cheek, but he waited to follow his devastated niece's lead.

Beverlyn whipped around. "Uncle Linson, I'm a lot more tired than hungry. Would you mind if we just went home?"

"Of course, honey," he said sympathetically. "That's what I thought we should have done in the first place. I'll have Joseph drop you off first." He cupped her hand under his elbow, leading her toward the front door. "Would you like to stop somewhere and pick up something?"

"No, I don't want anything." Beverlyn shook her head, fighting to hold back the tears as she looked back over her shoulder, past L.W., to the table where Dwayne and Nina sat, heads close together.

"Let's get out of here." L.W. led her through the crowded restaurant.

Thinking about it later, Beverlyn leaned her weight against the back of her front door. Twenty-four hours ago, she was onstage, captivating more than fifty thousand people in Miami who sat on the edge of their seats, hanging on her every word. Two standing ovations had followed, and even so, after exiting the stage, she'd had to return to quiet the crowd before show organizers could go on. Anywhere else, she'd been appreciated and adored. But tonight she was alone.

Scanning the house her success had built, she stepped into the living room. Stylishly decorated, it could have been pulled from the pages of *House Beautiful*. Her eyes rested on the framed photos atop the fireplace mantel. The frames were filled with pictures of her mingling with various dignitaries, politicians, and other celebrities. The photos were meant to provide an account of all she'd accomplished, but instead, they showed what was missing. While her life was full of important people, it was devoid of anyone truly special, like Dwayne.

Suddenly, she wondered why they hadn't taken pictures in New York or the Bahamas. She didn't even have any family pictures. She had none of her mother. She didn't know her grandmother and had no other family to speak of.

Having spent her early years in the orphanage, she'd always dreamed of having a big and loving family—a house full of kids, a husband who loved her. She would cook, shop, and do all the things wives did.

Not that she did any cooking or cleaning now, but she was beautiful, successful, in great shape, and had a great home. What man wouldn't want to be with Beverlyn Boudreaux? Sure there were men who were intimidated—who would rather be with someone they could overshadow in order to build their ego. But those weren't the kind of men she'd desired anyway. And Dwayne hardly fit that category. So what was it? What did Nina have on her?

Oh, Nina was cute and she had a nice figure, but she was a has-been, and with Omari in tow, she seemed to have a lot of baggage. Besides, surely Dwayne could have had her if he'd wanted her. After all, they were friends before Beverlyn came on the scene.

Perhaps she was overreacting. Maybe it was just a friendly dinner. After all, everyone had said how much of a dynamic team Beverlyn and Dwayne made together. And then there were his own words: "We're good for each other, Beverlyn."

Still, in her heart of hearts, she knew there was something deeper going on. Dwayne and Nina seemed to share an intimacy that she couldn't duplicate. She tried hard to put out of her mind the suspicion that they had become physically involved, but she was certain that there was a definite connection, and she was certain that it troubled her.

Beverlyn clicked off the living room lights and retired upstairs to her bedroom. She undressed slowly with images of Nina and Dwayne bombarding her mind. What was she going to do? She'd been sure that Dwayne was the beginning of the next chapter of her life, and she was used to getting exactly what she wanted—and she wanted

Dwayne Grandison. But she also knew that he wasn't a man who would bow to her demands.

How ironic, she thought. To run a multimillion-dollar corporation . . . to be able to draw and motivate thousands . . . to be one of the gospel industry's most sought-after performers, and yet not be able to win over one man. If she could only focus, she'd find it—the perfect plan.

She got down on her knees and began to thank God for all the blessings He'd bestowed. To pray for others who needed blessings of deliverance, salvation, and healing. And to pray for the one thing that would make her life complete.

She pulled back the white down comforter and climbed in between the satin sheets, letting the events of the day settle in her mind. This was a setback, but it wasn't over. All her life, she'd had to fight for what she wanted. Why would this be any different?

L.W. twisted the cap from the bottle of his imported cognac. He couldn't have been happier about the recent developments as he thought about how the sight of Dwayne and Nina together just might do the trick. The rope he wanted to coil around Dwayne's neck might not be necessary. The doctor was hanging himself. And this way was even better, as Dwayne would be able to stay with the network.

This was his private celebration. He laughed out loud thinking of his good fortune. He thought about how tonight almost hadn't happened. How he had tried to persuade Beverlyn to stay in Miami and not rush back. But Beverlyn hadn't seen Dwayne, and she'd insisted that instead of a good night's sleep, what she wanted was Dwayne.

It was the glow on her face when she mentioned Dwayne's name that had made his skin crawl. His niece had been getting too close to Dwayne and he'd been helpless in stopping it. He knew about the time they spent together when he was out of town, and after the Bahamas, he began to feel like he was losing his hold. But that was days ago. Oh, how things had changed. Once again, the control had shifted back to his hands, where it was supposed to be. And what made it all the sweeter was that he'd done nothing at all.

Nothing could stop him now. Everything was going as planned. Beverlyn was the star, but behind the scenes and in the boardroom was where the real power lay. With the success of the Jubilee Network, he was on his way to becoming one of the most powerful men in the Christian community.

# Chapter Thirty

Dwayne browsed through the list of topics for the upcoming season of *Higher Ground*. He felt good about the fact that his show was entering its second season. He'd arrived early to prepare for the first meeting of the year, and began to highlight topics that interested him: teen prostitution, guns in schools, and family secrets, among others.

He raised his head when he heard the knock on the door.

"Dr. Grandison, Ms. Boudreaux is on line one."

"Beverlyn," he exclaimed, genuinely happy to hear from her. "How are you?"

"I'm fine now that I'm back home."

"When did you get back?"

"Last night."

"Why didn't you call?"

"I'm calling now," she said sweetly.

Beverlyn wasn't coming to the meeting, opting to get some much-needed rest. Instead, she would prepare a romantic dinner for the two of them at her home.

Dwayne was surprised at how much he was looking forward to it. He marveled at how very much his life had changed in such a short period of time. While it was Nina who had helped him to emerge from the fog that surrounded him, it was Beverlyn who was taking him to new heights. Anxious to get his day over so that he could spend the evening with her, Dwayne gathered his papers and notes and eagerly rushed down the hall to get the production meeting started.

In Hancock Park, Beverlyn nervously looked at her watch. It was a quarter to seven. The caterer had just finished with the table settings, and everything was ready in the kitchen.

Guy, her hairdresser, floated down the stairs. "Beverlyn, darling, you're set for tonight. Now I have to go," he said, punctuating every word with his hands. "A lot of people are very angry with me for rearranging my calendar to accommodate you. I hope you're pleased."

"You know I am. Thank you, Guy."

"Anytime, darling. There is no one as important as you!" Guy paused, lightly licked his finger, and then smoothed down a stray strand of Beverlyn's bangs. He had trimmed her hair today, tapering the back, but keeping longer layers to give her hair more fullness. "You look fabulous, honey. This man better be worth it," Guy called over his shoulder as he dashed down the front stairs to his waiting car and driver.

She inspected everything once more, seeing that everything was in its place, checking on the food in the kitchen, then checking herself in the hallway mirror. The lavender lounging ensemble was perfectly cast for this occasion, and though she felt worn down, she looked good. The soft chimes of her doorbell rang, signaling Dwayne's arrival.

From the moment he walked through the door, Dwayne noticed something different about Beverlyn. He couldn't put his finger on just what it was, so he just let it slide as the evening passed, without acknowledging his concern.

"That dinner was really something," Dwayne later said, lifting the napkin off his lap and onto the table.

He got up and put his arms around Beverlyn's waist as she kissed the tip of his nose.

"It's good to have you home," he said.

"I'm just happy to be here with you."

Dwayne put his arm around Beverlyn's shoulders and led her into the living room. She dimmed the lights and sat on the couch, kicking off her silver mules and stretching her legs.

Dwayne crouched in front of the stereo, punching the power button and selecting the CD player. Instantly, Beverlyn's voice filled the room.

"Turn that off. I hate listening to myself."

Dwayne raised his eyebrows. "I didn't know. I love hearing your voice."

Returning to the couch next to her, he sat down, lifting her feet to his lap. Beverlyn leaned back, closed her eyes, and moaned softly as he began gently massaging the balls of her feet. He asked about the Miami Crusade, but Beverlyn recoiled. The thought of Miami conjured images of him and Nina together the night before. Instead, she kissed him and then leaned her head against his chest.

"What's wrong?" Dwayne asked as he nuzzled his face in her hair, taking in her whole scent.

"Do you know how special it is to be here with you?"

"I hope so." His arms closed tighter around her.

"I couldn't have imagined this a year ago."

"So you want me to believe that you didn't have men chasing you—"

"There was no one," she cut him off. "I was never interested. My only concern was singing and speaking."

"Why?"

She shrugged, though images of her earliest days came to mind—times when she'd cried herself to sleep, longing for her mother. Longing for someone to rescue her from the prison everyone told her was home. Longing for someone to hold her through the horrid dreams that filled her nights.

"It's different now," she said. "You've opened sealed doors in my heart."

"That's a good thing, I hope."

She turned around and kissed him, then pulled his arms around her again, leaning back on his chest. She took a deep breath as she thought about her next question. "What about you, Dwayne? Did you think you'd be here a year ago?"

He let a year's worth of yesterdays flash through his mind. "No." His eyes searched hers. "You . . ." He brought his lips to hers before he could finish the sentence, and they kissed deeply, discovering each other in ways they'd not known. Their tongues and hands explored, searched, and found. Several minutes passed before they pulled away breathlessly.

His fingers traced her face. "I was just thinking how long it's been since I kissed a woman like that."

"I can't say I've ever kissed a man like that."

"Then we should do it again." He skimmed his lips over hers. "Don't you think?"

She nodded. "I love you, Dwayne Grandison."

His eyes widened, but before he could speak, she covered his mouth, parting his lips with her tongue. A second later, the doorbell's chimes interrupted them.

Beverlyn tried to pull away, but Dwayne locked his arms tighter around her. "Don't answer it."

Beverlyn knew that the only other person with access directly to the front door was L.W., and that it was quite likely that he heard their arrival from his quarters. Dwayne grimaced as Beverlyn walked into the foyer to check the security screen to see who it was. A moment later, she returned from the foyer with L.W. at her side. Even in the dim light, Dwayne could see L.W.'s beady eyes and pursed lips.

"I think it's time for me to leave." Dwayne rose to his feet and reached for the jacket he'd laid across the couch.

"That would be a good idea," L.W. said.

"L.W.," Beverlyn exclaimed furiously. "This is my house and Dwayne is my guest."

"That's okay," Dwayne said.

"No, it's not," Beverlyn reprimanded.

"I'm sorry," L.W. said, interrupting her. "But I have to talk to you about something important . . . something private, and it may take a while."

"Apology accepted. Good night, L.W." Dwayne took Beverlyn's hand. "Walk me to the door."

She glared at her uncle but followed Dwayne.

"I'm sorry about L.W.," she said, straightening his jacket lapel.

"I told you not to apologize for him. Your uncle knows what he's doing."

"I had such a great time tonight."

"So did I."

"It's ending much too early."

"There will be many more nights like this to come."

Beverlyn held the door open until Teddy steered the car around the driveway, then disappeared through the front gate. She closed the door and stood a moment reflecting on the intimate moments she'd just shared with Dwayne. Until, that is, she saw L.W. standing with crossed arms under the arch of the living room entrance.

"Are you out of your mind?" Beverlyn screamed at L.W. in astonishment. "What on earth possessed you to do that?"

"Beverlyn, what is going on between you and Dwayne Grandison?"

"None of your business," she said angrily, rolling her eyes. "I stopped answering to you a long time ago."

Realizing he may have overstepped his boundaries, L.W. changed his strategy, taking Beverlyn's hand. "Oh, honey, I didn't mean to upset you, but I was upset with him after seeing you so hurt last night.

"Let's sit down," he continued, sitting beside her after she'd settled onto the couch and folded her hands.

"Uncle Linson, please don't ever do that again."

"I just want what's best for you. Besides that, I'm responsible for your career."

"No, you're not," she snapped.

"Yes, I most certainly am, and I take great pride in my duties as president of Beverlyn Boudreaux Ministries, and as your uncle. There are rumors flying around the company about you and Dwayne." He paused and held up his hand, stopping her from interrupting. "Now, I don't care what people say, I care about the truth and how that truth is going to affect Beverlyn Boudreaux, my niece whom I love very much. But I would like to know what's going on between you and Dwayne."

She waited a moment. "Uncle Linson, I understand this is all about business for you, but I've discovered much more than that with Dwayne. At thirty-five, I'm in love for the first time in my life."

L.W. forced a smile. "I'm happy for you, honey."

"Are you?" She really wanted to believe him. "I really hope you are, Uncle Linson, because Dwayne is coming to be an important part of my life and I think he would be a major asset to the company."

"What are you talking about?" L.W. was dumbfounded.

"Well, with his background, he'll bring so much to our company."

"What does your being in love have to do with the company?" he asked incredulously.

"Well, if he's my husband . . ."

"Whoa, wait a minute!" He was floored. "You're talking about marriage already?"

"Not exactly." She edged closer to him. "But I believe we're heading in that direction and I've spent so much time on my ministry, I think now is the time to concentrate on getting married and having a family."

"I am your family, Beverlyn." L.W. sat frozen.

"Of course, Uncle Linson, you'll always be, but Dwayne satisfies other needs. Besides, it's time for me to get a life away from all of this traveling and evangelizing and the Jubilee Network. I need some balance. Maybe you should think about that as well."

"No, no . . . Taking care of you and this ministry is quite enough for me." He stood. "I need to go."

"I thought you had something important to tell me."

All of this had caught L.W. so off guard that he couldn't muster the energy to come up with something clever. "It was a bit of business, dear, but it can keep until later."

"Are you sure?"

He kissed her forehead. "I'm sure. Have a good night, sweetheart."

As L.W. retreated in the cool of the night air to the guesthouse, he allowed the weight of Beverlyn's news to settle in. After last night, L.W. thought he wouldn't need to implement the plan that would stop Dwayne Grandison dead in his tracks. But it seemed he had been wrong. He would have to move ahead now and do it sooner than he had first thought. No one would come between him and Beverlyn; certainly not now, when everything he'd worked so hard for was coming to fruition.

It saddened him to think of how the plan might affect Beverlyn. Then again, he would be there to pick up the pieces just as he always had. L.W. leaned back in his plush leather desk chair. There was no need to worry. In a few weeks, Dwayne Grandison would be little more than a bad memory that would—with time—fade from her mind.

# Chapter Thirty-One

The studio was frantic with excitement as the crew prepared for *Higher Ground*'s first live production. Doing the show live had been Beverlyn's idea. She'd wanted to kick off the new season with something different. Dwayne had to give it to her: Her argument was persuasive. A live show wouldn't look rehearsed, and it would be less predictable and thus more interesting to the viewing audience. Finally, as hardly any of their competitors did live shows, *Higher Ground* would be more edgy and the show could be billed "Live with Dr. Grandison."

"We can even take live calls," she'd said. "Do you know how many people will watch and call in if they have the opportunity to talk to you directly?"

Still, Dwayne had thought it a better idea to wait until they had a few more shows under their belt before trying it. Maria, the show's production manager, sided with Beverlyn, noting that she'd done many live shows and all had gone well. L.W.'s approval had been the nail in the coffin, and with that, Dwayne had bowed to the team's experience.

"We'll still plan down to the minute and scrutinize every caller, but that's part of the excitement." Beverlyn paused before adding, "I'm convinced this live format will make the show even greater."

Now, as Maria barked directions and the camera and the lighting crew conducted sound and video checks, Dwayne sat in the makeup chair, reviewing the last-minute script changes and guest introductions.

"Maria, what is this?" Dwayne held up the page.

She rushed to the chair and looked at the paper. "Oh, we had a last-minute substitution. Reverend Powell will be here instead of Pastor Williams."

"Why?" Dwayne asked sharply. "I don't know anything about this Reverend Powell."

"Well, Pastor Williams called with an emergency. We were fortunate to get this fill-in because he's a friend of L.W.'s."

"Maria, look at this sheet. There's no information on this guy. How am I supposed to interview him?" He stopped. "He can't be part of the show."

"I thought it was all there." Maria flipped through the pages to the last stapled sheet.

"What's he supposed to talk about?"

"Let me see what I can find out." Maria dashed off.

Dwayne went back to the script and continued his review of the background information on the other guests. Everything else was complete; just Reverend Powell's information was sketchy. All he could see was that the Reverend Andrew Powell was an evangelist who lived in Los Angeles. That was all. No church information. No personal facts.

"Tori, get Beverlyn on the line, please," Dwayne said to his assistant.

"No need; here she comes."

Dwayne watched Beverlyn's approach in the mirror. Tori whispered something in her ear, and a moment later, Beverlyn walked over to Dwayne.

"Good morning." She spoke to his reflection. "Tori said you wanted me," she said seductively.

"Give me a second." He turned to his makeup man, then back to Beverlyn. "Did you know there's been a change in the guest schedule?"

Beverlyn shrugged slightly. "No, but that shouldn't be a problem."

"Well, this show is kind of different, Beverlyn, being our first live show. Not only do I not know this Reverend—"

"Dwayne, you really don't know any of the guests."

"But we always have background information. I don't even know what this guy's expertise is. I'll look like an idiot."

Beverlyn glanced at the paper. "He's an evangelist."

"So what's he doing to add to the subject of family secrets?"

"Who booked him?"

"L.W."

"Well, then, Reverend Powell must be okay. L.W. would only book someone who's good for the show."

Her words did little to soothe him. He'd never liked the idea of a live show, but he chalked his reaction up to nervousness and relaxed with Beverlyn's assurances that everything would be fine. Now Dwayne took a deep breath and held the back of the makeup chair, silently praying that he would make it through the next forty-seven minutes. Then he headed onto the hotly lit set.

The applause lights flashed and the camera zoomed in on Dwayne.

"Hello, I'm Dr. Dwayne Grandison and welcome to *Higher Ground*."

The applause from the 112 audience members continued, and Dwayne tugged at the bottom of his suit, straightening it. He glanced again at the sheets on the small table in front of him and took another breath before the floor director gave him the signal.

"Family secrets. Are there secrets in your family that have remained hidden because you're afraid that if they were exposed, your family would be destroyed? The Bible says that we bring to light the hidden things of darkness. That's what we're here to discuss today: freedom from the bondage of secrets tucked away."

Camera one slowly pulled back from Dwayne, giving a view of the entire stage with the five other purple suede chairs, lined up next to his.

"Help me welcome today's guests. First, Tanya Roberts is a woman who has held a secret from her family. And though Tanya has not come here to reveal this secret, she wants to discuss steps to take to begin the healing process. Please welcome Tanya Roberts."

The applause lights flashed and the studio audience cooperated.

"Next," Dwayne continued, "we have Christopher Johnson and his wife, Joan. Christopher says that a family secret, hidden for twelve years, almost ripped them apart, but with prayers and guidance, they made it through the storm. Welcome the Johnsons."

Again, the crowd applauded.

"Please also welcome the Reverend Andrew Powell, who says that nothing should be kept in the dark . . ."

Dwayne paused, not knowing what else to say.

"Finally, welcome Murray Ladd." The applause started before Dwayne could continue. "You know him as the Self-Help Guru, but he prefers to be known as a simple man who loves God. Murray says that while it was a family secret that destroyed his family, it was through its revelation that he found the Lord."

Dwayne waited until Murray sat at the end of the stage and then said, "Welcome to all our guests.

"I'd like to start with Christopher and Joan. You say that a secret devastated your family, but you were able to stay together."

Christopher took his wife's hand. "Yes, but it was only through the power of God."

Joan nodded. "You see, I kept a secret from my husband for many years. Our second child . . ." She bowed her head. "I was never sure that our daughter was my husband's. I was tortured every day of her life. After she was in a terrible car accident and needed a transfusion, I had to face the truth."

She paused as the crowd moaned.

"But you weren't sure what the truth was?" Dwayne asked as he lifted his head from his notes.

"No," Joan continued. "We needed a DNA test to tell us."

"It was terrible." Her husband, Christopher, picked up the story. "But if it wasn't for that, I don't know if we would have found the Lord. We went to a Christian counselor—by accident, quite frankly—and he set us on the road to true recovery. We were saved, and it was only through praying that I was able to forgive my wife. And frankly, there were things she needed to forgive."

"I'd like to ask a question."

Their eyes turned to Reverend Powell.

A guest had never posed a question, but Dwayne didn't stop the preacher. "Yes, Reverend Powell."

"Mrs. Johnson, why did it take you twelve years to tell your husband?"

Tears came to Joan's eyes. "I was afraid. I didn't want to break up my family and I was afraid for my daughter. Christopher was the only father she'd known. What would her life be like if Christopher was not her father?"

But Reverend Powell shook his head. "That's what's wrong with this society." Dwayne took a glance at the reverend, marveling at how much he sounded like L.W. "The devil has such a stranglehold on us," he said, making a fist. "The devil controls through the fear inside of us that holds us hostage."

"I understand what you're saying, Reverend. That's why we're here. There are so many people like the Johnsons who want a way out, but in the natural, it can't be done."

The reverend shifted in his seat. "You should know," he mumbled.

Dwayne frowned and the wrinkles on his forehead deepened when he felt the wrenching in his stomach. He waited a beat, then said, "The question is, what kind of solution can we provide to those in need? The Johnsons prove that you can come out delivered and healed on the other side—but how do you get there?"

"By telling the truth," the reverend boomed through the studio. "The truth will set you free."

"That's why we're here," Dwayne said, feeling more discomfort with each of the reverend's words. "Murray, why don't you tell the audience your experiences?"

"Before you do that, Murray," the reverend said, turning and patting Murray on the arm, stopping him before he could start, "I'd like to ask the doctor a question."

A rumble began to rise through the audience.

Dwayne clenched his teeth and turned his head slightly. Through the curtains, he saw L.W. backstage. His wide smile made the muscles in Dwayne's stomach tighten even more.

"What would you like to add?" The question moved through Dwayne's lips in slow motion.

The reverend smiled and leaned forward in his seat, as if he were about to jump on his prey. "As a Christian, the best thing you can do, Doctor, is lead by example. Before you counsel anyone to tell their secrets, you must tell your own."

"Cut," Dwayne almost yelled, wanting to do what he'd done many times before—when the show was taped. The audience buzzed with both excitement and confusion, and the guests turned to him as if he had pertinent information.

"Reverend, this is not about me, but I can honestly say that I'm not harboring any secrets . . ."

"Oh, come on, Doctor." The reverend chuckled sarcastically. "Tell the world."

Dwayne leaned forward in his seat, glaring at Reverend Powell.

"Tell the world you're a homosexual!"

Dwayne wasn't sure if the gasps he heard were from his own throat or others. "Reverend, I don't know where you get your information, but that is not true."

"Doctor, not only is it true, but your lover is dying from AIDS. Are you also HIV-positive, Doctor?"

It was his professional training that kept Dwayne calm, though friction from the highly charged tensions mounting onstage spilled out into the studio audience. He clenched his fists and measured his options. He couldn't do what he felt like doing—jumping up and decking the reverend, which would surely thrust *Higher Ground* onto Jerry Springer turf.

Though the reverend's statements didn't deserve to be dignified with a response, he knew he couldn't allow the lies to stand, particularly not unchallenged. "Reverend, your statement is false, but we are not here to discuss my personal life. We are here to help—"

Reverend Powell interrupted, "Sean Wiley is your lover and he is dying of AIDS."

With that, murmurs from the audience escalated into full-scale disorder. Dwayne's head snapped back in surprise, but a moment later, he realized his reaction was a mistake.

"Look at him," the reverend charged. "You know I'm telling the truth."

Dwayne could feel eyes burning into him, waiting for his response. He cleared his throat.

"Reverend Powell—"

"Cut!" the floor director yelled, and the camera lights were turned off.

Dwayne blinked in confusion. "We are live. We can't cut."

The floor director looked at Dwayne, then dropped his eyes. "Those were the orders," he said, pointing to his earphones.

In just moments, a producer rushed the guests from the stage, while four others escorted the audience from the studio. Dwayne stood as if frozen in place.

The first thing he noticed was that no one looked at him directly. The second was that every part of his body was shaking. At least two minutes passed before he took a deep breath in an effort to calm himself. His eyes scanned the studio for Beverlyn or Kim, but he didn't see either of them. As the delirium continued, Dwayne searched until he found Maria.

"Who gave the orders to stop the show, and where's this Reverend Powell?" he demanded.

"Reverend Powell is gone," she said, dropping her hands to her sides. "And the cameraman told me the order to stop the show came from L.W. It's a mess now. The telephone lines are clogged . . ." She held her hands to her forehead. "I don't know what we're going to do." Maria turned and rushed toward an assistant who was screaming for her to answer a call.

Dwayne looked around. Just fifteen minutes had passed and the studio was now empty except for the production team. He gathered his papers. Maybe it was best to go back to his office. That's probably where Beverlyn had gone to handle damage control.

He left saying good-bye to no one. Teddy was waiting as soon as he got off the elevator. Without a word, Dwayne got into the car. He just wanted to go home, and as quickly as possible. He kept replaying the nightmare he'd just lived through over and over again. Who was Reverend Powell? Did he hate Sean? What was going on?

He felt a familiar stirring, and the image of L.W. sprang to his mind. He had something to do with it, but what? Surely, he wouldn't risk the reputation of the show or the network. No, L.W. wouldn't hurt the network that way.

But—Dwayne shook his head—L.W. had something to do with it. He felt it in his guts. And he would get to the bottom of this.

"He was outed on television," he heard Tori exclaim as she looked up and saw him returning and then abruptly cut the telephone call short. Her mouth had still been wide open as he cleared his throat and asked if Beverlyn had left a message for him.

"No, but I can call her office."

"No need. I just went and she's not there." He moved toward his office. "Have her call the moment she gets in."

He could feel Tori's burning stare as he walked past her desk. Surely, no one believed what the reverend had said.

The intercom buzzed and Tori announced that Lafayette was on line one.

Dwayne picked up the phone at once. "Lafayette."

"Dwayne, what's going on, man? People are saying you confessed on the air that you are gay."

Dwayne leaned back in his chair and closed his eyes. "I can't believe this. I consent to do the show live and some reverend I've never heard of—I don't know who this guy is—accuses me of being gay and involved with Sean. This is the most ridiculous thing I've ever heard. Man, I could kill somebody."

"Now, calm down, baby bro. Who knows this guy? What was he doing on your show?"

"I don't know, but I sure am going to find out. This is just crazy, man. None of this makes any sense. I still can't believe it. And this nut also announced that Sean has AIDS."

"Does he?"

"Yeah, but no one knew. He'd wanted to keep it private, fearing what would happen if word got out."

"Man, this is too much. What are you going to do? What's Beverlyn saying?"

"I can't seem to reach her."

"I always had a bad feeling about that show."

"I don't know, man, I just don't know. Will people really believe these lies?"

"Don't be naive. From the calls we've been getting here . . ."

The buzz of the intercom interrupted Lafayette.

"Laf, I have another call. I gotta call you back."

He didn't wait to hear his brother's response before he picked up the other line.

"Beverlyn."

"No, son."

Dwayne closed his eyes. "Mom. You saw the show?"

"What is going on? My phone hasn't stopped ringing."

"I'm not sure, Mom, but we'll handle this. I've really got to get back to you, though."

She was silent for a moment before she grudgingly agreed to let him call her back.

He buzzed Tori. "Have you found Ms. Boudreaux yet?"

"No, Dr. Grandison, but I'm overwhelmed out here. Newspapers are calling, all kinds of reporters . . . Do you want these messages?"

Why would the newspapers care about something like this? Dwayne wondered.

"Tori, take messages. I'm going to be out of the office for a few hours."

"Yes, Dr. Grandison. And if Ms. Boudreaux calls . . ."

"Tell her to call me on my cell."

A moment later, Dwayne noticed heads dropping—and no one making eye contact—as he walked past the other cubicles to the elevator. This was all a lie. Surely, the truth would come out and this would be no big deal in a few days. But as the elevator doors opened and he stepped in, he knew this was little more than a pipe dream.

# Chapter Thirty-Two

*B*everlyn searched the papers for at least the fortieth time, scanning the documented record of meetings, affidavits, and pictures. She carefully examined specific dates, wondering how many times she'd imagined Dwayne had been with Nina when he'd really been with Sean. She stopped midstream in thought. What was she thinking? Dwayne couldn't be gay. Neither, she thought, was Sean.

Turning to her uncle, she said, "Uncle Linson, are you sure?"

His face was solemn. "It appears so."

"I don't believe it." She threw the papers across the car seat. "This doesn't make sense. Where did Reverend Powell get this information?"

L.W. shrugged. "I don't know. When I confronted him, he handed me the folder and said he would pray for us."

"You know, right before the show," Beverlyn said, thinking back in her search for answers, "Dwayne asked me about this man. There was no fact sheet on him. How do you know him?"

"He's been a friend for many years."

"I've never heard you mention him."

L.W. coughed. "Well, maybe *friend* is too strong a word. Over the years, we've bumped into each other at various conferences and conventions. While I don't know him that well, I do know that he's a man of God who can be trusted."

"I don't know, Uncle Linson. This just doesn't add up."

L.W. looked at Beverlyn with sad eyes. "You have to face it, sweetheart," he said, taking her hand. "It's hard for me too. I don't know what effect all this will have on the show or the Jubilee Network, but for your sake, I'm glad the truth is out."

She crossed her arms. "I need to speak with Dwayne. I just can't believe this is happening. It can't be true." She reached for her cell phone.

"No." L.W. snatched the phone before she could finish dialing the number. He clicked the phone off and put it in his suit pocket. "Before we do anything, we have to carefully think this through," he said, his voice softening with each word as if he were considering her feelings.

"There's nothing to think about." She pushed the privacy button, and as the window opened, she called out, "Joseph, please take me back to the office."

"Never mind, Joseph." L.W. spoke over her words. "Just keep driving until I tell you otherwise."

"We should talk to Dwayne," Beverlyn suggested.

"After keeping so much secret from you, do you really think he will tell you the truth now?"

"You don't know Dwayne. Besides, I love him and I owe it to him to at least get his side of the story."

L.W. cringed at her words, but remained composed. "Beverlyn . . ." He stopped as if he didn't know how to break what he was about to say to her. "I never wanted to tell you this . . ." He stopped again.

"What?"

He looked down.

"Uncle Linson, you're scaring me. If there's something I should know, please tell me."

Finally, he turned to her, clasping her hands inside his. "I know for a fact that all of this is true." He looked away, his face twisted with pain.

Distress covered her face and L.W. hesitated, not sure he could say the final words. The sting had worked better than even he had planned, but how could he continue to hurt his niece? He had hoped the reverend's words would have been good enough. But if not, he'd been prepared with this story. It was the look on her face now that he wasn't prepared for. The words he was about to say would destroy her, but that couldn't deter him.

"Uncle Linson, what is it?" she asked, her voice almost trembling.

This was the perfect opening L.W. was hoping for.

"I never wanted to tell you this, but"—he took another breath as if he needed air—"I saw Dwayne and Sean together once at a restaurant."

"So they're friends. I've been out with them," Beverlyn protested, though L.W. didn't detect any real conviction in her voice.

"They were huddled together in a corner, hand in hand. It was . . . intimate."

"I don't believe it," Beverlyn said to herself, covering her mouth with her hand.

"I prayed that I misread the situation, so I confronted him," L.W. continued. "Of course, at first he denied it, but when I told him I'd seen the two of them together, he started stuttering like he did tonight and became very protective of Sean. That's why I acted the way I did at your house that night, and that's—if you remember clearly—why he left without a fight."

Beverlyn gasped as the words began to sink in, like pieces of a puzzle beginning to fit together.

"How could you not tell me?"

"I assumed wrongly that knowing I would speak to you, he would back off. That's what I was coming to tell you that night, but you were so upset with me, I was sure that you wouldn't believe me, so instead I went to him later and told him to back off."

Beverlyn turned away, staring out of the car's tinted window.

"Beverlyn, I need to ask you something. I know this is personal, but I need to know for your protection." He paused, but she didn't turn back to him. "Were you two ever intimate?"

None of your business, she wanted to yell, as L.W. hammered the final nail in her chest. But she simply shook her head, thinking of how close they'd come.

"Thank goodness." He slammed back into his seat. "At least, I don't have to be concerned about you coming down with AIDS."

"Uncle Linson," she moaned.

"I'm sorry, honey, but you're my first priority—you and the ministry. And we've got to think about the ministry. I know this is probably the most difficult thing you have had to face, but you need to think this thing through clearly.

"I know you don't want to hear this, but it's important to say. The ministry has to come first. We can't let the way we handle what just happened undermine the trust we've built in the loyal followers of the ministry and the Jubilee Network. We can't allow people to doubt who we are. We have to make it clear that we are not people who preach one thing and practice another.

"Besides, Beverlyn, think about it. Severing ties with Mr. Grandison and Sean Wiley is the only way to spare them further shame and embarrassment and end this nightmare. I know it's hard, but you've got to think clearly," he repeated himself. "As it stands, we'll have to do a huge PR effort. And, Beverlyn, you're going to have to trust me on this one and let me do the fighting for you."

I have no fight left, she thought, continuing to stare out of the window. "I want to go home," she said, suddenly feeling sick. When she turned to address him, her eyes were glassy with tears. He took her in his arms and held her as he'd done so many times before.

"I'm sorry, Beverlyn, but we are going to make it through. But we'll have to work quickly. There is so much on the line."

That, Beverlyn did understand. The ministry was the fulfillment of all her childhood dreams. It was where she was at her best. People counted on her and she thrived on the interaction, not just for what it brought her but for what it gave them in the view she shared of herself as a vessel of God. She reveled in the role and validation it brought her.

Their business side gave them a lifestyle they could never have imagined—the cars, private planes . . . the money. But at that very moment, none of that seemed important. She closed her eyes, dissolving into tears.

Beverlyn kicked her shoes off at the door as L.W. continued to talk about the best way to handle the situation. For a time, she'd tuned him out, replaying the moments she'd shared with Dwayne.

L.W. rambled on. There would be an announcement to the press distancing the network from Dwayne. A statement proclaiming that they had been unaware of Dwayne Grandison's sexuality and that his behavior and lifestyle were not in line with the spiritual and/or moral fiber of Beverlyn Boudreaux Ministries.

Beverlyn stood and walked to the bar, scanning the beverages that lined the shelf until her eyes rested on the bottle of cognac L.W. had brought her from a trip he'd taken to France.

L.W. looked at her and celebrated inside. But his veneer remained sober. "We should call a press conference ASAP. I'll work with Daisy in marketing and we'll have a statement prepared for you in the morning."

She took a sip and grimaced as the cognac scorched her throat. Maybe it would burn her vocal cords away and she'd never have to speak again.

"When you speak tomorrow, you have to be calm, unemotional, and unattached. Dwayne Grandison was just an employee who fooled you and everyone else; the Jubilee Network will continue in spite of him, and Beverlyn Boudreaux Ministries will move forward in the spirit of what we've set out to do for God."

Beverlyn let L.W. ramble on, talking about security to keep Dwayne away, meetings with lawyers to review contracts and offset any impending lawsuits that could rise from the fallout.

Finally, L.W. said, "The most important thing, Beverlyn, is that you stay away from Dwayne. We don't know who's watching, and this thing is bigger than you, and bigger than what you thought you had with Dwayne. We employ hundreds who will lose their jobs if this isn't handled correctly. Then there are the children you're committed to helping with the success of this venture."

He watched her through intense eyes. "You'll also have to steer clear of Sean Wiley."

Almost oblivious to what he was saying, Beverlyn looked at the clock. It was almost six. Hard to believe so many hours had passed since this nightmare had begun.

"Beverlyn, did you hear me?"

"Uncle Linson, I need some time alone."

He was startled by her words. He couldn't leave now. He wanted to make sure she was all right. To keep check on her actions and ensure that nothing interfered with his smoothly executed scheme.

"Honey, you don't need to be alone."

"Please, L.W.," she said, leading the way to the front door.

After a brief pause, he gathered up his jacket and his papers and reluctantly moved toward the front door. He leaned forward to kiss her, but she stopped him.

"Good night, Uncle Linson."

He backed up, hurt that she was pushing him away, even if temporarily.

"I'll see you in the morning," he said, quickly recovering. "There's no need for you to use your car for the next few days. I want to be with you in case any reporters try to contact or harass you."

"Okay."

She opened the front door, and without another word, he walked out. Beverlyn closed the door the moment his foot hit the porch, and she rushed to the bathroom, the place that since childhood had always been where she'd go to think, and to keep anyone from seeing her cry. The day's events passed through her mind like a video in fast-forward. She recalled the look on Dwayne's face when Reverend Powell mentioned Sean's name. It was a look of recognition, mixed with surprise, as if he were relieved the truth had been uncovered. She leaned against the sink and began to sob uncontrollably.

Her insides cringed as she thought of the many kisses they'd shared. What could it have meant? Was he bisexual? Or was he simply using her, like so many other men had, to try to get his name in lights? By the time the ache rose to her throat, she had already turned to the toilet.

*       *       *

L.W. pulled out his cell phone the moment he opened the guest-house door. He dialed Kim's private cell, which was picked up on the first ring.

"Kim, did you disconnect the phones in the main house as I directed?"

"Yes," she said reluctantly.

"Turn them back on tomorrow while we're at the press conference. I'll call you with the time."

"As you wish."

"Has Andrew Powell left the city?" L.W. asked.

"Done," Kim reported. "In fact, everything's done. You pulled it off," she said in a tone that reflected her distaste.

"Kim, do we have a problem here?" L.W. had become annoyed with her tone.

"No, we don't. Everything has been done as you instructed."

L.W. pressed the "end" button and leaned back in the recliner. It took months to plan, and now that he was in the middle of Dwayne's fall, it didn't feel as good as he had thought it would. It was Beverlyn's face that stole his joy. He hated that she was so hurt, but in a few weeks, she'd be fine. And Dwayne Grandison would be gone from their lives.

He pulled Beverlyn's cell from his pocket. It would be a while before his niece noticed her missing phone. He clicked it on and grimaced. Just as he thought, Dwayne's number appeared as the last missed call.

He returned the phone to his pocket. There was still a lot of work to do.

# Chapter Thirty-Three

The moment Dwayne walked through the front door, his phone was ringing. He closed his eyes and said a quick prayer that it was Beverlyn. Instead, it was a reporter from the *Los Angeles Herald* wanting a statement regarding his relationship with Sean. The thought alone seemed so foreign to him that he angrily slammed the phone down without saying a word.

As he tried to unwind, the phone rang again. He answered after recognizing the number on his Caller ID display.

"Hey, Laf," Dwayne said, trying to sound more up than he had in their earlier conversation.

"It's me, Dwayne," Robbie said. "Are you all right?"

"Hey. I'm still trying to figure it out."

"Lafayette and I were talking. We want you to stay with us for a few days."

"I'm not sure that's necessary. I'm hoping this will blow over."

"I don't think you understand the impact, Dwayne," Lafayette interjected from the extension. "I believe this is part of a major effort to ruin you."

"But who and why . . ."

"I don't know."

"Listen, let me get back to you. I've got to sort some things out."

The phone rang as soon as he set down the receiver. He was about to let it roll over to voice mail when he recognized the number as Nina's. He was hoping that she hadn't seen the show but was glad she was calling to check on him.

"Nina."

"Dwayne, are you okay?"

"Dazed would be the operative word," Dwayne said, relieved that he could finally share this nightmare with someone who knew that the revelations contained little truth. "I can't believe what's happened." He paused. "I haven't been able to catch up with Beverlyn, and Lafayette seems to think this is part of some grand scheme. Did you see the show?"

"No, but I've been getting call after call—from some of the women and the people at church."

"Oh, no . . ."

"Don't worry, all the calls have been from people on your side. None of them believe a word of this."

He doubted that and said nothing, contemplating the notion of always having to address the question of whether or not he was gay. Always wondering who had believed this trumped-up story.

"Please assure everyone that none of what they saw on TV was true and that I am grateful for their concern."

"I will."

"What gets me is that this only happened this morning. How could so many people know already?"

"Bad news travels fast," Nina said with the authority of one who'd gone through it.

"Yeah, but it's not like I'm some big celebrity . . ."

"Maybe you're bigger than you think. Besides, it happened on live TV and cameras were able to capture the shock on your face. And the lies—well, they make for great sound bites, which is what drives the ratings way up for the network news. I've seen it replayed on at least three news stations. These people have no shame. It's just a story to them." She paused. "Do you want to get together and talk?"

"Thanks, Nina. I'd like that, but let me get back to you. I need to handle some things first."

"Remember, Dwayne, I'm just a phone call away—any hour of the day or night. And Dwayne, the truth will come out."

Though still restless—the adrenaline running rampant throughout him—Dwayne was somewhat hopeful as he hung up the phone from Nina. He sat on the bed and took a deep breath. There was another call he had to make. He didn't know what he would say, but he dialed the number anyway. He tried every number, but like Beverlyn, Sean was missing. Dwayne couldn't even reach his assistant.

Leaning back against the headboard, Dwayne closed his eyes. "Why is this happening?" he said aloud. He covered his face with his hands, but the ringing phone took him from his meditation. Wanting to keep the line open for Beverlyn—and Sean—he'd resisted the temptation to snatch the cords from the wall.

Two more hours passed before Dwayne could take no more. The phone had not stopped ringing, and neither Beverlyn nor Sean had called. He threw on his jacket and marched out, driving around aimlessly before finally ending up at Lafayette's.

"Lafayette, it's your brother," Robbie said, opening the front door. "Come on in." She welcomed him with arms stretched wide. "We've been so worried about you."

"Hey, man." Lafayette extended a hearty embrace.

"I needed to get out. The phone hasn't stopped ringing. I was trying to keep the line open for Beverlyn and Sean, but I haven't heard from either of them."

"Let's go in here," Lafayette suggested, and the two retreated into the den to talk.

For the next two hours, they alternated between going over what had happened, praying, reflecting, and sitting in silence. By the time Dwayne returned home at midnight, he was exhausted both mentally and physically.

Still, there was no call from either Beverlyn or Sean. He sifted through the mess he'd created earlier, undressed, and then reflected on the scripture that Lafayette had left him with: *"The effectual fervent prayer of a righteous man availeth much."*

He got down on his knees and prayed.

Ten minutes later, he turned off the light and laid his head on the pillow, but he could get no sleep. Instead, all he could do was think of Beverlyn and Sean. He knew Sean would know that he hadn't betrayed his confidence, but he was still concerned about his friend professionally. About what it would mean to his career.

He turned over on his side.

Could Beverlyn have believed what Reverend Powell had said? He kept telling himself no, but as the hours had passed without a word from her, he wasn't so sure.

Though mentally exhausted, Dwayne tossed and turned throughout the night, only really falling asleep at about three-thirty. Less than three hours later, as the morning sun began to peek through his windows, Dwayne was up—eager to set the record straight and to find out what exactly had happened and on what side of the fence everyone stood.

In the bathroom, he allowed the steaming water from the dual showerheads to pulsate against his skin. By the time he dried himself off, he was rejuvenated and determined that by the end of the day, he'd have answers to all his questions. He was fully dressed when the phone rang, and he picked up when he recognized the number.

"Monique?"

"Dwayne, I'm sorry to call you so early, but I just got a call from Mr. Daley. He says the office building has been overrun by reporters . . ."

"I don't believe this."

"They've been camped out since yesterday. Building security held them back so I could get out, but Mr. Daley said that reporters have contacted him and are asking all kinds of questions, especially about Sean."

Dwayne fell back onto his bed. "So now Sean is the story," he said, finally making sense of the insatiable appetite the media were demonstrating for the story.

"Must be. They've asked Mr. Daley questions like had he ever seen the two of you together and . . ." She paused.

Dwayne closed his eyes. "Go on."

". . . if he'd known that you two were lovers," Monique whispered, as if saying the words softly would make them less painful.

"Well, do they know that Mr. Daley is just the landlord?"

"Dwayne, I don't think they care. I'm so sorry for all of this."

"So am I, Monique." He stood. "Okay, this is what we have to do.
Before I do anything, I've got to find out what's happening with
Sean."

"Do you want me to call him?" Monique inquired, matching the
renewed energy she heard in her boss's voice.

"No, I'll find him. Secondly, you and I should stay away from the
office for a day or two. I don't trust the newspapers and we can't give
them anything—not even a photo—that they can find a way to
twist."

"Gotcha. I'll reschedule your appointments, but how should I
handle the questions?"

Dwayne paced the length of his bedroom. "Tell anyone who asks
that I will meet with them next week and personally answer any of
their questions. I'll give you a call in a couple of hours to update you
on what's left to be done."

Dwayne hung up the phone and shrugged his jacket from his
shoulders. He rolled up his shirtsleeves, but as he reached for the
phone, the concierge intercom buzzed through the apartment.

Dwayne couldn't remember the last time the morning concierge
had called him. Perhaps reporters were downstairs as well.

"Yes, Samuel," he answered.

"Dr. Grandison, Mr. Linson Lejohn is here to see you. He says it's
urgent."

"Send him right up," Dwayne said without hesitation, though his
hand shook from the returning anger of the day before as he returned the intercom phone to its hook on the wall. *Finally, I'll get to
the bottom of this nightmare,* he thought—still reasoning that L.W.
had played a key role.

The idea of L.W. coming to his home did not appeal to him, but
at the same time, Dwayne was desperate for answers and news of
Beverlyn. He thought back to the image of L.W. behind the stage as

Reverend Powell began his attack. When the elevator doors parted, the look on L.W.'s face confirmed his suspicions.

Like a lion about to devour his kill, L.W stepped from the elevator into the impressive entry hall to Dwayne's condominium, scanning the elegance of the circular foyer and the massive living room before he looked Dwayne squarely in the face.

Realizing that L.W. had not come with answers, but instead to perhaps deliver a final blow, Dwayne cut to the chase. "What is this about, L.W.?"

"I thought that would be obvious. It's about the embarrassment you've caused the Jubilee Network and Beverlyn Boudreaux Ministries."

"You know better than that, L.W., " Dwayne said angrily.

L.W. cleared his throat. The doctor had caught on, he thought. Well, so what? He had the upper hand now.

"There is no way we can move forward with what we've planned—"

Dwayne cut him off. "Why do I feel like you had something to do with this?"

"We only need to discuss your resignation and the terms of agreement." L.W. was determined not to get off track.

Dwayne slammed his fist on the marble table, wincing slightly in pain, but the brief uncertainty he saw in L.W.'s eyes made the angry gesture worthwhile. "I will not resign and make it easy for you, L.W. If you want to get rid of me, you'll have to fire me."

L.W. took another step away from Dwayne but kept his eyes plastered to his. "That can be arranged."

"I have a contract, L.W."

"One that includes a morality clause, and with your lifestyle, we have a right to exercise our option to terminate your contract."

"Well, we'll just see what my lawyers have to say about that."

It was now L.W. who was being caught off guard. There was a moment of silence before L.W. said, "The truth is out about you. Why would you want to do my niece and the Jubilee Network any more harm with this scandal?"

"There wasn't a shadow of truth in Reverend Powell's words. You know it, I know it, and believe me, a court case isn't the sort of thing you want, L.W., because I'll win."

"Really? Are you telling me that Sean Wiley doesn't have AIDS?"

"I'm surprised at you, L.W. There is a religious saying: 'The devil will flood you with the truth just to float one lie.' You know very well that Sean does have AIDS, but the lie is that neither of us is gay and you know it. The problem for you, L.W., is that you had the contract with me."

L.W. couldn't believe his ears. The good doctor was still giving him a fight. "As long as part of it's true"—L.W. smirked—"it's enough to bring a cloud over you, Mr. Grandison. Believe me, there's enough doubt to have people debating your sexuality for a long time. If you're a real man, do you really want that, and why should Beverlyn—whom you claim to love—have to endure it?"

With that, L.W. proceeded to remove an envelope from a small shopping bag he held. "It is in the best interest of everyone for you to sign the letter of resignation in this envelope." He laid the yellow envelope on the foyer table. "There's some other papers in there you need to review as well. Of course, you no longer have access to our driver or credit cards or any of the other perks you squeezed out."

L.W. turned toward the elevator, then suddenly turned back to Dwayne. "We would prefer to have you resign, though it would be more fun for me to terminate you." He paused, letting his words sink in. "So it's up to you. Return the resignation letter to us within twenty-four hours."

He pushed the button to the elevator, then continued, "And send the letter by messenger. A security company has been hired to make sure you don't get anywhere near the premises. Oh—" He turned back. "Don't worry about your things. This afternoon we'll send over your belongings."

Dwayne's eyes narrowed. "Were you that threatened that my relationship with Beverlyn would leave you out in the cold?" When L.W. didn't respond, he continued, "I wonder what Beverlyn would think if she knew what you've done."

Through clenched teeth, L.W. cautioned, "Don't even think about it."

"Do you really think you're going to get away with this?" Dwayne steamed. "By the time I hunt down Reverend Powell and tell Beverlyn and the world about you, you'll be as worthless as I already know you are."

L.W. kept his cool, though he couldn't help but wonder if he had underestimated Dwayne Grandison. But even facing the rage in Dwayne's eyes, L.W. remained steadfast. "You can attack me if you wish." His voice was barely above a whisper. "Make my story more believable."

"Get out of my home, L.W." Dwayne charged toward him as L.W. stepped back into the hall. Dwayne's fist shook above his shoulder like a ripple of waves through the sea. But suddenly, a calm moved over him and he slowly lowered his hand. In that moment, Dwayne saw L.W.'s guts in his eyes. He was staring straight at evil.

"Get out," he commanded once more.

"Gladly." L.W. chuckled as if he had no fear, then stepped into the elevator. Just as the doors began to close, L.W. put his hands between them, holding them open. "One last thing, Mr. Grandison. You'll also find a restraining order inside that envelope. So don't try to contact or go anywhere near my niece."

Dwayne watched the door close. Turning back into his condo, his eyes fell almost immediately on the package. With slow steps, he walked toward the table, staring at the golden envelope. It was thicker than he'd thought, and when he lifted it, he could tell a videotape was inside. He returned to the living room and opened it. He pulled the tape out first, then two smaller envelopes.

In the first envelope, just as L.W. had promised, was the resignation letter. It was addressed to the board of directors of Beverlyn Boudreaux Ministries. He glanced through the letter, focusing in on several key phrases: *apologize for the embarrassment I have caused the Jubilee Network . . . my personal life has affected my ability to perform as host of* Higher Ground *. . . relieve Beverlyn Boudreaux Ministries and the Jubilee Network of any legal liabilities.*

His name was typed on the bottom, and there was a space for his signature. Tossing the letter aside, Dwayne now turned his attention to the other document. His eyes scanned the restraining order. Having known what it was before he opened it had lessened the hurt.

It was all very predictable. *Dr. Dwayne Grandison is restricted from . . . home, work, or any other place where Beverlyn Boudreaux may frequent . . .* There was the legal terminology that told him how far away he would have to stay. *All contact is prohibited: telephone, postal . . .* At the bottom was a declaration that the temporary restraining order had been registered with the local police.

Dwayne held his head in his hands and asked himself the question he'd repeated at least a million times: How could this be happening? And how could Beverlyn do this without talking to him? Without asking his side? It didn't make sense.

"There is no way Beverlyn knows what L.W. is doing," he said suddenly. He was about to pick up the telephone when the video caught his eye. Hoping it carried clues, he inserted it into the VCR and pushed the play button, then sat on the edge of the couch. It took him less than a minute to realize it was not what he had expected.

"This is a very sad day for Beverlyn Boudreaux Ministries and for myself personally." Beverlyn stood in the center of the screen, absent her usual flamboyant attire of brightly colored chiffon or vivid silk sheaths. For this appearance, she was dressed in a conservative navy high-collar suit with gold buttons. She spoke into a bank of microphones, and when the camera panned back, Dwayne could tell that she was in the studio conference room. He wondered whom she was speaking to.

"We are not here to judge either Dr. Grandison or Sean . . ."

Dwayne flinched at the mention of his friend's name. This was painful enough for him, but what this would do to Sean's career made him shudder.

"As you know, our network holds our employees to high personal and professional standards. Mr. Wiley has been a mainstay at my conferences and crusades across the nation, and Dr. Grandison was a new associate who joined our staff recently . . ."

So that's what I've been demoted to, Dwayne thought.

"However, while I and everyone at Beverlyn Boudreaux Ministries

respect both Dr. Grandison and Mr. Wiley, with the recent revelations concerning their choice of a personal lifestyle, a choice which
is contrary to the standards and values we preach, with sincere regret we announce the termination of our professional relationship
with both gentlemen."

Though he was watching her lips move, he couldn't believe what
she was saying.

"It is important to note that we've accepted the resignation of Dr.
Grandison, and Mr. Wiley will no longer be performing with our
crusades."

Anger and shock overwhelmed Dwayne's thoughts, as he still
couldn't believe what he'd just heard. With each word, he became
more and more convinced that Beverlyn was part of the decision.
But how, he wondered, could L.W. have gotten her to go along? Still,
the tape held the truth. Beverlyn may not have been a contributor
to his setup, but she was certainly a big part of his downfall.

"While we do not stand in judgment, our company's principles
take us in a completely different direction from what Dr. Grandison
and Mr. Wiley believe . . ."

"What are you talking about?" Dwayne yelled at the large-screen
television.

What kind of relationship did we have? he asked himself, becoming more astonished with each word. He had opened his heart
to her. She should have respected him enough at least to talk to
him.

"In closing," he heard Beverlyn say, "while this is a disheartening
setback, we see this as a forecast of a bright future for Beverlyn
Boudreaux Ministries and for the Jubilee Network, which will continue to do well in the coming years. Thank you for your attention."

Beverlyn gazed solemnly into the center camera as the screen
faded to black. Using the remote, he turned off the television. This
morning he had prayed that this day would bring answers. He
glanced at the grandfather clock that had been in Yvette's family for
three generations. It was just ten o'clock, but his prayers had indeed
been answered.

Armed with the answers, all that remained was what he was going to do. Now that he knew the enemy, defining his battle plan would be much easier. He lifted his legs, stretching them forward onto the table, and closed his eyes. He'd take a quick catnap, he thought, as the sleep that had resisted him last night conquered him now.

# Chapter Thirty-Four

*B*everlyn twisted in her chair, turning to face the window. There were stacks of messages to respond to, yet she'd done nothing but stare out of the window. It had been that way ever since she had taped her statement to the press. When she heard the insistent door chimes and rushed down the stairs, she was aware of feeling hopeful that Dwayne was at her door, and that somehow everything could go back to how it was—or how she believed it was.

When she opened the door to find L.W., she'd wondered if there would be any end to the nightmare that had ambushed her hopes and dreams for a personal kind of fulfillment she had never known.

L.W. had been up all night with the advisers who'd determined that the best way to thwart reporters, minimize the risk of damage to the network, and relieve some of the emotional distress she was under was to produce a pretaped video of Beverlyn's press statement. The taping had been set for 6:00 A.M. Pacific time, which made it nine o'clock on the East Coast.

She read the statement as she rode to the office, protesting the termination of Dwayne and Sean without talking to them. But L.W. assured her it was the only way to avoid further scandal. "Beverlyn," he'd cautioned, "the media will be hot on this thing. If anyone catches you with Dwayne or Sean, it will ruin us."

Kim, too, had only reluctantly agreed, all the while wondering why Beverlyn couldn't see through the act. But she, too, had been caught up in the snare. Perhaps it was time to look for another job.

"What if these are all lies?" Beverlyn pressed, still not quite sure of what to believe.

"Beverlyn, we went over it all last night. I told you how I confronted Dwayne. It's true whether you want to believe it or not. We cannot take a chance with our company. Too many people will be destroyed if we don't handle this right."

Beverlyn's gaze dropped to her hand and the four-carat diamond ring that she'd had specially designed. On one wrist were two tennis bracelets that sparkled brightly, and on the other was a Rolex—her casual one. Her uncle was right: Many would be affected if Beverlyn Boudreaux was involved in a scandal, but most affected would be the two of them.

L.W., riding in the back of the Lincoln Continental limousine he'd just recently purchased, was at least dressed for the occasion, looking impeccable in the three-thousand-dollar handmade suit he'd flown to Milan to have specially made by Paul Zaleri. When he asked if Dwayne had tried to contact her, she'd been unable to look into his eyes.

L.W. had struck a nerve. At the very least, she thought, Dwayne could have called to explain, and, yes, it did mean something that he hadn't, though she wasn't sure what. L.W. had surmised that perhaps Dwayne hadn't wanted to compromise her any further. That he knew the best thing for him to do was to stay away.

She wondered then, as she wondered now, if that was what Dwayne was doing. She didn't understand it. Surely, he knew they needed to talk. Maybe he was embarrassed. Or—her heart sank—he had used her and deceived her like no one ever had. Now he was deserting her, just as she always feared he would.

The light knock startled her as she faced the door.

L.W. laid a sheet on her desk. "I wanted to give you a list of where the tapes were sent."

Beverlyn scanned the listing. "Do you think all of these people care?"

"Because Sean is involved, this is big news."

Beverlyn felt sadder at the mention of his name. "I wish I could talk to him. If he has AIDS, he needs his friends."

L.W. leaned on the side of the desk. "Beverlyn, you are not his friend. You've got to get back to thinking like a businesswoman." He took her face into his hands. "Please, I'm counting on you."

Tears streamed down her face. They were the first since she vowed not to cry last night. As L.W. rushed to comfort her, she tried to compose herself, swallowing the lump in her throat.

"Okay." She nodded as if she were making a pact with herself. "Don't worry anymore, Uncle Linson. I know what I have to do."

"That's my girl."

She forced herself to return his smile. "Thanks for everything."

"There's nothing to thank me for, sweetheart. I'm just doing what I have to do."

As L.W. walked out the door, Beverlyn decided it was time to stop wallowing in this real-life drama. It was getting obvious to her that Dwayne had moved on. Now it was time for her to do the same.

Awakened by the intercom buzzer, Dwayne sat up straight.

"Dr. Grandison, Pastor Grandison is on his way up."

By the time Dwayne returned the intercom receiver to its hook and retrieved the package from his tabletop to put it back together, Lafayette was walking off the elevator.

"You look a mess, baby bro," Lafayette kidded.

"I dozed off for a while. What time is it?"

"Noon, man."

Dwayne returned to the position he'd been in before the buzzer awakened him. "Still getting calls?"

"Yeah." Lafayette leaned back on the couch. "I can't believe the interest in this story. Did I say that I saw you on the news last night?"

Dwayne grimaced.

"So have you figured out what this is all about?"

"Didn't have to. Linson Lejohn came to see me this morning," he said, handing Lafayette the package.

"Are you telling me this man planned the whole thing?" Lafayette began to read the letter.

"That's right. Pretty good job too."

"But why?"

"The way I see it, he never liked me, and when I got involved with Beverlyn, I became a threat. I knew this man was scum, but I underestimated the depth."

"How did he find out about Sean's having AIDS?" Lafayette looked up from the papers briefly.

"No idea. But it's Sean I'm most worried about."

Lafayette gave a long, low whistle as he read the resignation letter and restraining order. "This man doesn't play."

"Then again, he might have underestimated me." Dwayne smiled, holding a microcassette in his hand.

"What's that?"

"I taped L.W.'s conversation. He doesn't come right out and admit he was behind this scheme, but even an idiot would be able to connect the dots after listening to it."

"All right!" he exclaimed, extending his hand to high-five his brother. "So what's the plan?"

"I'm not sure." He paused and stood, walking past his brother to the view. "More importantly, I realize now that I had a lot to do with what happened. This is what happens when you go after the wrong things."

Lafayette remained silent. Many times in the last few months, he wanted to go to his brother and warn him.

"I got too caught up," Dwayne continued. "The money I was making had become just as important as God. I gave up the men's fellowship at New Covenant so I could make more money. Then I started spending it in ways that weren't really me."

"This happens to so many people. They get financial and material blessings mixed up with God's real plan for their lives."

"It's a thin line, isn't it?"

"It is because God wants to bless," Lafayette explained. "But He makes it clear when Jesus says, *But seek ye first the kingdom of God, and his righteousness; and all these things shall be added unto you.* That scripture gives us a formula. What comes first and then what comes next."

"Well, my mind is clear now."

"And things will work out for the best. You've learned an important lesson."

"Yeah, but at what cost?"

They sat in silence for several moments before Lafayette rose and said, "C'mon, there's something I want you to see."

"Where are we going? I'm not up to seeing people."

"Relax. Get your jacket."

At one o clock in the afternoon, they pulled into Lafayette's driveway. Dwayne didn't recognize the car in the drive.

"Whose car is that?"

"Clarence Milsap's. After seeing the news last night, I gave him a call and he agreed to meet with you today."

Dwayne hadn't thought of Clarence Milsap, an elder at New Covenant Assembly, who had been a much-decorated police detective. Now retired, he did private work for members of the church.

"I didn't know how you'd want to follow up, so I thought the two of you should talk."

Dwayne nodded in agreement. But as they walked inside, it became all too clear that the real surprise had little to do with Elder Milsap. Sitting silently, with full smiles, were Robbie and their four children, his mother, Nina, Monique, and Elder Milsap, and standing next to the fireplace was Sean.

"This is a different kind of family council, son." Bernice walked toward him, drawing him into her warm, full embrace. "The people who love you most have gathered to show our support for you, to pray with you, to let you know that all is well, and to remind you that we will not allow you to go through this alone."

Overwhelmed, Dwayne shook his head in disbelief.

"Well," said Lafayette, "let's get this party started. You know the boy probably hasn't eaten."

The children cheered and rushed to their uncle. Robbie followed with a kiss before disappearing into the kitchen. Then Dwayne turned back to his mother.

"I'm proud of you, son."

Dwayne thought about what his family had endured over the last twenty-four hours. But here they all were, full of love and support. He hugged his mother tightly.

Monique came to him next.

"Hey, kiddo," he said. He could tell that she'd been crying.

"Dwayne, I'm sorry that I didn't handle things well in the office."

"What are you talking about?"

She blinked in confusion. "Lafayette didn't tell you?" She lowered her eyes. "Some of your clients want to cancel their appointments— permanently."

He squeezed her hand. "Don't worry about it. We're going to be fine. There are clients who will stay, clients who will leave, and new clients who will come. Everything is in God's hands."

"Well, I really admire your faith. I don't know if, in your position, I would feel the same. I suspect that man L.W. has something to do with this," Monique said, sniffing back tears. "I knew there was something not right about him or his niece. I just knew it."

"No matter what, we will get through this. All of this . . . with God."

They hugged and she headed for the kitchen. Then he turned to Nina, who, without saying a word, put her arms around his neck. He had forgotten how good she felt in his arms and he held her longer than he knew he should.

"How are you, Dwayne?"

"Better now."

"You have good friends, Dwayne, because you're a good friend. And I think there's a friend over there who is very anxious to speak to you." Nina motioned in the direction of Sean, who had not moved since Dwayne had walked into the room.

Dwayne kissed Nina's cheek and walked across the room, stopping in front of the fireplace.

"How are you, my friend?" Dwayne said. The two men hugged.

Dwayne couldn't help but notice his friend's pallor and that he seemed to be thinner than just a month before.

"Will anyone miss us if we take a walk?" Sean asked.

Dwayne looked around the room. "I think we can sneak out for a moment."

He led Sean toward the back of the house, but by the time they walked into the yard, Sean said, "Let's just stay here."

Dwayne's high spirits dissipated, noticing that his friend was short of breath as he pointed toward the patio chairs and they sat.

Sean felt Dwayne's stare and met his gaze. "It's started, Dwayne."

"I suspected that when you didn't show up for Beverlyn's New York Crusade."

Sean nodded. "Well, I won't have to worry about missing any more of her crusades. My long-standing invitation has been withdrawn."

"You've heard from Beverlyn?" There was hope in his tone.

"Not a word. But I got an earful from L.W."

"He paid you a visit as well?"

"Yup." Sean leaned back in his chair. "L.W. met me in the hospital this morning, right before I checked out. Did you get the videotape?"

"Yeah, and a few other things. I can't believe that man."

"I'm not surprised," Sean said. "I knew he would try to take me down. I'm just sorry he pushed you off the cliff with me."

"I'm the one who's sorry. I know how hard you've worked to keep your private life out of the news."

"Maybe this was God's way of showing us that was the wrong move," Sean said. "You know the saying, the truth will set you free."

Dwayne just sat, saying nothing.

"I've called a press conference for tomorrow at noon, Dwayne. I'd like you to be there for support. Perhaps I can turn this around and show people how to live through all kinds of challenges with the grace of God."

"You got it, man. I wouldn't miss it for the world."

Sean began coughing. As the seconds passed and his cough intensified, Dwayne jumped from the chair and knelt at his friend's side.

"What can I do?"

Still coughing, Sean shook his head. Finally, he sat up slowly and Dwayne waited until his breathing steadied before he returned to his chair.

"How bad is it, Sean?"

He was silent for a moment. "Let's just say I couldn't have sung at a crusade if Beverlyn had asked me to—at least not for a while."

"I'm sorry, man."

"So what about you, Dwayne?"

"I'm not sure yet. I want revenge, and at the same time, I want to cut my losses. I recorded my conversation with L.W., but I'm not sure what to do with it."

Sean began coughing again—a dry hack that made Dwayne cringe. Dwayne resisted the urge to touch his friend—to pat him on the back or just hold him. Instead, he watched from his chair and silently prayed that God would comfort his friend.

"Let's go back inside," Dwayne said when Sean finally settled again.

Sean stood, but shook his head. "No, I need to rest up for this press conference. Give everyone my regards. Let's talk tomorrow morning."

Using his cell, Sean instructed his chauffeur that he was ready, and by the time Dwayne walked him around to the front, the Lincoln Town Car was waiting. Dwayne watched as Sean lowered himself into the backseat. He stood on the curb, simmering with myriad emotions as the dark car moved down the street.

For the first time since his ordeal had begun, Dwayne faced all that he was feeling: His lips trembled with the thought of loss, and inside, he was still rocked by the betrayal. Yet it was his compassion for Sean that had brought him to tears.

He stood for a moment, contemplating all that Sean was facing, and realized he had another very important meeting to conduct with the one person he had not yet personally greeted—Elder Clarence Milsap.

Back inside, Dwayne took Milsap aside and they began brain-storming. Milsap theorized that Reverend Powell had indeed been a plant—a hired actor or a con. Either way they would never be able to discredit him without locating him. It would be equally difficult to tie Powell and L.W. together, as Milsap was sure that L.W. had hired a middleman to arrange the transaction in order to keep his hands clean.

The microcassette did give them some leverage in dealing with Lejohn, but there were numerous ramifications: Did he really want to replay the whole scene for the world to hear, or should he just let it become yesterday's news, as it surely would? Did he want his battle with the Jubilee Network duked out in the media? Did he want to further demean a network that had meant so much to the Christian community? Did he want to hurt Beverlyn? And finally, did he really want to play Linson Lejohn's game?

Still, he felt better holding something in his hand that bore out his story. With it—if he wanted to—he could bring down Linson Lejohn, the Jubilee Network, and Beverlyn Boudreaux Ministries.

When Dwayne returned home, he knew he had some important decisions to make, and the opportune time to make them would be before tomorrow's press conference. Last night, he'd gotten little sleep, and as he'd watched Lafayette drive off and made his way to the penthouse elevator, he realized the prospects for tonight wouldn't be much better.

He arrived at the church an hour before the press conference was to begin and drove in the back gate past a swarm of reporters. Though they shouted out questions, he drove past them into the lot, church elders holding them at bay. Lafayette said that they'd been camped out at the church since eight.

As Dwayne entered the conference room, he could see that Sean had not yet arrived, but everyone else seemed to be in place. He was greeted by Lafayette and then pulled into a corner by Mark Mansfield, a prominent attorney who attended the church and not only handled Lafayette's affairs but also had a thriving corporate practice.

Mr. Mansfield went over some final details as Dwayne scanned the room, confirming the presence of Nina, Elder Milsap, Monique, Robbie, and his mother, all decked out in their Sunday best. Standing near them was a group of clients who had become friends, some of them high-profile entertainers there to lend their support—and get their famous faces on the six o'clock news. Among them were Jasmine Charles, Harrison David, the actor who'd first introduced Dwayne to Sean, Jade, and others Dwayne only recognized from Christian television. Then to the left of them was a number of local pastors—friends

of Lafayette's, some of whom he knew, like Dr. Beverly "BAM" Crawford and Bishop Kenneth Ulmer, and some he didn't know; all representing the leading black churches in Los Angeles.

For the first time in forty-eight hours, Dwayne felt that everything
was going to work out just fine. Moments later, Sean arrived, looking much better than he had the day before, though Dwayne surmised it was taking every bit of energy Sean had to put it on for the
cameras, which twenty minutes later began to roll.

As the contingency of his supporters who'd gathered in the conference room now stood side by side on the pulpit, Sean walked
slowly to the microphone to read his statement.

"I have come here today to make two announcements. The first is
to confirm that I am HIV positive, the result of a heterosexual encounter more than five years ago. I had been symptom-free for two
years, until recently when it was revealed to me that my condition
was progressing. The doctors say that my symptoms may worsen,
but there is no timetable. However, for the time being—and under
doctor's orders—I am suspending all performances. I will not be
singing for a while. But I remain optimistic about my health and a return to the stage as I worship a powerful and merciful God who has
blessed me with success, with talent, and with the love you see in
this pulpit today.

"I did not come to this way of thinking on my own," he continued. "In the depths of my despair, having first been diagnosed with
AIDS and at the time suicidal, I was referred to Dr. Dwayne Grandison. My life has not been the same since.

"That leads me to my second announcement. It is because of this
man's"—he paused and pointed to Dwayne—"professional services
and friendship that I stand in front of you today. What many of you
saw on TV the other day was a friend who had been sworn to protect
the private affairs of another friend. A friend who had only recently
come through the tragedy of losing his wife in an automobile accident."

He turned to Dwayne. "I want to announce to the world today that
Dr. Dwayne just happens to be the best friend one could hope to
have, and quite a capable therapist."

Sean paused—his voice had begun to crack—while he composed himself. Amid the silence of pounding thoughts and the free-flowing spirit of God, admiring the spirit of his weary soul, members of the media were touched by a courage they had never before witnessed.

Sean Wiley turned to the audience. "Any questions?"

Hands flew up, and Lafayette, who'd been introduced earlier, pointed to a heavyset woman wearing thick TV makeup.

"Samantha Steele, *Around Hollywood*. What about your resignation from the Jubilee Network?"

"I'll direct that question to Attorney Mark Mansfield."

Before Sean could answer, Mr. Mansfield quickly stepped to the podium and dramatically declared, "There were no such resignations."

"Can we deduce from your presence here, Mr. Mansfield, that there will be a litigation?" came the second question.

"First of all, let me clarify that, at this time, I am simply an advisor to Dr. Grandison and Mr. Wiley. Mr. Wiley did not have a legal contract with the Jubilee Network. Dr. Grandison did. Legal action has not been ruled out, but for the moment, nothing has been decided."

"Will you file for slander?"

"While my client has indeed been slandered, as I said before, nothing has yet been decided. We have contacted the network and fully intend to meet with their lawyers."

"Sean, do you believe you will ever sing again?"

"I certainly hope so," he said, looking a bit weakened by all the commotion.

"And will you now be speaking out for AIDS causes?"

"I have always done that, but, yes, whatever I can do to advance the cause against the spread of AIDS and foster a greater understanding in the Christian community, I will do."

"Dr. Grandison, will you sue to be reinstated with the Jubilee Network?"

"I have no desire to be anyplace I'm not wanted. I have a thriving practice and hope to continue my work with Man-to-Man, a men's fellowship right here at New Covenant."

Although just thirty minutes had passed, Sean was visibly tired, and his doctor motioned to Lafayette to cut the press conference short.

"I'm sorry, ladies and gentlemen, that's all. On behalf of my brother, Dr. Dwayne Grandison—of whom I am very proud—and Sean Wiley, one of the most incredible singers in music today, I thank you for coming here today."

# Chapter Thirty-Five

*B*everlyn didn't know what to think as she caught clips of Sean's press conference on the afternoon news. She'd been right. Dwayne was not gay. And Sean must hate her as well. Immediately, she felt in her gut that this was not good for the ministry. Kim had not been optimistic either, confirming that Sean's press conference had been quite a coup.

Though the Jubilee Network had not been prominently mentioned at the press conference, it was clear that the network had not only allowed Dwayne to be slandered but also jumped the gun in announcing his resignation and publicly disassociating themselves from Sean. In facing the press, Sean looked like no less than a martyr and Dwayne a saint. But what disturbed her most was what the attorney had said—and what he had left unsaid. She should have gotten Dwayne's side of the whole incident. Now it was too late. She was sure he had seen her taped statement.

Her heart sank. Perhaps he hadn't called because he was disappointed that she had not known any better than to believe L.W. Why oh why hadn't she stuck with her own intuition about Dwayne? And where was L.W. anyway? It had been more than fifteen minutes since she'd asked Tori to tell him she wanted to see him. Just as she was about to pick up the phone, in walked L.W., slamming the door behind him.

"L.W., what is going on? Did you see Sean's press conference?"

"Yeah, I've just been with the corporate lawyers, who've said we may have a fight on our hands. Grandison, it appears, is threatening to sue us. I guess that's his way of saying I love you."

"Have his lawyers said they'll sue?" Beverlyn countered.

"Not yet. There is a meeting set for tomorrow . . ."

Beverlyn shook her head and brought her hands to her face. "This is terrible. I knew something wasn't right—that I should have waited to talk to Dwayne—"

"I'm sorry, Beverlyn," L.W. cut her off abruptly. "I just don't buy it. Sean's press conference was little more than a ploy to buy sympathy."

"Well, it worked," she screamed. "Even I feel sorry for him and wonder how as a Christian I could have contributed to his downfall. As to Dwayne, no wonder he didn't call me. If I had believed in him, I never would have believed what that Reverend Powell said. And what about that, L.W.? I thought you said you confronted Dwayne."

"I don't care what has been said. I know what I saw, and what I saw was a man you were going out of your way to please, while he was gallivanting around town with Sean and that Nina Jordan. Why was all the burden always on you in this relationship? Think about that. You did most of the calling. You did most of the giving, and now you are expected to do most of the understanding too. Why hasn't he called you? Was it so easy to scare him off?"

He calmed himself before going on. "I know you have your doubts. I have mine too. This is, no doubt, a bad situation. But the last thing we need right now is to second-guess ourselves and not put forth a united front. I'm on *your* side. Do you really think I would want to do anything to hurt the business empire we've worked so hard to build?"

"No, I'm sure you don't," she said with the resignation of someone who'd run out of options.

"Look, we'll get through this. And, Beverlyn, neither I nor anyone else can stop what God has for you. If Dwayne Grandison was meant to be your mate, nothing can stop that."

He was right, Beverlyn thought. How many times had she stood in a pulpit and admonished audiences to get out of God's way and turn over their lives to Him—to let Him provide their needs; to let Him choose their mates; to do their part and let Him do His part.

"Beverlyn, for you this thing has been about you and Dwayne, but I want to remind you that there's a lot more at stake. Look, I have to get over to the studio. I'll check back with you later."

As he walked out of her door and down the hall, he was silently cursing Dr. Dwayne Grandison and Sean. Boy, had he underestimated them. That Grandison just wouldn't die.

And that press conference was a stroke of genius, particularly the part where Sean's voice cracked as he spoke of Grandison. That was the clip news stations had played again and again. They looked like saints.

L.W. was sorry that he hadn't finished Dwayne Grandison off. Now it was too late to make another move against him. He needed to stabilize things with the network. There were rumblings from the legal department that his and Beverlyn's actions had left the network vulnerable to legal action. A settlement meeting had already been slated with Grandison's lawyers, since he had stated publicly that he did not want his spot back with the network.

He was sure Grandison would not be there, so there was no reason for him to fear the good doctor making an attempt to speak with Beverlyn. Besides, she wouldn't be at the meeting either. He would make sure of that.

Within a week of the news conference, the Sean Wiley Affair, as it had been dubbed, had faded from prominence in both the mainstream and entertainment news, though it remained a banner item for some of the tabloids. Dwayne found himself picking up the pieces. His lawyers had called earlier that morning to let him know that they had come to a settlement with the Jubilee Network, eliminating the need for further legal action.

Dwayne had signed off on the settlement, which awarded him close to a million dollars. It had been the Jubilee Network's first offer, and his lawyers had been against accepting it, arguing that no one settles on a first offer, that they could surely get more. Especially since the microcassette had been more effective than first thought.

Network attorneys first argued that the tape—recorded without the knowledge of Linson Lejohn—was in violation of California state law, and grounds for a criminal prosecution as well as a civil lawsuit.

"It is true the taping of a private conversation is illegal under California law," Mansfield told the lawyers. "However, there is an exception to the use of taped conversations. Maybe you haven't kept up on the latest case law, but a taped conversation can be used to prevent the commission of an act injurious to a person's economic well-being. Further, in such a case, that tape can be used in the event of a trial. It's called defamation, gentlemen.

"Additionally, our client was handed a restraining order which we believe could only have been attained illegally. So, let's stop playing games and get down to business. Put an offer on the table."

While they were free to argue the defamation issues, lawyers for the Jubilee Network began to view the microcassette as a smoking gun and opted to settle.

Dwayne had been more interested in the principle than the money. The press conference had restored his integrity and credibility. With the exception of a very few, most believed that Dwayne was not gay, and while he lost about nine clients, the phones were ringing off the hook from prospective clients moved by Sean's testimony of how the doctor had helped him. So much so that he had to have Monique screen the calls. Finally, he had to turn people away. He'd even gotten an appearance request from Oprah Winfrey, but he declined the offer, opting instead to keep a low profile.

Things were also going better for Sean. Thousands had written letters of support to the ailing entertainer, whose prognosis seemed to be growing worse, but whose spirits couldn't be higher from the outpouring of love from fans around the country.

And within a month, Dwayne had settled back into a comfortable rhythm that included long hours at his thriving practice, Man-to-Man, and time with family and friends. He spent little time in public places, still wary of the stares from those who seemed unsure of what to believe with regard to the Sean Wiley Affair.

For that reason, Dwayne was hesitant when Nina invited him to dinner at Dulans. He enjoyed the eatery's down-home cuisine but was worried about running into people he knew there.

"What, no business?" Dwayne asked Nina after they were seated and had given their orders to the waiter without one mention of New Covenant from her.

"Now that you bring it up . . ."

"I left myself wide open for that one, and here I thought you wanted my charming company."

"Well, that too."

He raised his eyebrows and lifted his glass to his lips, taking a sip of water.

Nina looked squarely at him. "We'd like to make you director of Man-to-Man."

"I never expected this." He coughed as he put down his glass. "That's *your* position, isn't it?"

"Actually, we'd be codirectors. That way, if something happened to me, you'd be the backup, and vice versa."

"If something were to happen to you?" He repeated her words as a question.

"You know what I mean." She brushed him off, realizing she may have erred in her choice of words. "This is an important program and it's better to have more than one person know everything."

Her words didn't convince him. "Is everything all right?"

"What could be wrong? I'm in your charming company and I've just made you a very decent proposal. So what's it going to be?"

"Do I get some time to think about it?"

"Just give in now," she said. "You know how persistent I am, and by the way, I prepared a proposal to show how much of your time it would take up, but I rushed out of the house and forgot it. We can get it on the way back."

"Oh joy!" he said sarcastically.

They laughed and chatted casually through the catfish, mashed potatoes, okra, and hush puppies. He paid the bill and they returned to Nina's apartment. As they walked to her door, he thought about how the night had been such a welcome relief from the monotonous routine he'd developed since *Higher Ground*. He couldn't count the number of times he'd laughed, and not once was Beverlyn or *Higher Ground* mentioned. The nightmare was at last behind him.

The baby-sitter was barely out of the door when Nina said, "I'm going to check on Omari. I'll be right back."

Dwayne touched her arm slightly. "Would you mind if I came with you? I haven't seen him in a while."

"Of course." Nina took his hand and led him down the hallway, which had been plastered with framed family photos.

They tiptoed into Omari's room. Dwayne smiled as Nina took her son's feet and positioned him in the twin bed so that his head was back at the top.

"I don't know why I do that. In twenty minutes, he'll be upside down again."

Dwayne leaned against the wall, watching as Nina picked up the checkered comforter from the floor, covered Omari, kissed his forehead, and then she and Dwayne quietly stepped out of the room, closing the door behind them.

"Do you want a cup of tea?" Nina moved toward the kitchen.

Dwayne followed, but shook his head. "No, I'm fine."

"Then let me get the proposal so that you can leave."

"No, get your tea. I don't mind staying."

"It will just be a few minutes."

He leaned against the narrow arch separating the kitchen from the living room and watched as Nina filled the teapot with water. He grinned broadly when she turned to him.

"What are you grinning about?"

"The really good time I had with you tonight."

"Me too." She took a cup from the cabinet and dropped a tea bag inside. "The proposal is right over here," she said, pointing to the table. She moved toward the entryway, but Dwayne blocked her path, standing steadfast, as if he had no intention of letting her pass. Their eyes held for long seconds, until finally Dwayne stepped aside. Nina smiled nervously—he had only given her a few inches. She moved past, careful not to touch him as she brushed by.

It wasn't until she reached the table that she realized she'd been holding her breath. "Here it is," she said, gripping the folder tightly.

She turned around and gasped. Dwayne was standing close behind her.

"I'm sorry. I didn't mean to scare you." He peered into her eyes.

"You didn't."

He took the folder but held her gaze. "Do I make you nervous, Nina?"

The teapot whistled and Nina rushed back into the kitchen.

Dwayne took a seat on the couch, opening the binder and scrolling through the document. Moments later, Nina took a seat at the opposite end of the long couch.

"Just like before, the schedule won't conflict with your office hours. And if it interferes, I'll understand if you leave—"

He cut her off. "I won't leave again. I've learned a lot in these few months and I now know what's most important."

"I don't know if I ever said this." Nina lowered her cup and moved closer to him. "But I admire the way you handled things. Even as your world was falling apart, your primary concern was Sean. I was so proud of you." She touched his arm lightly.

He looked down at her hand, still resting near his elbow. "Thank you," he said softly, lifting his hand and letting his palm cup her face. When she didn't protest, he moved forward, his lips angled toward hers. But just as their lips touched, Nina pulled back.

"Dwayne, no . . ."

His eyes questioned her.

"With everything that's going on," she started to explain, then stopped.

"Nina, this is about you and me. There's been something between us for a long time. We haven't faced it."

"What about Beverlyn?"

He shook his head frantically. "That wasn't real. I can't explain it," he said. "Maybe it was the glitz and the glamour. Maybe it was the whole Hollywood thing. Or maybe"—he paused and pulled her closer—"it was because I couldn't have *you.*"

This time it was Nina who raised her hand to his face, and there were tears in her eyes. "Dwayne, I can't do this." Her hand was still in place. "You should go."

He stood, following her lead, then reached for her, but she stepped back, folding her arms across her chest. When he moved toward her, she turned away. He stood in place until he heard her whisper, "Please, go."

He swallowed the lump in his throat and walked to the door. As his hand covered the knob, he glanced over his shoulder. Nina had moved to the window, her back still to him. He stepped into the hall-way and closed the door.

Dwayne glanced at the clock on the dashboard again. More than thirty minutes had passed and he was still roaming the streets of L.A., playing the evening over and over again in his mind. He turned onto Wilshire, driving almost mechanically, his mind still seeking answers to the questions Nina had left hanging.

Dwayne was as sure of Nina's feelings as he was of his own. He could tell by every exchanged glance, every inadvertent touch, every tentatively spoken word. From the beginning, sparks sizzled just beneath the surface, waiting for them to concede to the inevitable.

He tapped his thumbs against the wheel, his eyes glued to the traffic signal. "Something has to change." The light turned green, and suddenly, he swerved his Jaguar across the double yellow lines making an illegal U-turn. A solo horn blared, but Dwayne sped down the street, ignoring the driver.

Nina was sitting on the floor with her back against the couch when she heard the light taps on her door. She sniffed, trying to compose herself. She thought it was the baby-sitter. Only she would come to her door so late. Nina looked around the living room searching for what Agnes could have left behind. But all she saw was the half-filled cup of tea and the proposal on the table where Dwayne had left it.

Wiping her eyes, she forced herself to stand. She frowned deeply when she peeked through the peephole, but still opened the door.

"Nina, we have to talk." Dwayne stepped inside.

"Dwayne, it's . . ." She moved away from him.

He closed the door and moved up behind her. "I know you feel the same, Nina." With his fingers, he gently lifted her face. "I'm not leaving until you talk to me. Until you tell me what's really going on here." With his thumb, he wiped a tear away. "Why are you holding back?"

Her eyes were closed as she shook her head.

Slowly, Dwayne dropped his hand. "Okay, Nina. I'm sorry. This won't happen again." He turned from her.

"All right, Dwayne . . . ," she relented.

When he turned and pulled her into his arms, burying himself in the softness of her hair, her head fell against his chest.

"I didn't want this to happen." She began sobbing.

"What?" he pleaded. "Nina, talk to me."

"I have cancer," she gasped, then covered her mouth as if trying to retrieve the words.

His eyes widened, and they stood waiting for the silence to reveal what should happen next.

Finally, Nina sighed and said, "I want to check on Omari. I'll be right back."

Dwayne's eyes followed her as she hurried down the hall, leaving her words hanging in the air.

*I have cancer.*

Alarms went off in his mind. What have you gotten yourself into? You've already lost one wife. But Nina couldn't be dying. She was so young and healthy and vibrant. This is too much, his head was saying. But it was his heart that he was listening to, and it was telling him that Nina was the one woman he was meant to be with.

He looked down the hall, anxious for her return, but there was only darkness. He needed her to come back—to fill in the blanks. Finally, there she was—walking slowly toward him, her eyes downcast, her arms folded across her chest.

He had so many questions, but he opened his mouth and uttered just one word. "Cancer?"

"Breast cancer." She sat in the adjacent chair, staring straight ahead.

"How long have you known?"

She dropped her arms but continued to stare straight ahead, expressionless. "It's been a few years. I've been in remission twice."

"Wait a minute." Dwayne held up his hand. "Are you in remission now?"

She nodded slightly and then began rocking herself back and forth. "The doctor said I have to be in remission for five years to be considered cancer-free. That hasn't happened. I was hopeful, but the cancer came back again."

He repeated his question. "But you're in remission now?"

"Yes, but I don't know what's going to happen. It would be unfair to get involved with anyone, especially you. You've only recently gotten over Yvette. Now here I am. I couldn't have you love me and then lose me."

"It's too late for that," he said, looking into her eyes. "I already love you and I know you love me. So regardless of what happens here tonight, if something happens to you, I've already lost."

She bit her lip and allowed her fingers to glide across his cheek.

"But we're not going to lose," he said.

"How do you know that?" Her voice was full of hope.

"Because of where we're starting. Nina, how many people have a chance at what we have? We've denied it over and over and allowed everything to get between us and yet here we are. Doesn't that say something?"

She wanted to speak—to unload the burden she'd carried alone for so long—but still she held back.

"Please don't fight me on this. I want to be there for you and Omari. Nina, we can do this together."

She opened her eyes and the floodgates at the same time. He pulled her to him and this time she didn't resist, closing her eyes and opening her heart. For the next several hours, they alternated between talking, kissing passionately, and holding each other close, while exchanging fears, hopes, and plans for the future.

When the clock struck three, both knew their doubts were gone.

"Omari is going to be so thrilled. He loves you already."

"Not any more than I love him."

He leaned forward and kissed her. "It's time for me to get out of here."

She followed him to the door, where once again they held each other, neither wanting to release the embrace, but instead to freeze the moment as if it were their last.

"I love you, Nina Jordan."

"I've always loved you, Dwayne Grandison."

# Chapter Thirty-Six

*B*everlyn looked at the certified envelope again, then reread the letter and its three-page attachment. Finally, she let the papers slip onto her desk and dropped her face in her hands. She didn't even look up when she heard the knock on the door.

"Beverlyn, I need to speak to you." L.W. stopped when he saw his niece's face. Closing the door behind him, he asked, "What's wrong?"

"We're in trouble."

Slowly, he walked across the massive office and sat across from her.

"Beverlyn Boudreaux Ministries, the Jubilee Network." She held up her hands. "All of it—we're in trouble, Uncle Linson."

L.W. took a deep breath. For the past month, they had battled the backlash from the *Higher Ground* fallout. Seemed there was a new fire to put out with each day. From sponsors pulling away to investors demanding reports and audits. Even their viewers had turned their backs: The network's ratings were dropping like lead balloons, and the private contributions that made up almost fifty percent of their income just two months ago had dwindled to a fraction of what they had been. The mail was indicative of the public's sentiments. Last season, praise reports flowed in—now the mailroom was overflowing with hate mail.

As if that wasn't enough, with word of what had happened in the lawyers' settlement meeting, there had been a move on the part of key board members to have L.W. ousted from the board.

"You handled this pretty badly, L.W.," one of the members had said. "We had to shell out over nine hundred thousand dollars to Grandison and just barely avoided a lawsuit."

While the motion to have him ousted died in the first round of votes, there was no doubt in his mind that this was only their first attempt. He swallowed as he twisted in his seat, waiting for Beverlyn to reveal the latest bombshell. "What is it now?" he asked.

Beverlyn handed him the letter from the board of directors of Christian Empire, a financial services and insurance company that was the network's largest investor. L.W. glanced over the first page, then looked at Beverlyn. "They're calling in their loan."

"How could this be happening to me?" she groaned.

L.W. sweltered beneath his niece's stare. He had miscalculated. Dwayne Grandison was the one who was supposed to experience ruin—not them. What was happening at Beverlyn Boudreaux Ministries was turning his long-term dreams into a short-fused nightmare. And the biggest disaster was that this had come by his own hands.

"They can't call in their loan, can they?" he asked.

"Uncle Linson, they can do whatever they want. To be honest, I just don't care anymore."

L.W. leaned forward in his seat. "You can't give up. We've worked too hard."

"Yeah, but it seems the longer we fight, the more we lose. For the last month, it's been one catastrophe after another. We haven't been able to repeat the success of *Higher Ground*, and everything else at the network is falling apart. It's like the devil has his hands all over this."

L.W. loosened his tie. "Beverlyn, you're blowing this up. Give it time."

"We don't have time," she snapped. "I'm sorry. I just feel so helpless. I am tired of fighting all of this."

"I am as well, but what is there left to do?"

Beverlyn raised her eyebrows. She couldn't remember the last time her uncle had asked her that. He was the one with the ideas—with solutions to every unsolved opportunity. But as she looked at him now, she saw the toll this tragedy was taking. The dark lines under his eyes were more pronounced. In that second, she decided. There was no way they would survive—emotionally or financially—unless they got out now.

"Uncle Linson, I'm going to sell the Jubilee Network."

"We can't do that."

"We have to."

"Who's going to buy it the way things are now?"

"I thought of that," she answered. "This morning I met with the accountants." She took a deep breath. "Ian recommends bankruptcy. He feels the network's hefty debt load would keep buyers at bay."

Besides, Beverlyn was not about to open herself up to a lot of speculative tire-kicking and skeptical press.

"Beverlyn, it's been just two months. It can't have come to that already."

"Yes, it has." Tears stung her eyes. "The numbers are so bad that I don't see any other way out."

"But where will that leave us?"

"We'll be fine," she assured him, fighting back tears. "I can still speak and sing . . ." Her voice faded. Then she said, "We may have to give up a few things. I'll have to sell the house, downsize, and liquidate some of our assets. But we can do it."

L.W. was not only stunned but speechless as well. Right before him, his future had dissipated into ashes. Where would they go? What would happen next?

"It would be better if we returned to New Orleans," she continued.

L.W. stood. He could hear no more. "Excuse me," he said simply, and walked from the office.

Beverlyn looked after L.W. She knew her uncle. Once he thought about this, he would see it for what it was—the best for both of them.

Dwayne Grandison had cost her so much. She stood and went to the window. This will never happen again, she thought. There is only one person on this earth I can trust. She looked up to the sky. "Thank you, God, for Linson Lejohn."

Darkness filled his office, but L.W. made no move to turn on the light. Hours ago, he'd heard most of the employees leave. Even Beverlyn had come by, knocking on the door. But she'd gone away when she found the door was locked. For hours, he'd been staring into the darkness. Still, there were no solutions. He leaned back against the chair. His world was falling apart and he couldn't even cry. He hadn't cried at his mother's funeral, and although there was everything to cry about now, there was nothing to be gained. For almost thirty years, he had carefully cultivated the rise of Beverlyn Boudreaux. Now, because of one mistake, his niece was talking bankruptcy.

"Damn you, Dwayne Grandison."

He returned to the desk, unlocked the left side of the credenza, and pulled out his cognac. He half filled a crystal brandy snifter and began sipping. He finished the first glass and poured another. By the time he'd poured his third drink, he had the answers he'd been seeking.

He was Linson Lejohn—the man who created this empire. Giving up was not an option. Even if they sold the network, there was still plenty of money to be made through Beverlyn—after all, she was the commodity. They wouldn't be the multimillionaires he'd imagined and there'd be no more private jets, but they would be able to get by on a million or so each year. She'd just have to speak more. And she could produce more than one album a year. He would even suggest that she write another book, maybe two. Finally, he would devise for her the perfect testimony to win back those who'd fallen out with her. Why, in a few months, it would be like this disaster had never happened.

He beamed as he thought of the options. Who knew what was out there waiting for him?

His cell phone rang. He was sure it was Beverlyn.

"Hello."

"Mr. Lejohn?"

"Who's speaking?"

"Reverend Powell." The voice laughed.

Slowly, L.W. lowered himself into the chair. "Who is this?"

"You heard me."

L.W. felt his heart beginning to pound. He'd never known the true identity of the counterfeit evangelist. He hadn't wanted to. And they had only met the day of the show.

"What do you want?"

"You're a businessman, like me. What do you think I want?"

L.W. said nothing.

"More money."

"You've been paid," L.W. said.

"Well, not entirely. I guess Mr. Allen didn't mention that the twenty-five thousand dollars was just a down payment."

L.W. took a deep breath. Allen was a shady private detective that he had asked to "hire" Reverend Powell. It was all supposed to be done through Allen; Powell was not to have any direct contact with L.W.

"Reverend Powell, or whatever your name is, I don't think you want to go up against me," L.W. said.

"I hope you're not threatening me. I'd have to charge you more for that. Besides, you have nothing to threaten me with. You don't even know who I am. Ah, but I know everything about you—right down to how much your company is losing because you miscalculated with your scheme against Dwayne Grandison. With a few phone calls to the press, I can finish off the job."

"If you do that, you'll get nothing."

"Then again, I have nothing to lose."

L.W. closed his eyes in an effort to review his options. There weren't many. Although the future of the network was no longer an issue, Beverlyn Boudreaux's credibility was still intact. A further scandal would indeed be the final blow. L.W. sighed. Just as Beverlyn was talking about cutting back, it appeared he was going to be shelling out some pretty big bucks.

"How much?"

"Fifty thousand dollars. I'll call you back with the arrangements. Oh, and it's nice doing business with you, Mr. Lejohn."

There was a click and the phone went dead.

How ridiculous this had all become! Today he found he might be filing for bankruptcy, and tonight he was being blackmailed for money he didn't have. His quest for power had brought him to this place, and suddenly, he found himself powerless. He controlled nothing. And by the time this was over, L.W. feared that control wasn't the only thing he was going to lose.

He laid his head on the desk, and, surrounded by the expensive mahogany furnishings, imported art, and the best cognac money could buy, he cried.

# Chapter Thirty-Seven

*N*ina squeezed Dwayne's hand as they proceeded up the concrete steps. He smiled, then pushed the large glass door open, and hand in hand they ventured down the long halls toward the elevator banks. When the elevator light blinked, signaling its arrival, they stuffed themselves into the chamber, along with nearly a dozen others who didn't want to wait for the next elevator. Nina and Dwayne stood stoically, their eyes glued to the lighted numbers that indicated the elevator's ascension.

People pushed past them, exiting and entering on each floor, until the light signaled the seventh floor. The hall was silent as they walked past the numbered doors to room 708. They paused at the entrance, exchanged a glance reflecting the challenge that lay on the other side, then with slight nods and deep breaths, Dwayne pushed the door aside so that Nina could step in first.

The private hospital room was stark white, though sprinkled with expensive floral arrangements. A low beeping drew Nina's eyes to the green lines that danced in a syncopated choreography across the monitor connected to Sean Wiley's chest. An intravenous tube was connected to his right arm. As the door opened wide, Sean turned his head and immediately smiled.

"My man," he said weakly.

Dwayne placed his hand lightly on Nina's back, nudging her forward.

"Nina, so good to see you."

Dwayne reached over the metal rail and took Sean's hand. "How are you, my friend?"

Sean pushed a button and the top half of the bed slowly rose. "I'm just taking it day by day, but today is definitely a good day." He coughed and pulled the white sheet up to his chest.

Nina moved in front of Dwayne and kissed Sean's cheek. "Good to see you, Sean," she said.

Sean touched his cheek where she had kissed him. "With that kiss, I'll be better in no time." He pointed to the single chair under the window. "Pull that over here and sit for a while."

Dwayne got the chair and Nina sat down.

"I'm glad you called and let us know you were here." Dwayne covered his friend's hand with his and at the same time, surreptitiously scanned his body. The short-sleeved robe left Sean's arms bare, but there were no visible scars or lesions, and Dwayne was relieved that apparently Sean's condition hadn't significantly worsened. When he got the call, he hadn't known what to expect.

"How are things?"

"I'm not in any pain, so that's good. The doctors were worried that I had pneumonia, but now they're not sure, so they want to keep me under observation for a day or two."

Dwayne nodded.

Sean reached for his glasses, which lay atop the Bible on the table next to his bed. "I don't want to talk about me. What's going on with the two of you?" He peered over his glasses.

"Good news," Dwayne started, taking Nina's hand. "We're getting married."

"Show me that diamond, girl." He reached for Nina's hand.

They laughed as Sean held her hand high. The emerald-cut, three-carat diamond (purchased with money from Dwayne's settlement with the Jubilee Network) shimmered a rainbow of colors against the white light in the room.

"Is this real?" he teased Dwayne and Nina as they all shared a good laugh. "I'm so happy for both of you." He turned to Dwayne. "Man, you did good."

"Don't think I don't know it," Dwayne assured him as Nina blushed. Then putting his arm around her shoulders, Dwayne continued, "It took us a while to find each other, but it was worth it."

"So when's the big day?"

"That's up to you," Nina interjected. "We're having a small wedding, but we really want you to be there."

"Yeah," Dwayne added. "Any word on when you'll be getting out of this joint?"

Sean hesitated, then said, "Just tell me the date. I'll be there."

The sound of Nina's cell phone interrupted their banter. "Excuse me, you two. It's probably Omari's baby-sitter. I'll take it in the hall."

Nina said hello as she stepped into the hospital corridor and walked to where she could find a private spot. When he and Sean were alone, Dwayne lowered the bed rail and perched himself against the edge of the bed.

"I knew the first time I saw you two together that Nina was perfect for you."

"I should have listened. I couldn't have imagined that I would ever be this happy again."

"Well, I'm really glad for you."

"Well, I can't help but be a little worried about you."

"Dwayne, you should know that it's all in God's hands. The doctors are hopeful. People are living out their lives with AIDS, and because of what you've taught me and the strength I now have in the Word, I plan to be one of those people."

Dwayne fought the swell of emotions that threatened to overwhelm him and was relieved when he heard the knock on the door. Both he and Sean stared at the entryway.

"Hello."

The last time Dwayne had seen her, she was flitting through the studio, assuring him that everything was all right. But she didn't look the way he remembered. Even her dress was different. She wore a tailored black pantsuit. And she was alone, absent the entourage that accompanied her in public places.

"I hope it's okay," she said, looking back and forth between the two men, unsure about whether or not she should proceed. "I found out you were here and I wanted to see you."

Dwayne wasn't sure whom she was talking to, and he was relieved when Sean took over, pushing himself further up in the bed. "It's fine, Bev. Come on in."

She walked slowly toward them, stopping in front of Dwayne. She reached across the bed and kissed Sean lightly. "How are you?"

"Okay."

She nodded, turning to Dwayne. "I hoped that you would be here," she said softly. "How are you, Dwayne?"

"I'm fine," he said, sounding stiffer than he wanted to. It wasn't until that moment that he realized he hadn't thought about Beverlyn in a long while, nor contemplated what it would be like to see her again. "How are things with you, Beverlyn?"

She shrugged. "Could be better." She paused. "I don't know if you've heard," she started, speaking to both of them. "We're moving back to New Orleans."

Dwayne and Sean had matching expressions of surprise.

"I didn't know," Dwayne said. "I hope that's a good thing." His eyes searched hers.

"It's what we have to do. Things didn't go well with the network and . . ." She shrugged, leaving her sentence incomplete.

"I'm sorry to hear it. I hope someday you find happiness."

"I thought I had." She looked up at him.

At that moment, he turned toward the door, acknowledging Nina's return.

"Hello, Beverlyn." Nina walked toward them and stood at Dwayne's side.

Beverlyn's eyes darted between the two. "Nina, what are you doing here?"

"Dwayne and I wanted to check on Sean." She smiled.

Beverlyn turned toward the bed as if she'd forgotten Sean was in the room.

Dwayne turned to Nina. "Are you ready, honey?"

Nina nodded and reached for her purse. She didn't miss the shock that registered on Beverlyn's face. She moved closer to the bed, forcing Beverlyn to step back, then leaned over and kissed Sean's forehead. "We'll see you soon."

At the door, they turned back at the sound of Sean's voice. "Call me the minute you set the date of the wedding. I have to get my tuxedo ready."

Shock was still visible on Beverlyn's face as she looked at Sean and then turned to Dwayne and Nina.

"Beverlyn, it was good seeing you again," Dwayne said before he and Nina stepped from the room.

They took a few steps before Dwayne stopped and pulled Nina into his arms. "Miss Jordan, have I told you that I love you?"

Nina glanced at her watch. "About an hour has passed since you last said that." She laughed, then became serious. "You know, we're going to have to do something about that 'Miss Jordan' thing," she said, waving her hand with her ring in the air.

Dwayne took her hand in his and they continued toward the elevator. Dwayne's thoughts turned back to Beverlyn, and to how for a time, he had placed his faith in the seductive rewards of her glitzy world, none of which held any real eternal value.

He silently thanked God for yet another chance to live his life for what really mattered, and especially for Nina's love, however long or short their time together might be.

RONN ELMORE is a relationship therapist, ordained minister, and author of the national bestseller *How to Love a Black Man*; its sequel, *How to Love a Black Woman*; and *An Outrageous Commitment: The 48 Vows of an Indestructible Marriage*. Much sought after on the speaking circuit, Dr. Ronn has shared the bill with Tavis Smiley and T. D. Jakes, among others. His insightful views frequently appear in national publications, including *Essence*, *Ebony*, and *Family Digest*. He and Aladrian, his wife of over twenty-two years, are the parents of three children. The family resides in the Sacramento area, where Dr. Ronn is the pastor of Faith Fellowship Church.